To Dam,
Enjoy th[...]
A[...]

# Spacer

A Novel of Space
by Alan E. Fields

PublishAmerica
Baltimore

First printing

ISBN: 1-4241-2765-3
PUBLISHED BY PUBLISHAMERICA, LLLP
www.publishamerica.com
Baltimore

Printed in the United States of America

To Margaret my wife

S tand at any point on this planet Earth and look outward to the heavens. See the vast and unending volume of space expanding high and forever above this our world. With the naked eye, on the clearest of nights, we are able to behold just a small segment of those many, many stars, which surround us on this planet. This is the planet, which we, humans, call home.

Stars, upon stars upon more stars that we can see. And beyond those, there are many, many more. Though unobserved by the naked eye, they are surely there, countless in their never-ending number. These same stars have persisted in their unchanged states in all of the comparably short time that we, who are of this race of Homo sapiens, have looked upward to the night sky. They, the stars, are those same and everlasting identical points of light which human beings have been admiring or worshiping, and sometimes observing with absolute awe, for centuries or no doubt even for millennia.

All of these celestial bodies have maintained their unchanged locations relative to each other for the numerous millions of years of recent Earth history. The only minutest of exceptions, have been an illusion sometimes created by the motions of this planet. Induced through its ever-changing position whilst it had continually and soundlessly circumnavigated our own star in this Solar System in which we dwell.

Our story begins in a future time when humankind has evolved many centuries beyond our present constraints of only watching the stars whilst still being bound to our home world.

After mankind had first entered space, more than one thousand years would pass. By this time, the very outer edge of our Solar System had been finally reached. By humans in the flesh. Exploration outward and beyond that inevitable point had to be placed on hold, whilst a new and more efficient means could be devised and one that would enable humans to propel themselves beyond that outer unseen boundary of space.

That device was a long time coming.

The name Maastersym has now been long forgotten by most. But the valuable key work, the precursor so to say, that was the commencement in the development of the 'Bubble' still prevails. Through his early efforts and the persistence of those of his family descendants who followed, humans now possess the mastery to make their own dynamic and illusionary changes to those star patterns. Now they move freely and at their own will throughout the depths of the void that lies between those stars. Forever they now transform their view of these same ravenous machines that generate cosmic energy. The stars.

Many hundreds of years have now passed since the people from Earth have been the masters of their ability to travel across vast expanses of space. During this time, hundreds of star systems have been visited. Their planets and half formed space debris have been surveyed and catalogued into the hundreds. They have been typeset into their categories, categories listing them as good, not so good and poor for human uses. Those of them having the required and correct characteristics have been colonized, with settlements that have flourished. Cities and towns have grown, each possessing such spectacle and such individuality that only visionaries could have forecast their development.

Just as it always was the ilk of mankind, occasional warring of various magnitudes had been fought. Battling over territory, battling over wealth, or sometimes battling just for ambition.

But now, warring belongs in the past. Some scars still remain but a final peace exists in all of this local galactic neighbourhood. And poverty and want have long been vanquished.

# Chapter 1

These few had all been summoned, to be here. And now they were gathered, here in this place.

"They are coming. Now!" said the first.

Another, who had not yet spoken, interrupted.

"But how is this possible, they were always so—primitive."

"They have progressed beyond belief since we last visited." The first one spoke, eyes looking in no particular direction. "Someone left something behind."

It was not said whom, those gathered here though, knew instantly.

The words spoken in this place were not as words, but the others were at once aware. The form those assembled took, was not their form.

"How far have they traveled?" The second needed to change the threat the silence now indicated. This presence needed the assurance that they were really coming. To that other place.

"A very great distance. Their journey is almost over. They have not far to go now before they will have arrived."

The reply came from the third in this large space that was nowhere and that was without substance. The assignment of this one had been to monitor their progress.

"And they are to arrive there?" It was the second again.

There was no reply, just the sensing of an answer.

"Can we not stop them ourselves?" The second asked again, though knowing the answer before the question had been formed. It had been asked before, often and for the very same reason.

"No." The first was definite and almost mocking in the quick response. "But," there was a pause, of no great length.

"—I." This presence had never before used the possessive. It was unknown, "—have arranged for an alternative."

The small fast ship was going nowhere. Its course had been just a direction chosen at random, not even aimed at any star in particular or even any coefficient in the surrounding space. The propulsion system had shut down earlier, after reaching beyond the speed of light. Acceleration would continue though. That was a slightly puzzling feature to its occupant. It didn't matter though. And its passengers were not in any really immediate hurry either way.

Small was not a true category for this particular craft of space and was unexplainable in real terms of knowledge. The exterior was small and that was true, but on the inside its spatial dimensions would strangely expand to surround the occupant with a sensation of unending volume. Mentally there was no comparison of the perception of the ships interior dimensions relative to its exterior shell. How this feature was manifested had been always an equal mystery to the pilot, but she had lived with these strange characteristics for so long, she now always took the effect as unfathomable and therefore for granted. There was a time long ago that she had endeavored to understand the concept when it had once been explained to her by its builders, but the mental technology required to begin to understand, was far beyond her own human adequacy. The closest she had arrived at the explanation had to do with shrinking to the size of a Proton for access to the higher transference wavelengths.

But then the beings who were the builders of this strange craft, they were also so far beyond those human accomplishments of this epoch. And that knowledge was all she had required to accept. She had finally put aside her own failings to understand their ideology.

The course, just randomly assigned for the craft, would take it through the deep and empty space existing among all stars. Take her away from her latest conquest. Even at its present speed of more than that of light, the ship could travel for years before entering the realms of any probability that it could collide with another body.

Any Terran who has traveled between the stars, knows space to be still that same measureless and timeless void it always had been. Nothing much changed. What was beyond this particular segment of the Galaxy was of little consequence to its new inhabitants. Beyond and far away from this place there were millions and millions of other stars, some had planets in orbit and some were without any form of offspring. And far beyond those uncountable stars, there were more, and then after those, the far off galaxies, greater in number than the stars each of them contained.

But now, at this present time, in this small and special ship, set adrift between these same stars is the human known to some as the original. She was The Spacer.

Her name?

Clysta Z'ee.

Since her earlier beginnings, almost likened to a Queen to this region of space, this section of our spiral galaxy. It was all her domain.

Since her early adulthood, Clysta Z'ee had spent most of her time ensuring the safety of humanity, using strengths and cunning and a few of her own un-metered advantages. That latest conquest which she had just completed had been a short one; it had not involved anyone other than herself and the protagonist. He, Maisal was said to be from the star system of Ruben. He was a large man and much younger than Clysta, but no match for her special talents and the strength and speed of her constant companion. This ne'er-do-well, Maisal, had been observed for months breaking the local laws of the group of five planets orbiting around Chaph. Chaph was a large yellow star in one of those constellations known since ancient times as Cassiopeia. Now Maisal had been out-foxed. Clysta had caught him red-handed stealing the 'Stone of Atonement'. It had belonged to the system's major planetary ruler. Maisal, a master of disguises and transformation had connived his way into the court as an advisor to the High Prince. He was now though on his way to serve his deserved time of life, on the penal world of Never, a rocky planet deep inside the distant star cloud of the Orion Nebula.

Now her work it was over, she would take a short rest. Maybe she would visit some distant world, far away from this region. Somewhere that she was not known, or for that matter did not know enough to become involved in its needs for assistance. She might even take a vacation of sorts. Lightsworld now entered her reverie from deep in her subconscious. Then the thought was moved aside by a slight feeling of inner sadness.

'Wait until Tomorrow', she thought. It would be soon enough to make the decision for their next destination. Then she would wait, as she had so many times, to be called again to attend to some new and deserving escapade or service.

If her services were needed, Clysta Z'ee would know. How she knew was always something of a mystery to those she helped. It was a greater mystery to those wrongdoers she would eventually dispense. But she would always be available. Prepared to serve and react for those being wronged.

Humankind and their priorities had changed from the much earlier times of space travel. Those times had passed when it had been the dream of every youngster of planet Earth, to travel at a breakneck speed through the cosmos and explore the unknown. For hundreds of years, those who had left Earth had migrated to become the Planet Breakers. They had grown beyond those same urges of that early youth. Most had become constructors, some became the miners and the farmers on the very worlds their own great-great ancestors had only dreamed of and had never seen.

Those millions were to now wallow in the satisfaction of becoming a small part of cultivating that unstoppable Terran expansion into space and the stars.

The countless population dwelling in this long since settled Galactic arm was in no real hurry any more to venture into those new and unknown territories beyond. Growth and expansion had ground to a halt for now. Perhaps it was time to take an accounting of its past and of its undoubted future.

Just as those ancient adventurers of old Planet Earth had done many thousands of years before, the early planetary colonists each had traveled their intergalactic distances into the relatively unknown, to find that small piece of 'Utopia'. Their own plans had long been to settle and build on those pieces and mold each of them into their own styles and designs. Now these plans had been or were now being fulfilled by the millions of people who had spread from planet Earth.

Clysta Z'ee though, she was of a different kind. She was not born to be one of these and would never be.

There were a small number of others, who in a small way could be called Spacers too. These few had been recruited by her, from time to time, to help eradicate various injustices. One here and one or two there had enrolled, to assist her in some of the escapades to protect civilization in its growth. They had similar goals to hers and were ready for all of the challenges of the ultimate adventure. But now, they had grown so few, she had not crossed paths with even one of them for at least five Standard Years.

It would appear that these accomplices in her duties had finally become settlers too. But as times before, not Clysta Z'ee. That was not in her making.

For Clysta, it seemed almost that she had been here in space for an eternity. It certainly had been the place she called home for the greater part of her long life.

And this particular day was special for her. It was the anniversary of her birth, the one hundred and thirty-first measured in the Galactic Standard Years. Clysta Z'ee had spent at least ninety of these years in and out of space. She had seen up close, more than a half of the inhabited worlds in these three neighbouring spiral arms of this Galaxy. And the rest, which she had not seen, she always made a vow that she would visit later.

But on this particular day she stood alone and, being the lone human on board, there had been no celebration. Only a personal recollection and the recognition of the years past, as she stood once more on the flight deck of her strange, sleek cruiser the Murayssa III. That name was chosen out of a special reason, born by melancholy for two good friends and much earlier times.

Well, the truth was, she was almost alone. For still at her side as always, was her good friend and faithful companion. Both were looking outward at the velvet blackness of space, pierced only by the stars she had always loved with a passion.

Clysta was silent. Thinking of those times so long past. She was remembering…

"Aren't you ready to go yet?" her father asked.

"Just give me a few more minutes will you." As most teens could, Clysta answered in that good hearted tone at which no one could take offence.

"I need to check if I brought enough of the right clothes for The Hunt." Her voice carried from the cargo area in the rear of the habitat area and beyond the galley.

He let his eyes roll upward, saying very softly, so she could not hear, "Just like your Mother." Then raising his voice so she would hear, he said, "And it is not 'the right clothes'. It is 'the correct clothing' please. Your English is being eroded by those people you school with."

"Shouldn't it be 'With whom you school'?" she responded to his correcting.

"Right, right!" he conceded.

Clysta's Mother, he thought to himself. His beloved wife. A pang of sorrow entered his thoughts. He hadn't thought much of her Mother for weeks. He carefully pushed it back into the appropriate mental safe for reflection later.

"Listen young lady," he said, raising his voice and in a comical attempt at laying down the present Galactic Laws and returning to the first topic. "We do not require that many clothes and anyway, we can purchase whatever you have not already packed when we get there. I am looking forward to this trip, and have been for weeks. I have my lift-off control patterns already dialed in and I do not want to go through any delaying procedures. It takes forever to recompute, you know that," he emphasized.

"Just one more container, then I will be satisfied," she answered, ignoring his efforts to speed up lift-off from the surface. Then, in less than fifteen seconds,"- -Right, we can go now. Wasn't that speedy?"

She pressed the pad, which would cause the trunk closet to seal as she was turning around to make her way toward the control area of the ship.

Clysta entered and brushed past her father's reclining chair. She bent over him to place a kiss on his cheek, then continued to her own form-fitting seat.

She said, as if in retrospect, "Anyway, forever isn't really true, is it? Even I can do it in 12 minutes. You know that," referring to the last statement about lift-off control patterns.

Her father smiled.

As the restraining force-field energized itself around her whole torso, she tried unsuccessfully to lift and wave her arms in mock gesticulation and a forward thrust motion.

"Ok – ok. Let's go," she said, smiling, "Lightsworld won't wait forever."

Thirty-three seconds later the craft had lifted off, soundlessly speeding in a vertical course through the spaceport's roof iris and into the surrounding ether and toward the stars above.

Clysta Z'ee was only now in her mid-teens. She had begun her training from early in her childhood for her future in life. Her father had begun his rise through the system as an Intergalactic Traveler, collecting and dissecting information for the old Galactic Bureau. Visiting far-flung regions, mostly alone. His responsibility had been to report on new and un-surveyed worlds and their prospects. He had made far greater plans for his only daughter.

In her younger years Clysta had been a skinny and gangly kid, never very tall and did not mix well with others. She was never very attractive either and with a nondescript mousy coloured hair, which, no matter how hard her mother would try, just would not stay in the same place for more than five minutes. In addition to this constant untidy and 'Tomboy' unfeminine appearance, her face was so full of freckles; it was sometimes difficult to see her real colouring.

Her eyes though were of a totally different making. They had the appearance of being deep and unusually dark blue. But they were also oozing with an expectation and anticipation. When she looked at someone, it was as if she could see into the very soul. This same effect remained with her all of her young years and she followed it with a questioning and constant curiosity in all that was around her.

As if to compensate for her minimal physical attributes, she was very bright and intelligent. During her early schooling she had shown a phenomenal talent for learning. At the age of six, Clysta had already grasped the many earlier mathematical theories. Relativity and Quantum Physics came easy to her. At seven years, she was well on the way through the five mighty volumes of the Yan Siong Proposition. It was then that tragedy struck, all too suddenly.

Clysta's Mother was an eminent specialist in the sciences on cures for interplanetary diseases. Earth and the development of earthlike habitats in the Solar System had been scourged of dangerous viruses and disease for more than one thousand years. As part of the necessary and rigorous defense procedure, she had been carrying out a series of tests on a range of samples of an atomically decaying soup-like formation.

These particular samples had been found in an equatorial swamp on a hot but promising planet orbiting the type G-O white star, Spica. Without any prior warning, she was stricken by an unidentified molecular virus-like organism. It was quite unexpected and at the time unknown. Luckily, if it could be said so, she had the foresight to instantly completely isolate herself from contact by her colleagues.

Even the Celamite Particle Wave protection screen had been unable to stop the atom sized viral seed. Unseen and with an unanticipated speed, it crossed the vacuum of duplicated space within the sealed crucible where this tiny molecule was under observation. From there it traveled magically and at high speed, along the fibres of the motion generator controlling the laboratory impulse dissecting equipment. She had only a fraction of a second to understand just what was happening as she watched its lightening like progress upward through the molecules of the surrounding minute sample of swamp growth.

Almost as if it had somehow anticipated its target, this demon advanced through and past the fail-safe retina screen. It ended its journey by invading directly the electronic impulses of the brain of Murel Z'ee. Unaccountably, it had leapt across the ionized antiseptic air to penetrate the iris of the eye she had up close to the finite electron microscope. Outside of the sealed area, Murel Z'ee was observed by her co-technician to stand upright for five seconds then she collapsed to the laboratory floor. That was the last movement she ever made.

Within one day, Clysta's Mother had slipped into an irreversible state of comatose. This tiny fiend had quickly and systematically cancelled the reproduction of the body's cells so necessary to life and had then begun to tear away at the rest. Within forty-eight hours she had been reduced to a hollow and decaying shell by the savagery of the further atomic deterioration of those remaining cells. Even with the efforts from the best of her own staff and the most eminent doctors available, she never regained consciousness. Her death came, finally and mercifully. As if by a further stroke of luck, the fiend itself died with her.

Clysta was then only seven and a half years old.

One year prior the his wife's death, her father had been appointed Chief Statistician for the Galactic Bureau for the Future of Expansion of the Human Race throughout the Galaxy. He often was known to joke that it took him longer to say where he worked than it took him to get there.

He found after the death of his wife and because of the commitment to his appointment and the continual trips the position forced him to take, he could not always be at home and at the side of his now motherless daughter.

Professor Z'ee finally made the decision of a responsible parent.

Clysta would be better able to develop her own future, lonely though it now seemed, in the best facility that teaching had to offer. In the eyes of many of her educators and teachers together with a few of Professors Zee's own colleagues, she was amply capable of handling the highest in education.

He chose the best in its field. It was the Jupiter Galactic Academy of Etheric Mathematics. She joined the Academy at nine years of age.

Clysta, young as she was, soon proved to be a very good student, exceptional in fact as all of her professors and lecturers often remarked. After she had reached the age of fourteen years, she quickly began to loose her earlier cosmetic inadequacies and was becoming increasingly more attractive and beautiful with each passing month. She was taller, much more feminine and her hair now fell, controlled, to her shoulders. It was a creamy blonde colour with red tones. She had an almost regal deportment but was liked by many or most of her peers.

Clysta Z'ee had by this time academically outstripped the fellow members of her class in their studies. That is with the exception of one co-student.

Kindra Nymralph was a male student who, for the last three years, had continued to keep pace with Clysta in their education and their grades. The two had become friends some years ago and that friendship had developed into one that was a continual but friendly competition in all subjects. Each of them had prospered from it. There was only the minor exception. That was in the studies of the Hyper-Nominal Equation Techniques. In that subject and that one only, where Kindra was just slightly behind Clysta, but, only slightly.

At the time Clysta became a teenager, the positions her father held at the Galactic Bureau had now been escalated to one of a higher management level. He now was able to arrange more of his own free time to fit with Clysta's schooling schedule. It gave them both better opportunities to see more of each other and make amends to his daughter for those lonely years since the death of her Mother.

In his own work in the past, he would frequently be needed to shoot off to some distant point in space to carry out an important report for his superiors. His latest promotion meant he himself was now one of these superiors. It was someone else's job to carry out those urgent inspections. He could arrange some time off to match Clysta's term breaks. On some of these occasions, he would arrive at the Academy in a rented Skipper III and they would take off to some distant star system.

The Skipper III became their favorite escape craft. It was small but it was still capacious and with sufficient space to accommodate four berths. This particular mini cruiser had the latest drive able to Jump into Hyper Space and then out, anywhere in the local sector in no time at all. It would take just a matter of a few Standard Hours to transport through hundreds of Light Years of distance, giving to Clysta and her father, good and easy access to the many now inhabited worlds in the region.

Quail Z'ee, Clysta's father, was a most quiet, gentle and smiling individual. He was tall, just short of two metres and slim. His dark almost black hair was sleekly combed backward and tight to his head. He looked younger than his years except for those few telltale graying hairs mixing in with his long, neat sideburns. His skin was evenly tanned adding to his most handsome charisma and his steel blue eyes were kind and all seeing. His smooth sculptured features gave light to the appearance of dignity. That with the intelligence that showed in a long record of ability together with his numerous qualifications made him an obvious candidate for upward positioning.

The Terran calendar was still operating and mandatory for space travel though local planetary calendars were used by the inhabited worlds. It was to celebrate Clysta's Terran dated eighteenth birthday that he had planned one of those trips. Her father had promised this time they would at last be staying at the ever popular resort world of Lightsworld II.

The space that surrounded the Skimmer III was filled with craft, many coming and going, soundlessly arriving and leaving this planet filled with many pleasurable things. The exhausted occupants of this Skimmer though were still sleeping soundly, parked in orbit and oblivious to all of the traffic passing by and around them.

Lightsworld II had once been a wasted lump of mostly rocky outcrops. It had almost no vegetation or areas that could be transformed in growing abilities. No qualities at all to make it fitting for mass colonization. It was too small to hold a dense atmosphere and not enough economic raw materials existed to make it a worthwhile attraction to any of the earlier mining conglomerates. This little planetoid did have one attribute though. It had a decently classed star and was deep inside the glory of the Orion Nebula. It needed only a meeting of minds of the controlling members then a quick voting decision by the one of the major and ancient Mass Entertainment groups of Earth. Then began the designs followed by some large construction investments and it was now the most popular pleasure world in this half of the Orion Arm.

The ship's monitoring robot checked all instruments and environments on board as it had each millisecond of the time since it had been assigned to this craft. Then it had roused Clysta's father just a short while ago and after enjoying his shower and daily toiletries, Quail Z'ee was now busy preparing his usual routine 'surprise' for his daughter.

Clysta and her father had just, the evening before, finished seven fantastically fun filled days going through the many entertainments that were available on this special planet and they were both thoroughly exhausted. The night previous, they had returned to their craft, prepared and ready to leave for their home system of Sol. They had decided to be shuttled back to their Skimmer III to sleep there that last night, parked at the orbiting Space Port, as an ending to their stay. Sleeping here in the space docking zone would also help avoid the line-ups to the shuttles and to give them an early start on their trip home on the day following.

The last three days of the vacation had been used in The Hunt. That was a popular and almost seriously life like action entertainment game and they were both fatigued from their strenuous ordeals, playing cat and mouse with computer simulated but almost lifelike holographic pursuers.

Clysta was awake now and stretched in her cot, removing the remnants of her sleep. She was smiling, awakened by the pleasant smell of breakfast. Breakfast would usually have been prepared by the 'auto', as were all the meals, but this morning the aroma was different. She stretched again, then skipped out of bed and headed across her sleeping quarters to prepare for the day ahead.

A minute or two later, the smiling face of her father came into view around the door as she was stepping lightly from the body cleaner sani' mold.

Before he could stop himself he spoke.

"Did you sleep well Clysta?"

His face became crimson in embarrassment when he saw his daughter's nakedness. He realized suddenly she was not a girl any more. Naked, and brief though his view had been, what he was planning to say today really did matter. But it could wait a little longer. He looked away quickly, saying.

"I'm ever so sorry Clysta. I didn't know you were out of the cot."

"That's o.k. Dad. As long as you didn't look," she answered, equally embarrassed.

She smoothed away the awkward moment as she answered his query, raising her voice slightly, having to talk around the archway and into the ships control room.

"Sure did, father-slept well I mean," she said pleasantly.

Then her father said, the awkward moment gone, "That's good. Breakfast is ready now, so come and get it. I brought along some real beans for the coffee. I have made it the old fashioned way, and it is still hot, so hurry before the whole thing gets cold."

She stepped into her brightly coloured and fresh one-piece body hugging garment. This was student standard dress in these times. The one she had, was of a material that had a sheen-like finish and it sparkled with a controlled static charge as she moved, generating a misty stardust like effect. She twisted around and gently smoothed the form-fitting tunic into place, whilst watching the full size holographic vision that showed a reflected model of her. Then she left her sleeping section and walked into the main cabin. Her shoulder length hair, neatly styled in fine gently twisting curls, which converged at the back in a geometric knot.

Her father had put on an apron as a mock precaution, to cover the all white loose fitting two-piece tunic of trousers and shirt like top.

"You look as if you are ready for work, father," Clysta joked as she moved around the nook housing the breakfast table.

"Thank you," he replied, noticing the innuendo. Then he continued.

"D'you know? You look more like your Mother each time I see

you, Clysta," graciously ignoring her last comment. He was beaming lovingly as she sat down at the opposite end of the small table.

Her father had set two places with bright silver utensils and a small vase of colourful and aromatic flowers, secreted from the planet surface below.

Clysta had an odd premonition something new was afoot. She often had a mysterious forewarning of forthcoming events, even at her Academy classes. Usually when these sequences occurred, she would put it down to deja vu. Lately though she had been very surprised at the items she would suddenly become aware of before they were spoken.

"Did you make all of this food yourself, father?" she asked as he placed a platter of his cooking on the table before her. She helped herself to some of the delicacies and started to eat. She wondered absently to herself what, if anything, this 'something' could be.

"Of course I did," he replied, and then continued as he passed her the other serving tray. "I told the food prep' to hold fast and have a holiday. Then, I sent the service robot to the rear of the craft to keep it out of my way. It is a sad day ahead, if I can't personally make this last breakfast of our trip. Is it not?"

Her father's statement needed no answer, so she gave none and continued eating. But again, she had a return of that odd feeling of something new and strange was on his mind.

She passed back the tray and continued to eat her meal. This was the usual routine on the last day of all of the trips they had taken since she could remember. They would obviously take advantage of all of the restaurants whilst they were down on the planets wherever they were visiting. Sometimes they would pick up picnic items. Other meals on board of course would be assembled by the ships in-built systems.

But for Clysta, this last breakfast meal brought all of their fun of their trips together and had become the final highlight of these outings.

The controls for piloting this compact little ship were close by, with the large viewing screen filling the wall, all at the blunt end of the key hole shaped area forming the main cabin. These, together with the habitat cabin were located at the bow of the vessel with the propulsion machinery and Hyper Bubble generator to the rear or stern. Separating these two sections were the sleeping quarters and a comfortable ancillary cabin.

As she ate, Clysta would casually look toward the screen and its vast display of the local space. She could see the closest section of the Nebula, far ahead of their ship, just a fraction of the glory that surrounded this area for many hundreds of light years of distance. One by one, she named in her thoughts, each of the many points of light in the local neighbourhood. She had learned of and loved the stars for as long as she could remember.

"There go the Sanravics," Clysta announced. A ship, much larger than their Skimmer, was leaving its orbit from close by. Her father turned on his seat to see it on the screen.

"Yes. That's them," he confirmed, "They said that they would be leaving early. Nice people they were too. I hope to see them again next year—." He stopped himself in mid-conversation.

Clysta was once again startled by a flutter inside her consciousness, as if she had suddenly become aware of an event of nothingness.

She watched as the craft left the screen's perspective.

The whole of the screen presently provided a view of the panorama of space directly ahead of their craft. By voice request, the screen could scan or turn that view through any portion of the sphere of space, to survey any sector, which surrounded this tiny and compact ship.

Her father once again continued with his light conversation trying not to be too serious in his manner.

"I never got to ask earlier, we have been too busy down there?" He indicated the planet below by pointing his fork downward. "So, tell me. How are things this session? How are you doing this year at the academy, and how are they all treating you?"

"Pretty fair, and good, to both of those. Why, it is almost fun!" she answered him with a pleasant smile. She continued, helping herself to more of the eggs. "One professor has been a pain, but I think I am getting the better of his studies. We are having classes on the causes for Hyper Space radiation this coming term, and do you know, later we get to carry out a few practical experiments on the use of the Johnsen Rule."

She was again aware of the same feeling of the 'something' in the background as they spoke. Words, not of her own statements, possibly thoughts from somewhere else even, were attempting to form inside her head but she was unable to decipher their meaning or reasons. She was confused but carefully hid her bewilderment. Her father interrupted her inner deliberation.

"That should be interesting," he said as he chewed on a strip of bacon and egg mix. "Do you know? When I was at Mars-Ac', even in my final year, the formulations to develop the Johnsen Rule did not exist. Now here they are teaching it to students at your Academy. Now I would call that real progress. You should enjoy it."

He finished the meal filling in with small talk again then picked up his cup and leaned across to the coffee dispenser for a refill. Clysta had finally finished her own cup and she refused more when he offered it. Turning back to the table, he took a deep breath, paused as if to gather his next words and then turned his eyes towards Clysta.

"Now that breakfast is over, I have something very important to tell you, Clysta." He started, trying to choose the right words. His voice had changed into a mood of seriousness as he spoke. "It concerns me and of course you. Us! So if you have finished breakfast, I will tell you what it is about."

Well, she thought. Here it comes. Clysta knew her father well enough to sense the urgency in his tone. He had always begun in this way when he had something significant to say.

"Just a minute then," she said.

She quietly arose from her seat, gathered the used dishes and utensils and placed them all in the recycling unit and then returned to sit down back at the table to listen.

"What I am about to tell you must not leave this vessel. It is a most secret and undisclosed plan and is for your ears only."

He paused to see Clysta's response. Seeing none coming, he continued.

"This all seems so melodramatic and perhaps unbelievable in our time, but those are the conditions under which I and many others have been placed for the future. This is the story."

"Two months ago, I was reassigned into a division of the newly delegated Intergalactic Exploration Group. He began. He twisted in his seat, stretching his legs outward to make himself more comfortable and relaxed.

"It is a new body of specialists. One with ever so much secrecy but also one that I feel must have lots of friends in high places. I have since been told that they, the Group that is, were only formed just about one Standard Year ago. It is most unusual for someone at my level in the Administration to have anything pass by in such secrecy. You know how I mean, at my level. This type of thing would have been brought to my attention at least. Or there would have been a meeting or two that I should have been attending or, if not, I would have known about." Clysta nodded her head in silent agreement.

Her father continued, "That there is no sign of it then suddenly, with no announcements, no enrolments, they have a craft and," he emphasized, "The candidates for its future commitments. I myself found it very strange. Never seen anything quite like it. Anyway, talk about speed. They must have moved pretty fast since whenever it was formed. Now, and without any fanfare or prior notice, a mission has been prepared with the objective to send an exploration team."

He stalled a little, gathering his next words.

"It,-the team—, is to cross the void lying between this and the next arm of our Galaxy. What it all boils down to is this. If things go as my superiors have indicated and also as I think I myself view them, I am very likely to be first choice for the appointment as Commander in Charge, for the mission."

He paused again for a second or two. Clysta sat still, trying to unfold these surges within her consciousness, but said nothing. Just milliseconds before he said the words, she knew what he was about to say. Then he continued, saying.

"There are three others beside myself, two male and one female. These others are part of the final selection to be in command of of the group to be sent. That selection is being made presently at the offices of Galactic Centre. Two of the others are good but I have been told that my experience and credentials will make me a favorite choice above those. The other one of the three, from what I also hear, hasn't quite the correct background." He drank from his cup and placed it ahead of him and held it with one hand and stroked the handle with his finger as he continued.

"If I am successful and they do select me to this commission, it is to be announced in camera by the ruling board——." Her father hesitated, then, "In just two Standard Days. That will coincide with my return to the Bureau from our trip here."

He stopped again as he selected his next words. Then he carried on, explaining.

"I have issued many reports on the topic in the past years, that our prospects for this segment of the galaxy we know as the Orion Arm, where it all began-Humanity, the exploration and colonization-has reached its maximum with the present drive systems. The drones we have sent to the Perseus Arm," he pointed with his thumb, to the left, "are suggesting that the largest percentage of the stars that we have reached out there are devoid of planets. And some of those few that do have planets are seen as being too old and others too young. They are mostly useless in our own plans for the Terran expansion. Not much of value to the future of Terran evolution is showing up."

He hesitated. "And up to now, definitely no signs of living or otherwise intelligent creatures."

"Reports on the other hand," he smiled at the choice of words, "from the arm in the other direction are really quite interesting. A few drones were sent there also, some years back. They show much more interesting results to their analysis. Good stars, and planets worth note." Then he added, "No life as we know it as yet reportable though. So, it has been decided by these people," he stressed, this time pointing upward, "at the top. We are now at the stage where we should go and see what our neighbour Sagittarius really does have in store for us. Like I said earlier, the status of the information we have to date has shown much more promise out there and it indicates there must be much richer pickings. Better resources and possible livable environments. Maybe better even than anything in this region of the galaxy."

Clysta still remained silent, letting her father tell his story. She found it a little odd, but anything that he was saying seemed not to surprise her too much. It was just as if she was hearing all of this for a second time.

Her father continued, "The next stage in all of this has now been reached. I was informed before I picked you up at the University, this Group or Committee has planned the expedition to move along quickly. The plan is real now. We are to go beyond the edge of our spiral and see what is out there and this time, see for ourselves. The main thing is of course, with the distance being so great I, that is if I am the one to go, will be away for at least two and maybe as much as four years. The journey is a long one but it should be speedy. We will be doing all sorts of surveys though. Actual planet falls and then analysis. You know, the sort of exploration stuff that I used to do when you was young."

He thought of those times when he would have been away from Clysta and earlier, his wife for months on end. He carried on with a little increased enthusiasm.

"The vessel they have built for this special trip is a completely new design. I have not seen it for real but from the crystals I have been allowed to see, it really is a beauty. It has a new and improved drive, which has far reaching prospects. And we will be carrying a crew of the finest technicians available. The Bubble influence has been designed to operate differently also. They have found a way of something akin to a reinforcement, to make it last longer and so completely removed the chances of flawing."

Clysta still sat in silence. He paused as he took a last draught of the almost empty coffee cup. Then.

"The amazing thing that I still cannot come to terms in all of this is—that the whole mission during the enormous amount of work in the preparations, has been such an extremely well kept secret. No one appears to have been aware, even in my own branch, that such an undertaking was afoot. I for sure did not know anything about it until my division head sent to me the viewing crystal outlining the development. Hardly anything was said between us, I just followed the instructions and found myself,"-he paused then in a question, "nominated? The vessel even, it is at this moment being primed to leave—," he choked slightly and swallowed, at his closing words, "Very, very soon."

Clysta, who still remained silent, could feel tears of sadness about to mount in her usually bright eyes. She had many questions to ask, but decided on the question she really needed an answer for. Deep down in her heart she did not want to hear the answer, though she already was somehow-once again, ever so mysteriously-aware of what it would be.

She swallowed and said, "How soon then," it was now her turn to falter slightly, "Do you think it will be that this expedition is to be leaving?"

All of the time he had been talking, the imaginary lump had grown in his own throat. He had long depended on these trips with his daughter as a replacement to both of them, for the loss of his wife who had died so early in Clysta's youth. He knew this new absence would be something he could overcome. But it would very likely be harder on his daughter Clysta.

"I have purposely kept all of this a secret from you since collecting you at Europa, and I must apologize for that. I did it so we wouldn't have our fun spoiled by other thoughts. This could be the last time we may be together for a very long period of time," he said. Then quickly and softly he answered his daughter's question.

"The answer to your own question is-that when I return to the Bureau, I will be notified of my future. If I am given the new posting, and it comes with no refusals, I am then to report to my new office at the Bureau's number Thirty Three Base. It is a new satellite station built at a small and inconspicuous star named I was told, by someone long, long past. It has an unusual name,—Mura." He paused again, then said quickly, "And all of that, the appointment, the approval and arrival at the base, is to be concluded in three days from now. Then again, and should I be the one chosen for the position, I get my appointment to full Commander immediately that I arrive there. The expedition itself will be leaving outward bound at fourteen standard days after they have made their selection. And from the moment of our arrival at the base, there will be no contact for the expedition's crew with anyone outside. Everything is to be in secret."

Clysta sat quietly, hiding her feelings and choosing a response that would satisfy both of them. She said finally, "But is that enough time to learn about the new ship and its new drive and be able to acquaint yourself with all of what this trip entails?"

He was ready with the reply.

"Those three others who I mentioned before, beside myself and who are part of the final selection, they have been learning most of the rudiments of the voyage too. Whoever does not become selected to receive the appointment of Commander is to have the chance and the option to be also a part of the Commanders aids in the specialist crew that goes with the expedition. A small part and requirement of the preliminaries was the knowledge of most of the needed skills. It has been just like returning to school. Really!

"Anyway, the larger parts of the learning processes are to take place during the trip out. It was not planned to waste time in too much more preliminary training. Just get familiar with the basics of the Star-craft here. As a part of its secrecy and speed of assembly mainly, or at least that is what I have been told. This is to be one extremely long trip, so there will be lots of time to assimilate."

"Well." Clysta said, not too resignedly, after listening to her father's explanations, "I suppose this has to be expected with the type of occupation you are in."

She said the last in a matter of fact tone, with her chin held high and bravely concealing the sorrow she was now feeling. Those tears she had at first felt, had now subsided. Also at the same time, she was so pleased that her father had reached to such a height in his profession. Now she felt not so sad at this long and imminent departure from her life.

This whole announcement, though she was still confused about the feeling of premonition, had come as a complete surprise to Clysta. She had, had only occasional contact with her father, mostly on these trips and in some letters and vidi'-messages. As it is with mostly all teenage students, she was not really aware of, or conscious of the importance of what her father's position was at the Bureau. His habit was not to load her with the details of his status. Now she felt, along with those strange movements within her own consciousness, she understood fully.

Trying hard to brighten and dispense the slight sadness that still lingered, she must not show the effort to hide the once more mounting sadness that they may be separated for so long a duration. She continued, suddenly sounding and feeling adult.

"I suppose it is only just a matter of time and then there is always some unforeseen new phase in exploration which is evolving. Just like this has now. And in the role that you hold, you are expected to move onto it when it does comes along."

Then she carried on more bravely, "We have been told at the Academy so many times, that without our outward exploration and following up with the inevitable expansion, the Human Race would stand a good chance of stagnation and possibly fade away within a few thousand years."

They both sat in silence for a second or two then Clysta perked up a little more as it occurred to her that she also had her own special kind of life ahead of her. The very best in education and the rewards those were likely to come to her later. When she graduated.

She said finally, "I am being very selfish. This is evidently a big step for you, father, the adventure, and then into the unknown. I should not feel I must try to stop you or try to make you turn down this intriguing opportunity. It is wrong to be so selfish. As for me, I am going to be fine. I will have lots of studies to keep me occupied. I have many good friends and lots of things ahead to plan for. And anyhow it isn't going to be for always. Is it?"

Though she heard herself say it, she was unsure of the truth of what she had just said. That feeling of oddness was again nagging inside of her mind. As she stopped talking, for the minutest span of time it was as if there was a scratching at layers within her consciousness, and then just as suddenly it was gone.

She brightened and smiled, saying.

"And you just might get back here in good time for my graduation. Don't you think so?"

Then she reflected to the beginning of her father's explanation. She added finally.

"Oh! And Dad!" She had so seldom used that term they were both taken aback. "The secret is safe with me."

He smiled.

"I know."

Those unknown territories in space were still regarded with the same sanctity as they had always been in the earlier days of space and planetary exploration. That exploration still was capable of surprises and sometimes its own little horrors. As it was, up to the present time, four dozen or more planets from the many hundreds visited had been found possessing their own range and variations of living beings of a high order and above the level of microbes and bacteria. There were of course hundreds of lower class creatures, some of them having strange and dangerous properties to test the visiting, early or even newer, adventurer. Of the planets found to have these indigenous upper intelligence creatures, just only five planets had creatures with intellect comparing to the type of intelligence or abilities of Earths own non-human creatures. Nowhere had there yet been anything, being or otherwise, discovered to be close or equal to Human, in intelligence or possibilities.

Luckily, these small few had their own forms of aptitude. These had evolved in the main from their survival of those environments on their own particular planet. Scavenging for food, battling with other similar habitants. Anything with any meaningful ability or upper state of intelligence turned out to be mostly passive, and all had in some ways been found to accept the visiting Terrans as if they were friends. Some appeared inquisitive by nature but that was all. The Terran colonists who followed the original explorers had learned from the old lessons of Earth's ancient history. To treat other newly found beings with respect, however strange and different they may appear. Don't try to change the aboriginals, whatever they may do to be registered as being different from the newcomer.

On some of the planets with living beings, there were those numerous natives of which there were still unknown details. Many of them had a much lower mental development, but some had compensated by having the strength and the power to inflict injury or even death to the unsuspecting explorer, innocently or by error. Occasionally, a menacingly ominous life form had been encountered on a planet, which was sometimes of an enormously diverse level of evolution. In many occurrences these native inhabitants would take their toll on first the explorers and then the colonist who followed, before finally the Terrans were able to understand and eventually learn how to exist with them.

The many dangers of venturing into strange places were still a force to be dealt with, even with the Terran advanced intellect and weaponry.

But in the distant neighbouring arm of the Galaxy? What changes or differences in evolution could be anticipated there? And so, so far away!

Quail Z'ee's own anticipation of the appointment to the rank of Expedition Commander did come to fruition. The appointment itself and the subsequent departure of Clysta's father as authoritative head of the expedition passed quickly and without any fanfare whatsoever. For reasons not clear enough to Clysta in particular, the whole operation was just as her father had inferred. It had all been planned in absolute secrecy, as if to screen the event from the public and of course all those ever present interplanetary news bands and bad news hounds.

To give herself some gratification, Clysta theorized the officials at Galactic Centre were full of wisdom and must have decided it was far better to maintain their complete secrecy about this particular mission. At least until it had departed and had achieved a safe distance and also be well clear of the objectors and their prying eyes. But Clysta found it hard at times to reason with this supposed intent.

There had been a variety of claims in the past to say, that expeditions of this magnitude were most unnecessary and are just a waste of time and talent. Clysta's own conclusions, again mostly to give herself some satisfaction, were that the planners of this mission had guarded against these and any other objectors. Some, she expanded in her reverie, could have gained sufficient media attention and would very likely agitate against its execution. Always there had been a number of misgivings stressed about the possible effects created by what had been termed loosely as 'The Zones of Rich Space'.

These volumes had been observed from a safe distance for centuries, without understanding their real content or possible effects on a space-craft moving within the Hyper Space medium. It was known that these elements appeared to exist outside the star producing vacuum of the galaxy. Pockets had now been detected within a number of small volumes of space surrounding the outside parameters of the helix of this galactic arm and mostly outside of the regions of the Terran Expansion. And it had been registered as a concern during plans for any future expedition that might reach to those extreme areas of space.

The Rich Zone anomaly had of late, been theorized to contain as much as quadruple the usual amount of Hydrogen atoms. If, as it was suspected, this material were to be encountered by an expedition, it may have a disastrous conclusion, particularly to their craft and its drive systems.

Probes had been long ago sent into the areas of the comparatively clear space that were between and separating the neighbouring Galactic spiral arms. Occasionally a probe had located almost by accident those un-plotted and sporadic 'islands' of this strange effect. The probe had ceased to transmit information until it had cleared these unpredictable areas of space, as though it were rendered inoperative for some even yet unexplained reason.

In some cases the probe would also report an encounter with what was described as a volume of enriched ether surrounding these same 'rich islands', which was equally unpredicted.

These two unexplained abnormalities in the fabric of clear space content still needed to be explored fully. Until recently the second abnormality had been speculated to exist only in the enormity of deep space between the galaxies themselves, at a distance too far for present methods of sampling.

This one item alone, Clysta had again speculated to herself, just had to be an argument in favour of an expedition of this magnitude. One giving its development the added credibility it required.

All of these thoughts went rampantly through Clysta's mind constantly as she tried to condone the need for the secrecy behind the launching of the expedition. Some scientists had at one time suggested, this enriched material may even one day in the far future be harnessed and used as a new source of energy, even as much as being used as a source of power for a new Ether Engine that could thrust vessels across the emptiness between the galaxies themselves.

`  Late on one evening, Clysta's disquiet and contemplation on the lack of release to the public of the expedition seemed finally to have been answered. Though it was only to be in a minor way. Clysta, luckily and really only by the oddest of chance, was to see one particular visi' news report.

At almost two months after the expedition had left the sector, a very brief announcement was made on the locally transmitted Sol news band. It made very quick note of the planned launch and direction of the new craft and then a terse history of its reasons for leaving on such a long journey. There was a short vidi' record from a dinner meeting held to commemorate the event. In a grainy visi' trans it was shown where some High Committee officials made a variety of speeches to laud the undertaking.

In his summary, the Chairman of the Deciding Committee in all of his eloquence had stated.

"We here, 'my honoured members and noble delegates', all understand the great and grave risks a new and untried expedition is likely to encounter. But in the cause of 'human endeavor' and its necessary expansion throughout the galaxy, we who are here must always consider—"

The Chairman paused, taking a long drink from his glass. Then he continued.

"—We are still not certain at this time if we are yet the highest of intelligence in this our Galaxy. It is as always, imperative we be ever sure that we be the first to encounter what ever there might be. It is also more imperative that if," he emphasized the word 'if', "there be those of a greater intelligence or strength, whomever and whatever— they must not be the first."

She was always mostly engrossed in her studies and did not spend much time with visi' scanning. But on this 'night' she had an urge to spend an hour of alternately hopping from selection to selection to find a suitable subject, and suddenly there was this item.

It was, for some time after, another puzzle to Clysta. Just why had the event still seen such a negligible amount of the media's attention? Why the delayed newscast? Why the late announcement of the departure of such an important expedition, which had taken its leave for the distant Sagittarius arm? And having no media follow-up. She could not find a way in which to rationalize the events and therefore had to let the matter slide from her attention.

It was later, much later, at Departure time-Plus Ten Months, that there came another visi' announcement that she again just chanced to see. She was with her friend Kindra, but it was he who was this time more unusually and sporadically surfing the many visi' bands.

It was just as brief and as inconsequential as before. This time announcing that contact with the expedition, which was by the usual Hyper-et-Visi, had ceased.

The article went on to elaborate, but only briefly, those technicians at the Command Centre had anticipated there would be the loss of transmission from the ship. Their excuse was, 'it is obviously and most likely due to the predicted interference caused by an increase in the density of hydrogen atoms.' This was conjectured to mean, the expedition had found one of the zones of the previously forecast medium.

Though seemingly apprehensive, the base technicians managed to fake a celebratory report.

The 'Director of Operations,' it went on to say, 'had immediately put the energies of those best available scientists to work, in an attempt at finding a means of overcoming this 'most annoying' problem.'

Clysta watched the screen in silence, almost mesmerized. Kindra broke into the silence after some minutes had passed. He too had watched the short newscast.

"That was an odd announcement. I hadn't heard of that particular expedition. They didn't have much to say about it, did they? I wonder where it is supposed to be going?"

He looked sideways and noticed the strangely concerned look of puzzlement on the face of his friend. He went on.

"What is it Clysta?" he asked, "Had you heard anything about that before?"

Clysta had not avoided saying anything about the expedition before this. She just did not have any real facts to pass along. That, together with her vow of secrecy she had given to her father. When she thought to say something to anyone, even to her friends, Clysta would be unable to form the words to begin. She thought very hard now, about a response of any kind, then decided she just had to say something to someone.

"Odd, is not saying enough," she blurted out. "All this is supposed to be a big secret, but after that and a short announcement in another news item, I suppose it is not a secret anymore. My father" she hesitated for a moment, "Is the Commander on that expedition."

Kindra was taken aback and showed his own genuine surprise.

"Your Father?" he stressed, "You haven't said anything before about it."

"Yes, I know. I have had to be secretive anyway. My father asked that I should. There just was not too much I was able to say about it really. And on top of it all, somehow not too many people seem to know of it, the actual expedition I mean. I have not heard a thing about its progress apart from one other very short newscast, which was released two months after it left. I suppose that should have ended the promise I made. And now there was that report. The one we just saw."

She felt a sudden release. The blockage that had been there, stopping her conversing about the events all of these months, just seemed to lift.

"Oh!" She started to explain. "I have made a couple of enquiries about the voyage, since it left. But no one, whom I could get through to, to speak to that is, knew anything about it. On my last try, I was shunted around and around until I finally stopped trying and gave up."

She then began to explain some of the facts, as far as she herself knew of them. She found that now, quite suddenly, she could tell Kindra everything. About the scant knowledge she had of the trip and about its intentions. Then, she told about those speedy plans that had been made in obvious secrecy. Slowly, she brought him up to date on the few facts that she herself had.

Kindra sat in absolute silence and listened to all she had to say.

# Chapter 2

More than a year had now passed by, since that last trip to Lightsworld II with her father. A new year of academics had begun and she was deep into her studies. At first she more than just occasionally thought of him and the expedition as the earlier months progressed. There were no more newscasts, strange or otherwise, or commentaries on the voyage, at the least that she herself knew of. Though now she did not get much time to do any viewing or checking into current events, Clysta had become so busy. Her time was spent generally in her education and in matters otherwise directed. Gradually as the months passed and for some unexplainable reason she did not find it necessary to think any more of her father, or even of those consequences of the reported 'Hyper-et-visi' communications breakdown. Then finally, as she became more and more involved in the mountains of work and her studies at the Academy, Clysta began to think even less and less of or about the matter.

Following the latest of the mid-term breaks, when she had been on a short vacation away from the Academy, Clysta once more returned to Europa. She had been enjoying a stay with five of her female student friends at one of those other of the Jupiter colonies. The students had stayed at a mining laboratory on Callisto, the larger of the many moons orbiting the large gas giant, Jupiter. One of the other young ladies had an Uncle whose position was Director of the settlement and ran the business of mining the many valuable metals. Clysta and her companions had all returned fully refreshed and she was ready to embark on this next session of studies with her usual enthusiasm again ready to become the hard-working pupil.

One morning, a few days after her return, she was standing in the student's viewing room with her friend Kindra. They were both working together as a team, on a hard task fraught with difficulties. It had been put by to them by one of the Professors of the Institution. Kindra asked amiably, whilst she watched closely the dancing output on the monitor display before them. They were both expectantly awaiting a result to the latest input from Kindra.

"Have you had any news of your father yet?"

Clysta was startled at the unanticipated question. She made an attempt to hide her surprise finding his inquiry quite unexpected. The topics, of either her father or the expedition had not been discussed between the two of them for those many months since they had witnessed the newscast. She thought quickly of a suitable reply. The mission had not taken up any measure of her own thoughts for quite a while. Except for some recent strange happenings.

Kindra Nymralph was a bright and energetic young man, just two months Clysta's senior. He had rich natural red hair, close cut and bristly, as was the style of the day for students at the Academy. With his infecting smile, mildly prominent but attractive features and bright blue eyes, it was always a pleasure to be in his company. Clysta and Kindra had been good friends for a number of years before and she always enjoyed that friendship.

His stance was upright and straight, with broad shoulders and a well muscled, but lean body. Try as he may though, even after many hours of body stretching exercises, he was still only those four centimetres taller in height than Clysta.

"No." She responded to his question as absently as she could and trying to be not blunt in her reply. Clysta was trying to withhold any response that might show the concern which was suddenly now renewed in her thoughts. She maintained her attention of watching closely, the results of his calculations as they were now beginning to develop on the display before her.

"Not yet." she added at length, but continued gathering her thoughts, and still a little hesitantly, she said, "There appears to have been an information freeze again on anything concerning the expedition. And I have not seen any more newscasts since that evening when we were together. I've been unable to get through to anyone with knowledge of even the journey itself."

She decided to continue and tell Kindra the rest.

"And I have not received even an official bulletin from Galactic Centre. Some months back, I sent a personal letter of request for news and haven't heard a thing in reply. I even put in that I was a related to the Mission Commander, but that does not appear even to carry any weight with them. Whomever they," she stressed," May be."

Since their first meeting in an early class, a number of years before, their friendship had continued to grow. It had grown into a dependable one where each helped the other at all times. Kindra and Clysta had also managed to temper the kinship with little friendly contests in their course results and marks.

Clysta quickly glanced from side to side, to ensure no-one was close enough to overhear what she was about to say. She then continued, now in a low voice, still concentrating on the screen, crowded now with her own input series of calculations.

"Kindra? Listen." She got his attention, then. "I have not spent any time recently thinking much about the expedition especially after I had no proper news for so long, or even of my father for that matter. Well— maybe that is not quite correct, there have been the occasional remembrances, you know, and then there were some other really odd," she paused to find the correct word, "Sequences? I suppose we have been so busy. My father and the expedition just have not been foremost in my thoughts—,"then she added in her uncertainty," Somehow."

She looked over her shoulder to check a second time, then again continued, in a low voice.

"But recently, about four or maybe five weeks ago, these other sequences started. Memories I guess you could say. I had a very peculiar dream and my father was in it. Very peculiar. And strange indeed. The details faded almost immediately, but I do remember vividly that my father's face appeared. That was the first dream, if you can call it a dream. Then it happened again later for a second time. Later, I had forgotten all about these two earlier occurrences then, it happened again.

This time, the last, it was just two nights ago, and I am not really convinced that it was only a dream. It seemed to be so unusual, almost eerie. But it was all, so…so real too. As if I was there with him, right there in the dream. But not a dream. You know? I cannot properly describe it, it was so strange and unexpected."

Kindra could feel the tension building in her conversation.

"Do you feel you want to talk to someone about it?" Kindra asked with real concern in his voice.

This kinship and trust between them had really taken a turn during the recent long hours of lab-work. They had studied long together on their present course topic. It was the time consuming study of Hyper-Effects, one of the major articles in the latest term at the Academy and each had begun to look out for the interests of the other.

"I don't know where or when it all started," she began, "But this last time I was at rest under Sublim Sleep Studies. I was going over those equations from four days ago, you remember, the ones which we had difficulty with, in the lab'."

She glanced around the area once more and, satisfied no one else was within hearing distance, she carried on with her story of the dream.

"This feeling! So strange it was. When I think about it right now, it all seems so stupid too. It came from out of nowhere. A cold and bitter kind of sensation at first, and then the face of my father just drifted by as if through a veil of mist. I could hear nothing but I could see his mouth was opening and closing. You know, like mouthing the words but in silence—no sound. His face though, it had a serious look. A look that, I have never seen before on my father. He always appeared to have matters under control. I got the feeling it was as if he was trying to tell me something. A warning. Something that was very serious too, by his look. Then just as suddenly it was all over. Nothing else happened. The odd thing about it all is that I remember each part of it so very strongly, but under the 'Sublim', you are not supposed to dream at all. Only the topic of the study is meant to come through to your awareness. You remember how it is supposed to be, your own sense of consciousness is switched off in the processing and nothing can interrupt the sleep. Short of a direct emergency from Central that is."

"What do you think it could have been?" said Kindra, keeping his own voice at a low level. "I mean. Do you believe it could have been anything but a dream? Perhaps you have your father on your mind a lot. Possibly. Deep down? Unconsciously perhaps?"

"I have thought of that too as a possible reason. But you know as well as I do," Clysta replied, "That interruption, or dreaming is not possible whilst you are in the instruction sequence, and anyway, why only my father's face. There was nobody to see or anything else for that matter. And especially under those weird and unusual conditions."

Kindra offered another reason.

"Could it have been possibly a malfunction, a system glitch maybe?"

She replied. "I doubt that could have come about. The system would have lit up had that happened. It is too much of an impossibility for that, and to have that effect."

Clysta was silent for a while, then, resignedly, "I cannot find an explanation for it but do you know, up until now I have never yet been very concerned or even worried about the expedition or my father. He is, or was," Clysta's face showed distress, "So capable as far as I was concerned. I hardly think of the expedition anymore. Then I get these strange dreams. Then I don't think of him again afterwards. It all blanks out generally. It sounds very odd I know, but that is how it happens. I have had so much confidence in him and found no need to worry. So why is this happening, now?"

Before they could carry the subject further, the signal sounded to announce the start of the next classes. Kindra made the appropriate function to avoid the loss of their work at the unit, and then they prepared to leave the area. Clysta's face still held the frown of concern as she gave a cursory wave of her hand and then resignedly shrugged her shoulders as they separated. Their next period was to take up their positions at the Ed-trans units for the next two hours of study.

At a time much later, Clysta was now well into her age twentieth year. Her education had finally begun to reach its pinnacle. This was to be the final year at the Academy too for Clysta and of course for Kindra, if all was to go as well as expected. The timing also coincided for the pair, with their final conclusion of the grueling two year course and its studies on Astrological Navigation. Those studies had begun to reach their completion and it was now toward the end of the course year. Following many weeks of extremely arduous instruction, the Professors for the course had arranged a practical and hands on application of what they had learned. This test was to have a great bearing on the students' final passing grades and on each of the successful scholars subsequent graduation.

The class had been arranged in teams. The exercise entailed the teams, groups of three students each, being transported by a spacecraft, to a point out in the depths of space. That point would be anywhere in a sphere of space of at least five hundred light years radius using the Solar System as its centre. The point was also not in any particular or recognizable direction either.

The groups were transported in a larger vessel, then each group transferred to their own test ship and then to be deserted, or in other words, left and set adrift there. The craft they were supplied with was one of the Academies smaller but well stocked training vessels that had been previously parked. It was at a location pre-selected by the Academy staff to be at a mid-point between two most effectively complicating and uncompromising stars. The stars chosen were as usual, to be a Blue Star and whatever else was in this secret sector of the void.

The general idea of the test was, after being stranded the team of three students were to find the shortest and speediest route that would lead the team back to the Academy on Europa. And do it effectively, completely alone and unassisted.

Adding difficulty to the exercise was the fact that they, the students who were involved, were not to be given any clue as to what point in the void each of these lonely test craft had been deposited. They were also not informed what were the names, references, or categories of the stars in that region of space.

The whole exercise was of course being monitored from one of the Academys' intercessor ships, hidden and undetectable in the neighbourhood, obviously in order to protect the students from any hazardous or disastrous results in their navigation. Onboard the craft, there would be all of the necessary equipment to calculate their position together with the records and charts and other materials with which to work. But basically, each team was to say the least, marooned and alone and wholly responsible for finding each, their own way back to the home base at the Academy.

The choice of stars was to set a further problem, which was, that a Blue Star has unpredictable extremes of gravitation not following the regular rules of space physics. This would create a curving of normal space leading to changes in the navigational perception of the local universe.

The three occupants gave a wave to the Academy pilot as he left their small craft via the air lock. They watched on the view screen as he then to took the short trip across space, to the other Academy vessel parked alongside. They then watched the screen in silence, as the other ship was powered up and gently left the neighbouring space, taking two other groups to their own test crafts in another section of space. Then it quickly dwindled in size as it accelerated into the nothingness of the surrounding space, leaving them all alone.

When a number of seconds had passed after the vessel of the instructor had disappeared from view, Clysta continued looking at the screen. It was showing in full, the splendor of the panorama that the millions of bright stars formed ahead and around them.

Then, she turned her attention to her two companion students, saying cheerfully.

"Well, what is first? Food or flight."

"I recommend food. We have the time."

That answer came from G'zin.

"And I, am going to make it!" she added with a bright smile.

G'zin DeVenouire. She was almost a newcomer to the duo's close friendship, although she had been a student at the Academy for nearly the same length of time that Clysta and Kindra had been there themselves.

G'zin was from the planet Fryl and it was the planet of her birth. Fryl was a particularly attractive world, having only two landmasses, large oceans, many mountainous areas with lakes and full of beautiful places. The land covered approximately forty percent of the planet with many native inhabitants and its oceans full of large and small living creatures. There were on this particular world, many, many indigenous plants and a multitude of land dwelling and natural lower intelligence animals and creatures. Fryl was one of those very few and strange worlds which had the Earthlike probabilities that mankind had sought for centuries of exploration. And it had been found to be instantly habitable by the Human explorers and colonists.

The planet Fryl rotated on a slightly wobbly axis as it revolved amongst three other less fortunate globes, around a yellow Type M star, just slightly brighter than Sol.

Tufel was the local name for their star, named after the Captain of the first ship from Earth to visit the system. The star also emitted a small percentage more Radions of the Ultra Violet wavelength than that of Sol, the star that had been the origin of all Terrans. This Ultra Violet factor was found by the specialists to be responsible for giving all of the descendants, after the first line who were born of Fryl, the bluish tint to their skin. It was also blamed for their red pupils and the green iris of their eyes. Another even stranger genetic anomaly amongst those females of the population was that their eye pupils would change their colouring and begin to sparkle like rubies, exposing their sexual attraction to the opposite gender.

They, again the females only, also grew six toes to each foot. For years this fact alone had many concerned genetic specialists continually searching for an adequate explanation.

G'zin's own exquisite beauty though was of more import than her twelve toes. Her hair was of the deepest black, styled tightly into two thick braids and ending half way down her back almost to her waist. The skin of her pleasant and attractive face was smooth and accented with high cheek bones and constantly smiling, full red lips around perfect and white teeth. She was smaller than the other two though, with her diminutive and neatly proportioned frame being ten centimetres shorter than her two friends. But G'zin DeVenouire adequately made up for her natural shortness by her voluptuously pleasant and infectious vigor.

The call for food was answered almost immediately. But of course, on this ship, as with all of the ships of the Academy, food prep' was no chore at all. Just zip a program into the dispenser and within a minute, anything from up to seventy items of food could be selected to represent the varied menus and dishes from almost eighty different inhabited worlds.

As they ate, Kindra started the conversation on the plans to fix their position here in space. This craft had most of the updated systems and devices of the age but, being designed for educational tasks, it lacked much of the roominess and comfort of the better commercial designs. There were none of the smooth lines and padding of better quality cruisers for general use and hard and lean seemed to be the rule.

The layout of the deck space was shaped like the leaf of the three leafed clover plant of Earth. There was a distance of just a few paces between each area. The cramped and open sleeping area was on the one side and the work and dining areas on the other. The area of the control console for piloting was central in this arrangement. The sleeping quarters and sanitation were both in only that one room meant for sleeping. It was quite small and would be shared by these three friends. Privacy was certainly not a consideration in the construction of these Academy craft.

"First," he began as G'zin handed him the snack he had requested, "I want to try a little game of astral' triangulation on some of the brightest stars. G'zin, if I start by zeroing in on those three," he turned and pointed them out on the screen, "There, there, and that one there. Can you take a spectral on them so you can identify them from the charts?"

G'zin did not answer. She just nodded and waited, listening.

He continued, "Distance is a factor which we may have to compromise on, but we can get a bearing to within I would say sixty five percent at the first fast reading."

He stopped as he thought of the next move. He took a slow draught of his drink. After a few seconds he turned again to face his two fellow students and continued.

"Then we approximate the time taken to reach this spot in space.

That will help confirm my suggestion. If it works," he added, more to himself than the others. "After that is done, we open up a sphere chart and radiate from Sol in parsecs. We can put those comps' to use that we worked with last month. I can remember taking three jumps in and out of Hyper on our way here."

The students had been isolated from the transporting craft's control room for obvious reasons. The physical effects though could be felt when jumping into Hyper Space.

G'zin took a sip and then placed her own glass on the small table. The glass contained a personal concoction consisting of a sweet and cool blue liquid.

She frowned, saying, "I don't think the Profs' intended this trip to be so direct and easy. Those jumps could have been faked, it has happened before to classes. And we cannot rule out the major possibility of a Star Curve somewhere during one of those jumps you mentioned. Someone remarked before we left that they had caught last year's class with that one. At least two groups had to be rescued from a gravity well out by Deuteronomy."

She left the table and walked across the craft's control area toward the large view screen. It occupied a major section of the curved wall over the guidance and power controls. Presently, it was showing a one hundred and eighty-degree vista of the black velvet of space punctuated by countless stars. G'zin was herself attempting to estimate by familiar star clusters, just about where the home system was likely to be.

"What is your feeling about this, Clysta?" Kindra asked.

Clysta had been sitting at the table, listening in silence. She gave a shrug and placed her now empty server into the slot. Clysta's marks indicated she was presently top student of this year. Though the other two did not intend to, they felt good that Clysta was here with them. Her knowledge could likely be a boost and a bonus to the end results of the exercise.

"I think you may be right G'zin. The Professors are very likely to try the same one again or something like it. What we need to do is pool our ideas. Your sphere chart concept may be a little laborious but with G'zin on comp' it might be the answer."

G'zin was their class's expert student on computer. She was fast at deciphering and applying the necessary input to any configured assembly of equations.

At one end of the screen's view of outer space, they could see the closest star, which was less than a half of a light year away. Clysta continued, looking at Kindra.

"I am sure that is a Blue Star we are nearest to. We can check it later; see if it has any bodies in orbit. That should help us to narrow the field by comparison in the star charts. If we cannot get results using your suggestion, or find them leading to a 'Blue' with a straight line, then we will experiment with a few curves."

"So! G'zin," she suggested, turning, "Do the Spectral check for Kindra. Then plot the jumps with all the time factors that Kindra remembers. Don't forget if you are to develop a curve in Hyper you need to have a star in the right place to cause it."

As the others cleaned away the rest of the dishes and utensils, Clysta added, "You two can use the main comp' to do your own calculations. I will investigate to see if this really is a Blue Star that they have parked us near. If it is, I will then attempt to work on a way out by the Bubble. If I can't, we will be some time escaping by normal Ether Drive. I remember some tables I can use. They are from those lectures we attended before the Christmas break. They may be useful.

Now, if you two are in agreement, we will work for about two hours. Then we will stop and get some sleep."

With raised eyebrows she nodded her head toward those small and cramped sleeping quarters and smiled.

"Let's get on with it then," said G'zin with her customary vigor and enthusiasm. She pushed one of a number of marked buttons on the smooth wall of the work area. It would activate the systems, which would collapse and fold away, then store, all of the unnecessary furniture.

Kindra, who was also just as eager to get started, took the Thought Trans Unit from a cupboard. As he did his mind wandered to remember those tables that Clysta had brought to mind. He had had a little more than difficulty with those. He and three more students had been using one of the large crucibles on Europa that had been left behind by the mining company. They were making an attempt to develop a star structure and things went awry when Kindra used the incorrect formulae for the flux transformation of hydrogen supplies to the tiny Helium mass. It was his own error and he accepted the fault. Those tables, he winced mentally as he imagine had he not recalled them correctly, halted the possible creation of a new star right there in the orbit of Jupiter.

The Trans' unit he had taken, was similar to a lightweight, delicate metallic dome-like helmet which covered completely the head and face of the user. Then there was a ribbon of sensors, which trailed down the users spinal region. Tiny fibre like antenna painlessly entered the skin and into the elements of the spinal cord, to make full use of the relevant control of the nerves.

Using sensitive brain probe transmissions, lines could be drawn inside a large holographic sphere chart showing the surrounding space and the stars. The spherical holograph was displayed in the centre of the control room, now darkened for the projection.

In simple terms, the wearer of the device was given a mental picture of the same scene by a reverse process. It presented to the Unit wearer the perception that he was actually standing there in the void of space, out amongst those same tiny points of light.

This whole picture and the holo' imagery was connected to the main computing device where G'zin worked on her calculations and then the interplay of conditions could be seen by both of them, enabling each to react to the others input.

Clysta sat quietly at her own worktable. She was reading through reams of record filament, plotting particulars of the local relevant gravity curves. It was her own effort to try to expose the specification to indicate the spatial location of this particular Blue Star.

Finally, and after two and some half hours of arduous mental effort, they still had not achieved those speedy results they, and particularly Kindra, had at first anticipated. The three friends, each a little weary, eventually voted to stop working and reluctantly agreed it was time for sleep. They retired to their cramped cots, turned down the lights and switched on the assisted slumber inducers.

Sleep came immediately.

# Chapter 3

Clysta awoke with a start. She had no idea how long she had slept to now, but she was feeling refreshed. There was a trace of perspiration on her forehead and arms but still she felt quite cool. Checking the environment monitor just above her head, Clysta noted the readout, it showed the atmosphere within the small craft as being quite satisfactory. She tried to understand then, why she should have perspired.

What had happened before awaking came back to her almost immediately. She had been through that strange but now familiar dream sequence again. She had seen the strange image of her father in her sleep, but this time it seemed more distinct than it had ever done before. It was more real, the outlines not so fuzzy and dream like as it had been on those previous occurrences. Also, this time she thought she had heard something. In the previous occasions the visions, if she could call them that, there had been no sounds. This time there was a sound, but very faint. And it was similar to having been caught in slow motion. She could not quite be sure what it was she thought she heard, but she was sure this time it was as if the image and the expression of her father had been trying to give her a warning. But why? She tried hard to remember as the details began to fade little by little. But she could only guess now. One word, that was all, it was drifting quickly from her memory. It had a sound almost like 'Beware', but by now it was so painfully unclear.

As she raised herself and sat upright in her cot, the motion of her movements caused the walls of the sleep area to illuminate automatically. The increasing light now disturbed the other two and

Kindra, who was the first to awake, turned over in his cot to face Clysta. He spoke when he saw Clysta's confused and startled look.

"What is it Clys'?" he asked, "You look as if you have seen a ghost".

She slowly rubbed her fingers over her now closed eyes as she answered him, "I hope not. I have just had another of those…those…dreams. You remember, I told you of one some time ago. The ones where I see the face of my father."

A chill coursed through her upper body forcing an involuntary and momentary shivering spasm. Her deep dark eyes were open now as she continued.

"This has to be the third or the fourth occurrence since then. I didn't say more since we talked that first time, but it keeps happening and it's beginning to worry me now."

She described the sequence and what she could remember seeing and finally commented on the word of warning-or whatever it might have been.

She then said, "Just lately I have suddenly begun to get the feeling that I miss my father and I have a slight fear for him, or his well being. And though somehow I feel sure that he must be safe, these visions in my sleep are becoming more and more," she paused, as if looking for the correct word, "So upsetting. It is like having a premonition, you know, of him being in peril somehow, or somewhere."

Clysta stopped pensively, letting her words trail, then, "And not hearing anything and especially with that darned foolish and unaccountable bulletin blackout…" Clysta's voice trailed off completely.

Then she mused, saying almost to herself as her eyes closed again. She now was lightly rubbing at her temples, massaging the area in a pensive and circular motion.

"Enough is enough. I must make an appointment to have a check up when we are back at the Academy, all of this is becoming too much. I have been putting off having tests for this for so long. Maybe it will give me some explanation of what it is that is happening to my mind."

Kindra and G'zin said nothing, but their faces showed a friendly concern for Clysta's situation. It was out of context for Clysta to show any kind of weakness. She was always eager to demonstrate command of any situation. G'zin had now become awake and was watching the events though not aware of too many facts of the previous discussions that had taken place between Kindra and Clysta. Kindra swung his legs out of his cot and sitting upright, quietly told G'zin a brief chronicle of Clysta's father and his involvement in the expedition. He found it necessary, though unusually awkward, not to give too much attention or explanation to what he and Clysta thought of as part of the secrecy of the mission.

Clysta herself did not add anything to Kindra's explanation and left it at that. She finally asked that Kindra and G'zin not concern themselves about her problem any more, and that they keep their attention on their more immediate problem. That was the one that they had left incomplete before breaking for sleep, the problem of leaving this area of space and passing the test.

It was now close enough to 'wake-up' anyway, so they all decided to rise and prepare for the task at hand. After each had used the minuscule body cleaner and all had finished breakfast, they returned to their work where they had left off before sleeping.

An hour or more passed of almost complete silence. There was no small talk now nor was there time for it. The only exception was that of a few occasional words accompanying the myriad computations, which were constantly being passed, between G'zin and Kindra. Clysta sat in complete silence at her own end of the small work area.

"Here G'zin," said Clysta finally, breaking into their work and calculations. She handed G'zin a micro disc, "Add these to your calcs'. Enter them under the 'Zc waves' column. I think they will give us some of the answers that we need in our direction puzzle."

G'zin took the tiny crystalline disc and slipped it carefully into the slot in the computer's receiving tray. Her fingers then began their dance. As if playing an instrument she used her delicate touch to skim and leap lightly across the pads of the input console. After including a few of her own additional calculations and some speedy correctional entries from Kindra who again wore the Trans' unit helmet, she sat back and waited for the results to evolve. Meanwhile Kindra manipulated the holos sphere using his expertise with the neural wave patterns to activate his own input control of the finished holographic picture.

Clysta's entries added to those of the other two were a success, but only in this the first stage. That led them onto the next of the many steps in their efforts. Now the toil began. It was after almost five hours of hits and near misses interrupted by another meal, when Clysta was about ready to cancel one of their recent routines. She wished to try another way around what was now becoming the final phase in the problem solving. Weariness was showing in all of them, although not a bad word had been passed and no tempers were showing. But the end was becoming a farther point in the distance.

Clysta was just about to call a halt, and perhaps stop for the time being.

Suddenly, Kindra raised his arms above his head and gave a cheer.

"Eureka, I see the path!" he said excitedly.

G'zin automatically pushed the control to save all of the final computations as all three watched their accumulated development evolve in the air before them. The red line of the path home so slowly but deliberately began to zigzag through the hologram of space that was still being displayed in the centre of the darkened compartment. The route it described showed those small green splashes meant to indicate the position of each Hyper Jump. There were a total of three in all. Then the red line came to an end at a tiny bright dot deep inside the holographic projection. Finally, the computer's soft voice began repeatedly to announce, as if in its own disbelief.

"This is the target star system, Sol".

"Ok," said Clysta happily, "That is it."

G'zin added.

"And there is that curve we were trying to find. And it is very well hidden too. Crafty if you say it kindly."

Clysta continued, looking at the hologram of deep space.

" Now we know which way we are to go. Kindra, you enter that route into the auto pilot then do a quick check through the course. And you G'zin, will you please plot those Jumps while I work on these other systems. I am close to settling on a way to escape the curving gravity around this Blue star."

Clysta had some hours previously confirmed her suspicions. Then she continued.

"If our luck holds out, we can be back at the Academy in five hours, or maybe even less if we turn on the heat. And then, when we do get back and whilst you two do some celebrating and I can be excused, I will make my appointment to see the Academy Psych' about my silly dreams."

"Yes boss," said G'zin pleasantly, "Oh, and also. Whilst we are en route, would you please refresh us on those tables you used to get us started? Questions will surely be asked when we get back."

# Chapter 4

Doctor Branidge was one of the best in his field of Neural Exploration. He had retired from his practice on Earth so many years ago and set himself up as a consultant on the mental stresses of space faring people. That work was not sufficient to keep him content, so one day he was commiserating with a colleague when he was told of a good position being vacant on one of the moons of Jupiter. He applied and found he could be Resident Psychologist at the Europa Academy. Here he would be most useful in putting his long experience and life's work to the problems of overseeing the molding of the brightest of young mentalities in the known Galaxy.

His surgery was typical of all commitments of the Academy. Nothing but the finest was sufficient, both in equipment and in technology. Automated apparatuses, neural diagnostic scanners and brain probe viewers. Anything, that was new, or the latest and more.

Doctor Branidge was now a man who was in his later years. He was tall, two metres exactly and skinny, almost bony. Always immaculately clean but slightly untidy with an unusually balding head. No-one in this era lost their hair. But that was how Doctor Branidge liked it. What was still left of the hair that he did have, always appeared to have been left uncombed from at least some two days previous. And it was greying, another of his personal choices, and worn long, still another. Facially he had no distinguishing features, except for a protruding hooked nose and the foreboding scowl across his lean face and beneath bushy bedraggled eyebrows. These were accompanied by very keen, sparkling and all seeing ice blue eyes.

He enjoyed those very antique clothing styles of Old Earth. Wearing a Tweed jacket and loose-fitting flannel trousers, he was always very noticeable when out and around this most modern of Universities. His shirt, also typical of the same ancient style and always a bright white, was uncommonly continually crumpled and looked un-pressed. A final embellishment was a tie of the old school of one of the universities of Greater England. Possibly just of his many heirlooms no doubt. The tie was always tied in a knot but not tight, so to hang loosely up to an unbuttoned shirt collar.

Clysta approached the door to Doctor Branidge's surgery. After speaking to the door robot, the door opened to give her entry and she walked inside. She had completed the formality of previously making an appointment and was surprised that she had received the response so quickly. Less than one day had elapsed since calling for the check up.

All inside the office, it was gleaming white and shimmering stainless steel. After she had entered, the doorway behind her silently closed. Another robot, a mobile one this time, led Clysta from the hall and into the surgery waiting area and then, quickly left. Yet another machine approached. The other robot had been silent but this one had a voice, a little mechanical but seemingly having feminine qualities. It announced,

"This device is the recorder for Doctor Branidge. It is programmed to take down the credentials of visitors to prepare the Doctor for those visitors."

The doctor's robot 'secretary' as it was, asked questions. None of them too personal but very direct all the same. It seemingly was devised and programmed to take charge, so after the last of the questioning, it then guided Clysta into yet another room. This one was different to those previous. The walls radiated in soft colours that swirled and changed into most pleasing patterns, almost hypnotic in their presentation. Not sufficient though, to make one sleepy. Just make them content to watch their ritual of constant and ever changing.

The 'secretary' traveled over to a chair by the wall. It pulled the chair across the room, placing it at Clysta's side of the large central desk constructed of real and natural oak. Clysta quietly sat down and viewed with interest first the rare desk and then the many framed photographs, diplomas and honours occupying the walls of this the Doctors office. Almost five minutes had passed by, in silence. She then realized, a little startled at first that a man was sitting in a large leather chair across the desk from where she sat.

'That's odd,' she thought, 'where ever did he come from. He certainly was not there when I entered.'

Clysta must have been preoccupied by those walls. She had been sitting in her place for many minutes and had not noticed the presence of the man at all. That must be the Doctor, she again thought. She had only heard of his description from other students who sometimes discussed having attended his surgery and sometimes those few lectures he had conducted.

At the other side of the desk Doctor Branidge, if it was the Doctor, finally looked up from his work on the comp' display which was located to his left. His piercing blue eyes mellowed instantly and took on a kindly look as he asked in a pleasant voice, the usual and unanswerable first question of all doctors.

"And what is it that seems to be troubling you, Miss Z'ee?"

His voice took her by surprise. It was kind, almost fatherly and soft. Not at all the voice of as old a man as she was led to believe him to be. Calming. Yes, even more than those walls. When she began, it took Clysta just a few minutes to explain to the Doctor about those previous sleep periods and then she described that latest occurrence while on board the Academy vessel. She told him everything, even though she did not intend to. His gentle presence was almost hypnotic.

The Doctor listened patiently and most intently to her description of her dreams and then, when she had finished, he rose up from his seat.

"Follow me," he said with a slight, almost imperceptible waving of his hand.

An archway opened in the middle of the otherwise smooth and seamless wall to his right. He stopped at the opening and to one side and let her pass through, ahead of him and into the space that was beyond.

They had stepped into an elaborately equipped and furnished laboratory. The opening in the wall remained momentarily and then closed silently. He then guided Clysta toward a piece of apparatus in the centre of the area. As they stood before it, he took a little time to explain some of the routines of that particular device, which he said would possibly be of help in diagnosing her condition. Although she listened intently, she found it difficult to really understand all that he was telling her, so she politely nodded occasionally, as he appeared to reach a point in his dialogue that should have some relevance.

Whilst he continued to speak, he half motioned half guided Clysta toward a slender rectangular frame, large enough that she could stand inside its parameters. The doctor then stepped behind the frame, out of her line of vision. Clysta turned her head to follow his movements, but he asked that she continued to face front ward. He had moved behind her and outside of her peripheral scope. She could not see the doctor now as he operated the small hand held controlling console device.

Altogether and in one fluid spinning motion, she next found herself laying flat, parallel to the floor of the room, resting and suspended in an anti-grav' plane and next feeling a sensation of calm as the energy field was made to sooth and caress her body from head to toe.

Next, four spheres of highly polished gold, about twenty-five centimetres in diameter, floated close to take up positions in a square pattern around her head. The Doctor mumbled quietly to himself for thirty or more seconds whilst her brain was being subjected to what his dialogue was describing as a Lanson Layer scan. Then he looked at the large viewing screen. Clysta was unable to turn to see it from her position, as her head was now held tight in the field of invisible energy.

Clysta next felt an itching sensation, inside the back of her skull. She was reminded of those strange feelings she had had when she was with her father on that last trip to Lightsworld. The room became misty and faded as she seemingly blacked out of consciousness with no inference of the time. Suddenly from nowhere, the room around reformed and she was awake and feeling refreshed and informed, her thoughts fully at ease.

It did not even occur to Clysta to question what had happened and she was not even slightly inquisitive as to just what if anything had transpired during that blackout of her senses.

The Doctor was still doing his work and still also out of Clysta's plane of vision, so she could not follow what if anything he was still examining. After a few more minutes of his extensive checking and double-checking, the Doctor stopped what he was doing. He moved around to where she could now see him. He looked directly at Clysta's with his piercing blue eyes.

"There is nothing fundamentally suspicious that I can deduce from these patterns," the Doctor said in a soothing tone. "You are reporting normal with the exception of what we will call a-a-brightness—." He turned away to write a note on a pad on his desk top, stopped, then as he turned back. Clysta noticed he appeared to be suddenly more absent than he had been before. His eyes had taken on a glassy stare, like he was listening to another conversation, then it was gone. Just as quickly he continued.

"For want of a better term, we will call them, the neural anticipatory frequencies. Not many humans have use of them. But some few—."

The Doctor's voice trailed into silence, as if in absent thoughts. He took the small control from his jacket pocket, pressed the appropriated pad, and the four spheres glided away from Clysta's head as he carried on again.

"The Principal in his weekly reports on you." Clysta noticeably stiffened as the Doctor paused. "—Now you need not become alarmed, I receive reports on all Academy students to keep abreast of each pupils stress status.—Anyway, now where was I, ah yes! You Clysta seem to have a fairly good grasp of all of your courses and your work. These abnormal systems—"

He stopped. Appearing absent again and to be thinking to himself or even listening to something.

He then continued, "—Ah, yes that is it, quite correct, we will call them systems for now—, Aaah," he paused again, "—systems that you appear to have within your cerebrum may be helping you in these results. This condition you say you are going through. It almost suggests to me, this brightness of which I speak may be also at work. Even being manipulated by someone or something. It may be quite unconsciously of course your own particular case. Something similar to a-a-well, a catalyst?"

Again he wrote in the pad. Bent over with his back to Clysta, his voice mumbled on, to himself again, until it disappeared into silence. Clysta thought about the pad. No-one uses paper and a scribe these days. Notes are taken automatically and directly by voice recorder. Very ancient methods, and odd, she added in her thoughts.

He returned to where Clysta was still suspended and carried on with his diagnosis. While turning dials and closing the equipment down.

He further explained, talking to himself more than to Clysta. "Of course, these waves which I spoke of previously still have secrets we need yet to uncover. My colleagues and I have been working on a theory. It is one in which we believe these patterns may lead to telepathic abilities in such a way that a subject is able to receive advances in information."

The Doctor's eyes once again took on a glassy and pensive appearance. He seemed to be drifting off to somewhere in his own thoughts again, somewhere deep and far away. Then he brightened and returned to his dialogue.

"I have been trying to prepare a paper on this for the Psyso-Psychology Journal for almost two years now. Ah. But I digress again."

The Doctor continued.

"Your particular pattern is one that is quite unique. It is the only one of its type that I have come upon in this Academy to date. But we, that is may colleagues and I, have been noticing certain changes in the mental patterns of some of the students and that these are by no means isolated instances."

Having seemingly completed the remaining tests, the Doctor manipulated the suspension frame, making it almost upright then turned down the anti-grav' and let Clysta step from the frame of the unit to the floor beneath.

"Tell me a little about your father," he asked when Clysta had stepped away from the frame and assembled equipment, "From what I deduce from these apparitions and what you have told me, you must have been very close."

She had a sudden thought that he, Doctor Branidge, amongst a very select few, might know a few facts about the expedition. And about what had transpired since its leaving for the next arm of the Galaxy. She could not reason why she could think this though, and she did not feel to have the will of the impertinence to ask.

Clysta moved a few more paces across the room toward the only other solitary stool and half sat, half stood facing Doctor Branidge. She mussed at her hair and then smoothed the one piece suit.

"In a way, I suppose we were-very close," she corrected herself as she agreed, "Although we had spent most of our time in separate parts of the Galaxy Spiral. My father would come here to Europa to pick me up about three and sometimes four times each year, and we would just take off and visit all of the nicer places in this sector. He even taught me to handle a Skipper when I was only thirteen years old. By the time I was fifteen he would let me handle all of the calculations and instrumentation for short Hyper Jumps. We used to have lots of fun together."

The Doctor handed her a small tumbler of liquid explaining it was a mixture of vitamins and a medication. She sipped as she spoke feeling more at ease as the medication seemed to take effect.

"Then he was appointed Commander of the expedition. I wasn't very concerned about the trip because, although there was to be every chance it would be a long journey, this would likely be the last. You know. Before taking a permanent desk position perhaps, or maybe an early retirement. Now though these dreams or whatever they are. I am not so sure anymore. I wish it was possible to really know something a little more positive."

There was a sudden sadness that took over her usually bright aura and tears were beginning to well up in her eyes.

Doctor Branidge, noticing the sudden change, made an attempt to convert his stern expression to a smile. He then said in a more gentle and comforting voice.

"You must take a solid and positive outlook on all of this you know.

This expedition wherever it goes, must expect to have many years yet, before a return is anticipated. The consensus is that in the history of all of our space exploration, there has been no unfriendly life discovered anywhere. In addition, there is the fact of which the expedition vessel is most likely the best that the Council has ever had built. And it will operate, no doubt, forever. These facts alone make the odds heavily weighted for its success—and its return," the Doctor added quickly.

That last statement. It had Clysta convinced that the Doctor was informed somehow about the expedition. Somewhere, the words echoed some that her father had used, before he left. But why he should have been brought up to date? That was a puzzle to Clysta.

He paused again for a second as though searching for the right words.

He continued, "Think on the positive side, My Dear. The expedition must be safe. Its timetable must have had at least two years before it reached any real density of stars to confront and explore on the other side of the gulf. That will only be about now in our time, when they are likely to begin searching or encounter any kind of beings. If there are any at all to be found on those other worlds. Be they friendly or otherwise."

The Doctor appeared to correct himself almost absently. Then he shrugged his shoulders and sat in pensive thought for a while as if unable to collect himself. He added a few more notes to the pad. Then he rose from his own seat to lead Clysta to another doorway that had now made its outline appear. It had opened up silently and led to the first passage she had entered outside the surgery. Clysta took it that the examination was now completed. There were no other patients waiting in this the outer reception area and the Doctor followed.

He opened the outer door himself, letting Clysta pass saying, "Now you must return to your studies and continue as you have. You have many, many adventures ahead. You must come to see me again soon, or if those dream sequences repeat themselves."

"Thank you Doctor Branidge," Clysta said. She walked away from the Doctor and his office to go back to her quarters. Then absently she said, "Yes. I will do that."

It was little time later that the last statement came uppermost in her thoughts. 'You have many, many adventures ahead.' Whatever did he mean by that she thought?

Later, in the same day, she approached the study room where she was to join her friends Kindra and G'zin. They were in the corridor leading from their meditation compartments, reading a screen in the corridor wall, full of announcements. It showed the results of the recent Astral class space Navigation tests.

They were both smiling widely as she approached them.

They both said a bright, "Hello," acknowledging her as she came up to them.

"It looks like we came home in the shortest time, making us first up to now, in the test," Kindra speculated, "And look at those marks which we have accumulated. They sure look great, don't they?"

G'zin turned from the screen saying gleefully," If you had not remembered those tables, we may still be out there trying in vain to figure out a route back to here." Then she added with some theatrics, "Or else waiting for a tow."

"Maybe," said Clysta, showing a slight embarrassment at the concealed praise, "But you both had your parts in the results, especially you G'zin and your speed on the comp', and Kindra too. We all contributed, did we not?"

"Thanks anyway," Kindra said then he changed the subject, asking.

"So what did the Doc' have to say about those dreams you have been having?"

"Oh, not very much really," she replied, trying to keep the topic on a low key. "He took a number of tests, mainly on my neural patterns. Looked inside my head with some of his machinery. And then a few more tests, but he did not give any sound reason for my dreams and had no real or firm conclusions to make."

Clysta, although knowing she was being a little untrue, she found she was having some difficulty remembering the things the Doctor had actually said. Then gradually, most of his comments appeared as blanks in her thoughts.

She continued, not consciously but omitting any of the details which were by now completely forgotten.

"He seems to think it has to do with anxiety or something like it. Anyway we shall see."

She felt that she could not find more to say. Then, at that moment, all was forgotten as the time signal sounded. It was to indicate the commencement of the next class.

# Chapter 5

This year was 3128 in the record of Standard Years and Clysta was soon to be celebrating her Twenty-First birthday. In the year 2700 by the calendar of earlier times, it was decided to begin again and start a new calendar from scratch and with a new year numbered one. The start was brought on by the many changes in humanity and the attitude to other people. No more wars, no more strife or poverty-on the planet Earth at least-and personal values were changed forever.

A much wiser and more beautiful Clysta had by now completed the final year of education in the Course Galactica at the Europa Academy of Spatial Sciences. She had accumulated a closing average mark of ninety eight percent. It had been a difficult toil for her but she had achieved the best mark the Academy had given in many years. The second and third to achieve the next highest marks after Clysta were her two friends, G'zin and Kindra. Each with equal marks of ninety-seven percent, an achievement in itself, for their own result for this the final year of their own Academy Course.

The ending of the years of strenuous and arduous study together with these final results was not only the culmination of their education but it was also the incentive for a lavish and glorious celebration put on by the students at large. The celebration was to involve everyone who was at the Academy.

The three friends, Clysta, Kindra and G'zin, were being recognized as the Academy's top students. They were each now carried, as was the usual tradition, high on the shoulders of large groups of their fellow students. Around and around they were carried, being passed on to one group after another. The almost endless procession marched first through the smaller halls of the Academy, gathering more members as it proceeded and they were continuously paraded at the fore of this long line of young people.

The train of students then wound its way throughout the Academy's widest corridors and finally ended their long and merry march at the Central Hall. It was here that the finale was to be attended by everyone. It was here too, where there was held a party to surmount all parties. Taking up the remainder of the day and evening and then on to the early hours of the following morning, by some. Involving the hundreds of rejoicing students, who were also secondly each rejoicing the end of studies for their own Academic year.

The feasting and celebrating were interrupted occasionally by the speeches of congratulation from most of the heads of the departments. Then the party was later held up from time to time when presentations were carried out. Some of the students were presented with commemorative plaques of solid gold. Then were given assorted medallions and diplomas to each of the years other and many bright and successful students. These valued baubles were each ceremoniously distributed by the Galactic Governments very official representative. The presentations were then followed by more similar speech making and lots more very energetic party making.

It was after many hours into the celebrations when Clysta, finally exhausted, decided she would leave the largest hall. It was where she and her friends finally had been allowed to dismount from the student shoulders. They had feasted for hours and imbibed somewhat and to excess. She had thoroughly enjoyed the party but excused herself from any more of the revelry. After bidding an equally exhausted 'Goodnight' to her group of friends and gathering up her diplomas and prizes, she left to make her way to her sleeping quarters. Time and again she would be met on her way by other students or lecturers and the accolades would pour forth in their own personal congratulations. Finally she managed to escape the halls and leave for the quieter passageways leading to the sleeping quarters.

She could still hear the revelry as she approached the area that contained the elevator system. Before entering the drop tube, she spoke into the plate of the controller telling it to take her downwards to the fourteenth level, the one on which her own room was located.

The moon Europa was one of the larger of the planet Jupiter and had been amongst the first of many off world Solar System mining colonies. Mining on this satellite had long lost its value and the crews and robotic tunnelling and mining machines had been dismantled and removed forever. The Academy had been established inside the main structure and throughout the vast workings of this old and disused mine. It was a large mine which had many years earlier, exhausted its quantity of the mineral Quoxite. This once valuable material had had its value in alloying with aluminum to coat the exterior of the now equally ancient interstellar spacecraft of many years ago. Quoxite's mining value had diminished in the Solar System once 'The Bubble' had been developed to such a degree that all transport to the stars was done in that way. These particular mines were once owned by a grateful entrepreneur who often made claims he had gained his first chance at his fortune making from having had a good and sound education. The mine, with all of its establishments, its buildings and docking facilities, they had been donated by his giant mining company to the authorities of education.

The original one kilometre wide hemisphere that retained the atmosphere had been left intact, though repairs and upgrading had been necessary. The internal systems were then completely modernized from a Foundation Trust Fund and the Academy Trust had taken over, afterwards building inside the controlled atmosphere the most modern educational facility in Terran history.

The mine's own network of many underground caverns and ore chambers had been ideal for use as education and lecture areas. Kilometres of tunnels led to vaults that could be developed to house the students and staff, with more room than was needed for all the other many activities normal in educating these, the brightest of students.

Clysta watched absently as the pattern of lights changed as she floated downward passing level after level, descending and finally stopping at the one that would lead to her own living area. She left the tube and turned to the right, walking quietly along a wide and pleasantly coloured corridor, leading in the direction of her room. She came upon a lone couple. They were approximately her age, completely engrossed in saying a long farewell to each other. They did not appear to even notice her as she passed them by.

The Plasti-concrete surfaces forming the corridors were as always, warm and smooth, and as she walked, the dim lighting was increased in intensity many metres ahead and for the same distance behind her. It was controlled by the presence sensors giving full, bright illumination around her position in these and at this time, empty hall ways. She was humming to herself, a tune she liked and had heard again at the party above, as she walked slowly upon the soft carpeting covering the floor of the main corridor. After a little while she turned to the left, the last corner before the door to her quarters.

She was startled as she saw something fully unexpected in the supposedly deserted corridor. It was about twenty metres in front of her. This corridor had brightened as the others all had on her approach.

A figure was standing by the doorway that was the entrance to her own rooms. It seemed to be waiting. It appeared to be metallic. She was a little more than surprised as, moving closer, she observed it must be a robot. What surprised her most was, if this was really a robot, it was most different to all others she was accustomed to.

The greatest and obvious difference from the normal robotic appearance was that it was standing upright and took human form. It was much taller too she judged, than the usual messenger types. Being easily one point eight metres to the top of its rounded head, which also took on a human shape. And it was standing on its own two legs and not floating on an anti-grav'. The metal seeming exterior was different also, looking much more humanoid in shape and with human like jointed limbs. Though it was apparently not meant to be an android as its finish was definitely metallic, slightly skeletal, highly polished and a deep bronze in colour.

She slowed her approach as she studied the strange object. More unusual still was its facial features, again almost human in style and likeness, but without any particular detail. Not seen at all on any robots of this age.

A decree had been enforced by a ruling of law made some two and a half centuries ago—,

'Manufacturers of robotic devices should avoid imitating human appearance and human features.'

But with this robot, those rules had been ignored completely. At the part of the head that would have mimicked a human's eyes, there were two slim slots and within them they appeared to have an inward glowing luminescence. There was no mark or contour that would suggest a mouth or nose. At least that part was consistent with the law.

Clysta approached now to within two meters and halted, to stand facing the robot. Somehow, she lost her apprehension and felt now she should not be at all afraid.

The figure did not move, backward or forward, it just stood to face Clysta.

'Most unusual.' Thought Clysta as she stood and listened attentively. 'What ever is it doing here?'

As if in an answer to Clysta's question, a before unseen opening appeared in the lower part of the robots headpiece and made an action suggestive of a kind of speech.

Discretely and in a soft but slightly metallic voice, the robot thing asked if Clysta Z'ee was the daughter of Commander Quail Z'ee and Murel Z'ee of the planet Earth.

This was the standard question from a messenger robot, so, though a little startled and now apprehensive, both at the device's knowledgeable statement and at the unexpected encounter, she tried her best to be relaxed. After all, this thing was not likely to be dangerous.

She answered as coolly as possible.

"Yes? I am Clysta Z'ee, the one you seek."

As if satisfied the voice pattern had matched whatever the device's internal records showed, the robot then asked her to place her right palm to the ident'-pad. A small panel slid to the side on the left of centre of the robot's upper body. The opening exposed a hand like impression.

Carefully, she did as requested. A slight but not too uncomfortable tingle worked through her hand and up her arm and then ended almost as quickly as it had begun. Clysta recoiled slightly at the strange feeling and stepped backwards a half a pace. The opening quickly closed after she had withdrawn her hand.

A smaller square panel slid to one side to the left of the pad she had touched. It revealed a small illuminated compartment in which she could see a cube about twenty millimetres each side.

'Clysta Z'ee, this is for you. It is from your father. We wish you a Happy Birthday!' The robot announced, then it became silent.

A smile was on her face as she now lost all of the anxiety of this unusual meeting, and she was suddenly overcome with an inward serenity.

Stepping forward again, she cautiously reached out and into the compartment, and removed the cube. Holding it carefully on her palm, she studied it not quite understanding what it was. She tentatively touched it with a finger of her other hand and pushed it around to reveal the rear side. It was solid to her touch and there were not any seams or buttons on any of its surfaces. The cube did not weigh more than a gram with a feeling similar to some kind of metal but by some strange visual technique, the exterior had an almost fluid appearance. Strange patterns and wave like shapes moved slowly and continually.

A soft musical sound was coming from inside but she saw no signs of a speaker or markings on any of its five exposed sides.

Clysta looked up to ask the messenger what it could be, but the robot had left and was already turning the corner further down the corridor and went out of sight.

"How very odd," she murmured to herself, as she fingered the enter pad at the edge of the doorway to her quarters. The door hissed open and she crossed the threshold as the walls inside illuminated automatically. The door closed quietly behind her.

"Well," she breathed, "It said it is from my father. But however did it get here? It wished me a Happy Birthday too. That was nice."

She crossed the room and sat down at her workstation, all the time studying the item in her hand. Still confused, she carefully placed the cube on her desk top to study it more closely and after a few minutes, sat back in her chair, more puzzled than ever.

The soft musical sounds were still emanating from the mysterious cube and the melody, though it was a little unusual, intrigued her. She could not hear it too well so she carefully picked up the cube from the desk top and turned it over a few times to see again if there was some kind of control. She could not find any so held it closer to her ear, to listen to whatever it was that was playing.

Almost instantly, there was a brilliant flash, then, a feeling of nothingness.

# Chapter 6

"Don't be afraid."

That was her father's voice.

For an instant, the dark nothingness had engulfed her then it had once more become light and she was in another place. She could not recognize any of what she saw and as she turned to look around her the view was the same, all unidentifiable. Then finally she saw her father. He was sitting in a strange mobile formation that appeared to be a chair. He was looking at her.

He repeated. "Don't be afraid, please be calm and I will explain. First let me wish you a 'Happy Birthday', my dear. I expect this is all very strange to you, but I should think that this is the first Thought Cube ever to be available to Humans. But I will explain all of those details too, shortly.

"I think that when you reach your twenty-first birthday, I will still be out in deep space between this arm of the galaxy, where you are now and the next spiral arm where I am going to. If it is still so, I apologize for not being with you to celebrate. Also this will probably coincide with the time when you will be finishing your education at the Academy.

"I know you will do well, so 'Congratulations' on that occasion too. I hope that robot that met you was courteous when it gave you the cube, he had to be sanctioned a few years ago and who knows, he may have forgotten his manners by now, or when, or whatever.

"Now to the cube," he carried on, "It works by using a Telepathy of a kind. It is able to record thoughts, but only then to be transmitted to the person it is meant for. Don't ask me how, but of course you couldn't do that anyway, could you? But it does it anyway, and very well I hope, or you might not be listening to this at all.

"The cube also conveys a kind of accompanying visi' of the sender also transmitted in the same fashion, you understand, by thought. That little trick with the music? Well it was my own input. I knew you would not resist trying to make out what the music was and to hear it better you would put it up to your ear. That would put it close enough to your temple and it is that, that is necessary for the transmission to work inside. You may feel a bit strange at first, but you are still where you were when you did that."

Her father smiled pleasantly as he continued. He remained sitting in the strange form of seating which appeared to be gently embracing his lower body. The surroundings in view now became more focused and obvious. The structures and items she could see behind him appeared to Clysta to be most strange. All of them quite unexplainable. With designs and features, which were very foreign and totally new to her.

"And now for your birthday present. Some years ago, before I set up this," he waived his arms to each side in a sweeping motion. She saw still more of the surroundings behind her father, equally as strange looking as those first views she had had of this unusual place where he was, "I was on one of those routine surveying and mapping trips. My technician who usually accompanied me was needed on some special work, so I took along two robots, one of them with some special attributes, the other one just a worker type. You know, the routine box of tools and tricks on an anti-grav'.

"We headed out for a region in the South East quadrant of this arm of the Galaxy, well into the direction of the galactic core. Our task was to recheck some areas where old records from earlier probes described some of the systems as being moderately less than habitable. By those older ordinances of course which had existed at the time a few hundred standard years ago.

"You and I have talked about the expansion requirement before. Well. The way that we are expanding, I was on this trip to recheck the degree of uselessness under the old definitions. Some of these have a possible usefulness by today's methods and I was on this trip to assess their real value now.

"Well, we were hopping around, in and out of Hyper, at the Outer Edge moving from star to star when, just as we were about to exit into real space, our systems somehow malfunctioned. Probably through overwork I suppose. It was not serious, it just took a long time to fix and re-tune.

"By the time we had done these repairs, we had lost our bearings and we had very little to go on. It seemed odd at the time, but as we coasted along, there on the view screen ever so suddenly and quite unexpectedly, appeared a star. I could find only one planet in the system, otherwise nothing else. Oh, yes. And it, the planet, had a small satellite moon. A little bit like Earth but alone, I thought at the time.

"I spent a few hours going through the chart crystals but I could not find a match for a system in the whole sector that was equal to the spectral analysis and readout I was receiving from that star. The star was not recorded on our crystals at all."

As her father spoke, an image entered her thoughts showing a view of space and a bright star situated close by. Not very far in the distance she could see a reflection from a blue looking planet.

Her view changed and the vision swung around to show a panorama view of the Hub that was the centre of the Milky Way galaxy. Although from where this vision was taken, the distance would have been many thousands of light years away. But she was able to take in that breath-taking sight of the millions of stars, all so close to each other approaching that centre and the intensity of light that she had never before seen. Again the vision within her mind changed and her father was there.

He continued, "We did a few wide orbits of the planet. It seemed to be worth checking and up to that time all appeared safe and stable. I decided to shuttle down to the surface of the planet you can now see and take a look-see. I took with me the better of the two robots, it was the same one which handed you this cube. The planet was a most beautiful place, Clysta. Vegetation, the atmosphere was perfect, water in abundance,—there I go, talking like a report—but the best of all, it was inhabited. And by a race of most handsome beings. They were humanoid but slightly removed from our physical appearance, in features and detail mainly. Their race, I later found out, is a very old one and their intelligence has gone far ahead of that of Earth by many hundreds or even many thousands of years. But there they were, the first intelligent beings ever met by humans. Ever."

A different view came into Clysta's thoughts. It was of a garden type of setting at the edge of a purple coloured sea, with an endless and clear gold coloured sky. In the foreground, there stood a group of what must have been the local inhabitants he had described, not much unlike Human in form and standing tall and proud.

The view changed again to show her father once more, sitting just as before when all of this had begun.

Her father spoke again.

"You must go there Clysta," he said dramatically, "I stayed a month or so, as a guest really. They asked me nothing really about our race, just a few insignificant questions. Like what part of the universe we lived in, what type of life we lead. Small stuff really. Funny people, I suppose at their level of intelligence, they didn't care too much about other life forms.

"Anyhow, whilst we were there I, we, this robot and I, did them a bit of a favour. That robot and I, well the robot seemed to do all of the work. He, or should it be It, repaired a small system malfunction, it was in a large central food processing device and in gratitude they promised that I should receive a reward. I decided to leave the reward behind when I came up with this marvelous idea. It is still there on that planet. I will not tell you what it is. That way, it will be a real surprise. I thought we should go there to receive it together, just the two of us. As a celebration of your own achievements. And your twenty-first birthday of course. Then this long expedition came up and now I have missed everything and the birthday too."

The vision changed once again to show the planet's inhabitants. Her father's voice took on a serious tone.

"These beings you are seeing had lived here for eons in complete isolation. They stressed a wish to remain isolated and their whereabouts a secret, at all costs. When I finally left, they used a device to erase all memory of their location from my brain. They even went through the crystals on the ship to do the same. Then, even the robots were tampered with. Their security was enforced farther by guiding us well out of the area. We were still under the influence of a mind block in order that the secret of where they might be, is still kept as a secret.

"Do you know? I can remember many of the details about that trip but try as I may, I cannot bring to mind anything with reference to the coordinates of that system. I even tried checking both of the robots, without any success."

Her father, who was still sitting, carried on, "This cube is all I have from that place to convince me it was not a dream. It was just a trinket to them, perhaps that is the reason I was allowed to keep it. I have managed to keep this entire episode a secret as they had wished and as I myself promised, even the cube, for many reasons. But mainly so that you Clysta, and I, we could go there together as I said, for your birthday present. You are now the only other Human who now knows anything of this planet so far as I know, and my story."

Seeing her father here before her after all of this time of uncertainty, even though he appeared only in her mind, had given Clysta a feeling of well being. Here he was, still the same confident and capable person she always knew. Even those visitations of her dreams did not seem to have the same meanings anymore.

Her father continued with his conversation, "Before we left for the other arm of the galaxy, I arranged for all of my credits to be transferred to a special deposit tied in, to your account. If I am still outside this galactic arm when you graduate and come of age, they are to become yours when you become twenty-one years of age. You must use some of it to rent or maybe buy a Skipper. You deserve it. One like those we used to use on our trips away, or, maybe something similar. Go to that planet any way you can. Find it. Use this cube to guide you to the spot in space where this all started. The coordinates of where we began our system malfunction are inside it, because those parts of the trip, I do remember. The rest is up to you and I am sure you are able to locate it."

He sat before Clysta, though only in her thoughts and looked lovingly at her for a few brief seconds. Then all too soon and hurriedly, he concluded.

"Well. I must finish now. It was only very brief I know, but I have told you most or all of the things I remember and that I know. So once again Clysta, 'Have a Happy Birthday' and best wishes and Congratulations".

He waived to her in a final gesture, as all around him was reduced to darkness again, then he himself disappeared. Clysta was left almost as if hanging in that same sudden darkened emptiness. Then, just as suddenly, there came a flash of brilliant light and she was back in her quarters sitting in her chair and very alone.

Her hand still held the cube close to her ear.

As she lowered her arm, she instinctively looked at the timepiece on her desk. No more than a mere ten seconds had passed since she had picked up the cube from the desktop.

# Chapter 7

Even with the sleep inducer set at deep sleep, Clysta tossed and turned on the anti-grav' that night. Finally the time came for her to rise. She was troubled and confused. However had that cube been held secret for so long. It must have been years, three or four at least. And that robot thing, where had that come from and into the Academy too, obviously unnoticed? If it had been detected at all, there would certainly have been a tumultuous hue and cry.

After a quick use of the whole body cleaner followed by a hurried but acceptable grooming, she made her way to have a light breakfast in the Academy Commissary.

During this time from awaking from sleep, she had come to a decision. Her mind was made up.

She entered the eating area, which was at the surface level of the complex. The immensity of it always brought astonishment to Clysta. It was so huge and spacious with a ceiling so high it was hard to make out the details of the structure that was above.

The chamber had a similarity with the cathedrals of old time Earth, designed with curves and columns to radiate from the centre point high above. The outer walls were of a large circular layout but with an undulating, and irregular but pleasing pattern with alcoves and offshoot passages. These walls of this structure were constructed of the same material as all structures of the age and carried an internal system which radiated warmth and an illumination, filling the whole of this enormous volume in shadow less light.

At floor level, which itself was vast, there were tables and anti-grav' seating, some in rows and others in groups. Occasionally in some areas, the seating and table arrangements were surrounded by an energy force field system, itself adjustable to a variety of heights and uses. This screening could be changed as required, from transparent to opaque to match the occupants wishes, enabling those who may need it a degree of quiet or privacy.

The large eating area to one side of the main floor was always busy, in use at all times by students, lecturers and staff. Visitors to the members of the Academy too, could be seen and always there were, the ever present service robots. They would be cleaning the spotless floor or removing used dishes, or collecting and delivering messages.

Clysta entered through the large doors and wove in and out between the tables and past screens where the many other people were having refreshments or a late breakfast. Occasionally, Clysta would see a group of fellow students who she recognized and would nod or wave to them, or say 'Good Morning', or other such pleasantries as she passed. Some would hold her in a short conversation then let her go on her way. This morning there were not many in what could be called a jovial mood. Last nights' celebration had taken its toll on most.

She finally found her way to the regular place used by her friends and herself and found G'zin and Kindra, both looking not quite their usual radiant selves. In fact they look terribly ragged.

"Good day you two."

Kindra looked up, grimacing. His facial colour was similar to that of ashes today.

"What makes you so perky?" He mumbled.

"Ooh!" moaned G'zin as she noticed Clysta had approached. Her hair was not too orderly and her one piece suit was definitely rumpled.

She managed to say, "Too much of something does not agree with something else, and fifteen hours of it makes it four times as bad."

"It's all because of your royal breading," Kindra quipped hoarsely, as he massaged his aching temples. They were evidently both suffering from the same complaint. Staying much too long at the party.

He was not far off the truth. G'zin was a true Princess by birth, actually the third in line to the Royal House of her home planet.

"You were not meant to imbibe on anything that was of a lower standard than The Regal Dew," he added in fun.

This Regal Dew he was referring to was a very sweet semi intoxicating nectar from a rare bee like insect on the same world where G'zin had been born. Fryl.

"Well," she parried, herself in a hoarse voice, "We don't export our best produce. That stays on the planet. I," she stressed, "Had to be satisfied with a poor alternative from a sick processor and that alternative just had to be that abominable local brew of this planetoid. But ooh! Please. Don't talk so loud. Ooh, my head!"

She stopped talking and nursed her head, moving it slowly from side to side.

Clysta interrupted the banter, "Listen up, you two and clear your heads. What are you intending to do now that we have completed our final courses? I have something to tell you, but first do either of you have any plans for the immediate future?"

The two looked at each other in puzzlement. 'Whatever was she going on about?' Kindra thought through his own private fog. 'Can she not see that we are dying here?'

Then he took a look at Clysta.

She was radiant as ever.

Kindra was first to speak, in a voice still containing its hoarseness from the previous nights revelry. He held back for a few seconds to form his sentences.

"Well. My parents are out on tour right now, trying to drum up some extra business out there in the Eastern Reaches. You remember don't you? They export Ryzidium. I am supposed to return to my planet now the course is over, but I will likely be alone there for quite a while. So there is no real hurry for me to go home. For a few weeks anyway."

Clysta looked to G'zin saying, "What are your plans, G'zin?"

"Nothing very special," she said trying not to make too much noise and holding her still buzzing head between her palms. "It's still winter at my own city on my home world and the celebrations for my graduation are not to be held until the first buds burst on the Zirsha Trees."

She winced at the agony still at work inside her skull. G'zin made an attempt to compose her next thoughts and began again.

"Let me see," her eyes closed tight, "That should be in about two months from now, Europa time."

Still pressing eagerly for information, Clysta looked again at Kindra, then asked, "What about the appointment that they granted you at Alpha Centauri? For the Assistant to the Master Geologist wasn't it. Isn't that due soon?"

"I have a few months yet to decide if I will be taking it," Kindra retorted. "I am sure that I will, but I have the time so I am in no hurry. Now. You have all the answers you are getting from us two. Now tell us! What do you have on your mind which needs all of these answers?"

"Ok I'll tell you. But first let's dial up a nice big breakfast," Clysta consented teasingly, as she pushed a button and dialed a few references. In about ninety seconds three breakfasts were in place on the table before them. G'zin and Kindra eased there plates away and sat motionless and, moaning occasionally, watched in disgust as Clysta enjoyed her hearty breakfast whilst their own just became colder.

# Chapter 8

It was just only two days later when all three of the young friends were sitting in Clysta's quarters.

Their allocated rooms were quite compact although very comfortable. They consisted of a decent sized formal room beyond the entrance and then a small area behind a single door doubling as a study and a single bedroom. A small cubical attached was the body cleaner mould.

The formal room contained the routine furnishings for living and entertaining and also contained on one wall a desk with the connection to the gigantic central comp' system which was in itself linked to the Galactic Network.

Another wall contained the apparatus for the mini-food processor and its recycling disposal system.

A messenger robot had that morning delivered a catalogue strip, which, Clysta had requested and had already threaded, into the holograph station. G'zin and Kindra had arrived earlier and, by this time, they all had enjoyed a prearranged modest breakfast together, here in Clysta's quarters.

The viewing equipment was now ready to take requests from them to display all of up to twenty-two of the various designs of those latest styles in the smaller size of space craft. The whole of the presentation was projected in a 'Three-D' holo', displaying in the area that was above the desktop. It was all to scale large enough to show adequately a detailed presentation. The visions could be controlled to rotate as required to show all facets of the individual designs.

Questions could be directed to and answered by the voice controlled system accompanying these displays. Any questions could be asked and these could be of the craft's drive ability, its interior finishes, or systems and qualities together with each craft's specification or any other relevant items. In fact any question necessary could be asked, to give a sales prospect all of the answers needed.

Together, the three friends covered each and every model in the systems library, debating to and fro the possibilities of each and every display. After two hours, they finally sat in silence, having narrowed the list of possibilities to four of the smaller models. They were though not quite resolved which one of these four craft suited their trip.

"What we should take is a ship like the one we had for the navigation test," said G'zin, finally breaking the silence. "The one listed number five is quite close to it, and it has some obvious improvements over the Academy craft. Such as, that well equipped gymnasium. There is also Ultra Drive for close space and the best in navigational robotics too!"

"It is also larger by at least thirty-five percent," added Clysta, remembering the cramped sleeping quarters, "We will need more space," she stressed, "The trip is undoubtedly going to be a long one."

"My father has had one of those for more than three years," added Kindra, "Or one very much like it. He says it is the best he has ever had. He goes all over the Arm in his."

"I like the comp' too," G'zin added with a smile, "It is top of the line."

"That one does seem to be the best of the group," said Clysta in thoughtful agreement. She reset the vidi' to have another look. "It has all the room we should need I suppose and there is as you say Kindra, a small but decent gym' as well." The others nodded in slow confirmation as they studied the holo'.

After a momentary silence, Clysta said, "That settles it then. We are all agreed?" The other two now nodded their heads energetically. "Then I will arrange the booking."

Clysta spent the next few minutes entering the details into the telecomp' unit, followed by each of their individual Galactic I.D. Lastly she entered with pride, their newly acquired Space Drive ratings.

"Ok. That's all finished," she said. They would need to wait a few hours for the final confirmation of their request for delivery of the craft. "Now let's start to make preparations for the trip. We'll plan to leave on the third day after tomorrow. It will give us time to close up our studies and gather together and store our personal belongings. By the way, you two still want to go, don't you?"

G'zin and Kindra looked a little sheepishly at each other, making mumbling sounds and showing some doubts, mocking Clysta a little. Then they looked up each with a final large smile.

"Just you try to leave without us!" they both chimed, gleefully.

# Chapter 9

The ship lifted off smoothly from the spaceport that was one quarter of a kilometre from the atmosphere dome on the frozen and airless Europa. Airless in human terms of course. An atmosphere did exist but only a thin, low density and mostly ammoniac one. Accelerating their craft quickly escaped the light gravitation of this large moon orbiting the gas giant Jupiter. Four hours and fifteen minutes into its flight was all this shiny new craft required to reach Quarter Light speed using the ships' latest Ether Drive propulsion units.

Their first Jump into Hyper Space would be in a further six hours ahead. Kindra had set its course to be at right angles to the planetary helical plane of the Solar System. This was primarily a short cut. It enabled the craft to be well clear of the effects of the Sun's massive elliptic gravitation stream, in an earlier space of time.

It was a constant threat. Though sometimes used as a slingshot by some more advanced travelers, that matrix of the Hyper Bubble could itself be affected by the closeness of any star above red dwarf classification. The ever constant and enormous stellar gravity had strange and distorting effects on the outer skins' waveband.

The three young companions would now have a little time to waste before the next battery of computations would need to be entered and ready for the Hyper Drive. They decided to spend some of it in the small onboard gymnasium, to test some of the newest equipment.

Dates in time and the recording of its passage had gone through a great change after the first major flight into Hyper Space.

The year of first enlightenment was 3066 if you were familiar with the now unused old Earth calendar, which outlasted its usefulness years ago. That calendar followed the solar course of Earth, set and dated from its beginning and in conjunction with, an ancient religion.

Time was to be everything to this one small family in the earlier days of planet Earth. Yet it was not at all important just what year in the far future this project would finally be completed, only that it must be. The succeeding years were just a mere passage of time and of no real consequence in this, the Project.

3066 by the older dating routine was the year in which the Project was first begun. Project 3066 was its title then and as the Maastersym family had known it for some generations to follow. It would very doubtlessly take many more years, at least another one hundred or even more to be anywhere near the final completion of this massive effort. This was the judgment which the patriarch, the brilliant Jaagard. P. Maastersym himself had foreseen when he first initiated its commencement.

He, Jaagard P Maastersym had been the Swedish born mathematician, who had begun the long task. It began in a secluded cabin type structure in the northern districts of the Rocky Mountains of what had once been Canada. Now it was a large and fortified citadel occupying that original and most secluded spot high in those same mountains.

Maastersym had gone to great lengths to provide the seclusion and privacy needed by installing the newest of security apparatus and many other screening devices to keep out those unauthorized visitors and their equally unwanted thoughts. These alone might lead to the interference and the jeopardizing of the immense work at hand in the Project.

In his youth, Maastersym had always been intrigued by a passage in an ancient manuscript he had seen early in his youth. It concerned the works of Pythagoras and one work in particular dealing with the subject of matter. Many of history's mathematicians and those scientists in the field of physics had long studied the ancient and famous doctrines of that Greek scholar and philosopher. But all had inexcusably missed what this particular bright young mathematician had himself found and refused to leave it un-deciphered.

He, Pythagoras, had first stated in a time when there was little public understanding of most of the sciences, that in everything, which was of the Earth and of the Universe around it, all of matter was numbers. In his ancient and extraordinary mind everything, he had said, could be equated on a numerical basis.

What Pythagoras meant, he never fully explained, possibly because he too was lost in its meaning. It was Maastersym though, who after almost two years of long and intricate study of these accounts, finally arrived at the fundamental truth of what Pythagoras had tried to reveal in his statement. The truth was that which lay not in humans views of the words as they had been spoken, but in a much deeper interpretation and their quasi-mathematical translation.

That is the real truth of what Maastersym had found. The long quest for a new meaning to everything could now begin.

Maastersym had been a hard taskmaster. He died at age one hundred and fifteen, never himself having accomplished that goal he had set. But he knew, when he began, it would take more than his lifetime to complete. Or even the lifetime of those who were his offsprings. A few of his earlier descendants had at first become resistive to the task, chiefly due to the demands which this program had imposed on their lives together with the continual seclusion. But that seclusion was essential in the precept foreseen by the founder.

This present line, the fifth of the generations of the family though had reared two descendants with fine minds who were ever eager to carry on the work initiated so many years before. After all, they constantly reminded themselves of what had been bred into the members of this family who had passed before them. This was important to the future of humankind.

Both understood, the Project long though it was to be, was one that would lead one day to a final conclusion. One that could release humanity from its shackles of solidity. The long passed Jaagard Maastersym had formulated in his most outstanding mind a method of inter-transportation previously so inconceivable it was beyond the comprehension of the common people, even of the brightest of this epochs scientist and professors. All of what was required, he deduced, would be acquired by what he himself had long ago named. Compressed Mathematics.

That was the eventual target of Project 3066.

A third member of this particular generation was Jake, just as his brother and sister, he was becoming a true Maastersym. He had though, in his earlier years been one of a few of those descendants who had occasionally tried to resist and even escape the constraint of his ancestors decree. Mainly, it was all of this enforced seclusion from others and outsiders. The task had enforced a constant avoidance of friends and what then led to the inevitable loneliness of each member, apart from these who were close and in the family circle.

Though now in his thirties, he had changed. He now always worked hard and long in his sequence in the routine. He was known to occasionally let out a scream of anguish in a halfhearted effort to complain of the senseless repetitive re-functioning of the mathematics. Then of course at such times of pain, he could always count on his older sister Maanu Maastersym to come to his aid. She would move to his side at those times and again transfer into him some of her own inner strength she found he so often needed.

Then fondly and coaxingly she would whisper as she stroked her long fingers across his head and through his black curls.

"Maybe this is to be the one last phase when you alone will find the end we seek, then we can all stop and sleep in glory," reassuring him once again as she always did, to think of what the end result would be like, managing as always to keep him at the task.

Maanu had held him in line in this way for many of his teen years. He had, on a number of occasions, slipped away from the laboratory to disappear from view and go his own way only to be sought out of his hiding place by one of the others. Most often though, Maanu was the one who found him. She would convince him to return again, and as was usual with some reluctance, to that monotonous and monstrous challenge.

Now finally Maanu, though not very late in her own years, was showing signs that she was failing mentally. Although parts of her mind had the same sharpness it had always held, the body of her brain was becoming weaker.

Those many years she had spent in constant brainstorming. The never ending studying, realigning and recalculating, as was her duty in executing parts of these one hundred and fifty-seven years long calculations and ciphers. These labours were now beginning to show their inevitable toll. The mental strain of those numbers of times she had earlier taken over for Jake's turn at the computron in his periods of absence. The interminable and extended periods of mind transfer using the Net. These had each produced scars within her brain cells which time could never repair.

The Calcx. That term had been accepted over half of a century ago as the present stage. It was a justifiable name as the soul of the Project. It was now consuming its fifth generation of the family Maastersym.

Just as the previous descendants had, all three followed the schedule of a rotating pattern where they each would sever contact after five years of work to take a two year halt in the order. A kind of sabbatical to help regenerate the ever precious cells of each of their brains. It served also as a means to search out the correct genes to replenish family stock and to prepare for the next future generation.

But Maanu had been a little more than foolish. She had most knowingly bypassed at least three breaks in the long routine, two having been on account of Jake. Now this slow unstoppable mental degeneration was her reward. Jake realized the truth and now blamed his own selfishness for most of her deteriorating health. Now he was the one to be of assistance.

It had been during one of those absences when Maanu had arrived at one of the many regularly and very crucial sequences in the processing of data. A mass mathematical compression was scheduled just at the time when she should have been handing over to Jake and taking her time away from the laboratory. But Jake had not been there. He was once more taking another of his many sporadic times of absenteeism.

Maanu had sat in on Jake's behalf. That session alone had begun the damage leading to the cerebral deterioration and it was to be irreversible and irreparable.

The other of the two brothers was Nepfh Maastersym. He was the more bright of the males. He had been the quiet stable type all of his life. He was the one who had accepted the 'Project' as a necessary part of growing up since their father had first initiated him to the sequence at the early age of twelve years.

As well as being four years older than Jake, brother Nepfh was always the taller of the two by some fifty or more millimetres and with his neatly groomed straight stature, looked very handsome even early in his teenage years.

Now at forty-two, he was still straight, although his hair was almost all gone. He still turned heads though at the purposely few selected science and physics dinners he attended when he had the time. He was personable and often shy and was usually most resentful of always being the one nominated to be the representative of the known but secluded Maastersym family.

Jake joined his brother Nepfh in the laboratory at daybreak. Nepfh looked drained, he had been at his station since the previous evening. Outside, the woods around the house and laboratory were still wet from the rain of the previous night. The weather in the mountains was of little consequence as no-one of this family ventured very far. But after a rain, Nepfh would enjoy seeing the sparkling cleanliness that was left behind. And when it was cold enough to turn to snow, the beauty was unbelievable. As usual though, their own life was one of enforced seclusion. No one outside of the family could ever share this beauty that surrounded their fortress.

No conversation passed between the two brothers for at least a half of an hour. Jake sat immediately at his control console. They both were pouring over masses of calculations and summaries. But Jake had something he had to get off his chest.

"I have been looking into the output of the multi-band vortex sequencing," said Jake, breaking the long silence. It was still early on this particular morning. He had something, which he thought of as most crucial. He was turning it over and over in his mind as he slowly sipped a mug of coffee.

He continued,"I know you studied it three times before now Nepfh, and I know you feel it is too soon. But I can see a new sequence evolving. I need to clear away a dark orange spot in the emuoscreen. I think there is something building behind it that we have not accounted for".

He put his now empty mug into the cleaner. Jake then looked up from the expansive table viewer and straightened in his chair.

Nepfh turned to face his brother. There it was again, that annoying condescending look crossing his face. His keen eyes were set deep inside their sockets. His face had a stressed and white pallor from the previous hours of toil.

"I have told you before-'Dear Brother',-a number of times," asserted Nepfh, "I and only I, am responsible for the emuoscreen and I cannot let your segment violate that data which I have building there."

He stopped the tapping of entries and placed both of his hands on the edge of the large display. Nepfh was indeed tired; he had been at the console and the mind scanner for almost fifteen hours and was overdue for his next long break.

Jake did not intend to be dismissed. He continued after Nepfh had spoken.

"But it is important that I get behind that blockage, I am due for a second breakthrough and this could help. Maanu has concurred with most of my theories and she says she has a few ideas of what might be behind the same block."

Holding his breath, he asked almost offensively, "Do you have any theories of your own to offer?"

Exasperated at his brother's constant reluctance to accept his evidence, Jake felt he might have gone too far. Nepfh was after all, the leader of this age of the Maastersym family. He had the final say, and thoughts, on all of the decisions. Jake returned to his controlled composure and coolness of mind. As always it was most important to not have these particular delicate and almost human computers sense if you were at a weakened phase of mental awareness. That could create ruin to many years of work.

"I do not have a clear view yet and you know it," Nepfh said in reply, "You also know, Maanu is seven years older than I and has run this phase the longest. Maybe she does know, but I say it is not yet ready to open, and also the Sallo guidance base is not yet complete. We need a safety valve and there is none yet. And," he emphasized, "It is my decision that counts at this present time."

Nepfh turned away with the arrogance of an older brother to his sibling and reached for the net that was a part of the mind scanner. Then after smoothing it carefully across his thin and scant hair he went back to his work.

With his back now to Jake, he continued his dialogue of rejection as he was still tapping at the consoles delicate pads.

"I have only fifteen more minutes of work left to do and then I am due to rest," sighed Nepfh. "Let me just complete this phase and I will leave you alone to work on your theories. But I must warn you. Please do nothing on your own. You have only second stage theories. It is most likely that your computations can and will be dangerous and I can see that only disaster will befall all of our work without some form of cushion. When she gets here, maybe Maanu will decide to let you in. I cannot and I have explained to you why. The topic is closed."

That said, he slowly closed his eyes letting the computer become absorbed into his brain's sensitivities and he returned to his task. He said not another word to his brother.

Jake released a long sigh of his own exasperation. Then inwardly he brightened

'Ah. Yes. Maybe—' thought Jake, 'Maanu is soon to take Nepfh's place. She will help me I am sure. She always does.'

Jake continued with his own thoughts.

'Maybe not on Nepfh's own screen, but she also has been working on a similar phase. And that together with my own work could be all that Nepfh will require to see that I am correct.'

'I hope she is well though.' He continued to think with a little sadness. He pictured in his mind those ageing and wrinkled features and an almost shriveled shell of the once lovely Maanu.

Eventually, twenty or more minutes later, Nepfh left the laboratory.

He quietly slipped from his chair and staggered toward the stairway, weak and exhausted. Jake was busy. He looked up from his work momentarily just in time to see the back of his brother as he left the laboratory.

Maanu did not arrive to take her place at the scheduled time. She had become just too weak to leave her sleeping place this morning. She had lain on her bed, just for a few minutes longer to doze and had fallen into a long light sleep.

Brother Nepfh had left his station without saying a word. He should have made Jake aware that he was leaving for his break in the days work. He should have seen to it that Maanu was available or even at her station before he left. But had become overcome with a drowsiness that he just could not shake. Sleep was more important to him now. He was also too weary to notice or even realize that error and that their sister Maanu had not appeared to take up her position.

Jake now found himself alone. He waited one hour unsure if the missing Maanu was coming to the laboratory or if she was not. He surveyed the screen of notes that would lead to his next calculations on the manoeuver his Brother would not discuss. After another half hour had passed he sat, still alone, before the emuoscreen and the projector tube. He was now trying to hold back the thrill of what he had finally decided he would do.

One week ago he had been planning some quasi-mathematical maneuvers and had an unsuspected flash of brilliant inspiration. It had not come at once really, these were the culmination of something much more strange.

One month ago, in his sleep, he was overcome by a series of foresight. It was unexplainable to him how it had come about but somehow he knew he was sleeping, but also he felt that he was totally awake.

Then magically, it was just as if he was being fed with phenomenal lists of calculations, equations and most of all, an understanding. As well, he felt all the time that he was not alone, that some presence was in the room where he slept though as if he was awake. And that presence was feeding him. The strangeness continued for what he imagined were hours, then he slept again soundly. Later, after he awoke, Jake had salvaged the memories and recorded most of the thoughts but had kept them to himself, until he was sure he could prove their worth.

He surely could not expose the real reason for having these masses of instructive calculations for fear of being proven an idiot who had been overcome with the pressure of the Calcs. But deep inside he knew, with conviction, that they were factual and would lead to some gigantic breakthrough.

From the inside pocket of the laboratory coat he was wearing, he took the coded and transcripted silver thread containing that sequence of enriched commands he had since been expanding and working on secretly, in his off station periods. He then connected the two terminals of the device, which would feed all of this newly derived information into the main computron. Then he went to work, alone.

It was almost three hours later that Maanu had finally awakened and gathered the strength to leave her quarters. She walked slowly and painfully, down the long stairway leading to the underground laboratory. She turned the corner in the narrow passage then passed through the arch and felt the familiar tingle of the scanning shield. Maanu did not at first see the new thing before the main screen of the enormous computron. Its translucence cast no shadow or brightness, even though it was suspended between the projector and the screen.

She walked slowly to her own work position within the giant apparatus. She noticed, somewhat absently and through her slight delirium, that her brother Jake was not to be seen anywhere in this subterranean cavern. She knew Nepfh was not to be here, it was far past her own commencement time anyway. Maanu knew she was late taking over. But Jake should be here. Jake always took over at this shift. It was important that some one should be here at all times with this enormous thinking machine. The machine was not ever to be left alone.

She mentally scolded herself for being at her station so late and could not bring to bear the concentration to give it another thought as she arduously climbed into the elevated seat that was her station. Finally, she was seated before that giant calculating device whispering absently to herself and shaking her head in derision.

"Where on earth are you Jake?" she said softly, mostly to herself.

The reality that he could be absent had not yet truly registered to Maanu. Her outer senses were too preoccupied by the strain of making her journey into the tunnel and then climbing up onto her chair. She could have used the elevator to this level, but she had decided to make the effort at a little exercise and had used the long stairway.

She reached out her hand toward the activation pad, but before she had passed half way across the board she halted the movement. Some thing, or some small sound of static brought her attention back to her surroundings. It made her look to where Jake should have been sitting at his own station at the other end of the enormous console. Some inner thought prompted her to look there. He was still not at his seat.

"Jake?" she said as loud as she could. Once again she had to be cautious. Loud noises, tones of excitement, or anxiety could affect that indomitable machine.

"Jake. Are you here? Where are you?"

His absence had not registered before, but now the fog of her inner thoughts cleared aside as she became curious and most of all, anxious. He should not have left the area before a replacement had arrived, if he indeed had been here at all. She squinted as her gaze dreamily traversed the large room. First she looked at Jake's post, he was not there. She then surveyed toward Nepfh's seating area, at the opposite side to her own. It was then that she saw it, a large and colourless, unreflecting sphere. Or was it a bubble?

The thing, the sphere, or whatever it was, was hanging, floating in the air about half of a metre from the smooth surface of the laboratory floor. It appeared to be pulsing off and then on erratically, though the pulse was at such a frequency it was almost always in view.

She slid down from the seat to the hard floor. Her legs were weak and she stood for a while trying to hold her balance leaning against the console. Then she slowly shuffled around the keyboard of her station and cautiously approached this new thing. It was positioned midway between the flux projector and the emuoscreen. As she advanced to a place where she was close enough, she found that she could see through the outer and almost clear skin. She stopped. Though Maanu was not afraid of whatever this thing might be, she decided she should be safer not to get too close. She squinted in an endeavor to focus with her keen eyes and to look into the flickering interior of the unusual and mysterious apparition. It was then she saw it. She could see a form inside the sphere. It was in the shape she recognized as that of her brother, Jake.

He was floating, or hanging, or was suspended from she knew not how, inside of this enigmatic bubble formation. He would disappear from view then reappear in sequence with the rhythm of the surrounding intermittent pulsing of the transparent sphere. Jake's pale face was smiling broadly and he did not move. His expression appeared jubilant, though she knew inside her heart that he was dead. He had one hand raised as if pointing in the direction of the large emuoscreen. She slowly turned her head, following in the direction of Jake's lifeless and pointing finger, to see calculation after phantom calculation pouring across a large spot on the giant screen. It was in a location to one side of centre and it was the same one, which the last time she had seen it, it had been orange in colour.

The spot had somehow changed. It was now of the same colourless and opaqueness as the sphere which now held Jake in his death state. The calculations poured on, for four days. Nepfh had been called when Maanu had gained sufficient strength and the courage to leave this strange apparition. They had each attempted to gain control of whatever it was, but in vain. Then suddenly the calculations, the spot on the screen and the translucent sphere were all gone.

Gone too was Jake.

"Gadzooks!!"
Jake junior could not take his eyes from the vision forming before him, and he dare not just in case what he could now see, were to all disappear.

It was a stunning sequence of designs and a marvelous accumulation of manifestations and numbers pouring in silence and incessantly across the wall screen. Equation upon equation. Formulation after formulation. All of it, with each sequence self-generating and with a never ending purpose.

Thoughts came to him of Maanu, the grand-aunt he never knew, now long dead. And there was his Grand-father Nepfh who had gone slowly mad. It was said it was from either the prolonged exposure to the ever and endlessness of the computations or the silent self-guilt for the disappearance of Grand-Uncle Jake. They would both surely have relished the sight of this moment they had all worked so hard to duplicate. And Jake would have been most proud of this, his ultimate moment.

But only Jake junior's aging mother Mandy was in the other room. She was with his much younger sister, Maanude. They too were working hard on their own meanings to this same conclusion.

The twenty three year old Jake slowly and without taking his eyes from the parade before him, cautiously pressed the signal. It was meant to summon the others into the monstrous chamber, which formed the laboratory.

"At long last."

He allowed himself to say the words softly in the lengthy and slow exhalation of a controlled breath. Afraid that an errant thought might destroy his many years of hard work.

Three years ago, it had been decided that Jake Junior would be the last. He was now the only one left in the long ancestral line of this family of super mathematicians to work in this room of the Project Laboratory.

Those others of what now was left of the decreasing lineage of the Maastersym family had become all but convinced the work could never be finally completed and this was to be the last year of the Calcx. Some had gone into industry. Two had been drafted into one of the ageless journeys to a distant star, to spread their special genes for the benefit of another beginning of human civilization. Some of the family felt that whatever the older Jake had found had been lost and, in the eyes of some other family members, could never ever be salvaged or duplicated. Wherever Jake Maastersym had gone to when the bubble had eventually collapsed into nothingness, he had taken the means to replicate it with him.

But Jake Junior was also a bit of a maverick, the same as his namesake. This enormous computron used the mountain as its storage medium. This place had been well selected by Old Maastersym. He had used the atoms within those thick veins of radium that laced itself through the pores of the thousand of cubic kilometres of granite. The radium would last and maintain itself for eons. Every vein by now had in it the millions of commands and computations, in deep storage. It was the depths of these that Jake Junior had plumbed to seek out any record of that memorable day long ago.

Jake Junior sat, secure on the inside of the remote and sealed cubicle where he monitored the computers actions. Even these actions were controlled through series of multiple and unconnected relays. This obvious precaution was meant to keep him out of harms way.

He, Jake Junior watched closely. He had succeeded. Quietly and cautiously, he whispered to himself. He was saying.

"This must be—, it has to be.—It?"


A quarter of the millennium had passed since the device had been developed to extract energy from the actual ether that was everywhere in all of space. The methods the machine used, was one that the uninitiated found most difficult to comprehend. Even unto the best and brightest of minds it was hard. But the apparatus that was finally evolved used what could be capsulated in simple terms as merely a push and pull process.

The Ether Engine, as it was termed for simplicity, could draw unlimited energy from the inexhaustible matrix of space itself. It, the device though not at all an engine, was perfected to a degree where, a vessel having the required Mass Containment field could approach within the final fractions to the speed of light.

Speed greater than that immovable boundary was impossible by an old order of physics and mathematics first envisaged and proven by an historical prophet of that same theme.

A further period of seventy years had elapsed following the now famous but still volatile Maastersym development. The volatility factor was from the actuality that no-one had perfected a method of retaining the medium in a safe and manageable state.

Two mathematicians had been working on a possible improvement by creating a new class of Hyper Wave generator. These two had stumbled on an important extension to the Maastersym Theory, which had been part of the initial foresight of its originator. Long periods of experimentation had led to their new principle. It was one that allowed previously un-calculated transformations through the use of these mere raw mathematics and in their own views, would eventually give access into another dimension.

Their theory developed into the still theorized formation of a small elliptical envelope. This new form had been changed from the original spherical envelope and could, only in theory, now be controlled for the first time since the unfortunate events of its original and lost discoverer. Their own plan, just like many others before, was to penetrate this new unexplored realm and extract possible endless energy from within the phenomenon's interior.

It was almost another eleven years after long and arduous representation to the scientific community that a practical demonstration was finally allowed to take place. The location chosen for this important presentation was to be in an isolation vault built at a lonely laboratory. The laboratory itself had been constructed in the midst of the Asteroid Belt to satisfy the obvious safety arguments. They used the interior of a large and long ago mined out chunk of pitted rock, to house their control and monitoring apparatus.

The complex devices for generating the new wave envelope were assembled inside the hollowed out core of another smaller chunk of asteroidal debris. This one was located at almost one thousand kilometres distant from where they themselves sat in their main laboratory. That would further isolate the two scientists in the event an unscheduled accident should occur. Inside this smaller asteroid, had been arranged a number of complex energy measuring mechanisms fabricated of the purest gold, each one levitated clear of the floor surface. The aim of these two scientists was to generate a model of a 'wave bubble' around these instruments, then to explore what if any new sources of energy could be used from its interior.

Now it was all ready and waiting.

The draughts of compressed mathematics were triggered and the real first development of a controlled bubble was observed across space, through the remote monitors. Watched and recorded, through every stage of its careful generation and growth, the translucent 'bubble' was expanded until it formed an enclosure around those measuring devices. After almost two hours of endless but necessary intervals of checking, waiting and monitoring, all seemed well and its expansion was proceeding as planned. The bubble had now grown to a large enough size that it was to surround the metering apparatus. Logan Metz, the leader of this partnership was smiling. He signaled for the next stage to commence. His partner pushed the pads whilst monitoring the screens around him, in readiness to evaluate the readings from those far away meters that might show any input of energy.

The command was sent, then within the next second and before the meters could respond, another bubble was seen to form within the first. There now began an unpredicted increase in the internal bubbles' dimensions. It grew slowly to a size, which was almost equal to that of the first, and then just as suddenly it overtook the first and absorbed it completely. Now the two mathematicians sat and watched as the new formation began a series of size fluctuations from small to large and back to small. The smile left the face of Logan Metz.

Watching the envelope they saw the groups of meters within begin to fade from sight. This whole fresh episode was not planned or even expected.

Knowing there must be a problem but saying nothing, both men frantically went to work on their panels in an effort to try to understand and then attempt to halt this new development.

Seconds turned to minutes. Then one of them broke the stunning silence.

"It is out of control. This should not be happening. Where did that other bubble come from?"

Ivan Sholtax, who was at the power controls spoke in a troubled voice whilst trying to change the effect by sending commands directly to the controlling computer.

"I cannot hold it in phase," he added.

"Try the power induction governor," his partner Logan offered. "Remove its power source and it should stabilize or at least it should shrink."

He tried to remain calm.

Ivan tried his suggestion, sending another command to the computer-controller. But the bubble was now behaving in a menacingly more erratic fashion. They had accounted for all events of uncertain results, with cut offs and by-passing circuits. But the events they observed now were not ever predicted. The readings they had hoped to receive were finally coming through and now being transmitted to their distant location. But those distant energy metering devices were each now proceeding off the scale, far beyond the top end of the marked red zone.

"It must be feeding its own energy from the other side," Logan said, realizing.

'Wherever that other side is,' he added in his thoughts.

They had both reached an agreement previously. Logan would be the leader of this prototype experimental process and it was now his decision.

"We must close it down. Now!"

Ivan was at first shocked at what his partners had said.

"Can we not hold for a while? This stage has never been reached or anything like this far before. We can learn so much."

These two friends had worked long for this moment. Whatever was happening now, this was a monumental occasion. He took his eyes from the screen to look at his partner for endorsement. But his partner's look of shear apprehension, even fear, was enough. He had to comply.

The recordings of energy transfer were enormous. Where they came from he could only speculate. They certainly were not from inside that tiny planetoid. Even a small leakage of such power could take away a piece of a planet. Without the proper control, which he knew now they did not have, anything could or would result. He waited for only a

ALAN E. FIELDS

fraction of a second then followed the order and moved his hand to
press the pad. He had not yet touched the control but as his fingers
reached the surface, the new elliptical envelope inside the tiny asteroid
could still be seen. Sholtax watched as it had now ceased its erratic
fluctuations and quickly expanded to a larger volume, seeming to touch
briefly the viewing devices for monitoring the actions. Then, just as
quickly the views on the screens were gone. Ivan's hand was still poised
above the console. The contact had not yet been closed.

"What the—?" Sholtax uttered, almost to himself.

Ivan Sholtax and Logan Metz looked at each other, both fearful that
they somehow had leashed some unknown power upon this universe.
They had been so convinced that they were able to keep the experiment
under control. Now it seemed their planning had failed them.

The eight monitors inside their own isolated laboratory station, which
had previously displayed a view of the distant asteroids entire hollow
and airless interior, had become totally blank.

The two men both formed their own similar conclusion. The asteroid
housing their experiment must have been completely atomized,
destroying with it all of their priceless equipment. Both Logan and
Ivan moved their eyes to view the three other monitors. These were
showing the volume of space surrounding the small asteroid. They had
been previously displaying views of the tiny planetoid's exterior, but
against the backdrop of stars and space. Both expected to see the lump
of rock being rent into fragments as it exploded into dust. But the
cameras on the three other asteroids close by, showed what could have
been a momentary view of that shimmering elliptical envelope as it
formed briefly around the asteroid. Then it was gone. Winked out of
existence.

The star sprinkled backdrop was all still there. The neighbouring
asteroids were still in view, reflecting the light from the distant sun.
But there was no sign of the anticipated destruction.

The asteroid that had housed the experiment was gone too.

Ivan Sholtax operated the fine focus of the viewing equipment. Their
equipment, the special chamber inside the large chunk of asteroid, they
had also disappeared from the space they previously had occupied.

100

There was nothing left, no debris, no dust, or glow of radiation. And definitely, there was no mysterious bubble.

Some days later there was confusion in that area of space out beyond the orbits of Jupiter, Saturn and Uranus and more than mid way past to the planet Neptune. Most puzzling to this one local miner, was a previously unrecorded planetoid or satellite. It was quickly charted, plotted, registered and claimed by the old prospector who, the day after his claim had been accepted and catalogued, coasted alongside to make an exploratory analysis of it for value.

This satellite was not large. It was less than one thousand metres in diameter. It's only feature was, it had one long and wide trench like crease in its surface. With his small Scudder type craft anchored to the course, curving and undulating surface, the prospector stepped down the ladder to check for its mineral possibilities. His closer scrutiny had surprise him when he found the satellite had a roughly formed landing pad, with anchors, cut into its surface. He had seen a bright reflection from somewhere down in the crease, so he made his way carefully toward its edge. Lowering himself down to the base of the wide depression and more to his surprise, he found what the reflection was. A small structure was down at the bottom, and a sealed door leading to what he was sure would be its interior.

The old man was not a locksmith in any way, but he was now determined to gain access. He worked for two Standard days on ways of opening that door. Finally he was successful. He found the interior of this stranger had lighting, heat and a vast array of computing devices and equipment, which he admitted to himself, were far beyond his own comprehension and evaluation. Otherwise, it was mostly hollow and contained no quantity of mineral of any value, except a small quantity of gold, spattered around the surfaces of its interior. The large cache of strange experimental equipment though, intrigued the old man. That may be of some value, if he could find out just what it was for.

"I cannot understand why it is there. I must have passed through that sector a hundred times and I haven't ever seen it before. We even made checks at the assay office and none of the others here at Neptune have either. It is in their area of jurisdiction, so they should know if anyone does," the old man said.

His grand-daughter was visiting with the old prospector. She was here on a short vacation from her college at The Mars Academy of Sciences and he was relating to her his latest discovery. He continued.

"I have gone through all of the records of satellites, those as small as this one, even for the last one thousand years and I cannot find one mention of anything even like this thing."

Mireema, his pretty and studious grand-daughter, listened to his words, then asked.

Could it be a ship? Maybe from outside, you know drifted here, unnoticed or unseen?"

"I thought that too, on account of that entrance to the chamber," the old man answered. "But there is no sign of any propulsion equipment, just the ether pile. But that is just for internal power. I checked the circuitry over. Nothing seems to be used as a propellant force that would move it. It just appeared there, is all I can say."

"Did you bring any of the equipment here?"

The old man just loved to have an audience and his grand-daughter knew how much he appreciated times like these when he could tell of some of his experiences. He answered.

"I have a few items in a quarantine cylinder fastened to the outside of my ship. Not much really but I thought it better to at least isolate it. I had trouble finding items small enough. There has been an explosion of some kind, but no radiation or burns, or any real damage at all. Just a small one it looks like really. Not much damage at all," the old prospector explained.

He had told her of the gold, splattered around in the central room. "There is that ether pile. It is small and very compact but too large to bring out through that entrance on my own. It's the most up to date pile of its kind I have ever seen too, so how that got there too, I don't know. Here, I have taken a vidi'-rec' of the whole interior and the stuff I have stored outside."

Outside. That meant the airless void beyond the insulated metal of the small, but efficient satellite he called home. And home was in orbit four thousand kilometres from Callisto's surface.

Mireema watched the vidi' carefully studying the equipment as the recorder scanned over it. She knew in seconds, just what all of this collection was?

Some days later the truth got to Metz and Sholtax. This was their mysteriously absent asteroid.

Its location was now in an almost stationary orbit around the planet Uranus. All of their devices were found undamaged and in as good a condition as that instant it had disappeared from the Asteroid Belt between Mars and Jupiter. Just those meters for recording energy had perished.

The How and The Why were to be the results of a further twenty-eight years of work and experimentation.

From this time onward, Human travel through space would become forever changed. The whole of this Galaxy was accessible to first the exploration and then its eventual settlement by Homo sapiens.

Hyper Space travel was born..


G'zin looked up effervescently from her comp' display.

"Well there is my part, all ready. Just check those readings on the visi' will you please Kindra?" she asked, then continued as Kindra took the calc' pad.

"I have plotted two short jumps then a third which will be a little farther. The last Jump will take the bubble into the region of Camrays Star and it is ready to go in fifteen point two five minutes."

"Looks just fine," Kindra replied after glancing over the readings quickly, then called, "Clys'! Anti Gravs in fourteen minutes."

Clysta entered the control room, looked around, smiled and said, "It's so good to be back in space again, isn't it?"

The others nodded their agreement and Clysta had heard what G'zin had planned. She paused and then continued.

"Why Camrays Star G'zin? That is not the direction we are supposed to begin our trip with. It doesn't matter too much, I know, just how we get there, but Camrays is not toward the Galactic Hub."

G'zin answered quickly, "You were saying yesterday you would likely feel more comfortable to have some weapons to take with us. We all three of us know that civilians and particularly people of our age could never get them around here. So I did a little thinking. I have an uncle who owns the Pleasure Satellite complex at Camrays Star and I know he has some small arms and weapons of his own there. Well, my uncle cannot resist or deny anything of his favorite niece," she said with a smile, her bright eyes twinkling, "And I too think we will feel safer in the unknown if we have something with which we can defend ourselves."

"Ok," Clysta said thoughtfully, "Then, in that case I can only concur. Camrays Star it is. But we must all agree to using weapons as the very final choice. Agreed?"

Clysta then lowered herself into the Anti-Grav and looked around the compartment, checking that all was ready. The other two nodded their consent to her last statement. A few minutes of waiting ended when the preliminary signal for the impending transport was sounded.

She added in finality, closing her eyes in anticipation of the coming transformation. "You really are, you know, the best of friends to have."

"I'll second that!" The other two chimed in, just as the formation of the Bubble outside the ship was coming to an end. Within milliseconds, the vessel made its first of a number of Leaps through the Hyper Space barrier.

# Chapter 10

"What in space is that doing here?"

Kindra was looking in the direction of the doorway leading to the sleep compartments. Through the arch he could see a tall humanoid robot and it was walking toward the control room.

The robot entered and in a very perfect, slightly metallic voice as if in answer to the question, it said.

'Good day to you Master Kindra and you too Miss G'zin, my name is 'Euclid'. I am a seventeenth class production of General Dynamics R.M. It is my duty to serve you!'

"And jolly proud to be doing it by its tone," chided G'zin jokingly, though she was equally surprised at the encounter.

Clysta started to explain.

"This is the same robot that delivered the Thought Cube to me. When I saw it before, I was left with the impression it was just some plain but old style messenger model. Then just before you two arrived, I was checking some of the details of the ship and the survival inventory. I opened a door of one of the storage lockers and there it was. Almost like a stowaway. He quite calmly announced to me that my father had instructed it to accompany us if we were to leave Europa. Somehow, and I am still not sure why, I believed it and here it is. I just was so surprised. Then I completely forgot about it being on board until we came out of that last jump. Well, what do you think?"

Kindra had a look of concerned perplexity and doubt.

"I know it is said, a robot cannot lie or do anything which will cause a Human any harm, it's all supposed to be a part of their psyche' of course," said Kindra, "It's just that they give me a funny feeling at the back of my neck, especially when they are like this one-almost human to look at and all metal. I have enough of a bad time accepting those little runabouts with their utility devices. They seem to be watching us, expecting us to fail or, something. This one looks humanoid almost too. And besides, they are always so, so perfect as well. I just hope this one works to those same rules of conduct."

G'zin listened then added, saying.

"As long as he does as he is told, I say, I don't mind one bit if it stays around. My father told me a few stories once of some of the old types, similar to this one. Some of them were very clever too in the old days. He said that some two hundred years ago they caused some kind of trouble, with humans. On one of the planets being Terra Formed I think it was."

Clysta had been listening to these comments. She let them have their say.

"I feel for my part, I am sure, it will do as it is told. Anyway let us find out what else it does. It may be very useful," said Clysta.

Then, turning to the robot, Clysta asked it, "Is there anything that you need to tell us about yourself, besides your automatic duties?"

'Commander Z'ee has programmed me to make use of the Thought Cube which you have in your possession and direct this vessel to a location close to the area of the Galaxy that he wishes you to visit,' the robot informed the three friends.

Then it continued. 'It is one of my programmed abilities to adapt the guidance computer of this craft to make use of its information and develop the coordinates. Is that your own wish?'

Kindra raised his eyebrows at the information. "That bit of work should come in handy. It may save us some of the time which we may need to finally find first the star and then that planet."

"Well we seem to be all in agreement. This particular robot will no doubt have its uses," Clysta said, seeing G'zin nod her approval. Then turning to the robot, "Very good then, Euclid. You are dismissed. Now go and park yourself in the closet again, we will call you when we need you."

The robot was about to turn and walk away, Clysta added. "Oh, and by the way, welcome aboard, Euclid."

The robot nodded its metal head ever so slightly, the vision panel seeming to glow in appreciation then it turned on its heel and disappeared through the doorway and out of sight.

It took less than a hundred years for the explorers from Earth to make their first visits to most neighbouring stars. Their task was to find those stars having planets of any value in this outer rim of our arm of the Galaxy and closest to our own star.

Most stars were eliminated from entry on the list of preferred systems due to their classification. These had been rejected centuries ago by the work of the early Earth astronomers using mostly the sciences of spectral analysis.

A scheme had always been ready for fulfillment of the dreams of colonization of space. Now with Hyper travel, most dreams could become reality. Mankind could now travel unrestrained by the slowness of Sub-Light speed. Star systems with habitable worlds could be accessed quickly and made ready to relieve the teeming population of Mother Earth and the Solar System, which at that time was measured at around eleven billion.

An unfortunate incident was the result of one of the many exploration expeditions of these earlier times. This particular group of explorers had been tracking ever outward in search of usable and valuable planets. After one of their trips, a virus like parasite was unknowingly transported into the Solar System by the returning vessel. The craft had later been traced to be one of those belonging to a mining conglomerate who had been scouting and prospecting in the twin star system of Epsilon Iridani.

This unknown and at the time unstoppable virus, generated a selective disease that ravaged the Solar System and carried on unchecked until it had lowered the population of Humans by more than two billion. Finally after some twenty years, the disease was isolated and conquered, then eliminated.

The system of Epsilon Iridani was afterwards posted with warning beacons at its perimeter to establish it as quarantine territory. The whole of the system was from that time made out of bounds to all space travelers.

Only a small number of the many star systems contained the occasional planet ready for immediate settlement by Earthlings, but many others were not. It was now that the teams of 'Terra-Formers' were detailed to spread throughout the systems nearer to Earth. They were to plant the necessary earth like environments onto planets having the best likelihood of success.

Approximately one hundred and ten selected planets were prepared. In most cases, first a base area of a hundred kilometres square was selected as the foundation. This was 'force formed' at first to give the 'Formers' a suitable place to set up their change machines for commencing the greater processes.

Though it was not perfect, this area was able to support the first immigrants with minor additional survival input from Earth, while the slower Terra Forming progressed. In many conditions more than two hundred years would pass before planets became totally self supporting. Then the population was allowed to increase by quota.

The first explorers visited many varieties of stars. Of many different magnitudes, ages and densities. Some would be double star systems some with planets of the correct workable specification but with incorrect or even dangerous solar radiation.

Many stars that would have had the correct qualities required for development were found to have no workable planets at all, just the occasional useless large lump of seared rock or dust particles in orbit.

Then there were those with nothing at all which was solid, just a wide band of orbiting celestial gases mixed with quantities of fine spatial dust. These would be the cause of much conjecture by people of science as to their history and their future.

There was though, a group of stars and celestial gases, which astronomers of long ago had looked upon from a distance as some of the most beautiful. This location in space had been known from ancient times as The Pleiades Cluster. Almost all of the stars in the group were still surrounded by the very gasses and particles that had helped in their birth.

One star in particular was a class G2 similar to Sol. Like some of the others, which were its neighbours, its evolution had formed no planets. It was conjectured that at some time, say a half of a billion earth years ago, before man had even evolved, this particular star had gone through a nova or even a super nova. It's evolution from then had been not quite the routine of others in the same classification.

What it now had though, was an almost perfect spherical shroud of opaque gases and particles making this star invisible from a remote galactic distance. The gas cloud totally surrounding this particular star was about one hundred and fifty billion kilometres in diameter with nothing but clear space within that shroud, the exception being just two small and mineral rich satellites rotating in a slow orbit. How so perfect a sphere could have been formed instead of the usual irregular or orbital plane formation, was the past subject of much additional astronomic speculation?

No matter, the panorama from within was one of enormous and breathtaking beauty. A truly spectacular view of the many hues of the star's refracted light, accompanied by an extravaganza of colours being reflected from the inner surface of the surrounding gaseous cloud.

That most beautiful phenomenon in the whole neighbourhood was the system, the home of Camrays Star. This was the first of the future destinations for these three friends, Clysta, Kindra and G'zin. And along with them, their robot companion, Euclid.

# Chapter 11

The exits, when they passed from the individual darkness of Hyper Space were about as uneventful as when they entered them. There was a slight shift of the senses, maybe a slight twisting in their abdominal region but in the main, as unrecognizable as an event in itself but definitely a shift. Then all was as normal as it could be once again.

The first to rise from her support was G'zin.

"Now that was just perfect. It took only two hours fifteen, in and out."

The view screen had changed from the deepest black of Hyper' to the sparkling panorama of stars and there, in dead centre was the dull glow coming from what was the target gas cloud, with the bright light of Camrays Star now faintly showing through the density of the surrounding mist of particles.

"The colours aren't so great from here," said G'zin, "But just you wait 'till we get to my uncle's platform."

"Kindra, would you please contact the station and establish a guide path?" Clysta said. "I'll see if Euclid can rustle up a meal, we may as well make some use of the robot. Then, when we have eaten, you can pilot us through the cloud and then onward to the platform."

The ship had left Hyper Space and was now coasting at a fraction less than the Light Speed necessary to safely enter any star system. It was being slowed by the reverse action of the Ether Engine.

The term, Engine, was perhaps incorrect for this propulsion device, as it had been given that title long ago and somewhat erroneously. The system does not use the aged and wasteful explosion principle as the word engine might suggest, but instead uses the basic atomic structure of ether and the matrix from which it was formed. Through sikrom-mathematics, each atom of the craft with everything inside its outer alloyed envelope is transformed to an ether base short band and then back again. These two transformations are completed at the speed of light, generating almost timeless and measureless motion without the earlier necessary Lightspeed containment envelope.

By the time their meal was finished the ship had slowed to a Half of Light Speed and was still fast approaching the outer surface of the gossamer shroud of gasses. After the passage of one hour they had passed into and beyond the thin layer of cloud and now exited that, into the pristine clear space within.

Kindra was once again at the controls. He was entering minor adjustments to the trajectory calculations to avoid the occasional piece of space debris or any asteroids which might have been caught in the stars gravitational attraction.

Kindra commanded the controlling computer it was time to slow the Skimmer to a Quarter Light Speed at the signal. He then called for view screen magnification as the tiny dot of reflected light became visible, orbiting the bright yellow star now ahead of them.

"It's unbelievable!" Clysta gasped in surprise at the view they now had of the station. "Look at the quantity of those dome structures and spheres."

She tried to count the separate structures, connecting in different directions by legs and tubes. "There must be at least twenty."

"Unbelievable doesn't cover it," echoed Kindra. "And your Uncle owns all of this?"

He did not take his eyes from the screen.

"Sort of," G'zin replied with pride in her voice. She continued, "My home world is full of rich minerals and it is that which made it a very wealthy planet. My Great-Great, Grandfather was once a Prince of one of the countries back on Old Earth. He did something of an unpopular nature, so he and his family were cast out of power for the same reason. Then later he and his family were exiled. They left the Solar System and toured the settled sectors to find a suitable new beginning and finished up on Fryl. My home world."

G'zin continued, "He started to do a little prospecting and found a considerable deposit of carbon crystals. They were found to be harder than the diamonds of Earth. That was just a beginning. They later discovered a vast seam of the material Vitileel on the planet, you remember, it is a major component in the assembly of the Ether Drives. It was in very short supply before that find and my ancestor was sitting on most of it. And then there were decent deposits of the other valuable metals. Gold, silver, lead. Though not an awful amount of that kind of stuff is mined by our family."

She finished, slightly embarrassed at her revelation.

"So apart from everything else, yes, my Uncle is, sort of, part of a family partnership, well sort of!"

As G'zin ended her story, a ringing sound came from the visi-con followed by a very correct sounding voice, accompanied by the image of a pretty young female. She announced.

"Welcome to the system of Camrays Star, the finest of all Pleasure Stations. We are at your service."

Then the announcer continued, "Would you please ensure your craft guidance system is monitoring Beacon Number Eight?" A signal reference was given. Then, "Your vessel has been tracked since entry into the region and its volume assessed. It will be guided automatically to a parking zone already allocated for your most welcomed visit."

The female then carried on to explain the routine of transportation from the parking arrangements to the entrance platform and that they could expect a forty minute wait before a shuttle pick-up.

"This will give us enough time to clean up and change," said Clysta, "Do you think Euclid will be allowed to come along, G'zin? I don't really know why, but I feel that the robot has to accompany us."

"When Uncle Zy hears that I am here along with you, I should think so," expressed G'zin over her shoulder. She was already making her way out of the control room toward her quarters.

The 'shuttle' vehicle which had been built on the same scale as the orbiting structure in this system, closed in on their tiny ship. It was very large and decorative. Designed as a space 'bus, its shape was an elongated sphere having six arms radiating from its equator. Positioned at the outer end of each arm was a cylinder attached and parallel to the crafts own directional motion. The three friends watched the manoeuver on their view screen and could see all of these cylindrical attachments were open at both ends.

Each of the individual cylinder structures was of a different radius and length allowing it to glide over and encircle a visiting craft, no matter what size of girth the visiting craft might have.

When this manoeuver had been achieved on their Skimmer, a sealing field, generated at the two open ends of the cylinder, made it safe for an atmosphere to be developed inside the surrounding and now sealed tube. The visiting passengers could directly leave their craft and pass in total comfort toward their end of the radiant tube leading to the central transporting sphere.

Clysta, G'zin and Kindra, followed two paces behind them by the robot Euclid, all left the Skimmer. They stepped onto the beltway and were each propelled comfortably through the tubular connecting arm to the lush appointments of the central sphere. There were, when they arrived, about sixty or more other visitors already on this shuttle, all having been collected previously. Theirs was to be the last visitor pick-up for this shuttle trip.

As the two female companions found a comfortable seat, Kindra crossed to a view port to watch the Skimmer appear as if to exit, from the rear of the tube as the tube itself, was thrust forward under the forward motion of the main central sphere. Then the shuttle was under way for the Pleasure Station.

Euclid moved as inconspicuously as possible to stand at another view port. It appeared, for a robot, to be strangely interested in the events outside.

A standard box like robot server was gliding across the deep piled carpeting, travelling to and fro amongst the passengers, busily serving refreshments and attending to each of the passengers needs. G'zin attracted the servers attention and called it over.

"May I make a call to central control whilst we are in transit?" She asked. "It is of a personal nature."

"You may," came the ever so perfect answer from the device. "A visi-con is located by the holograph art feature at the green wall. It also has a vibra-screen for privacy if you so require."

"Thank you," G'zin said, unnecessarily, as she was rising to cross the room.

"You are most welcome," the robotic server replied.

# Chapter 12

The four companions disembarked along with the other visitors into a large receiving hall. It appeared to be almost on the scale of the Commissary back at the Academy. The walls were hung with many decorative tapestries depicting a variety of scenes recognizable by the three as being from the history books of old Earth, all moving as if live, with a holographic style of motion.

Whilst the other two stood in awe at the spectacle, G'zin was trying to see through the accumulation of people to locate the one person she had contacted whilst in transit.

Looking across the polished gold and marble floor, and beyond the crowd of visitors straight ahead, it was impossible to miss him.

Uncle Zy was a huge and portly man, with a large, plump and jolly face. He was dressed in a full length flowing robe of the finest spun fabrics covered in patterns and swirls of many colours. His head, devoid of hair, had a highly polished sheen. The pupils of his eyes were pink, of a slightly darker shade than G'zin's, beneath a set of the blackest, bushiest eyebrows. The eyebrows were each complemented by an ample and equally black moustache.

"Uncle Zy!" squealed G'zin, joyfully, running toward him.

He placed his large hands around G'zin's slim waist and effortlessly picking her up with his strong muscular arms and began spinning around and around whilst he placed many kisses on both of her cheeks.

"My, oh my!" he exclaimed in a jolly voice still holding her high in the air, "Haven't you become a beautiful lady? It must be at least two years since I last saw you. No it is longer, more like three."

"Too long Uncle Zy, too, too long," she answered, beaming and out of breathe from the gyrations.

He let her down to the floor carefully and, turning to look at her companions, he continued. "And you. You must be Clysta?" as he stooped low, grasped her hand from her side with the lightest of touch. He then placed a gentle kiss on the back. He then straighten to his full height and looked around..

"Ah! And you are Kindra."

He took Kindra's hand next and pumped it up and down enthusiastically in a long and vigorous handshake. Then with a jaundiced look through one eye in the direction of Euclid, he remarked. "And this has got to be the robot whose name is,-Euclid?"

The robot moved forward.

'It is so kind of you to permit me this visit Uncle Zy,' said the robot.

"There he goes," muttered Kindra. "So perfect!"

"It is my pleasure," Uncle Zy said without the slightest hesitation.

Turning again to face the three friends, his long arms encircling all three. Then, he shepherded them across the floor in a direction oblique to the flow of the other visitors. Euclid followed close behind.

"Please," Uncle Zy said, grinning widely and explaining, "Walk this way. I have a short cut through this entrance stuff. You too, Euclid, come along."

A piece of the wall ahead opened up and they passed through to the other side of the regular entry points. The opening quickly sealed shut after them. Then Uncle Zy ushered them through a few entrance formalities as he talked.

"Your visit was so unexpected, G'zin you naughty young lady. You should have called ahead and I could have planned my day a little better. I do hope you will excuse me not being with you for a few hours right now, but I do have some very important matters requiring my personal attention for the next little while. After that is over, I will be free to spend lots of time with you.

But for the interim, I will put you all in the very capable hands of my number one aide who will look after you and your needs. He can take you to the Centre and show you around until I am free."

He brushed his large handlebar moustache with the back of his hand, bowed with an elaborate flourish and turning on his heel, disappeared at speed into the crowd.

The three young people stood for a second, watching the figure of Uncle Zy go from view. Just as Clysta was about to ask, "What now", she was stopped by a gentle touch on her arm by the robot Euclid. She turned to see why.

A young man, not more than just a few years older than the trio, appeared out of the now thinning crowd of visitors and was walking toward them.

"My name is William," he spoke as he approached. "I am to give you a tour of the Camrays Pleasure Station until 'The Boss' is free once more to be with you. If you will please step this way."

The man who stood before them was tall, straight and well proportioned. His height was a little less than two metres, with fair but tanned skin. His hair was blonde and neatly groomed, he was good looking, handsome in fact and dressed in a sleek and tight fitting one piece uniform of the same type as was worn by all of the station staff. Where others were of a variety of colours, he wore black. On the right front below the shoulder as others of the staff, there was a badge designed in the shape of the Station as it was seen from the outside.

William's badge in this case was of gold. Obviously it was to show his rank at the Station.

The usual routine hand-shaking introductions were handed around between the visitors and William. When it came the turn of G'zin, she gave William one of her special smiles with glittering pink eyes. She held onto his handshake for a split second longer for effect and releasing a soft moaning, "Mmmnh," as she slowly removed her hand from his.

"Now if you will please step this way," William said, his cheeks colouring slightly as he indicated the opening to a small tunnel leading away from the docking and reception area.

Clysta gave G'zin a sharp nudge as they followed behind. "That will do," she said, "We don't want to be thrown out of here now do we."

G'zin just smiled. "Only funnin'," she whispered, her eyes still retaining the glow.

The tunnel was short. It opened into an area smaller than the one they had left though still large and cavernous and not quite as well decorated. It was obviously a parking area for the many transport units here, which were of a variety of sizes. Most had arrangements of seats. Those which had, were also obviously used to carry the stations visitors around the complex.

William guided them to a Hover Car parked in a place to the left and separate from the others. On the side of this car there was the same badge insignia that William wore on his uniform, denoting once more, his position and indicating to the group it was his car.

"You have your own vehicle," Kindra asked if only to confirm the fact and to break the silence which had followed their first meeting.

"Yes," William replied, not too strongly so not to offend. Then with a courteous and sweeping motion with his arm. "If you will just step in and find yourselves a seat."

As the three friends filed into the vehicle, William explained, looking slightly uncomfortably when his eyes finally faced toward G'zin.

"Your uncle has planned that you stay in the Presidential Dome but it is not yet prepared for the three of you," then he added, "Or should I say four."

He looked at the robot still outside the car, then continuing, "So, as we will have a short amount of time to spare before taking you there, we can show you a little of our Station's features. If it is ok by you, we can begin with the first quick tour," he continued, asking, "Is the robot to come also? It can be safely stored here if you wish."

"If you don't mind, please. We would rather he accompany us," Clysta answered without hesitation.

William was a little confused by the use of 'he' but thought it best to make no comment.

"I don't mind at all," was his answer. "Does it have a name or maybe a number?"

To William's surprise, this time the robot gave the answer. "My name is Euclid, I am a product of General Dynamics R.M."

William hesitated in obvious surprise.

He then said, "Pl—pleased to meet you,—Euclid. Step right in."

The robot replied. 'Thank you William, I too am pleased to meet you.'

Kindra just smiled and shook his head from side to side as he looked down at the floor.

By now they were all seated and ready to move off and William dialed a code and took the controls. The vehicle levitated fractionally and did a circuit around a group of other visitors who had since entered the area. Then they were on their way and leaving through the mouth of another tunnel. This new tunnel turned into an intersection of the connecting arms leading away and toward the many domes and spheres of the Station.

"Would you have a particular preference of what we should visit first?" William asked as they approached a holo' directory showing pictorial representations of the pleasure station and its contents. He then had a thought and said. "Unless you would really rather that we go straight to the Galaxy Hotel and wait there for your quarters to be made ready."

"I think we should leave that to you, but we will have lots of time later to see our rooms and unpack," G'zin replied, again with her special smile to William. "Everyone else agree?"

"Ok by me," the other two voiced together, Clysta smiling to herself.

"Well, we can take a small tour of the domes that are almost on a line which will lead us eventually to the Hotel. If you don't mind then, I will first take you to see the Dome of History."

As he spoke, William was dialing the coordinates into the cars control console.

"I always think of it as my favourite place to visit. I majored in Earth History at the University Galactica at Cygni. I suppose you all know where that is. It was from there I received a recommendation for a future at the Station. They even set up an interview with your Uncle Zy, G'zin," he looked and then smiled in G'zin's direction. "I have been here ever since, that is almost for eleven years now."

As William was speaking, the car whisked along through the various large tubes forming the connecting legs they had seen from outside. Each tube terminated at an intersection of other similar tubes. These were the entrances to the large domes and spheres housing the exhibits and pleasure areas, demonstrations and the many other parts forming this Station of Fun.

Many of the entrance areas were in a totally transparent dome specially designed to let in the view from outside, and it was spectacular.

The cloud of gases and dust they had penetrated to gain access to this star, reflected the light of the star in fantastic arrays of colour. The random arrangement of those colours came as bands in some areas and in swirling patterns in others. Then there were areas seeming as though an artist had painted them with a giant brush. Swirling and writhing in million miles long streams of colour. In and around and between these spectacular views there were the incessant and repeated colossal flashes of electrical energy, evidence of the enormous turmoil, taking place, all within those distant clouds.

William stopped the car to give his passengers the opportunity to take in more of the view.

"Fantastic," Clysta and G'zin said together in awed agreement.

"Stupendous. It is as if we are looking at Jupiter from the inside," Kindra said, then he added, for the benefit of their guide. "That is where we three met, at Europa Academy."

Euclid just sat as a statue, in his seat, his view slot hardly glowing.

# Chapter 13

The Dome of History was a flattened semi-spherical transparent structure of enormous proportions. William took a few minutes to explain to his charges that it was one kilometre in diameter and the material of its transparent construction would filter the dangerous direct rays from the star that was always above this area. But it also maintained absolute clarity facing away to give unobstructed views of the beauty displayed by the distant surrounding gas clouds.

The volume of this dome was scattered with platforms of many shapes and sizes. Some were at floor level and many were afloat in a random pattern throughout the dome. On each platform was a depiction of an individual enactment of a phase of Human history. Each platform's display was a moving holograph and in life size.

Their car which was open and roofless, was guided by William from level to level and area to area, giving his passengers a view of each of the portrayals. A clear voice came from the car's console carrying on a dialogue, describing the events as they related to the scene they were watching.

"If a visitor so wishes," began William, "He or she or both may even take part in these programs just as if they actually were there in history. The system has the ability to make it all so real and lifelike. Your Uncle recruited the most advanced technologists in Holographic Art to design this system," he said proudly, once more noticing G'zin's sparkling eyes.

An hour had gone quickly by, while seeing some of this domes exhibits. William halted the car and suggested.

"Now that I have very briefly covered some of the platforms in here, how do you feel about seeing a little of our Zoo?"

"You're the guide," suggested Clysta, then asked, "Are the animals there all in holo' too?"

"By all means no," exclaimed William politely, "and of course we have many. Our zoo is noted as one of the largest collections off the Planet Earth."

Visiting a Zoo was something the three students had not had much time to take advantage of, even if the opportunity had arisen. The visitors appeared to be in agreement, so off to the Zoo it would be.

Once more William punched a code into the console then piloted the car toward one of the openings leading out of the dome. They noticed as they left one excited group of the many visitors had parked alongside a platform and were preparing to climb out to take part in one of the scenes.

"That looks like it could be fun," Kindra had time to remark, looking backward as they entered the exit tunnel. "I would like to return here when we can."

The car made its way once again along the network of tunnels leading through the Station finally exiting into another dome. It was much larger in area compared to the one they had left, but with this one the curvature of the dome was not so high.

"The air in this dome has a strange aroma," suggested Kindra, as he suspiciously sniffed and smelled at the air around them. "Is it possible that the recycling system is malfunctioning?"

"No, nothing like that," said William with a smile, "That is the genuine odour of authentic live animals. We keep it that way to give it more authenticity. I should suspect that this is one of the few places where you can see and actually be up close to so many real live animals. Especially of the variety that we have here at the Station. All of them are live," he said, once more with the same pride showing through.

He slowed the car to let the group take in the view, and carried on his dialogue.

"Do you know that many of our animals we have here, don't even exist in their original habitat, particularly in places like Earth and a few of those earlier settled planets. There were never many on the outside, as you probably know. The exploding population of Earth squeezed out many of their species. Luckily, Zoologists managed to save many before they were made extinct. Those which were saved are the ancestors of most of these which we have here."

The floor of this dome was designed to be undulating with some small and natural looking hills. It was covered with many types of greenery, trees and grasses. Here and there were dotted miniature lakes and in some sections there were areas representative of barren desert regions.

All gave a variety of scenes. Some of them were identical to areas from Earth and other of types from distant and outer planets, where some varieties of animal like life had been found.

As they proceeded to enter into the dome, a force field shield was generated removing and covering the openness of their car.

"Why the shield?" asked Kindra, as he was turning to have a better look at a group of small animals they were passing.

"I expect it will be for our protection," Clysta knowingly offered in answer. She was watching the same exhibit, the first in the dome. It was of a typical farm-yard scene from a world orbiting Ceti. There were sheep like animals closely similar to an Earth hybrid and a few creatures comparable to goats, both indigenous to the Ceti system and even some of their rare four legged chickens.

"That is just what it is, Clysta." William confirmed, "The enclosure is an automatic function in this dome. Really it is not only for the safety of the visitors. It also of course makes it less tempting to try to touch or feed the exhibits."

They traveled farther into the dome and each scene showed animals becoming more exotic and varied. For all of this time Euclid still sat in absolute silence in the rear seat of the car, next to G'zin. The robot's visor panel continued to show little change, except the slightest fluctuation of brightness at each scene, seemingly recording the information.

"Whatever is that creature? Over there?" Exclaimed G'zin pointing toward some dense greenery. "It looks almost human but so huge and—well, different."

"That," began William in reply, "is one of our most prized exhibits. It is a Ceti Gorilla. It is the only species that man has yet found which remotely resembles any other from Earth. And that one you see is also known here as a Silver Back. It is very similar, almost identical, to an animal that was once a native species of Planet Earth. I have been told its resemblance is most remarkably exact, apart from some peculiar characteristics. The others of Earth are now extinct in their own original habitat. This one and its family were in danger of dying also. Through some virus they had caught from eating some Terran strain of plant they were not able to digest. Uncle Zy found out and went to fight for their lives. But they had no chance in their own world and we are lucky enough to have had the whole family of them brought here and they are all doing fine."

The large animal sat, quite unconcerned that it was on view. It was sitting on a large flat area of rock covered with fine sand, at the edge of a large area of a cane like growth. It held a thin straight piece of the nearby plant in its hand and looked to be in deep concentration as it scratched a drawing in the smooth and flattened sand, that it had carefully prepared with a hand like front paw. As William spoke, a number of the same animals, each smaller than the first larger animal, congregated behind it. They were noticeably all of differing sizes, as they each cautiously came out of the bushes surrounding the area. They all looked at the car and blankly returned the visitors stares, then moved to gather around the first animal, each of them interested in seeing what it, the larger animal, was drawing. Then, after some minutes and a few noises between each of them, the whole group ambled lazily back into the tall bushy undergrowth and disappearing from view. The last to leave was the larger animal.

"I wonder what it was drawing?" Kindra queried, "It looked interesting enough for its companions."

William waited, and then answered.

"We can go to look now they have left, but it may surprise you. We will give them a few more minutes because if they do return, they are very playful but extremely strong, and their games do hurt."

William waited then softly brought the car to rest on a small bare hillock of soft greenery close to where they had seen the animals. He waited a few seconds more then opened up the enclosure and they each followed him out and walked toward the clearing where the large animal had been sitting and scratching in the sand.

Their surprise was just what William had anticipated.

The scratchings were clear and bold. The degree of scale and artistry was unbelievable. There was no possibility for error in what they saw. Inside a large rectangle, a number of lines drawn in the sand described a neat and clearly framed sketch. It was of the outline of their Skimmer craft that they had come to this system in. The area inside the corners of the outer lines of the rectangular area was large enough to hold also a number of words. Written or scratched with an equally unmistakable neatness one, to each corner were the words,

'Clysta' 'G'zin'

'Kindra' 'Euclid'

As the friends stood in stunned silence, trying to fathom what trick had taken place, William broke into their thoughts.

"It has beaten many specialists. That one does it all of the time, though we do avoid having our visitors see the results. It can be somewhat disturbing."

Some minutes passed, then William advised they continue. He suggested that the animals may come back, so the friends conceded and returned, still very confused and a little unsettled, to the car. They had left Euclid inside and the robot was still in his original position when they returned. As soon as they were all inside, the protective screen once more closed over them.

Moving on through some other settings, they approached a sandy, rocky scene. It took a short time for their previous experience to leave their thoughts.

This area was barren except for a scattered growth of a tall tree-like plant, each standing in isolation some nine metres apart. The plants had a single straight yellow trunk at least twenty metres tall and at the top of this sprouted a series of deep green branches which became a rust coloured fern-like growth toward the ends, each growing horizontally.

Equally strange were the three creatures that next came into sight. About the same height as a table top, each had long loose multi coloured fur and a long prehensile tube like mouth projecting from the top of the body. Even stranger, and their only other feature, they had six arms spaced equally around their torsos at the three quarters point of their height. The arms terminated in claw like appendages, probably to use as tools. There were no legs to be seen and what could have been eyes were three large black dots, to one side of a fuzz covered dome on the top of the body.

"I know what those are," said Kindra in excitement, as four more came into view from the top of one of the trees. "It's a Blocklix, they are the original inhabitants of the planet where I was born. There were thousands of them up to a century or two ago but now, unfortunately, they live only in certain protected and mountainous regions and are becoming extremely scarce."

"Those trees are all they seem to live on and in," he continued. "All day long they just go up and down, up and down. Then they go to the next tree and do the same all over again."

As Kindra spoke, two of the creatures stripped a small bunch of the fern from the tree and proceeded to eat it. Within a half of a minute the missing growth had magically regenerated and the area of fern was back to normal.

William interrupted. "You must be from Bambiron then?"

Kindra nodded his head to answer. "Yes," he said, "Do you know of it?"

William continued, a little surprised.

"My sister, she is two years younger than I am," he explained, "she has just started in a career on that world as a Hecto-Chemist. She is employed by a mineral exporting organization and she seems to be doing very well."

"Well, isn't that a coincidence?" Clysta suggested. "Kindra's family is in that same business on Bambiron. Isn't that so, Kindra?"

Kindra started to answer, but before anything more could be said, a small red light began to flash on the console. It was accompanied by the sound of a buzzer just loud enough only the car's occupants were able to hear it.

William pushed at a pad on the side of the console and an urgent voice could be heard coming from a hidden speaker.

"Director William, it is important that you please contact the Security Offices. This is an Emergency One. Please contact the Security Offices."

The message was repeated again.

# Chapter 14

William quickly turned the car toward another grassy knoll and came to a halt. Once more he pressed the pad and spoke this time.

"Security? This is Director William. You may speak."

There was urgency in the reply that followed.

"Director. There has been a breach through the exterior skin to Pod Number Six. So far we can only make a guess what is the nature, but it is most obvious that it is a criminal entry and they are humanoid. We have been monitoring the intruders the best we can by visi', but since they were first seen, they have been destroying the scanners just as we are putting them in focus."

"How did they enter," asked William.

"We are unsure at this time, Director and I do not yet have all of the facts," said the voice rather timidly. "Our exterior monitors show a small craft anchored to the outer skin, so we are suggesting that it is their ship. They are carrying weapons and they are also carrying a device that has been able to counter the Stunners and the exterior Shock Plating. Everything we have as a defense on the exterior seems to have been powerless to keep them out. They even avoided the docking routine and passed unnoticed until it was too late."

"Have you dispatched any additional guards?" William asked. William's demeanor had changed completely. He had now taken on a whole new personality, one of complete control and command.

"I have made contact with troupe five and troupe six. They are heading in the direction of Pod Six and the intruders, sir," was the reply.

William went into silent concentration for a second or two, then to the console microphone. "Pod Number Six. That is the commerce and banking section. From your tracking, where do you think these people are heading?"

"Without a doubt sir, I'd say there target is the Valuables Vault."

"I am presently at the Zoological Sciences Dome with guests," said William after a few seconds of thought. "I will be leaving immediately through number three arch. Clear a path."

He quickly dialed a series of instructions into the pad on the guidance panel and waited as the car levitated. He thought again for a moment, and then added, again into the console.

"Seal off connecting arms Fourteen, Five A and Five B. Pad out the energy and immobilize all of the ground cars in this area where we are now and also on my route to the vault area. I will use the over-ride in my car. Call the security in transit and have them do likewise. I will get back to you shortly."

As he fingered the control to lift their car high above the surrounding scenery, William turned to his guests who had sat in silence through the dialogue.

"Sorry, but we will need to cut the tour short. As you have just overheard, we seem to have something of an emergency. I cannot take a chance leaving you here; there are some dangerous animals in this area. If you don't mind, I will take you to a more secure location where I can leave you in safety and I will arrange for you to be collected and taken back to our starting point."

By this time the car was in sight of an arch, which had a large ornate number three in gold magically suspend overhead.

Clysta spoke up, "Don't bother to stop. It will be much quicker if you keep going. You will be saving valuable seconds and who knows, we may be able to help."

William looked around as the car closed in on the opening. He saw G'zin and Kindra both nod their heads in agreement. Euclid was sitting as usual, silent and unmoved, but its dimly glowing visor panel faced directly at William, as if looking into his eyes.

"Ok" He said with a sigh of agreement, "You are possibly correct."

He looked back at Euclid, then. "But you must please stay out of harms way and it is most essential that you all carry out my orders to the letter."

All three visitors nodded in unison signaling their total agreement, as their car shot at speed through the arch with number three overhead.

Once again, William fingered the pad.

"This is the Director again. I am en route and presently at interchange Three C. Security. Is their craft still outside the Pod?"

"Yes sir," was the reply. "I have it on the exterior skin monitor-cam'. It looks like the ship is equipped with some kind of energy weapons, Sir. And one of the maintenance shuttles that passed close by has been monitoring it. They report that those guns are now facing and it seems are aimed at the wall of the Pod. Sir!"

"And we know what they can do," he said, more to himself. Then he said back to the com' set.

"And how far have the intruders advanced?"

"They are now at the wall forming the rear of the Visitors Valuables Vault," came the reply from the dispatcher in Security. "The section leader has reported they are well equipped with powerful weapons and have killed two of our guards who were in the area and tried to stop them. There are also three others of our people who have been wounded, one very badly. They were trying to close in and hold them back and a weapon fight broke out. The three wounded staff members have since retreated and are now outside the area."

The dispatcher continued, "We are trying to bring in some energy shields, but they are stored at the other side of the station. It will be quite some time before we can transport them to the Pod Six location."

The dispatcher ceased his report then the car's occupants heard a whispered expletive from him. Then.

"Sir. I have just received a report from the Depository. Their monitoring cameras inside the vault have shown the Intruders have entered through an opening. It appears that they have cut through the rear blast wall with one of their devices. Those cameras have now also been put out of action."

"However did they manage to get through that wall, the builders told us it was impregnable," said William in a low voice, more to himself as he bit on his lower lip.

The dispatcher, who had this time overheard, tried to explain. "They have with them something like a particle splitter but it must be more powerful than those I have seen. That is possibly the device they used to gain entry through the outside hull."

All of this time as the interchange continued, they had been passing over the tops of the previously grounded tour cars. The passengers inside their vehicles could be seen looking upwards, puzzled, as William's car careened overhead at its high speed.

"They are being given entertainment on the car's internal holo'," he explained in answer to the unasked question. "Also there is a refreshment dispenser and a standard announcement that a malfunction is holding up their progress. Perhaps it can be termed a little lie, but most necessary under the circumstances."

William continued, talking fast as he negotiated a tight turn.

"Shortly after we have passed them and all is clear, they will be allowed to carry on with their tour, but they will be guided away from the area of trouble."

"What is the strength of the security on the Station?" Clysta asked.

"That is the immediate problem. We don't have a large force, it has just not been seen as necessary," said William with a frown. "There just hasn't ever occurred something like this. No one has broken in before. About four years ago we had a guest who tried to hold up one of the restaurant cashiers, and that was quickly solved without much ado. We do have twenty-five security personnel who are arms trained and a Sergeant-at-Arms in charge of Security. He is presently in sick bay though, suffering from a broken arm and collar bone. He got those injuries in one of our-ah, training exercises," he ended a little sheepishly.

His facial expression accompanied with a shake of his head showed the humour in his analysis of that situation.

He continued. "The guards are usually spread out around the Station. At the present most of them luckily, are stationed in the quarter close to the area that we are headed for."

His uneasy close was. "Not counting those who were put out of action, I expect there are now only eight security staff who will be in the area or close by."

William stopped his dialogue for a second as he thought, his brow creased in the realization as he then added. "Humph! I suspect that figure may not be enough."

He fingered the pad again and ordered. "Security, contact all the guards there. Instruct them they are to keep a safe distance, whilst trying to limit the intruders' movements. We do not need any more casualties," then he asked. "What is the latest information on their craft?"

"We have it on vidi'-con now, direct from the shuttle," came the reply. "It looks to be attached to the outside skin by magnetic grabs and with its airlock up tight. That almost confirms the suspicion that they have made an opening there for an entry into the pod."

Clysta spoke into the console, "How big is this craft of the intruders?"

The confusion in the Security Station at this unknown voice could be appreciated, so William added, "It is ok to answer. That is one of the passengers I am escorting. Carry on and answer the question."

The security dispatcher complied, "It appears to be a Flitter craft from its profile, so far as we can see. The shuttle pilot is confused a little by those armaments though. It is not a combat vessel. He suggests they must have been added at some time since it was built."

Clysta pushed at Williams arm to lift his hand from the contact. It was meant to sever the contact and its transmission.

"Listen," she said, earnestly, "I have an idea. It may be of some help. You must have a stock of Breach Patches. You know, the ones which are used if one of your pods is damaged or even holed by space debris."

William nodded, slightly confused.

Clysta added, "What would be the dimensions of the largest patch you have?"

"We used some small ones about a year ago," William answered as he thought, "I know there is one that is one hundred metres square and it is still in its compartment. That one is the largest. Why do you ask?"

132

"From the information I can recall, they are self propelled are they not? Piloted by remote control too," Clysta answered.

William nodded his confirmation, still a little puzzled.

"Those I am familiar with are very strong and will fuse automatically to any surface. Are yours of that same type?" Clysta continued her questioning.

Once again William nodded, adding slowly, "Yes?" And he was beginning to see her direction of thought.

"I can see where you're headed," interrupted Kindra. "That type of patch is able to seal to any surface, and it will include even securing the intruders vessel on the outside skin. Right?"

"Correct." Clysta agreed. Then taking the initiative. "Have your personnel launch the large patch as quickly as they can and then guide it to the area of the Pod where these people have entered."

William now was becoming cognizant and fully understanding Clysta's idea.

Clysta continued. "Your shuttle should be able to pin-point the target from the outside and the patch will cover the craft and seal it tight to the Pod. It will also limit their source of ether energy because they act also as a radiation barrier."

"At least then they will have no exit by their ship," she added finally.

Within a few more minutes they eventually approached Pod Six leaving the last intersection through the connecting arm.

William was finalizing the instruction to the Maintenance Section who would be responsible for launching the patch. Then he instructed Security to pass over control of the patch to the shuttle pilot after briefly detailing Clysta's plan. Half a minute later William lowered the car onto the mosaic surface covering the floor of the large hall outside of the Pleasure Station's Bank. This bank held the vaults that were also the main Depository for the security of visitors' valuables.

The area had already been cleared of any visitors and station workers. A few one and two seated security personnel vehicles had been left around the hall's perimeter farthest from the large etched glass doors, which formed the elaborately decorated entrance to the bank.

Clysta counted seven uniformed guards crouching behind the staff cars and two more against the large and ornate circular fountain. The fountain was the centrepiece of the large expanse of a polished marble floor encircling it. The walls surrounding this area were high and adorned with works of art and sculptures of many worlds. High above was a dome of equal proportions and beautifully inlaid with semi transparent coloured graphics.

William dug into an almost invisible pocket on his tunic and withdrew a small disc, which he held in the palm of his hand. He spoke into the disc.

"Security. Director William speaking. Who is in charge and what is the present status here?"

"Azmere here sir, at your right by the fountain sir." The voice came from the same disc. "I have temporarily taken charge."

"Good man, Azmere," William interjected.

Azmere continued. "I can account for only four desk attendants, and one shift manager, who are still inside the bank. They also have reported, via personnel discs, to have two of the wounded security personnel in there with them, one female and one male. Those are the ones who are too badly wounded to move far. They are attempting to tend their wounds. I have instructed them all to move as far as possible from the area as they can. So they have locked themselves inside the staff's lunchroom. The only monitor in there shows the front desk area only, so they are unable to give me an update to where these,-these people are at present, or what they are doing."

Azmere was heard to take a deep breath and continue with his report. "So far that I am able to estimate, sir, the intruders are the only other people who are inside the bank. Sir!" He added.

"Very good Azmere. That was quick thinking. I will now take charge," William responded. "One question Azmere. Have these people, the intruders, taken any hostages?"

"Not that I can account for sir," was the reply. Then he added, "They don't seem to need any, judging from the speed they are going and the equipment they seem to have with them."

Clysta interrupted. "William. Check on the patch, it should be in place by now."

William nodded and spoke with Maintenance who confirmed that it had been dispatched. Then he got a relay through to the shuttle.

"The patch has just fifteen seconds ago covered the intruders craft. The fusing process has started and the outer skin is solidifying," the shuttle pilot replied. "In another two minutes, they will be stuck for good."

"Good work," praised William. "I need you to continue to monitor it now and report anything that may be unusual."

"Will do!" Answered the pilot, almost enjoying the excitement of this diversion from his usual tasks. "Out."

Clysta asked William when the communication with the shuttle had finished. "Do you have any decent weapons or armaments?" As he was finding a suitable reply, she continued. "When these people realize they have lost their planned way of escape, they are going to be very angry and are likely to come out this way. And shooting!"

Whilst they talked, Clysta and William had left the car and positioned themselves crouched around a corner about twenty-five metres from the entrance to the Depository.

G'zin and Kindra had also left the car, keeping the vehicle between them and the glass doors. Euclid, the robot, remained where they had left it sitting inside on the rear seat, not showing any visible interest in the passage of events. The vision patch, still glowing slightly, being the only indication it was active.

# Chapter 15

"Fox!" That was the name of the tallest of the intruders. He was also their leader.

"Fox, come in," urged the voice over the 'talkie. It was their pilot.

Inside the Flitter, the pilot had felt a shudder pass through their craft as, unaware of what it could be, the breach patch made contact and moulded around its exterior. The patch's radiation proof composition, designed to protect against cosmic particles, also had caused the small ship's visi screen to black out.

"Fox here," was his answer. His companions halted there progress through the large vault and angrily waited to hear what it was that the pilot had to say. Fox glared at the tiny instrument attached to his grubby tunic at his left shoulder. "We are all supposed to be keeping radio silence, are we not?"

"I know," said the pilot, back at their craft. He nervously rubbed at an old radiation scar on the side of his neck, "B—b—but this is an 'Urgent'. You said if it is urgent, we break communication silence. Didn't you? Well, I felt something touch the ship just a couple of minutes ago and now the screen has gone dead. I am trying the scanners and they don't respond now either. Now I'm thinking that is urgent."

"Check the drive," said Fox, trying to ignore the man's remarks and control the outburst that he felt mounting inside, against the fool he had left in charge of the ship. "Make sure that is working, but for goodness sake, be careful you don't go and pull away, whatever you do or find. You know what that will do. I hope," Fox added, "We are almost finished here. Now 'please' keep that radio silence like I told you to."

They were quickly loading a Grav-sled with valuables and treasures. Mostly it was high quality jewelry with a few cashable documents and some Galactic Credit discs. They had been selective in their choices and had only chosen items of the greatest value in relation to their volume. The female member of the intruders was guiding them in these choices, having spent her earlier years working as a clerk at an exchange house.

Entering the strong room from a corridor had been easier than they expected. It was via an opening they had cut using the particle splitting device. The splitter had made a neat circular hole two metres in diameter, through one of the Dycanstel reinforced bulwarks that surrounded the compartment on all of its six sides. All that remained of that section of wall was a small pile of ash and some fine dust on the otherwise and previously spotless shelving and deposit boxes.

The splitter, a custom made unit, was a cumbersome item with its generating tubes and bottles, but on the sled it had been maneuverable. It was now discarded as useless because they already had gained their access. They would now need that sled to transport their 'booty'.

"Here is what I have been looking for!" Fox exclaimed after blowing off a compartment door with two short blasts from a handgun, "This item is the most valuable piece of jewelry for at least a hundred light years."

He held up before him a container. It was a transparent sphere three hundred millimetres in diameter. It was made from a synthetic material, tougher than diamonds.

"I knew that she would go nowhere without it," Fox mumbled to himself. "These baubles will get me a good new ship. And much more."

This man Fox was tall and strong looking, but he was robbed of any handsomeness through his mean looks and badly scarred face accompanied by a misaligned eye. His clothes, which were grubby and unkempt, appeared to have at one time been a uniform of some kind, stolen no doubt. As he tucked the back of his grubby shirt top into the waistband of his stained trousers with one hand, he held the sphere tight up to his chest with the other.

Fox had been in trouble with the law all of his adult life together with most of his juvenile years. This raid on the Station vault would make up for all of the time he had spent running and hiding. It would also help, he was thinking, to get him a respectable start far away from the lawmakers who knew him. And far from this motley gang of useless hangers on, he willingly added in his thoughts.

Inside the sphere he was holding were a necklace and a number of matching adornments belonging to the Duchess of Belva. Belva was a planet revolving around a star situated at the outer edge of this arm of the Galaxy. It had been colonized long ago and had developed a heraldic style of planetary government. And its ruling classes were very wealthy.

These precious items in the sphere had long been in the hands of the Duchy and were known to be priceless. Battles had been fought many times for their capture and the winners always held great pride in their possession.

Fox had himself received the knowledge earlier from one of his contacts that she the Duchess would be on the Pleasure Station at this time. It was most certain, his contact had said, that the Duchess would have them here, with her. Most likely it was in order to show them off to her favourites.

Fox unnecessarily wiped the top of the sphere with his shirtsleeve and then carefully placed the item on top of the pile accumulating on the sled.

"This we will open on the ship when we are far away from this place. It will no doubt take a little time but then when we are away from this area of space, we will have lots of time to learn of the codes to get access."

Then he said, to the others, "Ok. That should be all. Its time that we should be getting out of here."

The others of his crew each took a few other valuables that were light enough to carry by hand and followed each other out through the opening and back into the passage. There they stood, timidly awaiting their leader.

Fox looked quickly around the vault to be sure they had not missed anything that might be of more value. Then he too exited, with only the rotund man left inside. As he stepped from the ransacked compartment, Fox looked over his shoulder.

"Ok Sluzzz. Do your usual," Fox said to the man inside. "Spray the place with your Blaster. That will slow down their inventory at least 'till we are at the other end of this sector."

Sluzzz, not really an intelligent individual, always enjoyed this part. Sluzzz was short and extremely overweight, which showed where his ample waist hung over the wide belt supporting his loose and dirty trousers. Perspiration ran profusely from his thick neck and wide shoulders and stained the skimpy undershirt hardly covering his upper torso. He first had to finish rummaging inside some of those boxes he himself had opened and pulled out more of the smaller valuables and stuffed them into large pockets on his trousers. Then he backed out and loosely aimed his Blaster, adjusted it to a low setting and began spraying its heat and radiation. It spat the violent plasma stream indiscriminately through the opening as he slowly backed out following after the other members of the raiding party.

He watched, with a smirk crossing his lips, as the heat melted the untouched doors of the safety deposit boxes lining the room and blowing some of them apart. The smirk changed to a wicked smile when next their valuable contents were spread around the room, some of it igniting in the fiercely developing heat.

He was satisfied in his low mentality that he was doing a good job of what he always liked the best.

The fire suppression system took over as the leader and the other three crooks now quickly made their exit, returning along the narrow passage, which was located at the rear of the banking facility. This passage led them to a jagged opening through now useless airtight doors, again cut by the stolen particle splitter. They had earlier blasted an opening through these doors to give them access. These doors had been an access to a comparatively narrow service corridor with a low ceiling that encircled the exterior walls and skin of this section of the entertainment complex.

To the left in the outer wall and about five metres along this corridor was the first opening they had cut with the splitter device. Cold and airless space would have been all that existed beyond this opening except the craft's airlock was anchored outside maintaining a sealed breathable atmosphere within. In that same opening, with one foot inside the ship, stood the ship's pilot looking pale and harassed.

"We are stuck," he said nervously as they approached, "Stuck just like Kloor Mud. Whatever the thing was that hit the ship, it is now holding it tight. The motors are sluggish and no power in them at all. Nothing is responding and I still cannot see a damned thing on the outside."

Fox released his hold on the sled, pushed past the pilot and strode into the craft. Clambering over the untidy heaps of disused items of clothing, tools and garbage, he made his way to the control room where he checked the dials and graphics, then the blank visi screen. He then turned to check the motion computer. He pressed a series of pads to bring up the readout of the status register. It too indicated exactly as the pilot had said previously. Nothing would work. Only the reserve of auxiliary power was illuminating the ship and maintaining the normal operational functions.

It took a few seconds before Fox had finally stopped cursing to himself. Nibbling unconsciously on his lower lip, he spun on his heel and returned to the air lock. The others had not moved and waited in silence for his conclusions.

The pilot had told them what had happened since the raiding party had left him there.

"Well," Fox said angrily, pushing the nervous pilot to one side, "We can't leave in this ship, that is obvious. We will have to get to the main landing area and leave that way. There was nothing wrong with her when we tied up. Whatever it is that is affecting my ship, has been done by the station. So I will fix them," he said vehemently. "They wouldn't dare risk a Blaster fight so we have the advantage. I checked it out before we left the city on Zanzan. They have almost no security guards and no police at all. And that means no proper weapons."

He reached over and stroked the muzzle of the Blaster that Sluzzz held cradled in his arms, as he said, "I am sure they have nothing here that is a match for this little baby. So, they have got to let us leave peacefully, or suffer the consequences of this whole damned complex being depressurized."

Clysta and William now each held a Stun Gun. It had been passed to them by a Corporal of the Security Guard who had arrived seconds before them. The weapon was a small hand held device which with variations of pressure to the handle, gave out a narrow beam which would on contact either stun, incapacitate or knock out cold, for up to at least five minutes.

"This is the only type of weapon we are allowed to have on the station and only for security purposes," explained William. "The charge is good for one hundred shots and it reacts on the nervous system with no real damage to the body parts," he added, "Rest assured. It may cause a person to become unconscious but it does not kill!"

The outer areas surrounding the location of the Bank Plaza and its adjoining passages and tubes had been cleared of Pleasure Station visitors and all staff earlier. The pod itself was now sealed off at the tunnel openings to safeguard the other domes. The only persons now in the forecourt of the bank were the security guards and the occupants of William's car. A total of thirteen, and of course the robot, still in silence and sitting alone.

Five minutes of quiet followed a brief plan of action. The dim silence was disturbed finally, by whispering sounds from inside the semi-darkened facility's foyer.

Thirty seconds of mumbling was followed by a loud and menacing voice coming from the interior of the Bank and Safe Depository.

"Anybody out there who can hear, hear this and be sure to understand. We are coming out and we have with us a Hazlo Blaster. It is fully charged and it is cocked and is ready to burn a hole right out and into space."

For effect, a short blast from the interior shot out the elements of an illuminating panel inside a short display wall on the inside of the bank entrance.

Whilst William was thinking out an answer and watching the smoke dissipate, his palm disc came to life.

"This is 'The Boss', William!" It was G'zin's Uncle. "I hear we have a gang of thieves aboard. Who are they and what is the situation?"

William explained keeping it as brief as possible all that he knew to have happened adding, "I don't know yet who they are or what exactly they have come for, but they seem to mean business. They just gave us a sample," he then explained the demonstration without the finer points. "We will have to try to work things out from here and I will keep in contact."

Uncle Zy said through the disc, "I have had operations send out an emergency call to the Galactic Security Forces, but by the time they respond it may be necessary to bargain with these-these-bandits. What do you think, William?"

"First, I will try to find out just what they want and then we can decide. If they will let us, that is," was William's answer. He thought it better to leave out the real two statements the intruders had just made from the darkened Depository.

"I understand that our visitors are there with you. I will take that up with you when all of this is over. I will rely on your judgement, but take no chances. Negotiate if you must. Whatever happens I must ask that you safeguard my niece and her friends. Contact me immediately of any developments. I will be in this meeting room waiting for a reply from Galaxy and I will be in contact as soon as I have a reply to our call for assistance." The contact closed.

William looked dubiously around the plaza at the small number of the security force members. Clysta saw the concern in his look and said just loud enough for only William to hear.

"Well, I suppose it is our game now and I think those people in there are going to play a little dirty," then she added defiantly, "That is of course, if we let them."

It was then they came into view. Their dim silhouette was all that could be seen inside the now darkened foyer behind the huge glass doors.

"Security!" William ordered into his palm disc in a low voice, "Hold your positions and don't anyone fire until I give the order. And keep out of sight, we do not wish them to know how many we are."

# Chapter 16

The Depository doors opened automatically. First through the doorway was Sluzzz. The darkness made him seem larger. His appearance in the dim twilight was almost Neanderthal with his head of sparse, greasy, black unkempt hair. He cradled the large and cumbersome Blaster in his thick arms as if it were a toy, waiving it to and fro with a twist of his body to indicate his ability to do lots of damage. As a sample of his imaginary power, he shot a charge at a small statuette by the fountain. The blast was just a twitch of his finger on the firing button but the effect was impressive as the ornament disappeared in a cloud of incandescent smoke and particles.

"That'll do, Sluzzz. We do not want the folks out there to be scared out of their wits now. Do we?" It was Fox chiding the man from a location just out of view of those outside.

Shuffling up behind the big man and keeping within his shadow was the pilot, Golog. In contrast to Sluzzz, he was diminutive, angular and with taught skin on his bony face and body. He was a nervous type with quick eyes that moved shiftily from side to side taking in all of the details of the scene around him. He held a mid sized gun, which appeared to be too large for his small hands. But all the same it was an explosive projectile type that was still effective when used in a fight.

Talking over his shoulder to the others, who were still standing out of sight from those outside, Golog whispered, "I can't see too well. The lighting has been dimmed, but I can make out a car. I think," he added squinting into the gloom. Then, as he took in more of the view, "And there are the heads of three of what I guess must be security guards. They are all behind a fountain in the middle of the area. The car there looks empty as far as I can see."

The third came into view, carrying two larger stun guns fully drawn from their hip holsters. They were being pointed into the gloom, waving from side to side in a threatening motion.

"That one's a female," breathed Clysta in surprise, as she peered over the shoulder of William. They had positioned themselves crouched at a corner on the other side of the plaza, almost out of sight in the darkened shadows.

The three in the lead now fanned out into the plaza a metre or two in front of the glass doors, the female standing in the middle ready for action. She looked almost as menacing as Sluzzz did, standing straight and facing forward ready to do battle with anyone who dared come into view. She was not attractive looking and was slightly overweight though much taller than Sluzzz, and Golog by at least four centimetres.

Her attire was the usual one piece tunic and had once been of a silver looking material, but that along with her straggly hair was grubby and greasy and in need of attention. She held the large handguns in each hand with ease and obvious authority. She had been chosen well by Fox as a partner in this escapade.

"I know that one," said William in a low whisper. "We had a bulletin from our main office security people to be on the look out for her. She just was rehabilitated from the penal colony on-on. I will recall it later. Now, what was her name? Anyhow, it really doesn't matter, we will no doubt find out soon enough."

William added after seconds.

"And those two guns that she has. They are Lancers. Very powerful. Watch out for them, Clysta."

Fox, their leader, followed close behind, one hand towing the sled and the other hand gripping a weapon.

"Ok Who's in charge?" Demanded Fox menacingly. Standing tall and looking like as much a leader as he could. He got no reply.

He continued forcefully, "Whatever you did to disable our craft we don't care now. We want a fresh ship and you had better make it quick! We don't intend to be kept waiting."

William had been ready for this to happen. He had arranged a plan where a series of signal words would be used that the guards would respond to. He stood up cautiously and still slightly out of sight from the criminals.

He gave an answer. "My name is William. I am the Director here. A ship will not be possible, Mister!"

The word 'Mister' was a signal to the guards to be prepared for combat. To two of the guards in particular it was the signal to fire. They were concealed behind a large fern type of plant, one on each side of the Depository entrance fifteen meters from the doors. Their orders were to bring down whomever it was that held the Blaster. The two guards opened fire on cue.

Sluzzz was hit by a stun-gun beam, one on each arm, from each side, exactly as it had been planned. But as the shots took the microseconds to take effect on the large bulk of the man, Sluzzz's finger tightened instinctively on the weapon's firing button as his body began to twist in the direction of the voice he had last heard.

Two seconds later another planned stun gun was energized and pointed at his mid section to make the man double up and become incapable of retaliation.

That shot unfortunately hit the buckle on his wide belt and had not the effect planned.

Sluzzz was losing control of his muscles as the stunners continued to fire. With his knees beginning to buckle through the effect of the first shots, a fierce beam of energy spat from the muzzle of the Blaster just as it had done in the Vault. The stream of super heated plasma traveled horizontally across the plaza passing over the large bowl of the fountain, angling up to a point three meters above the smooth tiled floor. Hitting the opposite side, it began cutting a neat deep gouge into the sculptured plasti-concrete wall just a very few centimetres below the base of the transparent dome overhead. The plasma beam wavered a little then, as Sluzzz swayed sideways finally being slightly affected by the third stun beam, it began to traverse on a course across the area to the left. On its way it cut through the enormous and elaborate crystal centrepiece of the fountain, bringing it tumbling down into the shallow bowl.

One of the guards stood up from behind the fountain to assist in stopping the Blaster and took aim with his stun-gun, only to be hit in the shoulder by a shot from one of the guns that the female was carrying.

Finally the beam of energy from the Blaster found its intended target, which was the corner where William was stationed. The searing charge stopped long enough to cause the sheltering corner to explode just as Sluzzz fell, finally having lost consciousness and onto the floor. The gun that had created little damage ultimately ceased its firing and clattered to the mosaic tiles.

The concussion and fragments of material from the blast though had caught William full in the chest and pushed him backwards to collide with the wall behind him. He hit with enough force to render him unconscious and he fell senseless to the floor.

Golog, the pilot had begun to shoot at anything he saw as a menace. But within a few second he had received a direct hit in his thigh from a stun -gun shot by another of the guards from across the plaza. Strength was not his main character. He was now writhing on the floor and moaning loudly in agony from the pain. His gun had spun safely away out of his gasp.

"You said they had no weapons," the woman intruder said over her shoulder to Fox as she was firing both weapons indiscriminately.

"This is nothing toward ours," he replied, then, "Move out, to the left. That is where that William guy's voice came from. It's him we need. He is our bargaining chip."

Cross firing had started with beams and flashes darting in every direction. Clysta cautiously looked around the corner disintegrated by the Blaster to see the female intruder make a move. She was shooting in a random pattern with both of her weapons as she ran in Clysta's direction. Fox was following close behind, sled still in tow and still filled with their treasure.

The other guards who were still active, two having been hit and downed by the females guns, were firing at the pair but with no success. As the two dodged the shots, firing back as they ran, they approached Clysta's hiding place, and she waited until they were close.

Clysta took a deep breath and stepped out from shelter to cut off their route. She had picked up the gun that had been dropped by the injured William and now held both weapons.

Raising the guns in her hands, she shouted.

"Stop. Stay right there and drop your weapons, both of you," then, shouting out to the guards, "Hold your fire, I have them covered."

The beams from the guns of the guards, that had illuminated the darkness, stopped.

Clysta, in the excitement, had not had chance to look to Williams condition. Suddenly remembering, she looked over her shoulder in his direction to check, still with her guns in front of her and pointing at the adversaries.

Fox, quickly seeing this distraction as his opportunity, gave his female accomplice a hard push in the middle of her back, sending her staggering forward. As Clysta returned her attention to the two before her, she knew immediately her error. The female hurtled headlong forward and into Clysta, catching her off balance.

With a confusion of arms and legs they staggered, struggled and then both fell to the floor. With the weight of the other landing on top of her, Clysta was momentarily stunned and lost the grip on both of her own guns. She managed to hold onto the wrists of the female and, as they rolled over and over on the floor each trying to gain an advantage, one of those two Lancers fell and spun out of reach across the marble floor.

Clysta was now fighting for her life as the other was trying with all of her strength to gouge out her eyes with the free hand. Clysta, with those few seconds of struggle seeming like minutes, found her strength begin to wain. Trying to protect herself and holding the wrist that had a grip on the other weapon, Clysta summoned all of her remaining energy and twisted her body, and then wrenched hard on the other's arm. She felt a sudden, soft recoil from the gun. The Lancer had been triggered and its beam on full charge had hit her assailant in the neck. The woman gave an involuntary shudder and then stiffened. The shot had rendered her unconscious and rigid as a board.

Regaining some of her strength and gasping for air, Clysta struggled to push the female from her as she felt around blindly trying to find one of the lost weapons, intending to bring it to bear on the man Fox.

But Fox was quicker. He was already standing over her, legs astride, with his own gun only a few centimetres from her forehead.

"Now. Very, very slowly," menaced Fox, "You will get to your feet, immediately. This my fine young lady, is not your usual toy stun gun. It will drill a nice neat hole right through your brain. So watch it little girl. I," he stressed, "Have had a bad day and somehow I think you might be responsible."

As she was being pulled to her feet by the strong male, Clysta looked around to see how many had been hit in the fight. William stirred slightly as he began to regain consciousness and she could see two guards standing, their weapons pointing at Fox from across the bowl of the fountain. There were a number of the guards around the area, in the gloom and lying unconscious or possibly even dead.

Kindra was crouched at the far side of the fountain. During the melee, he had told G'zin to stay put and crossed the area from the car, ducking shots as he went. Now he held a stun-gun from one of the downed guards and was also pointing it at Fox.

Fox turned to face the area, his back against the wall.

"Now don't anyone make any foolish moves," said Fox angrily through his clenched teeth, "This young lady is my ticket out of this damned place. This gun is a laser. If anything goes wrong, even the slightest thing, then she will die."

Fox pushed the muzzle of his gun tight to the base of Clysta's skull and with his other arm wrapped around her neck, stood up close immediately behind her, so no-one could make a shot without hitting her.

While Fox was making his demands, Clysta, who's mind had been racing to make up a plan to defeat these people, was suddenly overcome by a cool feeling of unsuspecting calm and confidence.

The tour car was in the darkness outside Fox's peripheral vision, and anyway, Golog had indicated previously it was empty. And so it was. But only at the very instant after Fox had said those words-'she will die!'

Euclid the robot had been sitting through the battle, not totally uninterested in the action, but due to instructions inherent to the mental patterns it was unable to take part or sides. Now the robot under specific imprinted instructions, had to take action.

It silently and at speed, stepped from the car onto the marble and mosaic floor and in the same motion became airborne as it noiselessly leapt in the direction of the fountain. In a movement, almost faster than the eye could follow, the robot touched the edge of the bowl of the fountain with one of its metal feet and launched itself toward the opposite side twenty-five metres away. It landed in an instant with ballet-like precision onto the other edge.

Fox, who was not looking in the right direction, sensed a blur of motion. He turned his head to see and caught sight of the robot at the end of its final leap. The journey had taken no more than a half of a second from leaving the car to a final landing in front of Fox's captive. In the same manoeuver as coming to a stop, the robot clasped the muzzle of the laser between its metal finger and thumb, squeezed carefully and ruptured the charge cylinder. With a twist, the robot then pulled the useless weapon from Fox's grasp and tossed it backward. It landed with a splash into the centre of the bowl of the fountain.

The leader of these intruders, his silenced mouth opening in shock, had only a fraction of time to gape in a stunned surprise at the metallic body standing before him in the twilight.

He had time only to think to himself, 'Wherever did you come from?'

Fox's strength was no match for that of the robot as his arm was unwound from around Clysta's neck. Next, after she had been carefully, and with gentleness, pushed into the clear by Euclid, Fox himself was picked up bodily and turned upside down. Then, though writhing and protesting loudly, he was held there dangling by the feet in the robot's immovable metal grip.

# Chapter 17

"I just can't thank you enough," said G'zin's Uncle Zy so full of gratitude. "That was one extremely brave thing you did, Clysta. Such courage. And the robot-'Euclid'-you call him? He really is one of a kind and something of a hero. He must be a very special model because I thought they all are built usually with those specific rules are they not? They are never to bring harm to humans."

The three friends and Euclid had all gathered in the lounge, which was often known as 'The Inner Sanctum' amongst the Station staff. It was so called because only a select few and very, very distinguished personages were ever allowed inside. Uncle Zy did not need convincing that this was one such occasion.

Euclid, as usual, stood in silence by the double doors, which led from the wood paneled and lavishly ornamented room.

The dull glow in the robot's visor panel gathered intensity as it spoke in answer.

'That is exactly so, Uncle of G'zin, but my master the Commander Z'ee has charged me with maintaining the absolute safety of his daughter Clysta.'

They all turned to look toward Euclid as G'zin added.

"Well, you sure made a darned good job of that."

The gathering all smiled in the direction of the robot.

Kindra looked thoughtful as he said, "Of course if you look at what Euclid did to the man Fox, all the harm he really caused was two slightly bruised ankles and an extremely bruised pride."

That took away the seriousness of the conversation and they all began laughing. Even the robot's metal facial features, usually blank and devoid of expression, seemed to be showing signs of giving in to the humour of the statement.

"Well," added Kindra with a smile, "He will have lots of time to heal the ankles, but his pride may take a lot longer."

"Now we will eat," Uncle Zy said as he signaled his own server robots to begin. "Then you can rest and tomorrow you can continue, or restart your visit. It is a great pity my director William cannot join us here, but you can call on him after breakfast.

"By the way, his nurse tells me that he has been mumbling your name," Uncle Zy looked at G'zin, his large dark eyes twinkling, "In his sleep. Now I wonder why?"

After the feast was over, they all retired to an equally ornate sitting room where they carried on with the conversation about the Academy and some of their exploits. Slowly the conversation began to run out of steam and the large man took the opportunity to ask a question that had been on his mind for more than an hour. Whilst the servers were busily humming about with the various edible delicacies and treats, Uncle Zy's probing eyes once again stayed on G'zin and he said.

"Now G'zin my lovely niece, you must now tell me truthfully. Apart from seeing this Palace of Eternal Pleasure, and of course saving it from those brutes," he waived his ample arm in display, "And apart from wishing to see your favorite Uncle Zy." He stopped for an instant as, with a flourish, he brushed a large finger past his moustache, then.

"What was it that really, and I mean really," his deep and growling voice stressed the words, "Brought you and your friends all those many, many light years of distance and out across the sector?"

# Chapter 18

The sleek Skimmer left the visitor's craft parking zone slowly at first and moved far away from the area of the orbiting Pleasure Station to begin its acceleration by Ether Engine. Quickly now, it had cleared the proximity zone to commence their outward course, toward that encircling sphere of cosmic dust far in the distance.

The three friends had each thoroughly enjoyed their stay, though when the fifth day came, they all had agreed it really was time to leave. By now they had been through almost every part and each dome the station had to offer during those four days of Pleasure and Joy. This had mostly been accompanied by a great deal of back patting and vigorous hand shakes from the guests who had been affected by the raiders and from many others who felt gratified at what these youngsters had managed to accomplish.

It had turned out to be almost like a mini vacation for the trio. The real reason for going there had been forgotten for the time being. They spent much of the time visiting and sampling the contents of the vast complex, each containing its own individual theme and performance.

William's injuries soon were mended and he eventually managed to join the group on their third day, spending most of it in the company of the sparkling eyed G'zin.

Even Euclid the robot, who accompanied them everywhere, appeared to find pensive interest in some of the specialty domes. In particular for the robot there was the Sporting Arena.

The robot appeared to be captivated in its own silent manner, by those of the sections displaying some of the finer arts in sportsmanship. There, a mechanical unit was intended as a piece of swordsmanship challenge equipment. Its inventors had designed it to be used to test a contestant's skill. The match was meant to be against a robotic synthesised and until then a believed unbeatable opponent.

William made a friendly challenge to the group as they were watching a number of competitors succumb to defeat.

"This unit has gone undefeated in the last nine months. Anyone like to try?"

The visitors looked to one another in silence hoping that the other would take up the thrown gauntlet.

Euclid asked suddenly.

'Miss Clysta, is it acceptable that this unit is allowed to try out this sport?'

Clysta first looked at William to see his unspoken consent, then answered.

"I am sure that it will be very interesting to see the results. Why not?"

Euclid took up the challenge. It had a little difficulty at first controlling the sword and understanding the balance. But finally, after two test starts, the contest began. It took almost two hours of blurring and incessant counter and parry but Euclid finally narrowly defeated the machine. Now Euclid had the necessary experience, it then went on to defeat it a further three times in a row.

Uncle Zy, when he heard this news, made arrangements to present the robot with a trophy, a small gold cup. It was inscribed with the particulars of this record making event, as the previous record had been only two consecutive defeats of the machine.

Finally, when the three guests had announced their decision that it was time for them all to leave and continue with their journey, almost all of the staff had a large party for these four popular and valuable guests.

Mid way through the morning after this party it was time to leave. A slightly tearful Uncle Zy stood at the shuttle dock. He had brought with him, William, the Director and a small party of his grateful staff. They had come to say their most cherished and fond goodbyes and watched, a little sadly, as the Parking Shuttle finally departed.

It was Kindra once again who was at the controls, piloting their own craft through the encircling spherical cloud of gases and then out into the void that existed all around and between the millions of stars. Setting the control guidance computer to take them to ninety-five percent of Light Speed he then left those controls to commence on automatic.

Kindra had taken over the task of Pilot right from the outset of the voyage. G'zin, mainly because of her proven skilfulness with the computer, had gladly accepted the responsibilities for Navigator. These arrangements had suited them both even though they each had fully learned the skills necessary to exchange posts if it was required.

Clysta was 'Captain' or decision maker on this trip. She occasionally helped the others with their tasks when help was needed. Her more permanent tasks included the supervision of the ship, its systems and its power plant.

Management of this ship was only in name and could become a little boring. The craft was in itself completely robotic. It had an integrated system, reporting everything to a central command computer.

This supervised and almost lived within the components of the craft. It would automatically signal the slightest malfunction, and then, if it should occur, send out its tiny molecular clone robots to carry out repairs.

During the last hours before lift off, G'zin had disappeared along with her uncle and William. Clysta, who had said nothing of it at the time, remembered it now and thought she would ask.

Clysta queried.

"G'zin, how did we fair on the weapons that we came to Camrays for? I noticed you and your Uncle Zy went off somewhere just before we left."

"My Uncle Zy handled it all," G'zin replied, smiling, "He promised earlier when I asked, that we should take the weapons which those criminals brought. He arranged for the Sergeant-at-Arms to have them checked out in secrecy and recharged. He said he would have them hidden inside the chest we brought on board with us when we were leaving."

"Won't the disappearance of those weapons raise a few questions when the Police Force arrives?" Kindra queried.

He had overheard the conversation and joined in. Weapons were seriously controlled throughout the sector and anything with the firepower of a blaster was strictly forbidden.

"I asked that too," G'zin said in reply, "He told me his answer would be that he had disposed of them immediately after the fight."

"Talk about bending the truth. I hope it will work, for his sake," Clysta said, with a smile.

"Uncle Zy also gave me this. He thought we might put it to good use."

G'zin showed a credit disc of a gold account and handed it to Clysta.

"He asked me to give it to you Clysta. He said those four are surely to be wanted by the law in other parts of this sector at least. He told me also, that any reward for their capture would be deposited to this when it is issued. He said too, that there were also some very wealthy visitors who have shown much of their ample gratitude, financially. On top of all of that he deposited ten thousand of his own personal gratitude."

Clysta looked embarrassed, as she answered, "I don't know what to say." She stopped to make up the words, then, "But as we all took part we will use the credit together whenever we need to. I have a feeling and I am sure it will come to pass, the adventure we seem to be onto has more twists ahead than a three headed Falco Snake."

Kindra, who had now completed making a check on his auto' switching, turned around on his anti-grav seat and declared, changing the mood.

"Well it sure was some place, G'zin. I really enjoyed our stay there and I would like to go back some day. By the way Clys', sorry to bring it up, but has anything new happened with those strange dreams you were having some weeks ago?"

Clysta was quiet for a while then explained.

"I didn't want to spoil any of the fun we were having, so I kept quiet about it while we were at the Pleasure Station. But two nights back I had another of my dreams. It was much the same as before. My father was there again. He was trying to say something, just as before, and this time he was mouthing more words than in the last few dreams. Although I still could not quite make them out, to be absolutely sure of what he was trying to say.

This time though there was something more tangible about the vision. After this latest one, I am now almost sure I know where it is my father is in the dream. The scenery and the background this time were strangely so much clearer. Clear enough to recall details.

I am beginning to see them now as being much more than a dream. It is as if it all is trying to tell me something. Unbelievable or even silly as it may seem, they are like what I could almost interpret as a telepathic communication. If these dreams have all really meant some kind of message then I now truly believe he is at or close to the star system we are supposed to find. And please, don't ask me why I think that way, because right now I just don't know."

# Chapter 19

Four hours of flight took the Skimmer well beyond Camrays Star's concealing shroud of dust particles and gases. Five hours later they were so far away that when they looked back at the vast panorama of stars amongst the background of the ageless Pleiades Cluster, Camrays was once again invisible to the unaided eye.

Clysta and G'zin had used some of the time to check the hidden weapons and then replaced them in the chest. Euclid was called in to move the chest after deciding to store it away in one of the small unused compartments to the rear of the craft.

Euclid had later served some refreshments and the three chatted about the experiences over the past few days.

Clysta changed the topic finally.

"Now we are clear and out in deep space," she said. The group were sitting in the control room, "I think now is the time to put Euclid to work. You remember. He told us he has the ability to extract the information out of the Thought Cube, as to the whereabouts of the starting point for our search for the hidden star system. I think we may as well test his abilities and see if he really can do it."

The others seemed to like the suggestion, so Clysta called Euclid into the room.

The robot had previously returned to its routine station in the passage connecting the control room to the sleeping area. As usual it was out of sight and awaiting its next orders. Euclid entered the area and stood to attention in silence.

G'zin looked up from the mini-visi. She had brought along some of the Stations entertainments on crystal and looked then toward the robot. A sudden unprompted thought entered her mind.

'Funny,' she thought to herself. 'Whatever made me come to that conclusion?'

G'zin was now suddenly overcome with random thoughts, about the robot.

'Euclid is such a lonely robot. Standing before us in his silence mode. Always awaiting the next command whatever it might be.'

Looking then at the other two, who were both busy with something or other, she took a deep breath and spoke her piece.

"Listen, Euclid!" Her eyes moved quickly between the robot and the others, still feeling a little confused at the unexpected formation of her inner thoughts. She started slowly at first, "I think-and I hope the others will feel the same and they will agree-that it is time you were to get more with us, say, be relaxed and easy. That's if it is possible for a robot to be relaxed.

"Anyhow. After the truly spontaneous way in which you handled the man Fox and without so much as a command from anyone there, it certainly indicates to me at least that you must be of a different type of robot than any I have come across. I think-and this is me only speaking-you are at least deserving of some very special considerations."

She then turned to face the other two friends, "Well, what do you two say? Do you agree?"

Clysta was first to speak.

"I have been thinking along those same lines myself lately and I couldn't have put it better. What do you say Kindra?"

He first looked absently at the desktop then replied thoughtfully, "I know that I have always had some serious reservations about robots and what they should and should not be classed as. But in Euclid's case he sure showed me a quality I never thought possible or practical. I'm all for him," Kindra stopped, looked up and straight at the robot, noticing his change of genus, "Being counted as one of us."

"Well," said G'zin enthusiastically and before anyone could say more, "That now makes 'three for and none against'. The vote is unanimous. Euclid, you are now one of the crew and on everyone's behalf, I thank you."

"Good. And thank you, G'zin," Clysta added, to conclude the vote. "Now. Let us get to it, and start on working out those co-ordinates."

Euclid's metal exterior at the time again did not show the slightest indication of his ability to understand the meaning of this acceptance as an equal. Somehow though, ever after this occasion, the robot continued to improve in its abilities to work with the three friends and offer much unsolicited conversation and occasional advice.

Through all of the improvements though, the robot did not loose its ever programmed and unending agreeable attitude that always irked Kindra.

Clysta re-entered the control room, very carefully carrying the Thought Cube. She had kept it in her locker for safety and security. Equally carefully, she now placed the Cube on the work table so to allow Euclid to study this most strange and peculiar device.

The robot had set his work area close to the guidance console and had at hand an array of instruments from the ships emergency repair devices ready for its use. The scene gave these three young onlookers a feeling they were about to witness the performance of some very delicate and advanced neural surgery.

Euclid began by first opening the access to the guidance systems console. The craft had been brought to a dead stop in deep space as a precaution, to enable the work to commence. Using the occasional instrument, some of which the three humans found totally unfamiliar, Euclid prodded and probed and studied readings in and about the boards and relays with astounding gentleness.

After a while and following some internal movements and crossovers, the robot returned all of the instruments to the work table as if satisfied with its labours.

To their complete surprise, they watched as the robot began pulling off the second and third finger from its left hand. After twisting the base of each, they magically began to grow lengthwise and take on a new shape. One of the detached fingers finished growing to resemble a probe with a lightly glowing spiral element at the end. The other was a fan of gossamer like ethereal substance radiating in varying colours of the spectrum.

The robot once more turned its attention to the guidance unit. Pushing on two sensors on the inside, the interior unfolded outward exposing the inward elements of the unit and its myriad intermittently flashing pathways and circuits.

Clysta and the others had each done work on similar units in the course of their studies but in this craft, these were of the latest design and some areas looked a little unfamiliar.

Clysta asked, "Can we do anything to help you Euclid?"

'It is very good that you ask and make an offer to assist me, Miss Clysta. But the work for which I am programmed to carry out is of an unusual nature and therefore makes it most suitable that I carry on alone and unaided. I trust you can accept my apology for not accepting your help.'

That having been said, the other two and Clysta realised they should sit very quietly and watch. The robot returned to the original position at the console and restored its full attention to the work at hand.

Euclid restarted by first taking the new object having the spiral and began by cautiously but accurately touching the various panels and terminals in the intricate overlay of fine laser-like circuitry. Occasionally, the robot would use one of the other tools to make an adjustment or move a connection. It appeared to the three friends, that Euclid was executing a masterpiece of finest art within the console, consisting of delicate and interconnecting webs which were being added to become an extension to the core circuitry of the unit.

After almost an hour of this work the untiring robot moved back from the open panel as if to check its masterpiece.

"Amazing!" Kindra broke the long silence now that he could see the work, "Wherever did he learn to do that?"

"Not back at the Academy, that's for sure," G'zin, replied, "I thought when I first saw it, that he was just a robot with a few special skills and a normal robotic intelligence."

Clysta added, "This surely is none of my father's doing. As far as I know robotics was never his field of expertise. Where the heck did he learn it?"

The robot was not showing any attention to anything in their conversation and offered no answer to their puzzle, as it continued with the examination of the intricacies of the delicate web within.

Without any indication of satisfaction in its progress, the robot collapsed the instrument it had been using back into the shape of a finger and promptly reattached it to the left hand.

Taking up the other instrument, made from the other finger and now which resembled a fan, it began once again to work inside the guidance unit. With the fine and almost invisible edges of the gossamer membrane, the robot lightly brushed across the various levels in and out of the minute laser beams and circuit elements. Tiny sparks of many colours, almost dust-like, moved to and fro caught up by the movements and were deposited in other areas as if to rearrange the system's network.

All of the motions by the fan were patterned in the direction of the intricate web that Euclid had built previously.

As if in conclusion, the fan mysteriously disconnected itself from the instrument and reattached itself to the web taking on the form of a small, cantilevered platform.

The robot pulled back once more, then it reconnected the second finger as it had the other one. It now broke the silence, which had lasted for almost a further hour.

'The addition is now completed. This unit has made the revisions necessary for the inclusion of the Thought Cube,' Euclid advised the onlookers, 'There is only one additional check to be carried out.'

With that, the robot reached to the ship's tool array. It took up a long and hair thin probe seeming instrument. When this new tool was pushed forward, it began to guide itself through the myriad of fine and intertwined laser elements within the console and finally stopped deep inside. A radiance emanating from the end held by Euclid was of a dull purple.

Euclid stopped, silent and void of expression on its metal face, as the robot seemed to be recounting and retracing the steps it had taken to this point. Trying and testing with the probe at three other areas around its work the results seemed to be favourable to the robot. Positioning it again at the original point once more, it gave the same purple dimness.

On all previous occasions, Euclid's voice had been bright though slightly metallic and mechanical. This time the robot's voice contained an emotion of undeniable sadness as in a troubled tone it reported.

'This unit must apologise to you Miss Clysta, but it cannot make this system complete the final work necessary for the location of the starting point of the search you have indicated! The radiance from this instrument should have shone a bright white. Instead there is only a purple dullness.'

"But you have worked with such skill," said Clysta in a surprised voice, "Surely nothing can have gone wrong."

'This craft is of the newest design,' answered the robot. 'There have been a number of improvements contained in this guidance device, which have been superimposed upon the original unit that formed a part of my education on this revision. I have now become familiar with one of the principal improvements which has been the redundancy of a component which was to have been a catalyst for the Thought Cube's resonance.'

Euclid stopped almost as if the robot was to take a deep breath, then continued.

'The item is only of a secondary importance within the guidance system. But I have confirmed, the replacement that this ship carries is incompatible with the internal workings of the Thought Cube. I am concerned that some irreparable damage will be the only result should I carry on.'

'Once again-this unit offers its apology.'

"What is this component then, Euclid?" Clysta asked more in shock than anything else. She felt suddenly terribly deflated by the robot's statement of pending defeat.

'The item is known to me as a Neuro-Phasing Injector,' was the robot's reply.

"Is there nothing else that you can do, like using some other part, or

SPACER

even make one of these-Neuro Phasing things?" Clysta queried more calmly now. Understanding that the robot was not at fault.

'I am not aware of any source on board this craft that has the correct materials suitable for its substitution or manufacture, Miss Clysta,' quoted the robot, still with a subdued voice.

Silence and gloom began to descend upon the group as they each pondered this new and unexpected obstacle.

G'zin broke the mood, "There is only one solution as far as I can see. That is to find one of these-Injectors. Right?"

"If we could find one of these Neuro Phasing Injectors, could you then make this system work in the way we need it to?" Kindra asked, turning to face Euclid.

The reply was in the same subdued tone.

'It is a possibility. I can attempt to make the system work if the correct component is obtained and some minor internal modifications are executed to this craft's navigational systems.'

"Well, the chances of first finding one of these, is likely to be a very long shot," said Clysta, contemplating their next suggested move.

"Then to be allowed to remove it from the unit it belongs to. Most likely it will be a ship that is at present in use. It will be next to the impossible," she conceded.

"On top of all that," Kindra broke in gloomily, "Explaining to the owners the reason for our need of this item, will require a lot of careful answers. Particularly when we roll up in a ship so new it does not need one."

Once again silence descended on the group.

"Ok gang!" G'zin took up the challenge, "Thinking caps on. We need a group discussion. It used to work at the Academy and we were never beaten there."

After an hour of brainstorming over ideas and suggestions, the end result was no solution to the location of the injector component. Euclid was included as part of the discussions as they threw questions at the robot, asking about the designs and the specifications, the size and any alternative components. They covered the question of any other uses for the injector if one were to have been salvaged. Just in case they

163

might find one elsewhere than in space and not being used in a spacecraft.

All of this information was fed into the comp' that had been set on listening mode. Space vessel command computers were automatically imprinted with instant updates whenever and wherever a craft docked. And that would take place, wherever it might be in space. There would be an automatic and immediate interchange of news, changes, status and policies of the known galaxy that was being continuously catalogued. It enabled the traveller to be kept informed at all times from an immense library of facts.

The comp' that was a part of the Skimmer then was put to the task of using its ability to then cross reference all of the details given. It then assembled a series of various uses of this component essential to the robot's revision. The final list, and it was a considerable one, lit up the whole of the ship's view screen.

Clysta asked the comp' to condense the list. She suggested it remove those variables that were likely to relate to a use in space.

"That was a smart move, Clys'," remarked Kindra with a smile, "You are looking for something that is merely planet-bound. Clever, clever, clever! Now add some locations of the owners," he added, directing the last sentence to the computer.

The list of alternative uses for a Neuro Phasing Injector was now much shorter, although the locations ranged sporadically over almost the whole of the inhabited sectors. In all, the comp' gave a list of thirty three types of major usage and nineteen of these had a use in tandem with a second or even a third component.

The group viewed the list of known owners of the type of salvaged Injector they needed. Clysta shook her head in dismay. No conclusion was evident as to where they would be able to find or obtain the much needed item without their having to disclose to its owner what their need was. The search was becoming more frustrating the longer they looked at the list.

"I'm tired," said Clysta finally, stifling a yawn, "I suggest we should eat and then rest or even sleep on it. We can carry on with our search later. I think we have done enough today and we will find it a lot easier to concentrate after we have had a break. Do you agree?"

Kindra spoke up, "That is true Clys'. But there was something in the final list when I first saw it. It is nagging at my brain and I cannot bring it back into focus."

His eyebrows knit together in a serious mood as he pondered for a while, then he acknowledged, "Oh, I give up. Perhaps you are right, let us rest now. It may be clearer after a break."

The three friends arose from their rest fully refreshed. They were once again sitting around the control room each checking a copy of the comp' short list. G'zin was first to speak.

"There is a slim chance my home world Fryl has a few older craft that are no longer in use. We could try there. What do you think?"

"That may be a good idea. But only as a reserve if we exhaust all of our other chances," answered Clysta, "The trouble is we still will need to explain what it is we need to take it from a ship for. I would still suggest we try to come up with or find some place or one owned by someone that is using the unit in another capacity."

"What about a space junk yard? There is one in the Alberni Group out on the edge of Sector Four," G'zin offered.

Kindra looked at G'zin and rebuked her.

"That place is full of scavengers and vagabonds. I heard that someone is killed or maimed there every week, over some minor argument or in a fight. I would expect nothing but trouble if we were to try to buy even a Wringle-Snort from there."

Silence once more overcame the scene and time ticked by as they each studied the list again, looking for an answer.

Euclid silently entered the area where the three friends worked. The robot stood behind Kindra and appeared to be focusing on the notes he had before him.

Kindra looked at the screen showing the latest copy of the list.

"Comp'. What is this item-'Art of Morn'?" He lowered the printed foil that had been prepared earlier and turned to his friends, "If it has anything to do with the planet, I know a little of that place. It's a planet in the Sirius System is it not? And that is closer to Sol."

The computer did not answer him in a direct way but simply went into a verbal description of the facts that was the closest reply to the first question. It described a new art form that had been developed on the planet Morn that had evolved through experiments on Hyper Wave distortions. During the computer's conversation, the view screen displayed some of the artist accomplishments.

An artists' name was mentioned together with a list of his better known works. Some additional information regarding the other parts of his question, were then put forth by the computer as its dialogue continued, but Kindra was not really listening.

"That's what I was missing. A name, The Name," Kindra was beside himself in excitement, as he once again looked at the list now on the screen before them.

"That name there. The artist. It isn't his real name at all. That is what had me confused last night."

Clysta and G'zin both looked at Kindra, not having any idea of what he was so excited for. Then Kindra blurted out.

"That—" he was pointing toward the screen, "Is my older brother!"

# Chapter 20

There was not much dialogue needed to make the decision before the trio agreed they would take this diversion. It seemed like it was a long chance, but a possible solution to the problem of finding the missing component.

Kindra was sure that a visit to his older brother, who was eleven years his senior, would give them the answer they needed. The possibility was also that they would certainly not require a difficult explanation why they needed the Injector.

His brother's name was Mirsha.

Mirsha, as Kindra started to recollect and explain, had been a student at one of the Academies, established long ago on the one selected planet that orbited Sirius A. It, the planet, had been made habitable many years ago. The Academy of Morn as it was called specialized in the field of Neurology together with many other subjects and was the favourite and probably the best in the sector. The Academy got its name from the planet on which it was founded and built.

Mirsha's majors had been in Physics and in Mineralogy, the second subject being in-keeping with his and Kindra's father's ambition that he, as the older son, eventually would take over the mining business.

Mirsha had also studied briefly in a recently developed science dealing with the elusive concept of telepathy.

Mirsha had eight years of progressive results in his education when almost overnight he took a leaning toward Art. It finally took its toll when he let the Mineralogy courses lapse for a year in its favour. 'To further my experiences', Mirsha had said. Then those Physics results began to deteriorate.

Kindra remembered vividly one occasion when he was on a mid-term break, he had returned to their home world. Their father had been very upset because Mirsha was becoming too deeply involved in Art subjects. His father had donated one hundred thousand credits to each of the Academy's Physics and Mineralogy campuses. It was an unwritten prerequisite to a students' nomination for admission to the Academy.

"It's such a waste," their father had screamed, "You was doing so well in all of your work. What are you going to achieve in Art?"

They had argued long over the topic until finally Mirsha had one morning, packed his belongings and left in silence to return to Morn. That was about three years ago and Kindra had heard nothing since except a private trans-et he had received at Europa from Mirsha shortly after. It was a short but pointedly self blaming apology, for the fight and final ruination of what was meant to be a pleasant vacation for them both.

Euclid, when asked, confirmed that the guidance system would still function correctly even with the new revisions and the 'fan' left in place. The robot was asked then to recheck and to close up the console to prepare for the trip to the Sirius system.

Kindra and G'zin quickly worked on the course with the comp' and while Clysta double checked the details, Kindra set the craft into motion. Within three hours, they had jumped into Hyper Space.

The best that could be said about Hyper Travel was that direction meant nothing. You first computed the co-ordinates and allowed for the densities of the stars between the start and the target. Then inject a series of formulas and the ship was ready to Jump.

Of course this is an over simplification of the technique. Knowing what to inject was where the skill in system navigation came into its own.

They had to avoid this particular target star by a much greater margin, as Sirius A was a class A.1 star, very bright and larger than Sol. The system also was a binary. The companion was much smaller although it was one hundred and eight times the density of the larger star of the two. Both had gravity fields, which were extensive even by Galactic standards. The interaction was so immense that the first explorers to the area had great difficulty escaping as their Hyper drive would not 'click in' due to the smaller star's attraction and interaction on the wave generator.

The planet Morn, either through good luck or good fortune, had emerged from those embryonic gasses on the opposite side to the small companion star. This paradoxically cancelled out the destructive forces which gravity would have brought on any newly forming planet.

The distance on this Hyper Jump was more than twice the span of their first, having done a double hop via the red giant Betelgeuse. The point of exit from the other dimension was in all cases most crucial and with this star it was imperative that the calculations be perfect. Their timing and position was almost exact to a half minute of spatial arc. That half a minute was all of what was required to make a dangerous difference in the exit at the target star. They, in their small Skimmer and unknowingly, were to exit closer to the target than they should be.

Too, too close.

Luckily it was their anti-grav couches and the stabilizing envelopes, which saved the humans any dangerous injuries. The ship left its transit through the comparative safety of Hyper Space, speeding onward into normal space and gravity.

It immediately began to buck wildly, pitching and rotating in a combination of ever changing crossed axes. The movements became so violent; it caused the sequential trip release to be delayed on each of their individual anti-grav cocoons. The end effect was to make it impossible for any one of them to leave their places and to reach and manually disengage or alter the controls.

G'zin screamed through closed teeth, "Do something—Kindra! I can't move."

Even inside the cocoon, the pain from the motions was still immense.

"I can't—reach my remote," he replied, gasping. "My arm will not penetrate the shielding. It must still be locked."

Then Clysta shouted out, "Euclid!"

Then she let out a long groan at the wrenching stresses in her lower body. "Euclid," she repeated, "Do something. Quickly."

Over the shrilling sound of the warning sirens throughout the craft, they all heard the robot's storage closet hiss open.

After what was like an eternity, the robot, using its added mechanical strength, finally entered the control room head first, pulling itself hand over hand. It used any corner or any fixed object to fight against the violent and gyrating motions of the twisting and rolling ship.

The humans could vaguely see the view screen and watched in terror as the light from millions of stars flashed quickly by, caused by the ships twisting spinning motion.

A painfully long two minutes had now elapsed since the Hyper Jump exit, before Euclid had finally reached the pilots control area. It wrapped a metal leg around the base of the console and gripped tightly to the workbench edge with one mechanical hand. With the robots other free hand it reached out toward the contacts operating the manual power balancing controls.

It began tapping, with lightning speed at the contacts, in an endeavour to enter stabilizing commands into the ship's systems. After fifteen seconds of anguish the pitching craft was stabilized and brought finally under control.

"That is it, right there."

Kindra pointed at the last foil he had requested to be run out by the computer. The three friends had spent the last hour and a half trying to find a reason for their violent exit. This policy had been ingrained into the students at the Academy. If anything goes wrong, find the reason and ensure it does not happen again.

"I don't see it," said Clysta, puzzled.

"The plasma readings, there," Kindra indicated three readings in the print-out. "It must have been a remnant from a very big corona burst."

"But we were making allowances for something like that," interrupted G'zin. The charts they used had indicated timings of such events.

"Yes but, with those twenty seconds gain on the Jump through Betelgeuse," explained Kindra, "We exited just close enough to land us in those irregular streams."

"And just enough of an event error to throw the comp' off balance," added G'zin.

"Luckily it was only a glancing hit," Clysta concluded.

They went through the calculation twice more to satisfy themselves that this really was the cause.

"Ok," Clysta finally announced. "Euclid and I will do another thorough check of the ship while you two take a break, then we will get under way to Morn. Next time we will take a little more caution."

"We'll second that," G'zin and Kindra said simultaneously.

# Chapter 21

The Sirius System, with the one large planet and three which were comparatively small, had become one of the first group of stars to be settled from the Solar System, due mainly to its closeness to the birthplace of Terran civilization. The major planet already had a type of water, slightly atomically different than Earth's, and an acceptable amount of land surface. Really the Terra Formers dream.

The path inward to the planet Morn had been found to be the safest if a craft were to follow in the shadow cone of the planet. This would give a ship the maximum protection from almost all of the major star's effects, both of gravity and of its damaging and fierce radiation.

"This is tricky," muttered Kindra almost to himself, as he carefully piloted the Skimmer through the cone. "I expected it to be difficult, but nothing like as bad as this is. There is so much debris."

The screen moved through the many views as the sensors were attracted by the asteroids and small planetlets caught by the wash of gravity and pushed into the cone over eons of time. A signal would sound as a body became close enough to be a threat. The other two, G'zin and Clysta, would guide the deflecting pulser device to either push the offender outside their course, or signal Kindra's panel to take evasive action.

"Clearing up ahead!" Kindra called out. "This must be the outer limit."

Many years had been spent by those who were the earlier inhabitants of the planet, clearing the 'wash' for a distance of a million kilometres. Now the area they were approaching was safe to navigate, unhampered by debris.

"It sure does make it a lot easier for visitors," added Kindra as they entered the area of now unobstructed space.

"Do you know?" He continued in an element of wisdom. "It is on record that most of the debris out there is all that is left of a satellite which had almost formed in orbit around Morn. You know, like Europa where the Academy is. Or the satellite Luna, orbiting old Earth.

"It is also said that after the satellite had finished condensing and was becoming almost solid, the effects of the star's savage gravity must have just pulled it apart."

The craft was now well into the area of cleared space when a pleasant female voice announced from the communication band, that they were to tune their system to a quoted tight beam. Then the same announcer informed them they would be guided to an area still on the dark side out of danger from the ever present gravity of the star. There they could park prior to their descent to the surface of the planet.

As a requirement and for their quarantine reasons the visitors were told to land only as and when instructed. That landing was to be only at Morn's one and only space port. Though the voice was not threatening, the three friends concluded that if they avoided these instructions in any way, the results could be most interesting. They decided it was better to conform.

Space around Morn was nowhere near as busy as that which was within the System of Sol. In fact, other than there being a few ore freighters and one decent sized transport parked stationary in an outer orbit, the Skimmer seemed to be the only other ship around.

Although there were four planets in the Sirius system, Morn had been the only one of the type capable of being Terra Formed. It had the correct diameter and density to give it enough gravity to first hold onto an atmosphere. Gravity was the most important component amongst many to the Terra Formers, one sufficient to hold and retain the atmosphere around it as the new elements developed. And one not too strong it would eventually turn its fresh elements into liquid.

Morn had gained an early start in space colonization by having had these correct qualities. The population at the last Galactic Census had shown a figure of four hundred and twenty-three million. Mostly they were adult, with females holding the majority.

The signal came to start the descent to the planets' surface and Kindra warned.

"Ok. Every one to the anti – gravs, and that means you too Euclid," as he looked to one side at the robot, "The manual says that the atmosphere here is somewhat different to reasonable planets and the entry can be turbulent."

The exterior of the ship was alloyed with the same material giving all Anti Gravitics the same capability. At the movement of a control, the ship would 'float' straight up or down as the effect of gravity was interrupted or balanced. In the case of Morn most careful use of this effect was essential, as it maintained their radial position in the shadow cone of the planet. Orbital descent was not recommended.

They approached the planet at speed with the autopilot tuned to the beamed transmission. The view from the screen showed the star filled blackness of the planet's dark side as it increasingly blocked out the lancing fringes of light from the star.

Clysta remarked.

"We have been coming and going from Europa for so long, I suppose we have lost some of our perspective on what a large planet is."

"See the line of daylight showing through the atmosphere!" G'zin said in awe. "And all the colours fanning outward, isn't it so beautiful!"

The ship continued with its descent toward the surface and G'zin who was looking closely at the screen observing everything, said in surprise.

"It's all liquid. All around. As far as you can see. Can that be water?"

In the reflection from the light beams from the Skimmer and whatever illumination was available from the stars around and above, it was true. Nothing but water with a slight diffusion from the star's own light creating a phosphorescent glow.

"Where is the land? And the space port?" G'zin asked still confused, "Hadn't you better check the guidance? We are supposed to 'land' somewhere, are we not?" She put an emphasis on land.

Kindra hid a wide smile as he let the craft drop further until within a few minutes the ship slowed and entered the top layer of the liquid and carried on downward for five hundred metres or more.

"Now I remember," said G'zin overcoming her original surprise. She gave Kindra a caustic glance, saying, "This is that planet which has a layer of a plasma like membrane around and enclosing its upper atmosphere."

"This is the one," Clysta said, breaking in on G'zin's revelation, "The first explorers thought they had found a planet with no land, just water and created quite a baffling problem for the planetologists. Up to that time it had been calculated as being impossible."

"Now I remember," G'zin, overcoming the realising, she had been had. "It has something to do with the planets' evolution. Hasn't it? The plasma matrix has created a barrier to the gravitation of Sirius and it also has cut down the harmful effects which might have been caused by the enormous bombardment of radiation from the star."

Kindra completed the dialogue.

"In the long past beliefs of Astronomical Sciences," he said, "This planet should not be habitable. If the layer of liquid like plasma were not in place, the surface of the planet would have been worn away, first by violent atmospheric storms and secondly through the tremendous pull of its stars gravity."

He continued.

"When my Brother started his schooling here, I spent some time reading it up. I had forgotten until we were close by in the cone. An atmosphere, if any had developed, would only have existed for a very short interval in astrological time spans. The planet, had it even reached the solid state, would then be left as a barren lump of rock being progressively eroded and dismantled by the undefeatable force."

# Chapter 22

"Now we are able to travel in horizontal flight," Kindra informed the others. "We are in the planets real upper atmosphere. You know, I have wanted to do this for ages but around Europa there isn't much of a chance."

"Just don't run into any high trees," answered Clysta mocking him, "First though, we report at the space port. Don't let us forget those instructions. They did tell us we must clear their quarantine, and that it is required of us as visitors to the planet."

"This world is enormous," interrupted G'zin, watching the screen as Kindra put the ship into a steep descent. "Even from here you can make out mountains higher than I have ever seen. My home planet Fryl is large but it is still not quite so large as this seems to be."

Whilst looking at the two hundred and seventy degree view showing on the screen, she carried on, "I can see a body of water and over there, see it's a town by the shoreline. And there," she pointed excitedly, as they slowly entered the daylight side of the planet, "Another one farther along in that bay."

Minutes passed, as the planet grew larger around them. The spaceport finally lay below them and the ship glided toward it. All of the time the craft was being guided by the transmitted homing beam. The area they saw now was expansive and flat, much on the same scale as the large planet itself. From this high vantage point they could see the enormous landing area, totally covered with what they guessed must be a metallic material. Not many other spacecraft were visible, just one large cruiser model and three smaller space yacht types. They could also see a group of low buildings over to the edge of the expanse of what they took as being the landing area. G'zin suggested those could be used as hangers to hold or even hide quite a number of vessels.

Close by and outside of the area they caught sight of a quantity of large transparent domes. Kindra made a guess they may have been a part of the original first settlement from the early Terra-forming immigrants.

Some distance behind these they could see a series of very majestic looking buildings with high towers and they could also make out expansive lawns and what could be gardens around them.

"That has got to be the Academy of Morn," said Kindra as if reading the thoughts of the others.

Minutes later, the ship had finally settled smoothly onto the now confirmed semi-reflective metallic surface they had seen covering the whole immense area of the spaceport. As they came to rest, the same female voice as before announced.

"May we welcome you to the World of Morn. We hope and trust that your stay will be a pleasant one."

The voice, which spoke in good Galactic but with a local dialectic influence, continued by giving the details of their required quarantine check and that they must enter a particular tunnel beneath the metallic surface surrounding the craft. They would then be transported in a sealed car to the Immigration Centre.

As the announcement continued, Kindra closed down the power plant and Clysta did a routine check of the ships readout of the outside atmosphere.

"The air seems fine, a little more oxygen than we are used to at Europa, but all the other elements are normal," she reported, speaking to be heard over the voice coming from the ship's speaker.

As the voice continued on with its dialogue, they watched the screen. After a short wait a large metallic umbilical appeared, as if from nowhere. It moved up and alongside the ship telescoping upward from the surface and attached itself to the Skimmer at the location of their airlock. They did as they were asked when directed, again by the voice from their speaker, to open the air lock. They were met by a flow of very cool and antiseptic smelling air that then filled the whole interior of their craft around them.

"Well," said Clysta, "I suppose we should go. They sure go to a lot of trouble on this world to keep it free from disease."

The trio entered the tube that was large enough so they could walk comfortably and Euclid followed behind after closing and securing their air lock. It would now only open upon a request by one of the three humans.

The interior of the tube was brightly lit from its walls, which were of the typical luminous material. A gentle slope led them downward to what they could see was the beginning of a passageway. Presumably the tube had led them underground and finally into an area where an earlier promised transporting vehicle would be waiting.

Kindra spoke next after a lengthy silence.

"They seem to have this quarantine worked to a fine art, don't they? We are the only people here."

They approached a waiting and unmanned sleek bullet-shaped car, hovering a few centimetres above the polished metallic surface of the floor. The same female voice returned from somewhere inside, to ask that they all enter and be seated. G'zin led the way by walking up and stepping into the car. After they were all seated, the robot too, the opening into the car sealed and the vehicle got immediately under way. The voice returned once again and went on to explain that whilst they travelled, they should all place the palm of the right hand on the illuminated pad alongside their individual seating. This way, the voice revealed, all of the necessary immunizations and tissue and blood tests would be commenced automatically and in transit.

They each did as directed. They could feel the various and unusual proddings and probings into their skin as the testing took place whilst the car whisked them along at a high speed down a narrow darkened tube to the next destination.

The robot brought a different response. The voice returned to ask, "Do you bring with you a robotic device?"

Clysta was the one who answered the question.

"Yes. He is of a humanoid design and he answers to the name of Euclid. He is able to give you his own credentials."

"'He'," the unseen voice questioned, with an incredulous note, "A He for a robot!"

"Yes," Clysta answered once again, smiling as she looked at the others, "He!" Stopping and not intending to say more.

Following a few seconds of pause the voice returned.

"The robot will need a full exterior and interior scan and also a bacterial elimination. Our system uses a light radiation which, we assure you, will not affect the circuitry of your robot."

"That all sounds very fine and your assurance is noted, but what guarantee do we have that no unseen harm will be done?" This time G'zin asked the question, "We have developed a great affection toward Euclid."

"We carry out this procedure very often with many styles of robot and machine. Our system will not do harm," the voice then added, sardonically, "Of course, you may if you wish, leave the machine in the quarantine holding area when you disembark."

They all looked at Euclid, whose metal exterior could show no response to the conversation that was deciding its near future. It was Euclid's knowledge of the missing component that was the reason they had arrived here in the first place.

Clysta gave the answer, "I suppose we are obliged to accept and agree to your conditions as we wish that Euclid accompany us during our visit to your world. How long can we expect to wait until we all may be finished with the analysis?"

"Presently the results of your own tests are being processed and they will be completed by the time you have entered the receiving area of the space port," the voice continued, "The robot will need to enter the quarantine chamber at the stopping point and then there will be a wait of fifteen minutes or less. That is all that can be expected."

"The testing and quarantine procedure for machines is not too complicated," the hidden voice added, with a slight note of sarcasm.

Almost as soon as the conversation had ended, the car came to rest. It had entered a large domed hall about fifty metres in diameter with an elliptical area of a glasslike floor. The lighting, though sufficient, was not bright. At the opposite end was an opening, the only noticeable feature to the otherwise smooth walls. It led out through a tube-like passageway. The easily recognizable shimmer of a force field closed and guarded the exit. Through it could be seen what must be the main foyer of the spaceport.

To the left of this opening, appeared a second opening, unseen until it almost magically developed from the smooth walls. This opening lead to what could have been an adjoining anteroom. Equally unexpected, a glowing sign appeared which read-'Mechanical Equipment Quarantine'. A dull red glow was all that illuminated the area inside beyond the entrance, possibly intended as a means of hiding from view the equipment used for the decontamination processes.

There were no other visitors in the arrival hall and as soon as they all had exited the car, it disappeared at speed back into the tunnel they had entered through. The mouth of the tunnel that remained immediately vanished as though it had never been there at all.

A new voice spoke from a concealed speaker directing them to send the robot through the opening and into the room at their left. The friends looked ominously at the opening.

Clysta turned to Euclid saying.

"It seems to be necessary, Euclid. We will be seeing you shortly."

The robot began to turn away toward the opening indicated. Clysta spoke in a whisper just loud enough for Euclid alone to hear. It was a phrase which came from somewhere inside her head but try as she could she had no idea where.

"Sub-mode C until we meet."

G'zin and Kindra did not hear it as they had become somewhat preoccupied with the view to the outside. Clysta's put her fingers to her temples, puzzled, as she murmured to herself.

"Whatever did I say that for?"

# Chapter 23

The formalities of passing through the spaceport were quite easy and relaxed in comparison to the almost severe and regimental treatment of the quarantine examination.

They had a wait of exactly fifteen minutes to the very second, when the robot appeared looking no worse for the experience.

Kindra had handled most of the formalities of entry, saying that they were graduates of the Academy Galactica. When asked the reason for the visit to Morn, he told them they were all here on pleasure and to visit his brother Mirsha.

Kindra and G'zin went on ahead with Clysta and Euclid trailing behind. Clysta asked the robot, "Did they treat you well in there?" Meaning the decontamination room.

'Yes Miss Clysta, they carried out the inspection adequately and did no harm,' was Euclid's reply.

She was about to ask what the strange words meant that she had spoken as they were separated, when the thought sequence cleared from her mind. She tried in vain to again formulate the words she was sure she meant to say but nothing was left.

They exited the enormous and decorated foyer of the port into the brightness of the outside world. It suddenly occurred to the three visitors that this was the largest planet they had ever set foot on in many years. Excluding Clysta the friends had come from small planets in relation to this one and it was only slightly smaller than the planet Earth. But her earlier childhood on Earth was long ago and she hardly could recall the times. Also, the early pain of losing her Mother had been effective in erasing most of those memories and any need to return.

The scale of all that was around them was so large and wide open. Almost all of the last twelve years for each of them had been spent in artificial atmospheres, either inside domes or space vehicles or generally never on natural outdoor surfaces.

G'zin broke up the first shock of experiencing the outside.

"Everything is so large and so unconfined. Just to be able to look up at that sky. Wonderful and gorgeous isn't it?"

The colour of the sky above them was of a light shade of green and very bright. It was dotted with very large and flat formations of an almost circular shape that was cloud like. These gently floated along at a height of probably eight or nine kilometres, appearing almost like distant islands in a smooth green sea.

The sun, which was the giant star Sirius, shone almost white but with a slight hint of green. Considering that it was a class A.1 the brightness was not as unbearable as it should be. Due mainly to the filtering action of that high liquid layer they had encountered earlier, encircling the whole planet. But then they did not take the chance of looking upward for too long. The change to them from the constant artificial lighting may be too severe and become hurtful to their optic functions.

They proceeded to walk slowly away from the spaceport watching with interest, all of the many people scurrying about intent on their business. The time of day locally, they had noted, was around mid-afternoon.

"What should we do first?" Clysta asked, "Do you think we should find somewhere to stay? A room or hotel maybe?"

"If we are able to locate my brother, he may have room to put us up for the night. Or suggest even a good place," Kindra said.

"That might be a better idea, at least until we become familiar with this enormous place," G'zin suggested wisely. She was still taken by the proportions of their surroundings.

"We should take a ground car to the Academy then," suggested Kindra, "We can probably find there some information about my brother. We can also ask about some accommodation just in case we are unsuccessful and after that we can have a try at the local food."

All around the spaceport and especially at its front, the surrounding area was meant for pedestrian use only. In the distance beyond the forecourt area they saw what could be a ground car parking section, so they walked, making toward it with the robot Euclid taking up the rear.

It took a little longer than they expected, as they were not accustomed to walking any great distances between two points. Slightly out of breath, they approached one of the cars. It was empty and there was no driver anywhere in sight.

'Step right inside and I will take you anywhere in town that you wish,' said a metallic and male sounding voice. 'Just state your destination.'

It came from a console on the inside.

"It's auto'," said G'zin in surprise.

'Of course!' Returned the voice, this time mimicking G'zin's tone and even the slight Frylian dialect, 'Where have you been, out in deep space? Please, just deposit your credit disc in the slot. It will be returned to you, when your destination has been reached.'

"How can we be sure of that?" Clysta asked the unseen voice.

'As sure as the day follows night after night after night,' was the quick and almost impudent reply.

As they all climbed cautiously into the car, Clysta started by asking to be taken to the Academy. After a confusing discussion with the car's voice and an explanation that the Academy had fifteen faculties, they settled finally for the one covering Art and its sciences.

The car moved off and through the busy traffic with ease. The car's voice commented occasionally on points of interest that they passed, often in the earlier sanguine manner. The car finally approached the Academy grounds and the voice made a final comment.

'Wow! This sure is one heck of a credit you have in this disc. There is oodles of value not touched yet. You can call on this cab any time you like.'

The car finally came to a stop in a parking area some distance from the entrance to the Faculty Reception Offices, and Kindra remarked that once again they were expected to walk a long way. The voice returned with a comment in response.

'The walk will be good for you!'

After they had all disembarked and it was pulling away, the heard the car's voice say.

'I hope you will all have a nice day.'

When the car had left Kindra commented, smiling.

"Now that was one heck of a Cheeky Cab."

# Chapter 24

The building housing the Art Faculty of the Academy of Morn had a beauty of tremendous proportions. Its design was an enhancement of artistic splendour. There were carvings and sculptures everywhere. All around the great and magnificent entrance hall, there were an extravaganza of glass mouldings and shapes, some of them blown glass, some solid and all of many colours and designs. Between all of these there were many paintings and works of art that would be the envy of some of Earths many ancient and historical galleries.

Clysta and her friends approached the reception desk area timidly, mostly in awe at its own spectacular design that was an extension of this phenomenal display of artistry.

The desk attendants were female, three in all, and they sat behind the large and ornate counter. Their attire was of the usual one piece uniform, but they each were of a material and composition with its own individual pattern of artistic development.

Euclid had moved to the side of the large doors after they had entered. The robot positioned himself as inconspicuously as possible and seemed to be taking in the view embodying the interior of the almost majestic reception area.

Kindra walked toward the reception desk, leaving the other two who were pointing out to each other the surrounding works of artistry. After waiting his turn in the short line of other visitors or students, he moved forward and stood before the one to the right who appeared presently to be unoccupied.

"I wonder if you are able to help us?" He began.

"My name is Kindra Nymralph, of the world Bambiron. My friends and I have travelled from the Academy Galactica at Sol and have just today arrived at your world through the spaceport. We are here on Morn intending to visit my brother. His name is Mirsha. He has been a student of this Academy up until a few years ago. His last name is the same as mine of course, Nymralph. That is Mirsha Nymralph."

"Is it possible that you could direct me to his present whereabouts?" He then added plainly in courtesy, "Please."

The female turned to the one next to her and whispered something that Kindra did not hear. The other then looked up and then at Kindra for a length of time that gave Kindra a peculiar and uncomfortable feeling. Hand signals passed between the two, un-noticed by Kindra, and then a further concealed control activated a recording device hidden within the desk.

"We will scan our registry records," said the attendant to whom Kindra had spoken first, "What were the courses that your brother was enrolled into?"

"I know he did well in Physics," Kindra answered, "That is one course. The last time that I heard from my father, my brother had started to excel in Artistic works. I remember he was to receive a degree a little while ago, in some subject or other in that same field of Art."

Kindra had an urge to speak about the work Mirsha had done in his involvement in Telepathy but trying as hard as he could, he found it difficult to form the words on his tongue and say them. Finally the idea itself drifted into blackness and became erased from his thoughts and he forgot about the subject.

Whilst Kindra talked, Clysta and G'zin were moving about the hall, viewing some of the many tapestries and art works while Euclid was still standing motionless. He seemed to be looking at everything but nothing in particular.

Clysta noticed absently that four or five older students, who were just hanging around near to the reception area, had appeared to be listening in to what Kindra had to say. They then made to move closer to the vicinity of the desk where Kindra now stood asking his questions.

The desk attendant spent a little time viewing her screen read-outs and finally she spoke, rather too brusquely and with a noticeably disinterested air.

"We have no record of a Mirsha Nymralph at this Faculty. You must be mistaken. Are you sure that it was here at this Academy that he was supposed to be attending?"

Kindra was taken aback at this unexpected reply.

"There must be some mistake," said Kindra with a look of shock. "He was made an honour student at this very facility. This is the academy from which he last wrote me a letter. It was my second last birthday. Have you perhaps miss-spelled the name?"

Kindra quickly spelled the name Nymralph letter for letter to make it more clear for her.

With a very haughty and superior tone the female in the middle of the three interrupted. She now answered his query.

"Our records use the most up to date phonic references and therefore a mistake is not at all possible. My screen also shows 'no file' which means the name you gave has no record. Therefore, your brother is not on record as being a student here. As my companion says, you must be mistaken in some way."

"How very odd!" murmured Kindra almost to himself? Not knowing what if anything to make of this development, "Very odd indeed."

Clysta, who had now moved closer, touched Kindra's arm saying,

"Let us try at the Physics campus, they may be able to give you some information."

The attendants having dismissed Kindra's enquiry, returned to their work of giving information to the others who waited in line at the desk. The attendant who had not spoken watched as the three made their way toward the enormous carved glass doors that were the exit and entrance of this colossal foyer.

Clysta and the others then made their way to the outside and slowly walked away from the large building. They did not see the third female close the contact on the recording device and then speak into a tiny wrist unit as she secretly watched them further through the glass facade until they had passed out of sight.

Once outside, Kindra finally said to his friends.

"I do not understand this. I know that Mirsha was at this Academy. I remember the name. And I know he was at the Art's faculty. This one. His last trans-et was from here. Why is it they have no record of him?"

After walking fifty metres or more, three of the five students who had showed interest in the conversation at the desk, came out of the reception and began following, slowly and appeared to be watching.

'Miss Clysta,' said Euclid low enough for only Clysta to hear, 'The group of students who were inside the building showed interest in Master Kindra's predicament and were using the name of his brother Mirsha in their conversation. Now three of that group appear to be behind and following our party. Does this have some bearing on Master Kindra's present problem?'

"I thought I noticed something odd in their interest too, but my hearing is likely not so good as yours is," Clysta answered. Then, saying to G'zin and Kindra.

"I'm getting hungry! We should find an eating place and think this out over a meal. We would also be wise to look for somewhere to stay now. Before it becomes too late. I don't feel we know enough of this place to be about and outside after the sun goes down."

# Chapter 25

Clysta and her friends followed one of the many walkways winding through the gardens between the tall buildings forming the Academy proper. Eventually they came upon a directory mounted on a pedestal set amongst an arrangement of brightly coloured flowering shrubs.

Clysta stood before the device and tentatively spoke into the disc in the centre. It appeared to be similar to the system in the Academy at Europa.

"We are strangers to the Academy and wish to find a moderate place to eat, preferably off but close to the Academy grounds. And also a suitable resting place where we are able to sleep for the next few nights. Not too far from the Academy if it is possible. There are four of us."

It took a few seconds of waiting but eventually an automated and this time female sounding voice replied giving directions to one eating establishment that it said was within ten minutes walk. The voice then directed them to an area where there were a variety of campus visitors quarters. Then a crystal magnifier disk type of viewer was produced from a slot tray. Inside the device was a map showing the local area with highlighted routes giving easy directions to number of places that were recommended to match both of Clysta's requests.

The group started off to follow one of those routes that were described to lead to an eatery.

"If the people would only lighten up," started G'zin, as she took in the view of the Academy and its surroundings. "I think I could get to like this place. See all of the lovely flowers and all these trees. And look at those lovely tiny birds over there. What beautiful colours they are. Up to now all the folks I have seen are people with such frosty attitudes. It's almost as if they are under some kind of stress."

Clysta was listening and looking, but she also occasionally glanced behind them to check if her suspicions were founded and they might be possibly being followed. Faking as if taking in the view, she spun around to observe that now just two of the students were still behind them, but keeping at a distance.

"Well there is the eating place," Kindra announced. "I wonder what kinds of food they have?"

Clysta was the last inside the establishment, ahead of Euclid. She turned once again to check. Looking back, she saw only one of the students, a male, heading toward the entrance that they had used. The other, along with the third was nowhere to be seen. Clysta decided it must have been coincidence and thought no more about it and followed the others.

The building's interior was larger than it looked from the outside and brightly coloured. Along the wall to the left were the food dispensers. Each had dial panels and push pads listing many types and origins of foods. The systems compared in general with those they had used before though some of the listed foods were unfamiliar. One addition to the layout was a voice receiver, which could take instructions verbally from anyone requesting changes or more unusual menus.

Kindra suggested they try something with which they were familiar. It may not be wise to be too bold on their first day here.

Euclid followed the others to a table and automatically stood at attention, as was his usual pose.

G'zin looked at the robot saying. "Please sit down Euclid. You are supposed to be learning how to have a relaxed attitude. Part of that means looking relaxed and sitting with us when we sit."

'Thank-you Miss G'zin. It is this unit's intention to learn to become relaxed as you say, but it will not affect my constant state of alertness.' With that the robot sat on one of the anti-grav seats spaced around the table.

At that moment the student who Clysta had last seen outside, sat down at the table next to theirs. Two others, one of them female, then accompanied this stranger. Clysta thought she recognized them by their clothing and was sure they were from the original group at the Art Faculty reception hall. Now and then one of them would glance at Kindra, then whisper something to the others at the table, and then quickly look away as if trying not to be noticed.

The other tables were almost all of them in use by students and their friends, eating and talking between themselves.

Kindra broke the silence at their table.

"Have you noticed that there are no adults around? You know, no one who seems to not be a student."

G'zin had noticed that fact also.

"I thought about that," she said. "This place is close to the Academy though. Maybe adults do not frequent this place, because of the students or something."

"Well it sure isn't the food that keeps them away. This is delicious, almost as good as Europa Ac'," retorted Kindra.

Clysta quietly continued to eat, but cautiously making mental notes of her surroundings and particularly of those three student types who had evidently followed them here.

There was a gathering of younger scholars who kept watching their group, with inquisitive stares at Euclid. It became obvious they had not been too familiar with so humanoid a robot. And one that was in the company of a group of humans and above all sitting alongside them.

Kindra had finished his drink and arose to go back to the dispenser to get a refill. As he turned, one of the students at the other table also stood, bumping into Kindra. Kindra felt something being pushed into his palm.

"So sorry!" The other said, and then quickly he made his way to the door and left the eating-place without looking back.

By the time Kindra returned, the other two students had left their table now empty. He sat down and, in a whisper so not to be heard by the others who might be nearby, told the others what had just happened. He displayed his palm secretively to show them a circular flat disk the size of a large button or coin. It was partially translucent with a metallic outer edge and was glowing internally with a dim and pulsing light. In the middle of the disk in slightly raised crystalline and gold letters was written the words—'Mirsha Freedom'.

# Chapter 26

G'zin was just finishing a sweetmeat that she had taken a chance on. It reminded her of a blue, honey-filled spiked fruit grown on a planet close to her home system.

When she had finished cleaning the stickiness from around her lips, she bent forward and said in a low voice, "There is something very funny here. There are two females behind you Clysta, no, don't look," she said quickly as Clysta started into a motion to turn around, "at the other end of the room. I am sure that we are being observed. They have had their eyes on this table almost since we arrived in here. I am certain they followed us in too. This whole episode is becoming spooky. I suggest we finish our meal and leave."

"Maybe we are starting to imagine things. There is very likely nothing to our suspicions," suggested Clysta cautiously and equally as quiet. "What can you hear, Euclid?"

'I have heard nothing conclusive in the direction that Miss G'zin is indicating. The two humans appear to be looking in our direction with some slight interest.' Euclid continued, 'I have noticed that they have been using a system of finger and hand motions. They are similar to the motions used by two of the females who were at the reception desk in the Academy.'

"I didn't see that, Euclid," whispered Kindra, then with a grin, "Good old Euclid. Sees everything and says nothing." Kindra then took on a more serious look.

"I agree with G'zin," said Kindra continuing, "Let's leave here and find a place for the night. We may get farther in the morning when we visit the Physics Campus. Beside all that, I can't figure out what this disc is meant to be. Mirsha, I think I know as my brother, but the Freedom has me totally confused."

The three friends took only a little while longer to casually finish off the meal and they all arose, intending to leave the eating place. G'zin stacked their utensils and passed by the recycling device then dropped them into the chute.

Once outside they walked a little until they found an auto-transport stand. The giant star, Sirius, was close to dropping behind the horizon and a glowing dusk was beginning to form.

"My! What a beautiful shade of green," said G'zin, looking up at the evening sky, "And see," she pointed, "You can see some stars in spite of that liquid upper layer. I can't make out too many of them from here, but I would guess that spot of bright light over there is the Andromeda Galaxy."

"Always the romantic," chided Kindra, then more seriously, "Get into a car and let's get away from here. The two females whom G'zin had spoken of on the inside have left the building and are right behind us," he added still more seriously. "Now I think we are being followed."

The friends were walking along the line of parked cars, as Clysta viewed the crystal guide for suitable quarters where they could spend the night. Kindra meanwhile had noticed the numbers and markings on the side of the third car in the line and instantly recognized it. He called the others over.

"This is the same number as that on the car we used to get to the Academy this afternoon. Isn't it?" He said to the others for confirmation. As he approached, the door opened automatically.

'It sure is,' announced the familiar voice, 'Get right in and announce your destination. Please.

Clysta spoke into the cars speech disc as it pulled away. They were quickly carried into the stream of other vehicles as she was using the disc to make transi-phone enquiries at a few of the listed establishments, checking for vacancies.

The first and second of the hotels reported they had no vacancies. But after a third try, she found one, which was able to offer accommodation for them all in a suitably comfortable unit. She then directed the car by voice to the address shown in the device and the car instantly picked up speed and left the area behind.

After a short while, the car and the passengers arrived at the chosen hotel and disembarked.

After a series of automated questions, they were allowed to find their allocated unit, unassisted.

The suite was indeed comfortable and clean and colourful.

"This isn't at all bad," said Clysta after her speedy inspection. "We have two bedrooms, a super cleaner mould, and it uses real water. That should be an experience. And see, there is a good stock of entertainment discs and a dispenser that will serve up whatever we wish for breakfast."

Kindra crossed the room to a wall mounted control. He was not too sure what it was used for as he turned one of the dials slowly.

The wall across the room was magically transformed from its smooth and illuminating surface. The whole area from floor to ceiling and end to end first changed to translucent. Then by degrees converted to a transparency and finally becoming crystal clear. The view now was of the city outside the wall from their room high above the street at the eighth storey.

The sky above was now fast becoming dark and more of the surrounding stars were visible. In the distance the spaceport lights were on and to the left the towers of the Academy had been illuminated in many coloured lights. Between and around these lay the myriad lights of the city with its avenues and gardens with tracts of illumination and decorative displays.

"Very pretty," said Kindra in a low and pleasant voice.

"I heard that!" G'zin said mockingly. "You old romantic, you."

Together they sat in the apartment's deep and comfortable seating, talking about the days' events, trying to make some sense of what they had been told by the desk staff at the Academy. And then there was that play at the eating place. Confusion abounded. It had been a funny day ever since they had exited Hyper Space. Those first memories, they would rather forget all together, and they did. But the other events, perhaps tomorrow would be time enough to clear up those.

Euclid stood with its back to the wall at one side of the closed door. It was the only entrance to and from the corridor outside which itself lead to the elevating chute.

The robot's vision patch glowed a little brighter signalling its increased attention. Euclid spoke, in a low tone.

'Some-one, a human, has walked along the passage outside this suite and is standing at this door. That one human has now been joined by another to become two.'

Their conversation stopped as they listened in an attempt to hear any sounds from outside. The room and the walls around it were of a totally soundproof material and they could each hear no sounds, with the exception of the other two, breathing.

After what seemed to them an eternity of silence, the door buzzer sounded. Clysta got to her feet and crossed the room to the control for the visi screen and some of the other equipment within the suite. She selected a pad and pressed it. A view of the corridor outside appeared, replacing the solid door in its opening. It was a one way only view.

The two who stood outside were recognized immediately. They were the same two who they were convinced, had followed them from the Academy and sat along with the other who had first entered the eating place. One of them, a male, looked straight at them, though he could not actually see. The door as seen from outside was not transparent. The other was a female, and appeared nervous, looking first to the left then to the right repeatedly, as if she was afraid that they might be discovered by someone.

Clysta spoke toward the disc on the table.

"We are just ready for sleep. What can we do for you?"

The male of the two strangers spoke, in the planets local dialect of Universal Galactic.

"We apologise for the lateness of the hour, but it is not what you can do for us, but what we can do for you. Please, may we enter? We might have been followed here and we must not be discovered."

"What is your business with us at this very late hour and why should we let you enter?" Clysta asked, this time firmly.

The female held up her right hand and displayed in her palm a disc, similar to the one that Kindra had been given at the eating place.

Clysta closed the contact for the speech disc and turning to the others, said, "What do you think?"

"Whatever it is, they seem to have gone to a great deal of trouble to find us and then come to our suite," Kindra said, "and there is the disc, it could mean something. They might have some information about Mirsha. I say we should let them in."

"Agreed," G'zin said, "and Euclid can also keep a close watch over their actions, of they should intend to harm us."

The view at the door still showed the couple, with the female becoming more agitated and nervous. Clysta nodded a signal to the robot and operated the control. The door slid open.

The two strangers rushed inside.

# Chapter 27

In the second of time it took the door to their suite to close and seal, Euclid's seedy hands had gone to work to begin searching these two strangers for any concealed weapons they may have with them. They each wore a cloak made of a thin but firm material. Even these could not have concealed anything from the robots delicate but thorough search.

No weapons were there to be found.

Their cloaks, with a hood, covered all but a few centimetres at the front and ended at a point between the ankles and the knee. Both had footwear typical of all students, a soft slip on type, with high heels for the female the same as was worn by most of the ladies of this planet. Not much else of their clothing was visible.

The strangers moved to the middle of the room and stood in silence, conveying a non-aggressive attitude to their entrance. Euclid returned to a position and remained there, standing behind the pair, positioned between them and the exit.

Clysta spoke first, "Please state your business and why have you followed us?"

The male, who had a pleasantly sculptured face, well tanned and with bright blue eyes showing beneath the hood, started to speak but not to answer. His hand exited the cloak, startling the three friends. With a wave of the open palm, he motioned it as a peaceful action. He raised the hand and touched his forefinger to his lips indicating silence, then in a whisper.

"Please. Turn on the visi' and increase the volume a little, then remain quiet."

Kindra started to ask why but was stopped by the same repeated signal. He condescendingly pushed a control and a part of the window wall showed an adventure program in progress.

The accompanying dialogue would have covered the next words but in the same low voice, the male asked Clysta, "Now make the door clear."

They all watched the corridor through the now transparent door. A short wait, then Euclid gave a signal. Two people entered the view and stood outside. Both looked around the area as if checking for any telltale traces of activity.

They were tall and each was dressed in the same style of cloak as the visitors, but they and the clothing that was visible beneath, were all black. Their faces, though not unattractive, bore a stern unbending facade, almost regimental and plain. With each of them being devoid of any artificial colouring.

They each now lowered their hoods to reveal the deep black hair of both which was tied to the back in a small tight bun shaping. It was immediately seen by the friends that these two females were at the eatery earlier. They each had a small star-like badge on the left shoulder of each of their body covering cloaks.

One of the two new comers pulled a small polished metal cylindrical device from beneath her cloak and held it against the outside face of the door. She stood listening intently as if trying to hear anything that might be happening on the inside of the room beyond the door.

G'zin took a silent prompt from the female stranger before them and entered into the masquerade.

"This program is quite something, isn't it?" she started in an even voice. "I wish we could have had a few programs like this on Europa instead of all of that straight and educational stuff they always fed us. Perhaps life would have been easier."

Kindra could see the idea of what the two strangers standing before them had intended and followed up with some additional small talk. During this time those inside could view the two outside as they continued to stand in the corridor seemingly listening to their device and talking between themselves, all of it unheard by the room's occupants through the soundproof door.

It took a few minutes but finally the two females appeared satisfied with their mission. They moved from view after first replacing the cylinder in a pocket inside the handler's cloak.

Euclid spoke.

'Those new persons outside have left the area.'

Kindra let out a gasp of relief as they all turned to face those two visitors who were in the room. He touched the control and made the door solid again.

"I don't think I could have kept that up much longer," he said. Then turning his full attention to the strangers and in a more serious tone, he demanded.

"Now. What is all of this about, and don't try anything foolish, because Euclid, who is behind you, is very protective."

The female ignored Kindra's question. She spoke for the first time since they had entered. She had finally pulled the hood down from around her head to fully reveal her face.

The female was modestly attractive in a singular way and her use of an artistic make-up did the rest. Her age could be anything from teenager to early twenty years, the friends had really no experience of the planet's aging processes. However she was young in appearance. Her hair, which was cropped all over her head to about twenty-five centimetres made her appear young also. It was styled in the form of spikes, which radiated outward and each spike was tinted in an array of many luminous colours.

"Where are you from and why are you visiting Morn?" She asked in an accent not quite Galactic and in a young voice.

"Unless you can show us a very good reason to answer that question, I don't think we need to answer," said Clysta, "After all, the Galaxy is free range. Is it not?"

"Of course," answered the male stranger. He, like his partner, had by now let his hood reveal his head. He appeared to be at the same age as his companion. "You are quite correct. But we were at the Academy today. When you were enquiring about a Mirsha Nymralph."

They each as if on cue unbuckled their cloaks and with a stylish flourish, swung them from their shoulders. Then with another flourish, almost a ritual demonstration, they lay it neatly across the left arm. Within two seconds, the cloak shrunk as if by magic into a much smaller bulk to be the size of small towel.

The cloaks had covered a standard one piece tight fitting garment which itself covered the body from the neck down. The female's tunic was an orange colour and was designed with a plunging neckline, down almost to the waist. Kindra drew in a breath as he took a little more attention of that than of the male. The male himself wore an outfit that was buttoned up and to the neck and of a dark blue colour.

"It was noted that this person," she pointed toward Kindra, "said he is supposed to be a relative of his and we know that the answer which you received would have been a negative one."

Kindra spoke up, "Why do our questions to the Academy staff need to be of interest to you? We are complete strangers."

"We have our reasons," the female answered, looking directly into Kindra's eyes.

Kindra responded.

"That does not seem to be a good enough basis. There were many others inside the reception, and any of them could have heard our conversation," said Kindra again, not at all satisfied and ignoring the look, "I am afraid your questions will still not be answered without more and better explanations. Now. Can we have an answer to my friend's question? Why are you following us and why are you here at our rooms?"

A silence descended in the room as Kindra and the female stranger looked in a kind of defiance, at each other. An amount of tension was beginning to descend. Clysta made to speak and ask another question.

G'zin held up a hand and interrupted.

"Hey! This is going nowhere. We," her arms spread to indicate her companions, "Have nothing to hide."

She paused a while then began again, to offer an explanation, "We three have just graduated the final year at the Academy Galactica on Europa in the Sol System. Clysta's father," G'zin motioned in Clysta's direction with a wave of her hand, "Rented a Skimmer as a graduation present for us to skip around and enjoy ourselves. We were in the neighbourhood and decided to catch up on some of the things in this sector. Kindra," again, she motioned toward him this time, "Told us he had a brother here on Morn and suggested we could pay his brother a visit and, well, here we are. You appear to know all of the rest. All we know now is that we appear to have been followed ever since our visit to your Academy."

After a short pause, she finished with, "Now you can tell us your story."

The two strangers looked at each other in silence. Their eye lids fluttered in some kind on speechless conversation, then the male spoke.

"It is very important for us to know if you are telling the truth," he said. "We carry with us a device which is able to check. We call it a fluctuation reader; a lie detector I suppose would be your description. But I hate to use that term."

"You won't take our word then? About what was just said by G'zin," said Clysta.

"We cannot and we dare not," was his reply whilst looking at all three, individually. He turned cautiously to check if the robot was still behind him. The robot had not moved.

"Well, as G'zin just said, we have nothing to hide, although this is becoming more and more mysterious," Clysta inferred. "We really want to find and to see Kindra's brother. All of this—this," she hesitated to search for the word, "intrigue, really has us baffled. Maybe this device of yours will be the only way we can do that. But beware, any treachery and Euclid will not take kindly to any action which is not correct, mark my words."

This time, both of the strangers looked over their shoulders and in Euclid's direction. The robot's metal face showed no expression as was usual, but the whole of its metallic exterior still gave it a very formidable appearance.

The male slipped his hand into a pocket inside his tunic and extracted a thin and flat rubbery pad of about four centimetres square. He then placed it onto the table. Then he told them.

"It is a simple thing but very efficient in finding out untruths".

He then instructed that each of them was to pick it up in turn, place it in the palm of the right hand face up. Then they were to recite the words inscribed on the face of the pad.

Clysta volunteered to be first.

"It doesn't make sense. There are words missing. What are we supposed to do there?"

"Where the blanks are, you replace them by your own spoken words," the female explained. She added, "If the device is satisfied, your answers will appear in those spaces."

The male then cautioned Clysta.

"If the words are to be found or translate as untrue, the pad will display a red glow indicating a lie is being told."

The blank spaces representing those missing words came after the engraved and minute inscriptions;

'name'-

'place of origin'-

'reason for visit'-.

"Let me go first Clysta."

G'zin moved a step toward the table but Clysta had a sudden thought that she should be first and held her back.

"No thank you G'zin," she said coolly and sincerely, "Me first, you second then Kindra last. After all, as you said, we have nothing at all to hide."

Clysta moved to the table and picked up the white pad almost cautiously and began to turn it over and over checking for hidden needles or devices. Satisfied with her inspection she then carefully placed it on her upturned palm. The group watched, her friends partly in apprehension.

During her inspection, Clysta had grown a little apprehensive herself about the final sentence, which would need to end with 'to visit Kindra's brother Mirsha'. Her apprehension was somehow unfounded. When she finally came to speak those words, her mind was overcome with a clear sensation of absolute composure, leaving her almost oblivious of the fear she had before of speaking an untruth. Then just as suddenly, as she replaced the pad on the table, the feeling of conscious calmness that had taken over was gone.

Though the real and true reason for the visit was omitted, Clysta wondered why the pad had not responded by showing a reaction to the partial falsehood. If this was really a lie detection device as was meant to be, it should have glowed. Although the answer was almost a truth, the omission of the other and real reason would surely have been noticed.

She listened with the same building apprehension as G'zin and then finally Kindra came upon the same last statement and again on each announcement, the pad refused to change its state or colour.

Clysta, some time later in the same evening, had brought up the occurrence and found that the other two had noticed a similar awareness, if that was what it was. It was decided they should sleep on it. And they did, later and then forgot it completely.

"It looks like you are all telling the truth," the male confirmed as Kindra, who was the last, passed the pad back to the stranger. "I know now that we ought to have believed you from the start, but we just had to be sure. Now it is safe to tell you of our reasons for all the secrecy we need to maintain in this."

His tone of voice had become less serious, almost friendly. Even his appearance had become mellowed, since the proving.

He began his story.

"My own name is Myron 11. My companion is named Syrea. Our last names are of little consequence at this time.

"We have been students at the Academy of Morn for all of fourteen years. Our whole background is of Morn as we were both born here on this planet. Both of our parents were also born here after their grand parents had been drafted here as earlier immigrants from Earth.

"Six years ago, a small number of students at the Academy, were selected from one of the classes. These were of a group who had proven their special abilities. They were deployed onto a new and previously unconsidered study of the human brain.

"It was a lead to the development of number of very unique discoveries. Their work was carried out mostly as an item of extra curricular study in the Physics Laboratory and reports and conclusions were handled by two of the Academy's professors.

"Their work lasted for almost four years. Later that class was taken off the exercise. Now we know their results were beginning to make headway. After it's disbanding, three of the top same group of students was selected to carry on with the work. It was still extra curricular of course. The work up to this time had become close to something the professors found very significant. Those involved, were still reporting to those same two professors."

All of this time the group had stood in the middle of the room, mostly un-relaxed.

G'zin offered, "It appears to me that this story is going to be a very long one. Why don't we make ourselves more comfortable? After all, we have been tested for your sakes. And we always have Euclid," she looked at the robot, "if you two have any desires to harm us whilst we are here in this room. So why don't we all sit down and we can serve up some kind of refreshment."

When they had all become comfortable and each had been served a drink by Euclid, the three friends waited for the rest of the story. The female Syrea took up the story and continued.

"Mirsha Nymralph was one of those final three. One of his friends, another of the final three, was my brother, Jhel."

She continued.

"Mirsha had been a little suspicious almost from the outset. The way the work was being monitored and then the after class detail. And now there was the new routine and detail. He finally confided in Jhel of his thoughts, just after the time of the change-over to only the group of three students. Then. Some time later, Jhel overheard, quite accidentally, a conversation by one of the two professors to an unknown contact. Threats and money were mentioned. That convinced Jhel too, there indeed was some kind of, shall we say, conspiracy of a sort.

"Their work in the laboratory meanwhile had evolved into producing details of a series of components which if ever assembled would put them close to the development of a mass mind control transmitter. The purpose for it, they now surmised correctly or incorrectly, would give the ability to control and manipulate the populace of the planet with far reaching ends. Almost even have the ability to make people as slaves. Mirsha established, that two of our more prominent industrialists were well connected with the whole connivance. But neither Mirsha nor Jhel had positive proof to go to the authorities with.

"Mirsha had gone farther ahead and alone in his work in the production. He found he held the knowledge and the answer to the final item essential to making the transmitter function, but he kept it secret. Even from my brother Jhel and most of all from the professors."

The female, Syrea became quiet.

Seconds of silence elapsed and then the male, Myron 11, once more took over and continued with the account.

"Mirsha had decided that if they had no firm proof of an illegal connection, now it was necessary to slow the progress of the work on the systems. He told his student associates the device must not reach completion whatever the professors or these unknown industrialists may do. So he used his academic leanings in the field of Art to delay more real progress.

"He had found he had a natural talent for the subject. So, he fooled around a little, in and out of the Physics studies. Acting in a mostly lethargic manner and making as if he had lost interest, becoming more and more interested in studies of art. Then suddenly, it was about two years ago, the other one of the three, a female student, disappeared. It happened after she had unwisely confronted and accused one of the professors of their complicity in some form of intrigue.

"Mirsha and Jhel decided it was best if they were to cut themselves out of the development of the device altogether. Jhel has since become a high profile administrator in the Academy and up to now has managed to keep himself safe. Mirsha on the other hand made a few sales of his works and did very well in his new field of art. He finally went into hiding.

"Before he did though, he did a most dangerous and of course brave thing. He removed from the lab', a few of the more final and important components. He also erased all trace of most of the work of the group from the Lab' comp'.

"We and a few other students who were recruited by Mirsha, later, are keeping the development off track in any way possible and to try to stop the device ever being finished.

"Along the way, we also divert the suspected industrialists from locating Mirsha's hideaway. Believe me, they would stop at nothing to find him. And now that you have surfaced," Myron 11 glanced in Kindra's direction. "These people would even use you Kindra as a pawn if they were to learn that you are Mirsha's brother.

"About a year ago after he had gone into seclusion, Mirsha's name was erased from the Academy records together with his many achievements during his years here. It appears those people have such an influence in the matters of the Academy and know how to coerce some of the administration. Meanwhile they are constantly trying to locate his hiding place."

Their story was complete and the two strangers now became silent. Kindra, who had listened intently, to all that these two had said, looked to the others to see their reactions. Then he spoke.

"Do you yourselves know the whereabouts of my brother? Of this hiding place as you name it?"

"We two don't, but there are others in our group who do," Syrea answered. "We must take every precaution because he has been successful in stopping the plans of these industrialists. They are most intent on finding Mirsha."

"This sounds too bizarre to be real," G'zin broke in," Surely you are making this whole story up. This type of thing is not allowed to develop."

"Our story is quite true," Myron 11, said earnestly, "I don't know what else we must do or say to convince you all."

Kindra was ready to say something when G'zin said.

"Ok then. If all of this did happen just as you have told it and these people need to find Mirsha. Then how can we be sure for instance, that you are not part of this so called conspiracy and you yourselves are trying to use Kindra in your efforts to stop his brother Mirsha?"

Syrea and Myron became quiet, unable to think of any other proof of their sincerity.

"Just let us suppose that we believe in your story of a conspiracy," Clysta volunteered. "Who were those other two people outside the door? I am sure I recognized them from the place where we ate this afternoon. They too, appeared to show an interest in us. And I don't think they were here at the door for nothing."

"There is not much more we are able to tell you in order to make you believe our story," said Myron, "I will tell you though, those two who were just now in the corridor after we entered, were not friends of Mirsha's group. I have seen them around the Academy only occasionally. I am also sure that they are not students there. And I can only suspect they are ensuring you are available and in sight."

Syrea suddenly came up with a suggestion.

"Would it be easier to believe us if we were to use the pad on ourselves?"

Kindra was shaking his head in disbelief of what he was hearing. Suddenly a thought came to him and he said excitedly.

"I know of a safe and sure way of which you can convince me of your honesty. Just get word to my brother that I am here on Morn. If all you have said is true, get this question to him. Just say to him—,"

"What was our father's favorite name for his second son Kindra?"

"If the answer is the correct one when you return, it is an indication he is my brother Mirsha. I am sure that only he and I on this world know the answer. Then and only then, I will be convinced you may be telling the truth. Although about all of this intrigue, he himself will need to explain to me. Just don't come back with the wrong name".

Kindra's eyes looked past the two visitors and toward the robot.

The two looked in the direction of Euclid, then at each other and nodded their agreement.

"We will try to arrange that," Myron 11 said in agreement, "Now we must leave, it is already late."

They turned to make a way to the door and Clysta stopped them, saying.

"You left it unclear what those two others have to do with all of this. Can you tell us anything more, if only to warn us?"

Myron 11 answered in a grave tone.

"These industrialists are very wealthy, and with that they have great power. We know they have employed the services of a group of security consultants or at least that is what they are calling themselves. Their job amongst others is to seek out our supporters and also locate Mirsha. As it is right now, three of our friends have disappeared for no apparent reason. Two more are in hospital brutalized, afraid to say how or by whom. I suspect they are two who have been approached by that same security force."

He continued, "We and some of the others are followed, regularly. You have already been advised, the records at the Academy show that your brother Mirsha did not attend there and in their information, he does not exist. Therefore, you are not likely to be asked questions by them. But you also will be followed from now on, having arrived on the planet Morn and showing an interest in finding him."

He paused, and then added looking straight at Kindra.

"Particularly since you have already announced your relationship with him. As far as anyone who is involved in this is concerned, you will be taken to be Mirsha's brother until they are convinced otherwise. That in itself makes both of you very vulnerable," then he added for effect. "If it is true!"

"Now, once again, we must leave. We have been here too long," Myron 11 announced, as he pulled his retransformed cloak over his shoulders. But before we leave, we must use a device which will remove any trace of our visit here, just in case."

He drew from another pocket inside the cloak a silver coloured slender tube, similar to a short baton and, pushing a button in the side, he waived it around as he spun in a circle. A bright and flashing strobe-like effect filled the room and then it was gone.

"This," he explained as he finished and returned the device to its compartment in his cloak, "neutralizes all of the traces of our presence. Like particles of dust and skin and even odours. Our protagonists have ways of identifying us and can know of our visits, from extracts that we may leave in the air inside a room. They have easy access to the DNA files of everyone on the planet. Even yours now."

As he paused, all three of the friends knew immediately what he had inferred. He continued, "We are forced to use it all of the time, when we are not to be traced. It should help to keep anyone who is trying to associate this contact at bay for a little while."

They both then stood to face the three friends. Kindra quickly asked.

"I am still a little skeptical but, if all you say is in truth, when will I hear from my brother?"

Myron 11 stood a little while then answered.

"We will need to pass on our findings to some of our contacts. Then you will be approached again. It may take a little while, possibly a full day. Maybe longer, we don't know exactly."

Then Myron 11 looked at them, saying with a recognizable sincerity.

"We will now bid you Goodbye and Goodnight and Good Luck!"

Clysta looked quickly at Kindra and G'zin who nodded their approval. With a slight movement of her hand, she waived Euclid away to stand to the side of the door.

The door opened and as they left, Syrea turned. She held up her hand showing the palm. In it, and visible, was once more, the small glowing disc.

# Chapter 28

They all needed the inducers to help them to sleep that night. In the morning of the next day they awoke within minutes of each other. Kindra switched out the wall before taking first turn as he entered the body cleaner mold.

Sirius was just starting its glowing ascent into a light green sky and had almost cleared the mountains in the far distance. A pale green light of dawn was spreading outward across the city below causing each of the tall buildings to resemble towers of glowing sapphire.

In the distance a craft was leaving for space propelled by the ancient type of infracted impulse drive. The early morning's green dawn light turned to sparkling shades of blue and yellow as it passed through the ascending ships generated stream of ionized molecules.

Euclid had served a prepared breakfast of their favourites, or as close as the Morn directory was able to duplicate. Sitting around the table, Clysta began the conversation.

"Did we all have the same dream last night or was that all real?"

"It was real alright," G'zin replied, sitting down to eat, her braids neatly in place. "Do you think they were telling us the truth? After all it seemed a little fanciful to me, all that talk of plans to alter the minds of the populace. You don't think this is all some kind of juvenile prank? It sure smells of that kind of deal to me."

"What is your opinion Kindra? It is your Brother they were talking about." Clysta asked. He was already sitting at the table.

"I can almost believe it," he began, "Last night I started to go over the sequence of events from a few years back and it all seems to fit."

He continued, "Do you remember what I told you on our way here? My brother Mirsha and my father both argued, even raged, about his future in Physics and Mineralogy and his drifting into Art. He never did get the chance to explain to my father his real reasons for the change. If what we were told is true, then it does make sense now. I remember how, when I was around during the arguing, Mirsha was always a little vague about why. I began to think he had found it all too tough for him. The strenuous courses, the studying and all that."

"But if this episode that Myron II related to was the true reason," Clysta responded. "Why then, did he not say something to your father about all of what was happening? He could have recruited his help to solve this problem, couldn't he?"

"Perhaps only he can answer that question," Kindra replied, "I can ask him when I find him. They were both very stubborn in the end, about the whole episode."

"Well, possibly time will tell." G'zin offered. She was sampling one of the local juices. "I would like to suggest that we give them a day to clear away the doubts. Let them sort out the details, if they can. Meanwhile, we should enjoy the trip here and maybe see a little of this planet, for today at least. What do you two think?"

"Good thinking G'zin," was Clysta's reply. "Let's have a walk through the city and see some of the sights, then find a way to the coast that we saw close by. Maybe visit the town you spotted when we were on our approach to a landing."

"By the way, Euclid," Clysta said, turning toward the robot. "What conclusions did you come to, with regard to the two visitors of last evening?"

The robot did not need more than a fraction of a second to give a response.

'This unit monitored the conversation and the tone of speech of the visitors and found they each conversed with a straight and unrestrained flow of verbalism. There were no inflections which ought to indicate untruths in anything they said.'

"Euclid appears satisfied," said G'zin, raising her eyebrows at the dissertation. "I say that is good enough for now. Now we should, after we have finished breakfast, get ready and go and see what we can find."

They finished eating a leisurely breakfast and later as the other two cleared the table and prepared to leave, Clysta was busy on the visiphone enquiring about some of the sights and to make arrangements for possible transport to the coast. She gathered together, the pile of filaments showing local places of interest that had popped out of the slot at the front of the module.

G'zin estimated the time they would be absent, then punched in a code so that an auto-cleaning drone would straighten up while they were away.

"Ok," Clysta announced waiving her handful of notes, "Let's go. This lot is sure to keep us busy for the day. Come on Euclid, you're coming too."

They had arranged, meanwhile, with the auto booking to keep the suite for their return and left the building on foot to walk down the wide landscaped avenue.

Both sides were busy with people, once again going to and fro about their business. The planet, they had learned, had a self supporting industrial economy and this was the major city in this, the major continent. Elsewhere on the planet the other landmasses were not quite so industrious which led to this one being the most important and prosperous.

No-one was taking much notice of the visitors, who were strolling along and viewing the sights. On the odd occasion, a passer-by would look suspiciously at Euclid then, having made a silent comment about robots, hurry on with their business. Humanoid robots had long since been phased out on this and many other of the Federation planets, in favour of more direct robotic devises. This is what made Euclid occasionally all the more conspicuous.

There were many tall buildings, of blended but individual styles, each surrounded by lush lawns of the same pink coloured grasses, manicured and neat, almost like a fine carpeting. Arranged around all of the buildings and down the long avenues were trees and flowers and shrubbery of many varieties and colours, all so unfamiliar to these three visitors from Sol.

In the almost clear green sky above there were a number of those same flat disc like clouds they had seen the day before. They appeared to be moving inland from the direction of the what they judged was the coast. A gathering of flying creatures were going from tree to tree and nibbling at the fruits of a certain type of growth that was common on this avenue.

Ground cars occasionally passed speeding by, some occupied, and others empty. Sometimes an air car would pass overhead zipping between the tall towers lining the avenue.

After much head turning and finger pointing, Clysta remarked.

"All seems at peace this morning, quite different from what we went through yesterday. We should take a car to the Hall of Discovery. I have some details on it here. It should be quite interesting from this list of information I retrieved from the machine in the room."

# Chapter 29

Buildings of Morn each had their own individuality. These were also the largest man made structures they had seen for years. But the building that was the Hall of Discovery was most unique. It was not tall as many. It rose only to three levels but it was lavish and covered a large area. The exterior was a modernist style, with curves and sweeping forms and swirls, designed as if to represent updraughts and currents.

Plasti-crete had been used as a base material and then the whole structure was encased in a veneer of metal the colour of deep burnished gold. Windows too, to let in the light of the local star, abounded and in lines and forms to match the exterior shaping. Materials similar to glass were in abundance everywhere in many random patterns, catching the sunlight and breaking it down into the full range of spectral colours. Showering these colours both inside and outside of the structure.

Fountains were in use profusely around the exterior grounds, each a part of the universal design. Water was made to perform contortionist tricks that defied the normal laws of gravity. Gyrating through loops and spirals and many unbelievable artistic maneuvers.

The group stayed outside for a while taking in the beauty of the structure almost in awe at the artistry. In their own time at Europa, time had been directed to Space Physics and the accompanying topics. Art and planetary construction hardly meant much. These views of structures were new to them and very pleasing. Finally they moved on and entered to see what sights new to them were being exhibited on the inside.

They took their time meandering through the various halls and from level to level viewing the displays showing pictorial descriptions and holographics of the history of the planet Morn. Kindra pointed out a large section on the top level where the inventions and discoveries were displayed. The items were credited to people of this world in the many years since its initial colonization.

They had stopped at an unusual artifact of some historical value when G'zin closed in on Kindra. Clysta was busy reading the information about its discovery on the unexplored planet many hundreds of years ago.

"I'm sure we are being followed again," she said in a low voice. "Don't look back right now, but two females dressed similarly to the two outside our suite last night are keeping pace with us."

"Well, you remember what Myron said. He told us it would be likely to happen," Kindra said. "So what should we do?"

"I think we should do nothing," was Clysta's comment. She had heard the conversation. "We are here to see the sights. Besides you are only guessing, they may not be following us at all."

As Clysta finished, they arrived at an area on the second level showing a sample of the multitude of items of Art produced on the world of Morn. At the centre of an area in a corner of the large room, a small crowd had gathered. They all stood around an item, which had been set on a raised dais.

The piece began with a large shallow dish of brightly shining gold of almost one metre in diameter. Out of the dish arose a thick mist of very tiny many coloured lights. Likened to fire flies, they were thousands in number. The mist of constantly moving lights continually swirled inside the parameters of the dish, forming an irregular but straight column up to a height of at least four metres.

As the small crowd watched, the fog of lights appeared to polarize and become retained inside its own cylindrical shape. The light within dimmed as it coalesced into sections and areas containing shapes matching visually what might have been the whim of each of the viewers. Just a thought would magically form a depiction or a sculpture in the same configuration that was in the mind of the single participating individual for the enjoyment of those others who were gathered there.

The paradox within the piece only shaped creations from the personal visions of beauty and art, displaying them for the other participants or onlookers to view.

Many residents as well as visitors to the planet, stood around the exhibit moulding the towering fog of light, commenting on each others achievements, whilst others just stood admiring their own feats of artistry.

Clysta, who had become captivated with the object, watched as the group ahead each manipulated designs or structures in the mist of light. One of the group made a most inartistic portrait appear, to the delight and laughter of her companions.

Euclid who was never far from Clysta, carefully and quietly moved up closely behind her.

Clysta's own view was now drawn downward as she saw a formation of letters, which were slowly becoming written in the haze at the bottom of the ever shifting, ever changing column.

The letters gyrated through a spiral then finally arranged themselves into the words, 'Clysta. Look to the base'.

"See," she whispered to the other two friends who had come closer, to see what was the commotion. Clysta could now see what it was that was being shown to her. "There on the base under the gold disk. That inscription."

A plaque was secured to the front of the display, which read, The Never Ending Dream. Under the inscription in smaller and almost unseen script a name, 'Mirsha Freedom'.

Kindra studied the plaque for a while. He then looked over his shoulder. He too had been aware of what G'zin had seen regarding those following their group. He touched the arms of his friends and said in a low voice.

"There are two more females, dressed the same as those two who where there earlier. And those two I am sure, are still watching us. And the new two are definitely making tracks in our direction. I vote that we cut this short and leave this place."

Clysta gestured to Euclid to follow as they calmly pushed a way through the crowd around the 'Dream' exhibit. They then made to move in the direction that would be away from the mysterious females. Luckily the crowd had multiplied during the time they had been at the exhibit, and now made it much more difficult for the females to close in.

An opening was ahead of the four visitors leading into the next area in the exhibition, and they passed through it quickly and out of sight of their followers. G'zin spotted a door to the far right and suggested they make for it.

Passing through the door, which immediately sealed behind them, they entered a lighted and downward ramped tunnel. Occasionally, they would try a door from the passage but only to find it was locked. Finally, after following the tunnel for some distance, they found a door unlocked leading into a short passage, then made an exit through a second unlocked door to a garden area outside of the building.

"Either we seem to have a head start or we have lost them," Clysta decided. "Let us get clear of the Hall before they realize we are not inside any more and find those doors."

The three friends and the ever present robot moved quickly but not so fast as to attract much attention. First turning right then to the left at each subsequent corner they made their way in a direction away from the Hall of Discovery.

They finally stopped, a little breathless, at an area far away from the structure and Kindra said, looking back toward the direction of the building they had just left.

"If they were really after us, I should think we have managed to loose them. Now we should get into a car and move far away from here, maybe make for that coast we planned to visit, and then try if we can to sort all of this out."

# Chapter 30

The rest of their day, which was spent away from the city, was uneventful. They visited the coast, making the trip by auto air car. The route took them on a journey along the foothills that led up and into the mountain range. It was the one that they had seen in the distance from their suite.

The ocean was a light green colour inshore that became a much darker shade with distance. In the background near the far off horizon, the colour changed and became a shade of light mauve as it finally met with the distant skyline.

Walking along the long fine sandy beach they were each entertained by the teeming sea creatures, all of them very exotic to these three young off-worlders. They sat for hours watching the serene and unfamiliar ocean and found interest in just laying on the beach watching the clouds they had seen passing across the green sky. In the distance, out and across the ocean, the friends could watch also as the clouds mysteriously rose from the smooth, gentle surface.

The white flat discs that were the 'clouds', formed or condensed at the surface, around three kilometres offshore. They then would hover a while before levitating and then drift lazily, straight upwards until they had reached a level of five or six kilometres, then to be carried inland by the prevailing breezes.

The ocean, they were told by the locals, contained many strange swimming creatures, all of them indigenous to this planet. Some of the types were said to be edible but were now left alone, as the food dispensers supplied all the needs of the planet. Others that were large, and the three friends had noticed some swimming close to shore, were said to be amicable. There were yet many other species far out in those deeper waters, which, as a local vendor had told the friends, had still to be catalogued fully.

Eventually, evening was drawing in and it was time to leave. They made their way back, with a little reluctance on the part of G'zin, into the city and arrived as the daylight was beginning to fade. It had been a long day, as daylight time on Morn lasted fifteen percent longer than a Standard Day. That was the usual day they been accustomed to for years at the Galactic Academy.

G'zin made a suggestion as they approached the avenue on which they were staying. Maybe they should leave the city ground car they were now riding in and walk for the remaining half of a kilometre to the building containing their suite. Her idea was to give them a chance to spot anyone who might have the building entrance watched.

Though they were fatigued both Clysta and Kindra thought it a good idea and agreed. They stopped the car and disembarked with the robot Euclid, and sent it on its way.

Dusk was now forming when they rounded, on foot, the corner of a building opposite theirs. A number of arch features hid their approach and Euclid overtook them and moved quickly half of a stride ahead. The robot then stopped and held the trio back with it's outstretched metal arms.

'Please go no farther. Two humans are across the square,' the robot explained in a low sound.

Kindra saw them first, after Euclid.

"There on the left, in the opening at the front of the stainless steel tower," he whispered. Two silhouettes were visible in the semi-darkness. "I wonder if that could really be someone waiting for us?"

"What do you hear, Euclid?" Clysta asked quietly.

Euclid did not move, its arms still outstretched and protective. The robot said, once again low, 'The two humans are silent and this unit can observe they are looking upwards in the direction of the area of the room you have been occupying.' The robot became silent. It still did not indicate that they should go any further. Its untiring arms were still outstretched. After a few more minutes it then continued.

'The human on the left is now saying. "Wherever are they?-Do you really think they will ever return?-It is getting late. They should surely be not foolish enough to stay out after darkness." That is the last of their conversation.' The robot said, repeating again the conversation it had heard.

Clysta looked in the direction of the two in the shadows, and then asked Euclid.

"Are they Myron 11 and Syrea the two who visited our rooms last evening?"

Euclid was quick in its answer.

'The voice pattern of the human who was speaking does not have the same resonance print as that of any of those same humans which you have referred to, Miss Clysta.'

"Whomever they are and whatever they are doing there," said G'zin, "we had better find another entrance into the building."

"Agreed," said Kindra.

Clysta added. "There must be a rear door we can use. We should backtrack and get around to the left of that park over there," she pointed. "In that way we will be out of sight of anyone at the front of the building. Euclid," she ended, "I leave it to your better sight and hearing to warn us of any others who may be watching."

'This unit thanks you for the trust that you are placing in it,' the robot answered.

"Jeepers," said Kindra, smiling as he made his eyes role backwards in disbelief.

They all set off in the other direction, Euclid once again bringing up the rear. Darkness was closing in fast and the two watchers across the square did not see them leave. When the three friends arrived, no one was watching the rear of the building. There, they entered through a small service entrance.

Within minutes the four were inside the suite.

"I need a spell in the cleaner," said Clysta as Kindra turned the control to make the wall transparent so he could view the scene outside.

"Euclid," she added from the other room as she was disrobing. "Please listen for any movement in the corridor outside this suite?"

The robot seemed to nod with its metal head in acceptance of the command and positioned itself by the door.

"I'll use the cleaner too after you Clys', then we will eat," G'zin said as she joined Kindra at the wall. In the fast approaching darkness they could not make out the two figures that they had assumed as watching for them to return. Or if they were still there, watching. Or seeing.

# Chapter 31

"Your brother has a very inventive talent. This 'Clear Crystalian' as he likes to call it, is his own work," said Myron 11.

Myron 11 and his companion Syrea had both returned to the suite.

The three friends had almost given up hope that these two strangers would visit them again, and especially at this late hour.

Then Euclid had heard their footsteps outside in the corridor. The time was late.

Their entrance had been not unlike the previous one. Those furtive looks up and down the passage and then quickly accessing into the room. Myron 11 had picked up his cloak that he had discarded previously. He had just produced another mysterious device from the pocket inside and now placed it in the centre of the table.

This time the friends had been a little less apprehensive about the visitors. They still had the protection of Euclid, whatever transpired on this entry. Now they all sat around the main table in the centre of the room. Euclid had served some light refreshments, and the discussion had been light. No mention was made about the events of earlier today at the Hall of Discovery

The new device was clear and appeared solid and hard. Disc like in shape, about thirty millimetres in diameter and ten tall. The top was almost flat, raised slightly to the centre and its edges were cut in an elaborate ornamental design. Inside and placed suspended centrally, they could see a flat square filament coloured bronze.

Myron 11 continued as the three friends all inspected the crystal inquisitively.

"Like many devices used here on Morn, it is able to decipher gene patterns, right from the holder's palm. Mirsha, because of the work on the special assignment we told you about, has records of the patterns of many, both on and off the planet and uses it to send messages very secretly. When, and of course if, an exact match is found, the hidden message appears on the filament that you see inside."

"Are you sure it is a brother to Kindra you are talking about?" G'zin joked, her teeth flashing through a wide smile, then to Kindra, "It appears that all you got were the left overs of the grey matter."

Kindra held back a return smile and just grunted his mock disapproval of the pun.

Myron II ignored or perhaps missed the comment and its innuendo. He then said as he turned to Kindra.

"Place the crystal in the centre of the palm of either the left or right hand. As you did when last we were here. I must warn you though; the Crystalian has a safety device. If you are not a match then it will leave a purple stain which also causes an itch lasting for weeks."

They watched as Kindra gently picked up the crystal and placed it in his palm.

"Now push down with a finger in the centre of the top surface. That ensures good contact. A message is visible on the filament inside—," he added in a sinister voice, "If you are the one meant for the message."

After doing as Myron II had said, Kindra then removed his finger and bent his head to look closer at the results. Clysta and G'zin moved in and both tried to get a closer view but all they could see was the filament turning black. Kindra though had had sufficient time to have seen a message in white letters too small for the others to see.

Kindra smiled first, then he began to laugh, the crystal item still held tightly in his now closed hand.

"That's it, my father's pet name. Now, how do I turn it off?" he asked.

"There is no need," Myron 11 replied. "The filament will disappear in two more seconds. Now we can carry on. It appears you are satisfied and therefore we are too. We must leave now and pass along the news.

We suggest that you get some sleep and wait here in your suit. You will be contacted tomorrow, no doubt before mid-morning."

The crystal disc was still sitting on the table, where Kindra had placed it after the message demonstration. He asked as he pointed to it.

"What about this, shouldn't you be taking it with you?"

Syrea was spinning around, clearing the room of the trace elements, using that same instrument as Myron II had on the last visit.

Myron II looked at Kindra saying.

"Mirsha told us to leave it with you. He also said, that before we leave we are to say to you, 'The key is in the Crystalian'. And that you must always remember that."

Before the door opened to let them out, Myron 11 looked in the direction of the three.

"Generally, on this planet, we are a peaceful and lawful people, although, we are a little security conscious. It is just that there are some who are not as they should be. Look out for those, they are very powerful and can do much harm."

"Well Euclid. We are becoming more and more reliant on the extra power of your senses." Clysta had allowed a couple of minutes to pass after the door had closed, "What did you conclude with regard to their truthfulness this time?"

'It was most obvious to this unit,' Euclid started, stopped, turned its head and looked toward Kindra. '—Excuse my dialogue Master Kindra, 'I' am trying to terminate and revise that particular code in my program—that both of the two humans were or believed they were telling the truth.'

"Believed?" Echoed G'zin.

Clysta had also noticed the term. She tried to explain.

"I suppose it is not impossible to be unknowingly preconditioned to react in a way where they tell the only truth they know. That is what Euclid is implying."

"Whatever they were doing, this crystal gave me the answer that convinced me my brother Mirsha is alive and not very far away," said Kindra. "Now let's see if those other watchers are doing anything."

Kindra walked to the transparent wall and looked downward to the area where the two females had last been standing.

"I cannot see them anymore," he said. "The avenue is completely deserted now. It looks like they have given up for the night."

"We've done it again haven't we?" said G'zin lightly, "Here we are, deep into intrigue once more. Tomorrow, you Kindra will receive news of your brother. Then we all can get to know first hand what all of this is about. Then after all of that, we can ask him if he can find for us, one of those 'Neuro Phasing' things. Remember? The thing we came here to get in the first place."

"I sure do hope so," Kindra replied. Then he added, "To both of those items."

Kindra became pensive for a few seconds, after which he announced.

"Anyhow, I am hungry and tired. It is time we quit for this day. I vote-eat and then sleep-what do you two say?"

"I second that," answered both Clysta, and a yawning G'zin.

Euclid, as was usual made no comment.

# Chapter 32

The morning that was the beginning of their third day on the planet was totally miserable. The light green and pleasant sky they had become accustomed to for two days and thought would last forever, had turned into an ugly shade of brown which completely hid the brightness of the sun. Gone too, were the pleasant circular clouds, which had been continually, and dreamily floating in from the distant coast.

In their place the sky was filled with many dark, blue to almost black and boiling, twisting streaks diving through the brown layers above. They were belts of suspended moisture, which in their stream like action would flow, in an undulating pattern, across the sky at a height of about eight hundred metres. Frequently and most unpredictably, each of these streaks would be rent open disgorging thousands and thousands of litres of water, pouring as if from a giant waterfall. This water was then whipped and whirled incessantly by accompanying high winds, which spread it around high above the city and then downward.

The direction of the gale force winds which were pushing the storm came from the distant ocean and carried it far inland, though in the ever present and ominous drenching gloom it was not easy to see more than half way across the city. Even the spaceport with its bright lights was not visible. To add to the appalling conditions the strong and turbulent winds whipped the moisture in every direction as it fell finally onto the city and the ground below.

"I shouldn't think there will be anyone contacting us until this horrible weather subsides," said Kindra. He was watching the deluge as a giant stream of moisture cascaded against the transparent wall.

"Unless they decide to call us on the visi'," G'zin suggested, seeing Kindra's look of melancholy.

"I have no doubt we must rule out any chance of a call on the visi'," he replied. "If this is as secret a conspiracy as we have been led to believe, then anything other than face to face contact is likely to be intercepted. No, I think we will be waiting until this storm is finished."

Once again Kindra continued looking through the transparent wall at the weather outside. Euclid was preparing a late breakfast.

The robot stopped its work and stood at attention and still for a few seconds. It then said in a low voice in the direction of Clysta.

'Miss Clysta! There is once more a human who is standing outside the door to this suite. This time the person is not someone with whom we have previously been in contact.'

Clysta looked up from the study scanner she had been using. Still confused at the way the robot could sense these things.

She said, "Make the door transparent would you Kindra? This may be the contact you are waiting for."

The transparency revealed a male. He looked about, ten or fifteen years older than the others they had met. He was shorter too and stocky, thinning hair with a round unremarkable face, but with very deep black pools for eyes. His clothes were also unremarkable, almost making him a person easily forgotten.

Clysta waited until the man had pushed the door signal, then spoke into the disc.

"Can I help you?"

The man answered in an unremarkable voice, matching closely his persona, speaking toward the still unopened door.

"I have been sent as a courier. May I enter?"

"We are strangers to this world and are unfamiliar with your customs," Clysta replied. "Could we see some identification, and please state what is the purpose of this visit?"

The man outside was seen to look furtively to each side then he said almost in a whisper, "I have news of Mirsha. For his brother Kindra."

"Let him inside," whispered Kindra quickly, eager for the news of his brother. "We have Euclid and there are the three of us."

The door to the corridor hissed open and the man once more looked along the corridor, then crossed the threshold into the suite. The three young occupants had missed completely, the hidden hand signal as he entered from the corridor. The door was now closing behind him.

Euclid stepped from his position at the side of the doorway. From behind, the robot started to quickly search the new visitor.

In the same instant the man, who was much shorter than Euclid, spun on his heel to face the robot. He swung his arm high and pushed a silver pencil like instrument at the robot and made contact with the side of the robot's metal neck.

The visor, which usually glowed in various shades of red, immediately turned green then blue then black. A buzzing sound was heard from somewhere inside the robot's head then all was silent. The robot stopped its search of the newcomer and stood rigid in an instant pose.

"Euclid," screamed Clysta. "What has happ—?" Before she could say more, the man quickly spun and turned to face the trio with the same device he had used on the robot waiving to and fro in their direction with a menacing motion.

"Keep quiet," he said through his clenched teeth in deep growling voice. His face had changed completely showing now an expression of malice and spite, "This is a Zinger and this little tool will do the same to you three at any distance, and with humans the results are very, very painful."

He waived them to the other side of the room away from the still transparent wall.

"Now, we will all be very good and do as we are told," he growled then continued, pointing at G'zin. "You clear the door, and quickly, or I will make your two friends squirm. My companions won't be too long. They are waiting right by the elevator tube."

As G'zin did as the newcomer had ordered, the man looked quickly through the wall to the weather outside.

"I hate that miserable stuff. It is so unpredictable and wet. I always get into a bad mood when the weather is like that. My home planet hardly gets any rain at all and never anything like that mess."

Two figures appeared outside the door and knocked on the outside. The man whispered into the disc and the two outside nodded an answer through the door. The man pushed the control to open the door, the two entered and the door hissed shut behind them. They were immediately recognized as two of the females who had appeared to be following them at the Hall of Discovery.

One of the females held in front of her a device, which had the appearance of a small metering apparatus. A soft hum was heard from its interior as she studied the readout.

"Nothing!" She said in a low voice to her comrade, in part exasperation. "No traces at all, except these three," then with scorn, "And that machine."

Some whisperings and hand signals were carried out between the two additional newcomers and the man, who still pointed the Zinger at the three friends. The two females still had their hoods up and almost covering their faces completely. Then after a furtive glance in the direction of the robot, the taller female pushed her hood back a little as she spoke.

"We apologize for the action of our friend Topo, but he did what he found necessary. Your robot is temporarily discontinued, or in human terms, unconscious. The machine will eventually recover." She looked sideways at Topo, "At least that is what I have been led to believe." She looked back, "In about two hours when the circuits regenerate."

Clysta demanded, "Why are you here and by whose orders do you have the right to do damage to my robot? We are visitors here and wish to be treated with civility."

The other female had completely removed her cloak by now, to reveal a smart regimental uniform type tunic. Her face was framed by the black sleek hair and devoid of makeup. She draped the cloak across her right arm as, in a voice of rank, she spoke in response to the question.

"Since your arrival here on our planet Morn and your visit to the Academy, you have been observed. We have true reason to believe that you have been contacted and possibly before coming to Morn, by members of a prominent group of radicals. These same radicals have been responsible for collusion against the government of Morn."

"This is ridiculous, " said Kindra. "We are here only on vacation. I remember seeing you or two others similarly dressed as you are, at the Hall of Discovery but I had no idea that we were being followed. Anyway, why us?"

The female who was speaking ignored Kindra's comment and continued, "These people, these radicals of whom I speak, though few in number, are a threat to the democracy and future of the planet Morn and must therefore be stopped. We think you are in some way connected with this group and we are directed to take you with us for interrogation."

"That is crazy," said G'zin, bristling and ready to fight, "We only came here to—" Clysta raised a hand to stop her saying more.

"We are citizens of the Galactic Federation," informed Clysta, "And therefore demand to be treated in a like fashion."

"Demand all you like," said the taller female, "When our superiors have been convinced if you are deserving of such, then you will be. Now we must take you with us to the place where they are waiting."

Clysta tried to resist by asking.

"And what about our belongings? And this apartment, it is still registered in our name. We will be returned here. Won't we?"

"That depends on your answers and of course your behavior. Now I seriously suggest. Please do not resist. Topo is an expert in his field."

The female who had done the talking now replaced the cloak about her shoulders and then pulled the hood over her head. She then motioned the other female to open the door to the corridor.

"Tell us one thing. Are we under arrest?" Kindra asked as the man Topo, grinning, waived the Zinger and motioned the three friends to follow the leading female.

His question went unanswered as they reluctantly made their way past the still stationary Euclid and out into the corridor.

'Do something, Euclid. Sub-mode C. Please,' Clysta thought from a peculiarly unconscious impulse, as she passed by and out into the corridor.

The door to their suite slid closed behind them as the three friends were led down the corridor, by the taller female, toward the up-down chute. Topo, who had taken on a totally offensive nature since his transformation, occasionally looking over his shoulder as he followed along at the rear.

After first dialing the destination floor and the number of users, the first female stepped into the empty tube. One by one they each stepped in after her. Momentarily, the suspensors held them stationary whilst calculating the mass being transported, then propelled them downwards to the basement level.

"Where is it that you intend to take us?" G'zin asked.

Just as the last time, their guides did not answer but instead directed them in silence toward a ground car, parked close to the exit from the chute. The female whom was in the lead touched a part of her belt and an opening irised outward large enough for her to enter the car.

This vehicle was of a much larger design than the others they had used or seen since their arrival and was completely enclosed. The interior, which they could now see, was more spacious than the others and its finishes were superior.

The other female entered first. The man, his face changing from a scowl to a menacing smile said, "Why doesn't one of you just try to escape? It has been a week since I made someone squeal with this toy. How about you, young fellah?"

"That will be enough Topo," remarked the female at his side. "Our orders are to deliver them all and in condition for interrogation. Just get them inside and we can get out of here before someone else comes to visit."

Topo shrugged his shoulders at that comment, saying,

"I just wish, I just wish."

The trio was directed to sit side by side with their backs to the direction of travel. Their captors were themselves seated facing them, with the man seated in the middle, the Zinger still pointed menacingly at the three friends. The interior of the car had room enough for ten passengers, very classy furnishings and like all vehicles here it was automatic.

The open side sealed as the leading female dialed a direction co-ordinate into the console positioned at her side. Then they caught the slight feeling of motion as the car slowly and silently made its way out of the basement of the building and onto the avenue above.

It was earlier, at the moment the iris closed and the outside world disappeared from view, that the three captives understood the lack of windows to this vehicle. Then the realization crept up into their minds, of the most inescapable predicament they now found themselves in.

# Chapter 33

Euclid stood motionless inside the room. The robot had received the enigmatic subconscious thought transfer from Clysta.

Clysta had not understood her automatic thought, or where it came from. But it was likened to a pre-prepared unconscious trigger. Similar to the command she had given when they had passed through the tunnel at the Space Station establishment. This trigger though was to be fed into the synapses within the now stunned robot's Nega-Fluid awareness. Almost it was as a stimulus. The stimulus was then to set in motion a series of built in repair codes. Again, these were pre-prepared.

Minutes after the statement from Clysta's lips, some of the internal mechanisms were beginning to operate, though at a very slow rate of regeneration. Almost like being in a large vat of glue. It was unable to move with maximum haste but still able to sense all that was happening around it.

However strong the weapons charge was meant to be, it had not done any permanent damage. Even the stunning effect proposed by Topo and his companions was not as severe as the strangers had suggested. The likelihood of happenings of this type had been anticipated and prepared for during Euclid's earlier adjustments. The atoms of the robot's exterior skin had been calibrated to dampen the effects of any external radiated, electrical or magnetic interference.

Some of the weapon's effects had broken through the defense nonetheless and, as intended, were wreaking havoc within. They were creating a series of altered reaction commands, which interfered with all of the signals sent out by the robots brain. When the brain decided to do something, two commands resulted, one positive and one negative.

Euclid, who was facing away from the door, perceived the three friends being forced to leave the suite, together with their captors. But it was unable to react. The robot was then forced to stand alone for many minutes as the repair sequences were initiated and begin their own work. It's awareness had reached a level where it could begin to compute the possibilities of first counteracting itself, the effects the weapon had had. The robot itself had found a solution, quite unconventional but satisfactory under the present circumstances.

At least ten minutes of valuable time had elapsed by now, since the humans had left the suite, as slowly the signals were passed to its control sequencers. The robot was just about satisfied it could now begin to experiment with its method of overcoming the problems when a signal at the sealed door interrupted the robot's activities.

There was stunned silence, then two more signals, and one after the other. Euclid very sluggishly and with a movement of two steps forward and a half a step backwards, moved in a semi-circular path across the room to the control, which was the operator for the door. The robot pressed carefully at the button to make the door transparent. A reactive and opposite motion made its left leg shoot uncontrollably outward, kicking over a small carved glass table.

Outside and in the corridor there stood what appeared or could have been a man, the cloak was wet and it's hood pulled over the head so to almost cover and hide the face. With him was another, but shorter in height and standing to one side. Again, as twice before, the second person was looking furtively down the now darkened corridor. Euclid could not be really certain of the sexes of either of the two as their heads and body were covered completely and out of sight.

Euclid managed to press the control for speech.

'Whowishestoenter' in a singing dialogue. It was all of which the robot could manage at that moment.

The face of the man outside, of what could be seen, looked in puzzlement toward his companion. Then he turned toward the door again and spoke. He had a voice that was of an educated Galactic and with a possible off world dialect.

"My companion and I wish to speak with Kindra Nymralph. We are good friends to his brother."

Euclid tried speech again. 'Pleaseshowsomethingsignthat—' the robot hesitated, computing the next words. 'youaarrfr—iends.'

The two outside spoke to each other in whispers but Euclid in its present state of discontinuity had difficulty hearing correctly.

Euclid repeated the sentence once more.

The two outside appeared to comprehend what was being said and the man then produced a crystal. It was similar to the one that Kindra had been given the day before. He said.

"Is this the proof you require?"

Euclid tried twice to make contact with the button control then with the third try it had success. The door lost its transparency. Next, as it hissed to the side, the two humans entered swiftly and the door closed behind them.

They both dropped the hoods of their cloaks to reveal their heads. One was a male, one was a female, both different than those others the evening before. They did though bear a close resemblance to those two in their youthful appearance.

Looking quickly around the room, the male returned his attention to Euclid with its metal arms in a most awkward looking posture. It was still stood by the wall and facing the controls. He spoke.

"Robot, you are alone? Where are the others? Where are the three humans?"

Euclid took its time and slow and jerkily turned to face the visitors.

'ThehumansthatIamaccompanying—arenothere—thetheyweretak—enbytwofemales—andonemale—I—I—. Mysystemshave—b-b-eenretarded.'

The male visitor took a few seconds to decipher what it was the robot was trying to say. Then he understood and spoke as he was unclasping the cloak and opening the front. His friend took the signal and pulled open her own cloak.

"Quickly Shara, " as he turned to his companion, "The robot, so far as I can decipher, is trying to say they have been taken. We must get word to the others and quickly. If those people are able to hold on to

Kindra Nymralph, our whole cause will be lost. And all the work will have been for nothing."

He looked at Euclid who was mumbling and fumbling trying to sort out the circuits speedily, but with not much real success.

The female companion moved to the control for the door. As the door began to unseal, the male stopped the other from leaving.

Then, after a pause, the male said quickly to the female, Shara, changing his first decision.

"No. It will be better if you go to the car and try to catch up with them and follow them. I will contact the others myself. We both know where it is that they will be going. It is likely to be the usual place. But be sure they do not spot you."

The young lady was fastening her cloak and putting up the hood, saying.

"Are you sure you will be ok? With that?" She nodded in the direction of the still dysfunctional robot.

"From what Myron II said," he answered, with confidence, "I am sure he will be friendly. Especially when he knows, we too are friends. Now go, before they get too much of a lead on you."

Shara had unsealed the door as they spoke and was shaking her head in puzzlement as she left the suite at a run. As the female left the apartment, the male pressed the control to seal the door again.

When the door had hissed closed, the man, who was now alone, crossed the room to the console and punched in a command for air car service. He ordered a craft to meet him on the roof in five minutes. He muttered to himself some derisive comments about the happenings, after the contact closed.

Now, the young man turned his full attention to the robot. He looked rather quizzically at first, as he circled around the device. Then he decided he should ask the machine questions even though he was not accustomed to this type of product. He was also unsure if the answers would make sense.

He began.

"My name is Fazaal. I am a friend of your recent visitor, Myron II and Syrea. Tell me robot. How long is it since they left here? The new comers and your companions."

Euclid paused for a second then gave an answer.

'Theeffectsofthestun—ning—deviceaffectedmytime—functiobut—but—but—bzzzz—twelvemin—uteseventy—, incorrectthirteen-min-utesfifteen secondswould appearto be the cor-r-r-rect-t-t interval. Buzzzt…—I have now regained normal speech.'

Fazaal moved again to the control console and making the wall clear, looked out over the rain soaked city. He was thinking about the air car as he spoke, mostly to himself, as he was switching off the view.

"We will have to take a chance in this weather, but it is necessary. The worst is yet to come."

Then he turned again to Euclid, not sure if he should explain.

"From what our friend Myron 11 told us, you seem to be a very sophisticated robot. I am told you answer to the title of Euclid. Is that so?"

'Yes,' the robot answered politely. 'May this unit use the title of Fazaal in reference to your good self?'

Fazaal's eyebrow rose in recognition of the eloquence and he said in reply, "Of course, of course and my last name is Ker. Now. Are you able to walk?"

'This unit's traction capabilities are presently most disoriented. By the use of a series of internal computations, mobility is possible, but it will be most erratic.'

With that, Euclid began to experiment and moved a short distance forward then rocked on his rear foot with a backward motion.

'It is most evident that acceleration to the pace will undoubtedly be required, if the necessary forward speed is to be maintained,' explained the robot. It spun around twice and quickly approached one wall. It stopped just in time after knocking over a large stone ornament and gouging the wall with its metal elbow, but finished up facing the exit.

'Please excuse any damage which might be done, it is purely without malice,' Euclid explained.

"We will overcome all that," said Fazaal, stepping smartly to the side as the robot made a to and fro dash for the now open door. "Just don't demolish the building on our way to the roof."

# Chapter 34

The large black sedan was not in any really big hurry.

The car carrying the three captors and their captives traveled smoothly along the stormy and extremely wet avenue. They needed to avoid attracting attention so they maintained the customary speed matching that of the scant traffic, if any that might have been abroad.

Because of the savage intensity of the storm, the amount of other vehicles on the avenues at the time obviously was at a minimum. Only those who really needed to be out in these torrents were. The constant deluges outside of their transport continued to pour water on the streets and buildings in such quantity that visibility was restricted to around only seven or eight metres. The car though, was running on the customary auto control, making the chances of a collision almost impossible. That is, almost and calculably, impossible.

Occasionally, another ground car would pass, travelling in the opposite direction hardly visible through the gloom, their automatics giving each a wide berth.

The taller of the two female captors spoke in a low voice to her two companions. Her hood was now pulled down onto her shoulders revealing her face. She was not unattractive; having a high and intelligent looking forehead, deep-set eyes and distinguished but prominent nose. Her face make up was coloured in the usual lighter pastel shades with deeper colours around and toning with her dark brown eyes. Her hair was now in the upstanding spiked style and very deep shade of red, possibly not her natural colour.

"I hope we are not taking too much of a risk, being out in this storm," she said.

The man Topo replied, in a smile showing his short stubby and cracked teeth, usually most uncommon in these times.

"Risk? Why worry about 'the risk'?" He repeated with scorn. "We have here in our possession what may be the only lever the bosses will ever need to rid themselves of that pest Mirsha Whatsisaralf." He mocked and looked straight at Kindra, "Whatever risk it is that we may be taking! And remember, with this vehicle there is none. It is surely worth the fantastic bonus we are going to get. Don't you two agree?"

"I am only worried about the bolts," said the female in reply. "I don't like them and it is always risky at any time."

The man replied with a growl.

"I don't care about the risk, or the Bolts, or from anything else for that matter. Take risks and live dangerously, I always say. I have taken greater risks than these conditions, many times. Anyways, there have been only two bolt hits this season. Something must be improving. Yes?"

Before Topo could get a response from his companions, Kindra, who had been listening to the conversation, asked a question, with a look of anxiety on his face. He said, hesitatingly.

"What are the bolts?"

He then wondered if he should have asked.

The man Topo scowled in Kindra's direction, as he thought for a moment if he really needed to give an answer. After all, he Kindra was the one who had caused them to be out in this miserable and, mostly to him Topo, intolerable weather.

He decided it would give him some weird, added satisfaction to maybe terrify their captives. He reached across the front of his female companion at his left toward the control and pressed a pad to one side.

In the middle of the wide area between the front and rear seating, there appeared a holo' imagery of the exterior surroundings in a miniature scale. It gave a view of the darkness and gloom engulfing the area around the car for one hundred or more metres with the constant downpour electronically omitted.

"I can see you have never seen this little visual idea before," the man said observing the look on the faces opposite him, "Well just watch. See if you can catch one. If you really must know what a bolt is,—"

At that very instant, a brilliant and vivid light was seen to illuminate the holo' image of the area shown around the car. In the view that was being transmitted, they could see the cause of the light. It showed as a perpendicular slim shaft of white energy coming from high above to connect with the ground to one side of the now instantly and brightly visible avenue of surrounding tall offices mixed in with some low industrial buildings.

The shaft of energy stood, vibrating slightly and slowly, then after two long seconds it disappeared. The three captives expected there to be a peel of thunder to follow, as they knew occurred on other worlds after such similar happenings. It did not, just a deathly silence followed.

The man gave out loud and raucous laughter at the look of shock on the three faces opposite him.

"Now, that my friend is a 'Bolt'! Brought down, especially for you," he said, tears filling his eyes, "And it was a small one at that."

The shorter female was removing the hood that had been covering her head.

She began, trying to ease the discomfort of the captives explained,"The Bolts usually mark the coming end of the storm. That one," she said hooking her thumb in the direction indicating the outside of the vehicle," Is probably the first of a usual total of only five. After the fifth," she added, "and sometimes there might be a sixth, the storm ends. And then it is over and the sky clears completely."

The man though, not to be robbed of his pleasure continued, wiping with the back of his hand at the dampness around his eyes.

"Of course in this area they have set up grounding pads at the road side to attract them and avoid damage to any of the property. Where we are heading for though," he continued, his eyes taking on a sadistic look of glee, "They don't have any grounding pads. So we are back to living dangerously. Eh!" Then he began his raucous and cackling laughter again.

Two or three minutes of silence followed, while the man Topo still watched the captives. Then equally unexpected as the first had been, another bolt this time some distance away from their location, dimly lit the area ahead still being shown on the central holo'.

The taller female broke in on the silence.

"We have picked up a tail," she announced. She bent closer to the holo' image to get a better view. "That last bolt lit it up. About a hundred metres behind us."

"How sure can you be?" asked Topo, taking attention. The smile left his face and he rubbed away the wetness on his cheeks.

"Up to now we are the only travelers on these avenues," was the reply, "What else would anyone be doing out here in a storm? Surely no one is as foolish as we are. We passed the last grounding pad at the turn."

"Ok," The man Topo ordered, "Dial out of auto' and we can give them the slip."

The smaller female did as Topo had suggested and took over the manual controls. The other female interrupted, protesting.

"You know trying to loose them will be useless. If they are following, they must be locked in to our route by now anyway. We must do a detour around the next block and back. That will show if they are really following us," then, to her companion, "I will take the control."

The controls were switched over and the car, now fully on manual control, was steered by the taller female using a hand shaped pressure pad at her side. She handled the vehicle with skill, observing as she did, all around the outside on the holo' scene still being transmitted in the area between the seating.

Their vehicle approached the next intersection at a slowing pace, then suddenly accelerated the car and turned to the right. As the car sped along the side avenue, a sudden flash brought brightness to the outside storm once again.

Topo said, whilst scrutinizing the scene before them.

"There goes another one. That must have been about two Kilometres away, not so close this time. They must be moving off."

"The other vehicle is turning the last corner and they are slowing, but see, they are still with us," said the female at the manual controller.

The vivid flash could be seen reflecting from a shape on the darkened avenue behind them.

Another flash illuminated the surroundings. The storm outside still continued its incessant downpour.

Topo looked grim and said. "It's time to loose them whoever they are. Turn left and speed up, that avenue is long and straight and not many buildings."

The only impression the passengers had of turning was by watching the holo', the vehicle moved with such smoothness. As the car straightened its course following the turn from the intersection, Topo reached across the females lap and slammed his hand on top of hers. He began applying more pressure to the motion controls.

"Let's go," growling his impatience, "Faster. Faster. You are travelling much too slow. You will never loose them at this speed."

The power plant in their car responded immediately and leaped into high speed.

The acceleration quickly pushed the car to a speed, which was close to one hundred and fifty kilometres when, the Bolt hit ground.

A brilliant flash was shown in the holo', so intense its light filled the interior of the vehicle. So bright was the flash it was vivid enough that all of the occupants were partially and momentarily blinded.

The Bolts were known to be of solid, silent energy with an outer texture that could at best be described as rubbery. This Bolt stood as all other Bolts, firmly grounded and attached to the surface and unmovable for up to the average two seconds. It's unpredicted appearance immediately in front of and too close to the car, gave not enough time for the inboard computer to react and take any evasive action.

The speeding car hit the firm and immovable Bolt a glancing blow with the front end, just off centre and bounced off in a sideways direction. Then it began to career, twisting and bucking wildly about the road surface on its anti-grav cushion, still maintaining the high speed it had already attained.

The two female captors instinctively gave out a scream and the male Topo, in silence, braced himself with his hand still unconsciously applying pressure to the vehicle's motion control. All was happening in the fraction of a second whilst the female herself was trying hard to regain command of the surging vehicle.

Clysta and her two friends held on tightly to the edges of their seats, mostly the in fear and the wild anticipation of the obvious.

G'zin could not retain the scream which was now rising upward in her throat, and let it out in a shriek from clenched teeth as they were all buffeted to and fro.

Kindra murmured more to himself than anyone.

"I think we are going to hit something!"

The car, still on manual, now had no control over its route. Almost airborne it quickly left the road surface that held the auto' guidance implants. The car's front facing collision monitors had sent an immediate signal to the interior restraining functions just as the system became fused by the cars absorption of the fierce energy emanating around the Bolt's exterior.

The signal was a warning of an impending collision with a solid object that was ahead—somewhere—and that was all it had time to transmit. The message was instantaneously received by the comp' and incomplete or not the comp' went to work.

The computerized systems reacted to save the occupants from injury at all costs. Clysta, Kindra and G'zin, were seated with their backs to the direction of the car's flight. Only a simple and straightforward enclosure by the automated force field restraints was necessary to safeguard their being.

The case for the captors was a little more of a problem. A minute spark of the energy from the Bolt had fed through to the crystal and atomized some of the protection statutes. The internal security field began to enclose the three who the comp' knew were now facing into an unknown but expected collision. What it, the inboard computer, did not know was that the vehicle had left the danger and was now only skidding drunkenly for a hundred metres or more, across the lawns at the road side.

Within microseconds the enclosing system began to apply an invisible pressure, cancelling the inertia within the bodies of those who were now its main charge. It had though, lost the ability to stop or balance that pressure. As the succeeding milliseconds ticked onward, the two females would receive just more than the balanced treatment due to their lighter structure. But the man Topo, whose short stocky build was now being calculated to require extra restraint pressure, needed just that only in his case at a rate now being vastly over compensated.

The ensuing crushing force on the females' bodies restricted their breathing and caused the two of them to let out a gasp as they passed into unconsciousness quickly but still enclosed. Fortunately, their unconscious state and non-resistance saved them any further pressure by this defective force field.

Topo, however, fought back against the restraint. It was a short fight he was doomed to loose.

He whispered curses to all as he twisted and turned to escape the restriction that was building around him. His useless struggles were to create a reaction that registered to those damaged controls as requiring threefold the usual pressure. With the almost mindlessly increased application of the restraining forces sent out from the damaged comp', a crunching sound was heard from the inside of the man's chest then from his skull then the arms and legs as he vainly tried to fight against the ever tightening enclosure.

A scream of agony was finally forced from the man's throat followed by a silence, as his whole body was crushed and compacted to a much smaller volume by the systems meant only for passenger security.

The careening car eventually slowed its travelling and skidded to a stop in a spray of mud and pink grass, finally becoming stuck amongst a large group of aptly lily-like flowering bushes.

The three friends could only look in horror at what had transpired before their eyes, each unable to move from the still active enclosure of their own rigid but gentle restraints.

"Now what do we do?" Clysta managed to say whilst fighting the feeling of panic and nausea.

Shara had taken a short cut through two stormy and luckily deserted pedestrian only areas. She screeched around the corner of one of the taller buildings and stopped the ground car to look down the avenue before her. Like a black streak, it was only visible for a split second as it passed between the buildings in the distance. She had luckily caught sight of the large black limousine in the flashes from one of the Bolts.

Quickly making a mental calculation, she assessed where she could join the other car farther along its route and then got under way.

To avoid arousing the suspicion of 'Topo's Squad', as it was often referred to, she had hung back a reasonable distance. After turning the car over to auto and dialing in the order to keep pace, Shara spoke into her disk to inform her contact of the kidnappers whereabouts.

She was becoming apprehensive after the second Bolt struck to her right.

"That one was a little too close," she mumbled to herself.

The violent weather was not improving at all up to now. Still following she saw the third flash some distance away.

In anticipation of the chance tactic of their turning and then accelerating out of the next intersection she luckily dialed more speed so not to loose the beam.

Turning the last corner she saw the glare of the Bolt that materialized ahead. She watched in shock, her own holo' of the large black car as it twisted and swerved across the pavement then, almost airborne, it careened skidding across a lawn and hitting two large fern like trees. Finally the vision showed it bounce twice and then come finally to rest amongst the bushes in the front of one of the large and low industrial buildings.

Water still poured downward from the dark sky when Shara heedlessly jumped from her now slowing car almost not allowing it enough time to come to a full stop. She ran through the stormy deluge across the lawn up to the side of the damaged limousine. Blue coloured flashes emanating from the dynamics flowed up and down its exterior skin as she cautiously located and punched the button.

Shara looked inside and first recognized what now was the dead and mangled body of the man Topo. She then saw the two female accomplices, noting they appeared unconscious and then looked toward their captives. A look of relief passed across her face when she could see they appeared unharmed.

"Quickly," she said, to the three, their faces still showing their horror of what had just occurred, "We must leave here. Now. An accident signal is being transmitted automatically. It will be better that the authorities do not find you here."

"What about these three?" Kindra asked, slightly stunned.

"He is dead, the females are unconscious. Here," she handed him a scarf from around her waist, "Clean all surfaces you have touched. Do not miss anything. The authorities need not know of your presence here, and those two are not going to tell, especially about your being here against your will. Now please. This way."

The three friends climbed from the car and into the downpour, as Kindra did as she had asked. Shara speedily waived the device to clear the cars content of traces of their DNA. She turned and motioned to G'zin and Clysta to follow her through the deluge to her smaller car and they squeezed inside. Kindra followed them after he had finished his task. He had spotted the weapon that Topo had named a Zinger and quickly palmed it saying to himself, "Now this may come in handy some day, and he doesn't seem to need it any more."

Once inside the other car and the opening sealed, the moisture that had soaked their clothing was transformed to its basic elements and dried away in seconds. Shara then dialled drive and as the car moved away she spoke into the disc to inform her contact of the accident and its results.

The torrential downpour outside was now finally reducing and the sky was beginning to brighten a little. They were zigging and zagging through the remnants of the storm, travelling along avenues and around industrial buildings so to avoid an easy trace. Their new companion ended her long silence and turned to the trio, saying as she opened the palm of her hand.

"By the way, I know all of your names so I should tell you mine. It is Shara Lexz, and I am pleased to meet you. I should think we are safe from any pursuit, so we can now go to our pre-arranged meeting place."

The storm and the sky had cleared by the time that they finally came to a halt. It was at an area easily recognizable as a parking area for air cars. The trio had no idea just where though. Their own car had stopped alongside a sleek six seat transporter. They recognized it as one of the many air cars that they had seen the day before, when they had gone to visit the coast. The larger vehicle had a top half of glass or some transparent medium, inside of which Clysta could just make out two silhouettes.

Shara answered the questioning glances almost immediately.

"Now we go on by air car. Everybody out please, quickly."

Shara once again waived the neutralizing instrument inside the small car they were leaving. She then dialled a delayed command into the cars guidance to move to another lot some distance from this one. When they were all out, the car then sealed and hurried away and out of sight.

# Chapter 35

"Euclid!" The three all chimed together, their faces taking on instant smiles of gratification.

When the door of the air car had opened, they had seen the robot sitting alongside Fazaal.

'This unit is aware of a great satisfaction to see that you are all safe,' said the robot as it watched the trio and their rescuer enter the air car. 'We appear to have found someone who is of a friendly category.'

Fazaal introduced himself as they all found a seat inside. The door sealed closed and almost immediately the craft became airborne. Fazaal explained as it skimmed over the tops of a number of low buildings.

"It is essential that we maintain complete secrecy as to the routes to our destination. Our adversaries, as you will have grasped by now, have ways of extracting information from their captors. I must ask that you use these to cover your eyes. The robot will have its visor covered also, the same danger exists for Euclid too."

He passed each of them two small discs that were sufficient to obstruct their vision. Turning them over and over, Clysta asked.

"Is this really necessary?"

Fazaal answered to say that it really was necessary even if only to protect the organization set up by Mirsha. Reluctantly, she condescended and started to cover her eyes. G'zin and Kindra followed her example and did the same.

The speed and direction was impossible to guess due mainly to the controlled environment inside the air car. The blindfolded passengers felt it come to land twice and then after ten or fifteen seconds they would lift off again. It was explained this was a ploy to confuse anyone who might be tracking their flight and their eyes should still remain covered for the entire journey.

After about a further fifteen minutes, the air car came to rest and they felt rather than heard as the power plant closed down.

"You may remove the discs now," It was Fazaal's voice again, "We have reached our destination." He then continued, "Now Kindra. You will soon see your brother. Shara. Would you take them from here? I need to relocate this transportation."

The group climbed out from the air car, stepping onto a wide lawn of the now familiar pink grass. It's pilot, the person they now knew as Fazaal stayed on board. The bright sun was shining again through the plasma many miles high above and the sky had returned to its pleasant shade of light green. The time by the position of Sirius was past midday. The now familiar and welcomed white disc shaped clouds once more were drifting inland across the otherwise clear sky. Here, wherever they were, there were no signs of the storm that had been.

They watched as the air car quietly lifted off and swooped low across the surrounding mostly barren and stony area then it disappeared into the distance.

"He will land again in a few other places around the city and then leave it somewhere and be brought back here later," explained Shara. In the far distance, high mountains could be seen. They were strange to the trio and they had no idea what direction relative to the city the mountains could be or were.

Turning, they faced the entrance to a large and beautiful garden. Behind it and quite close there was another range of lower mountains. They appeared from here that these could have been the same range they had seen from the city. It was hard to be sure, being strangers, so neither of the three friends was able to make the connection with certainty.

"Where are we?" Clysta asked.

# Chapter 36

"It has been known for centuries as The Garden. Some of it is real. Some, it has been explained, is converted using the personal brain waves of the visitor viewers," Shara tried to justify.

"To each individual visitor here, these conversions project their own designs and colours. There appear to be slight variations in the output, but the background seems to be set in a basic and simple but regular pattern, which stays throughout the whole of the gardens. That is only the explanation that is given by the archaeologist at any rate. Otherwise the whole area is a deep mystery. I am not sure if anyone really knows the whole truth about it."

They walked on along the pathways leading through the gardens, coming upon enormous varieties of flora and fauna. Euclid still was having trouble with the mobility commands but was able to keep pace easily.

"Who built this place?" Kindra asked.

"No-one seems to know," replied Shara, "This is not the only one. There are two others of them around this particular land mass and there are suggestions they have been here for at least twenty five hundred years. Some historians who developed this theory think they were here long before the Terra Formers started. They tell that it possibly just was not seen when the planet was first surveyed.

"Then there are stories that they developed from a mystery strain generated by the Terra Forming Company. As a kind of experiment that maybe just cost too much to use elsewhere. I myself like the former explanation. It has more of a feel of intrigue. But, who knows, I really don't."

"Well, whoever it was," interrupted G'zin, "They sure made something they could be proud of."

"How is it there are no other people around? A place such as this would surely attract more than just us," Clysta suggested.

"I suppose the locals have lost the desire to come here too often but there are times when it is busy," answered Shara, "Then that solitude also is ideal for our purpose. This is Mirsha's hideaway. It is also the one thing going for that ancient development concept. This garden has a special area. One, which we are going to come up on soon."

They had walked for a distance of around a half of a kilometre. They had come along narrow paths and across small bridges over musically tinkling shining streams and musical pools. There had been all around, indescribable growing things, trees and blooms. Ahead of them they now saw a silvery mist rising vertically from the pink grass at the edge of an area the shape of a 'T'. It was at the end of a meandering pathway, along which Shara had led them.

The strange apparition was maybe three metres square and appeared to rise and swirl then disperse into nothingness at the top edge. G'zin, always ready to explore, walked to the edge and stepped behind to look at the rear.

"What—?" A sound of surprise was in her voice. "I can see you, all of you, clearly. Can you not see me?"

Clysta and Kindra followed her to see what G'zin had found that was so surprising.

From behind, the mist was not visible and the view was clear. The substance, whatever it was made of, was hard and warm to the touch, even from the transparent side. They too were puzzled and like G'zin, tested the view, bobbing from front to rear. Finally they gave up, puzzled and convinced. This was some phenomenon that they should try to work on later.

"I don't understand it either," said a smiling Shara as they all returned to face the still flowing, swirling mist, "Now, do you still have the crystal? You know, the one given to you by Myron II?"

Kindra dug into the concealed pocket in his suit, pulling out the item and quickly checking to see if the message had somehow regained its visibility. It had not.

"We must move quickly through the mist after the next action. The effect lasts only ten seconds," Shara instructed them, "Now Kindra. Over to your right. There, about one metre from the mist edge. See that flat disc in the paving tiles. Set the crystal in the middle of it."

Kindra cautiously followed the instructions. He looked to Shara awaiting something to happen or her next words.

She said, "Now press the centre and then follow me through the mist quickly. Bring the crystal. Don't leave it behind."

"But it is solid," said Kindra, "I felt it."

"The crystal is the key," answered Shara, "It will be ok."

"I have heard that before somewhere," said G'zin with a little touch of sarcasm.

Kindra did as he was instructed, pressing the centre of the crystal but the mist was unchanged. It still appeared to be the same, roiling and rising to the top of its expanse.

Shara stepped up and put a hand out ahead of her. The trio could not believe what they saw as her arm disappeared up to the elbow whilst she looked back smiling at the look of disbelief on their faces.

"Come," she said, "Before the effect dissipates. We have only six or seven seconds now." Then her body passed into the mist leaving her other arm with a hand waiving them through.

The three friends looked at each other. Clysta spoke first.

"Let's go! You too Euclid! Max' ten seconds she said."

They each stepped forward with the robot a half a stride behind. A tingling rush was felt through each of their bodies as they entered this unique medium, then there was a momentary feeling of oblivion.

"Wow!" G'zin said as they all passed through, "What a sensual feeling. Now I like that, I must do it again. Often," she added smiling widely and turning to watch Euclid step last from the mist. This time it could be seen from the reverse side. Only in this new place the mist filled all of the opening or whatever they had passed through.

Clysta listened to the others relate the momentary feeling of static and expansion as they passed through this strange formation. She though, found it hard to keep her feelings to herself, but she knew she should. If it was only to avoid any non-understandable descriptions of what she had witnessed. Clysta had a distinct memory of having been to some place else and not a direct passage into this new location. What she had seen or done there was a mental mystery to her now, but she still retained the memory of being there.

Clysta looked around at the place they had all entered. The gardens had vanished completely. She had no idea where they were now. It was inside an almost cave like area, a tunnel maybe. Brightly illuminated, with a shiny black floor, perfectly flat and smooth. The walls appeared hewn from rock and sloped slightly inward at first then curved to form the ceiling. So fine had been the carving that it was almost smooth.

Shara stood ahead of them by two paces, facing a male who looked a little older than the visitors. He was slightly smaller than Clysta, possibly stocky build but that was hidden by a flowing and brightly coloured overgarment. He was smiling radiantly as he stepped forward.

"My brother, Kindra," The male said as he was striding and passing around Shara, spreading his arms wide. He walked up to a startled Kindra, and then held him in a hugging embrace. Then he let go to stand back and look him over.

"Mirsha." Kindra said in reply. "It really is you. But you have changed. Maybe a little more handsome than you were," smiling and looking the other young man over, "It is so good to see you though. And safe. Come, meet my very good friends."

He began to introduce them.

"This is Clysta Z'ee," They both shook hands.

Kindra continued, "This is G'zin DeVenouire."

She flashed her smile with the sparkling teeth. Kindra added, "Watch out for her. She has a smile that can break hearts."

G'zin started to blush and her eyes began to shine as their hands connected. But this time it was only slightly.

Kindra then indicated Euclid.

"And this is Clysta's robot, our very friendly Euclid."

Mirsha looked at Euclid not able to balance a response to the introduction.

Clysta interrupted, "It is a long story but he belonged to my father. He has been with us since we left the Academy. He sort of attends to our good health."

Kindra once again took up the conversation, feeling he should explain, "He was sent by her father to accompany Clysta on her travels. And I for one find him very puzzling at times. But he really is our friend, robot or not. Now, what about you."

"I am very pleased to meet you all, but first," said Mirsha. He raised an arm through the folds of his garment and indicated an opening at the opposite side of the area, "Please, you must come this way. Through here," he directed them toward an arch, "This entrance area is a little austere. You will find that beyond that arch, it is much more comfortable."

# Chapter 37

"So what is all this about, big brother?" Kindra asked eagerly, "Why all the secrecy and talk of a conspiracy? Can the planet authorities not handle it?"

"I will not try to answer your questions right away," Mirsha said as they walked on.

"You have met Topo I hear. And thankfully for the last time," he added with a smirk, "I have been told what happened to you and of the outcome of your capture. He will not be missed by us that is for sure, or anyone except those people he did his dirty work for. But for now, we must go onto better things.

"First we must show you to your quarters and make you comfortable. You will be staying here with me for the remainder of your visit to the planet. It will be much easier and of course, safer. Then when you have freshened up and are ready to, we will eat dinner. After which I will try to answer as many of your questions as I am able."

Clysta was just about to ask a question when Mirsha in anticipation interrupted with, almost in answer.

"Oh, I almost forgot to mention. We have arranged for all of your belongings from the suite to be brought here. Does that answer the question that was on your lips, Clysta?"

Clysta looked puzzled, then decided to respond simply saying, "Aaah! Yes."

They were shown to their new accommodation, which were rooms with exquisite furnishings, immediately taking advantage of the body cleaners and a change of clothing. After an hour or more they emerged sparkling and refreshed, feeling better than they had all of that day.

They were guided into a room that was obviously meant for dining. The room itself was circular with a dome shaped ceiling. The illumination was from an unseen source, not much unlike the type the visitors had been accustomed to but still, not quite the same. The walls were covered with tapestries and the floor was covered with deep pile carpeting. All the furnishings were of natural wood, an item quite unusual for these times and hardly ever seen.

Everyone became seated and, as they began dinner, Kindra said, "Ok Mirsha. Now, please tell us just what all of this espionage story means and whatever it is that is really going on."

Mirsha began.

"Very well, I understand that my friends have already told you most of the reasons. I will attempt to fill in some of the gaps. You will probably have a hard time understanding why or how this has been allowed to continue, but you must remember, this is not the Solar System. We, as each of the occupied planets are, are independent and like them have run our own courses of advancement for many hundreds of years. So long as the population is not thrown into a state of war or conflict, the Central Galactic Government will not intervene. So now my story."

As the auto-servers went about the business of distributing the food, Mirsha explained, as he had promised. He began to relate his story.

The whole matter had come to his attention when he was the top student in the Academy's Physics Campus. His work and studies had progressed very favourably and his results for each year up to then were indicating that he had become an exceptional student. He had a firm grasp on the concepts put to him and was advancing into territory not normal for a student.

Mirsha went on to tell of two professors who were involved in experimenting with a device which could isolate brain wave patterns from animals in their experiments and some time later, they moved to those wave patterns of humans. Mirsha and subsequently two other students from the same study class, were recruited to work on these experiments on their off-study periods. The other two had greater than average minds, but Mirsha being a little ahead became the project leader.

But all three had all shown a special leaning in there own categories in a variety of classes leading up to this work.

"Somehow," Mirsha continued his dialogue, "These professors had been rummaging in a collection of very old documents in the Morn archives and stumbled onto a record of pursuits into a series of experiments. These experiments, it was said, had been carried on with only partially conclusive results about three hundred years ago. These previous dealings had been discovered during archaeological diggings in two of the gardens like the one you passed through into here. This was the basis for the work of which we three had been selected.

All three of us were quite enthusiastic to be a part of these findings and we gave it our fullest energies. The others and I were coming close to completing a device, which we knew would work, when Suma, he was one of the other students, stumbled onto some frightening but conclusive information. It was this. Someone, who was outside the Academy circle, had coerced our once innocent professors, one by one, into developing a scheme. It was their, the professors, intention to hand over the findings to these others who could put the final device to use on a colossal scale."

Clysta interrupted, "This is the mind control Myron II told us about." Mirsha nodded. Clysta continued, "How did they intend to get away with that type of thing? There are Galactic Laws against tampering with peoples liberties, aren't there?"

"That is true," answered Mirsha, "but as I indicated before, handling of a planet's problems first is to be dealt with by the people of that planet."

He then carried on, "We were not sure at the first. We were so taken up by the chance of working on the very thing which had eluded countless other scientists of the past. Jhel and I ignored the facts of Suma's suspicions for a while. Later though, we found other implications and were becoming suspicious that the whole exercise was really being funded secretly by someone outside of the Academy. Our friend Suma again overheard something and one day confronted one of the professors with his suspicions. Two days later he was missing from our regular class, then he did not turn in at the lab' detail after the day was over. We haven't seen or heard from him since."

"What do you expect happened to him?" Kindra asked, almost suspecting what the answer would be.

"I never did find out. The real truth that is," Mirsha replied, "It was implied that he had left for home, off world. On a personal emergency, it was said. All I knew was that we were, all three of us, so close in our every day lives, he would have surely told us of any intentions to leave. He never did."

"So all of this is the reason you quit Physics?" Kindra suggested, "Why did you not explain it all to father? He maybe could have been some help."

"You know how father would have treated a thing like this," Mirsha replied. "His favourite Academy in some kind of subterfuge. Unbelievable. He would need absolute proof and I was in no position to give it, nor the mood to. After our last meeting that is. Besides, there is another side to the story. I began to like Art. I enjoyed the freedom it gave me. I was becoming good at it. And then there was all of this." He spread his arms indicating the place they were sitting.

It was G'zin who interrupted this time.

"And all this is from your Art?"

"Some of it is," he replied, touching the side of his nose with his forefinger, "Some I will tell you at another time. Jhel and I decided our suspicions had been correct. We knew we were close to an enormous and final breakthrough. Our consciences were giving us trouble. We needed to put a stop to the whole thing. Meanwhile, I put up a charade that I had become disenchanted with Physics. I changed my image, wore some outrageous apparel and took up artistry full time."

Clysta said, "That artwork at the Dome of Discovery. The Never Ending Dream, it has a name on it. Is it one of your pieces?"

"Yes Clysta, it is," he replied, then explaining, "Before we got out of the scheme, I had the solution to an important section in the 'Mind Machine's' development. That is the name we gave to the experiment we were working on at the Academy. I secretively brought most of the system and the important parts with me when I quit. I experimented with one of them for some time on my own and have been able to develop it further. I have put some of its abilities to work. The Never Ending Dream is a piece that uses it, to enable that particular item to function.

"I also took the liberty of removing a few of the most important notes and crystals from the records at the lab' to slow down any others who might be recruited to follow in our footsteps. These people dare not come out into the open and accuse or remove me, or friend Jhel, for fear of the consequences. That 'Dream' item did bring me a little added fame as an artist and it was all down hill from then. I now have customers off the planet and even an enquiry from Old Earth. Would you believe?"

"And those two professors and their work," G'zin asked, "What about them and their backers?"

Fazaal, who had arrived just as they had finished dinner, had joined them at the table. He answered G'zin's question.

"On the whole, Mirsha really did a job of sabotaging their scheme. They still try to build a group that is equal to Mirsha, Suma and Jhel. We continue to stall them by various means, mostly unknown to the students the Professors select. Sometimes we hold them up by getting them involved in some other activity.

"Occasionally we take them to a party instead of having them get to the lab'. Things like that. Just mess them up, continuously. I can say at present they are having very little success."

The three friends all smiled, each imagining the frustration created by Fazaal's methods. Mirsha arose from his seat at the head of the table and suggested they now all retire to his sitting room, forget all about the troubles of the mind control, and the three visitors could now tell of their own experiences at the Academy Galactica.

The morning after, the trio awoke to the aroma of breakfast being prepared by Euclid. Clysta arose refreshed having slept well and after the cleaner walked into the kitchen to find G'zin already up and assisting the robot.

Shara and Fazaal had left the night previous to start early in the morning checking on a new recruit in the lab'. That left only the three friends and Mirsha, and of course Euclid in this strangest of locations.

Over breakfast they had covered all of the small talk and finally exhausted every simple topic there was. Finally G'zin reminded Mirsha about his answer of the night before, that he had avoided, about this place they were in.

He turned to Kindra and asked.

"Can you and your friends keep a lifetime secret?"

The silence that followed lasted only for less than a second then Kindra answered truly.

"If the secret is to be ours alone, then I can guarantee it will be kept."

Mirsha would never understand why, but the statement from Kindra carried deep down into his unconscious and he received an overwhelming feeling of immediate trust about the other two. It erased any doubt about confiding in his brother or his two friends. Even including the robot.

"The truth is, I was not at all involved in the building of this place we are in and I have really not the slightest idea who if anyone, did." Mirsha said. Then, "Those gardens that you passed through on the outside must have been here for hundreds of years and possibly more. No-one alive actually knows who made them and these days luckily for me at least, not many who are alive really care."

He continued, "It is most peculiar, but people who come to visit those gardens on the outside, usually arrive filled with interest and begin to roam around and explore. But as their stay draws on, they begin most strangely to loose their original inquisitiveness. Then later, they just leave, conceivably fulfilled and having forgotten about their original impulse to investigate."

Kindra interrupted, "Shara referred to something in relation to that yesterday, about the locals losing interest. What about this," Kindra motioned, "—place—these caverns we are in now? You say you did not make them?"

Mirsha continued, "No," he said in derision and shaking his head from side to side, "That part is an even stranger story. Let me tell you that one. And don't have any misgivings. Although it is hard for me even to believe it sometimes, it is quite true."

Mirsha sat back in his lush, form fitting easy chair.

"A few years ago while I was into one of the extra studies on Physics, it was the Science of Mineralogy studies. I thought perhaps I might find something of value in these gardens. I had had a couple of trips before just to see them, since moving here to attend the Academy of Morn. Maybe I would even develop a thesis, I thought at the time. As no-one else was on record as having ever done it.

"There are two other gardens like those outside you know, and there may be more elsewhere on the planet, not yet discovered -," Kindra interrupted him, saying that Shara had also made reference to that too.

Mirsha once more took up his narrative, "So I set up a series of tests. The customary things, you know, like father would. Make tests on the chemistry of the plants, the soils, and the sub strata. Then I did some tests on the strata around the three of them. Two that are at the farthest edge of this continental land mass and this one we are in now. This was the last of which I worked on.

"I had found nothing of any proper consequence in any of the other two and was getting nowhere here either. Baffled is a good term for the way my results were coming out. I finally decided to give in, pull in my probes. I was getting really nowhere, except many dead ends. I had thought up another idea. I would move into another area of exploration that needed searching out from some previous notes that I had started with. It was to be in the mountains north of here. During that night, I was camping just outside the gardens, when, in the night whilst I slept, I had a most peculiar dream.

"I could not recall too much of that dream on the morning after. All I knew was that I needed to go back and remember something. What I did remember from that dream guided me the day after to a particular spot in those gardens that are just outside."

G'zin turned her head to look at Clysta and remark about her recent phase of dreams, but she was stopped by its almost immediate erasure from her consciousness. Mirsha continued, not following the movement.

"I found the spot exactly as I had dreamed of it. I had never been to that particular location before in my previous research. There was nothing to see that was obvious, so I started to scratch away at an area of soft soil. And it is there where I dug up the trigger. The first crystal. That is what I called the device, which let me inside this place. It was one of those crystals, like the one that I sent to you Kindra. Since that time, I have given it the name Crystalian, it is more artistic a name. And it keeps it intriguing. Anyhow, the find was just a few millimetres below the surface. How it had been missed, by earlier archaeologists and geologists baffles me?

"The whole thing I found by degrees was in that dream. When I had located the trigger, the transporter mist came to mind-that is what I have come to call it-and then I remembered that cave," he pointed in the direction of the entrance cavern, " All in my dream."

"That appears to be the only entrance as far as I know. The rest, I found when I got inside. Oh, these areas, where I live, they were all empty when I first found my way in. All of this, the furnishings and my own equipment, I put those in myself. As I said, I have earned many credits on art pieces. There are other areas beyond this, stranger still. I will show them to you later."

"But where exactly are we?" Clysta asked, interrupting, "Are we below ground? On the outside, in and around the gardens, there was no indication of any ground high enough to hold these caverns."

"That," Mirsha answered, "Is another strange thing. I just do not know. We could be anywhere and I mean, just about anywhere. I have tried many ways to work out exactly where this place is but up to now I have had no success at all. I even tried one time with a beacon but either the signal will not pass through the surrounding rock or where we are now is too far away from the gardens. It really is a puzzle.

"I didn't know exactly what to do about my findings and the access trigger so I decided to keep it all a secret and have only my most trusted friends in on some of it. I was the only one with a real key crystal up until now and now you have the one I sent to you."

Kindra interrupted, touching the pocket where he had the crystal.

"But Fazaal and the others? Do they have one each?"

"Theirs are similar but built by yours truly, with a slight difference. There were two types of key systems. The ones they carry are only a rather sophisticated signaling device and do not work as the original one did. When I earlier found my way in here, I did a little reconnoitre. I could say that I was a little afraid. The place was mysterious to say the least. There is a small area, like an anteroom at the side of the main tunnel. It has a shelf carved into the wall. There were six more triggers inside there on the shelf, when I first entered these caverns. And try as I may, each time I think of handing one of those out to another person, a terrible feeling of dread comes over me. It is as likened to a reminder of some kind of trust put onto me personally, to maintain the secrets of this complex."

The breakfast was by now all but over and Euclid was busily clearing the table. Mirsha watched momentarily and somewhat absently as the robot moved to and fro, then he suggested he show them the workshop at the rear of the refuge. As they left the table and followed him out of the dining room, G'zin asked.

"Have you found out yet who did build it all?"

"That is still another different puzzle," Mirsha replied, "There is not a sign of any kind indicating who or what might have done it. I even scoured the archives of the Terran history of the planet but I was unable to find a thing which was on record of anything like the work that this place must have involved."

As he spoke, Mirsha guided the three friends, with the robot following behind, along a wide passage. It curved downwards to the right and was brightly illuminated as all of the other areas inside. Off the left side of the passage were rooms of various sizes and heights, all with walls as smooth as glass and each room radiating in a light of a different but pleasant colour.

The first three of the rooms were full of materials, which appeared to be parts and equipment of Mirsha's work in art. Large areas of fabric canvas, metal canvasses, huge workings in metal and glasslike substances. All of Art work in progress.

A puzzled look was on the faces of the three friends. Mirsha answered their question.

"I use these first few rooms as my studios. These three had a soft white light radiating, so it was more suitable for a workshop. You see I really need for nothing. As I said earlier, I have sold quite a few pieces of my work, which has made me quite wealthy and I can pick up materials as and when I need them."

"Are the other rooms empty?" G'zin asked.

"I have used six of them for my own purposes. I have one room that has a red lighting. That I use for my savage art, the red gives me an amount of passion," he answered smiling, "But there are more. Lots more." He pointed to the apparent end of the curving passage, "That wall ahead is not real, just one more enigma about this place. It is some kind of illusion, like a screen and behind it there is a passage, just like this one we are in now, and more rooms. All of them are empty too. This passage carries on and on, curving right with the rooms always to the left."

Clysta asked.

"Just how far does it go? The passage behind I mean."

"I have tried on a few occasions to reach its end," Mirsha answered, "But on each time I have failed. I just somehow loose interest because the passage, it never stops going on."

The rooms had no doors that were visible and Kindra had entered the larger of the first three to look around. The room illuminated instantly. All around him were items of art in varying stages. Some were paintings, some mechanical, others of them that were hard for him or the others to characterize.

The group approached the last room before the barrier.

"This room is where I work on mostly optical and illusionary pieces, similar to 'The Dream'," explained Mirsha. "I am trying a new theme for that client I mentioned from Earth. It involves some mind and senses transmittal ideas that I think I can put to good use."

The light here was dark green, but visibility was not impaired by the lack of reflective light. The others along with Euclid had entered as he spoke, each examining the room's contents as Mirsha, changing the topic, asked.

"Anyhow, little brother Kindra. That is enough of my story. I can appreciate you have missed your big brother," he smiled at his attempt at sarcasm. "Now I think it is time. I don't imagine for one minute that you came to here just to find me. You can now tell me the real reason for your visit to the world of Morn."

The trio had continued to avoid discussing with anyone what their real quest was and at this question they looked at each other, unsure who should be the one to explain and if the real reason should be given.

As Clysta, who was always recognized as leader, was about to speak, Euclid turned to face a secured sparkling crystalline cabinet. Inside and in the centre behind the shimmer of a security field, was a small gold sphere with many hair thin wire attachments radiating from its surface.

The robot began to speak, just in the instant that Clysta opened her lips.

'If you will excuse the interruption by this unit, Miss Clysta, and also into your conversation Mirsha Nymralph——.'

The robot raised its right arm from its side and pointed. They all followed the direction indicated by the robot's metal index finger.

'——That,' said the robot softly in his metallic voice. This being the first it had spoken in almost an hour.

'There is the item we require, Miss Clysta!'

# Chapter 38

It surprised both Clysta and G'zin that Kindra did not find it necessary to tell his brother Mirsha, the whole and true story.

In some way, and it was not at all evident to them how he thought it up at such short notice, Kindra explained to Mirsha why they needed that particular item.

"We were on our next to last Jump out around Betelgeuse and must have been a little too close. You may know the rules about giants, we certainly do. You just don't get too close. Well, I still cannot say why, but our Neuro-Phasing injector became unpredictable after our pass-by. Euclid here is our service robot amongst other duties. It was Euclid who found the problem and informed us we required a replacement and must find one quickly, before ours finally collapsed. Luckily we were able to hop in and out of Hyper, a little erratically I must say, until we made it close enough to this system. And that is how we eventually arrived here on Morn. I knew you were here somewhere. The progression since that, you already know."

"Well Brother," said Mirsha, with a smile, "I can't say I believe it all but I will accept it as true. That," he indicated the part inside the cabinet, "is one of the many components and parts which I have accumulated during these few years in the Art profession. There are many items that have double use and that is one that has some amazing side developments. I use stuff like that unit in my illusionary and mind wave items."

Clysta was not the only one confused that the explanation had been so easily accepted. She herself though was of course happy it had and did not require any awkward maneuvers to avoid exposing the Thought Cube back on their ship. And she needed to most of all, keep it a secret that their own ship did not have a need for this old style component. That would have created a very delicate lie.

"Can we borrow it?" Clysta asked quickly, so not to loose these unusual responses. "We will replace it or even return it later. Euclid can put this one to use to make our system work. We can then return to Europa. We will need to return to the shipyard at Europa," she added to the untruth, "to get our own ship's systems properly checked and serviced there first. Then we will -"

Mirsha stopped her in mid sentence with a raised hand. He did not even question where Clysta's explanation would be ending. He said, turning and looking straight at Kindra.

"I don't have any use for it at the present time anyway, little brother and if you need it, for whatever other purpose, you are welcome to take it."

"Now that problem is out of the way," Mirsha continued, "We must plan a course to get you all safely off the planet. You are still in extreme danger on the outside you know."

Kindra started to object but as Mirsha touched his arm he stopped himself. Mirsha explained.

"Please," he said, "I myself am continually sought after by those people who want to retrieve that which I have taken from them. We have been most lucky so far. When ever I travel, I disguise myself," he noticed the looks of surprise cross the faces before him. Again he looked to Kindra, "Yes, disguise. You know. We used to do it regularly when we were both of us very young. Dressing up and taking on different personalities. Well, I haven't lost my original flair for it. In fact I have become quite good at it. Anyway, if you and your friends are to remain here on Morn, you cannot go outside of here in absolute safety and if you should ever fall into their hands again." He added with concern, "They will not cease, you know. Even though they have lost their brute. And the next time we may not be so fortunate. If you or your friends were taken, I would have to capitulate and that will lead to serious circumstances. For us all."

It was in the evening of the second day later that the Skimmer lifted off from the Space Port at Morn City.

Dressed in one of his many necessary disguises, Mirsha had accompanied the trio and Euclid to the departure area.

The 'Freedom' group, as they were called in their ranks, had a contact in the management of the spaceport. It was with her assistance they together had planned a way of reaching their craft without being seen or even passing through any of the normal and rigorous formalities. Two 'special' guards, who were also supposed to be keeping their Skimmer under very close observation for the adversaries, had their attention diverted.

The five of them were now finally at the entrance to one of the underground link tubes that would converge with the one leading to the Skimmer. They were saying their final farewells.

"Do you want me to tell our father about all of this?" Kindra asked his brother.

"It would be better if it came from me," he answered, "One day these matters will be over and then I will go to him and tell all of it myself. Agreed?"

"Can I return to help? I really do want to Mirsha."

Mirsha became quiet as he thought, to be sure not to upset his only brother.

"When you have finished doing the things you have set out to do, then return and, if these villains are still here, we will stop these people together."

Ten minutes later, darkness was drawing in fast. The trio stood in the control room of the now levitating and speeding ship, looking at the view screen as the lights of the city below them were becoming smaller.

Clysta looked toward Kindra, saying, "I must thank you for not saying to your brother anything about the Thought Cube."

"It just never entered my head to tell him." Kindra said his face blank, "I wonder why? Anyhow I still have that crystal key. That will give me an excuse to return and explain. Well maybe later will be soon enough, if we ever reach that place. Apart from my Brother being there, the place does give me the creeps. For now though, let's get away from here and out into the wide-open Galaxy. Why. I am beginning to feel at home already."

Then he looked over his shoulder at the robot standing at attention awaiting the next command.

Kindra said with a smile, as he changed the topic.

"I sure hope we do have the correct part for you now, Euclid."

G'zin, who had been watching the planet as it fell away below them said nothing but, from the corner of her eye, she was sure that she saw something. It was very similar to the appearance of a smile crossing the robot's rigid metal face.

# Chapter 39

The Skimmer began to accelerate now it was far away and clear of the spaceport. No other craft were showing up anywhere around them on the view screen. It was as usual, just a regularly quiet night over this particular continent. Mirsha had reminded them before he finally parted, of the requirements of lift off clearance. It was a caution to keep their speed in the atmosphere at one that was less than the speed of sound until they were up beyond two kilometres above the planet surface. They had had it explained. It was with regard to something about the sanctity for the indigenous underwater creatures occupying the planets vast oceans.

At two kilometres, Kindra increased the signal to the grav-shield causing the ship to then escalate its rate of ascent. Within minutes they had entered the plasma layer above and around the planet. An eerie green glow was reflected from the ships exterior lights that Kindra had switched on before their entry into the peculiar medium. The ever romantic G'zin commented.

"It is just likened to the effect of the viewing a diver would have when diving upward into the bottom of a lake."

Clysta and Kindra looked first at each other and then toward G'zin. They were both of them puzzled.

After their exit had thrust the craft into clear space, Kindra set up and engaged the Ether Drive and the ship leaped away from the planet Morn. He again piloted the Skimmer skillfully through the cone of debris that was the remains of what had been that forming satellite of the planet ever so long ago.

Breaking the silence that had been up until now almost tomb-like, since G'zin's dissertation, Kindra announced.

"We are almost clear," Then, "I am about to increase thrust now. We ought to be at half light speed in four hours. Anyone like to suggest where we should go to try out Euclid and the Neuro-Phasing thing?"

"Perhaps we should find a spot at least two light years distance away, and well clear of the effects of Sirius," answered Clysta.

"Hold it a while Kindra," interrupted G'zin. "We are not yet clear of this lot yet. I can still see a few large asteroids ahead at one degree left and three degrees vertical. I show them as being about the size of Martian Melons."

Clysta immediately zeroed in on the closest boulder of the two and using the narrow beam deflector deftly worked to push the boulder to the side.

"Just a nudge will be enough on the second rock," G'zin confirmed, "All ahead is clear now." She said decisively, but still continued to watch as Clysta took care of the second obstruction.

G'zin then said, changing the mood.

"When we are clear of this piece of space, maybe we could set up the Hyper-et-visi' and find out if we have missed out on any news of your father's expedition. They may have had some success by now with the missing transmissions. What do you say, Clys'?"

"Good idea G'zin," agreed Kindra still at the controls and plotting the acceleration codes, "In all of the excitement, I had forgotten our other lives. What do you say Clys'?"

"I agree, very much," Clysta added. Then, "Although, I feel more and more we may have very little news on the expedition. I have kept quiet all of this time but those dreams; they are becoming more frequent now, not just on different nights. And my last dream was even clearer than any of the earlier ones. The night before last, it was only for an instant, but there was an image that was of a shore of a sea, one similar to the sea that was in the Thought Cube. I am so sure that all of it is some kind of omen."

Kindra offered an explanation, "Do you still not think your

subconscious is doing this? You know, bringing up thoughts of the last contact you had with your father again?"

"Maybe," Clysta said doubtfully, "But each time now, when these dreams or visions occur they are so real, and not at all like they first started out. And I feel so odd when I awake afterwards. Silly, but I feel like I have lived through it. Not really slept through them, you know."

"Anyhow," interrupted G'zin, trying again to dispel this serious mood they were falling into, "It will do all of us a great of good to have some contact with the Solar System and become up to date with events. There is also the likelihood there will be a few transmits from home for the two of us." Meaning herself and Kindra.

"You're right G'zin, I am inclined to forget you two have your own families" Clysta agreed apologetically. She too, realizing it was better to think of brighter things, "Ok Kindra, set the course to a suitable spot to set up for Hyper-Visi'."

The Hyper-Visi was the name given to a system that had been perfected less than a century ago. It operated on a method of the transmission of certain wavelengths via a Hyper Bubble.

The best of students could spend many, many years trying to comprehend the mathematics of Hyper Space first perceived by the Maastersym family. There were several who had grown old in the effort of trying.

It had been fitting that some had survived the tremendous mental gymnastics required to grasp even the beginning of the system.

The entire history of modern space exploration had owed its existence to the few who overcame and finally developed what had become the Science of Hyper Space.

One of these few, in his later years, had been studying the effects of a number of deviant bar waves in a developed Hyper Space void. He, George Benner, finally came to a conclusion that the hereafter called 'Benner Wave', could be contained inside a 'Bubble'. This particular wave had been found to have its uses in storing computations such as those that a disc or crystal would. The wave's performance was similar to the old-fashioned radio wave but that its information could be, in simple terms, held in a frozen stasis and last indefinitely when it was suspended in a vacuum.

This capacity made it ideal for the transportation of voice or visi' information, from point to point, through the correct generative transmitter and receiver.

If a Hyper Bubble was generated to surround the vacuum containing the Benner Wave together with its recorded information. Then the whole idiom could be sent and received anywhere more or less Hyper instantly. It would enable transmissions to move infinitesimally faster than at the ancient restrictive pace of light speed.

To receive a Bubble transmit though, it was essential for a vessel in space to come to rest and remain in that same position until the transmissions in both directions had been completed.

An additional factor was to be in an area of space as close as possible to being exactly between stars in all directions. This was in order to cancel or balance the gravitation of each star.

"This should be right," informed Kindra. They had come to rest at a selected location between Sirius and an insignificant Brown Dwarf. The second star was small and had no planets or even asteroids. A third and a fourth star had come slightly into play but their distance was enough they were considered only to be a minor factor.

"Let me send off the requests. I have never done this," said G'zin eagerly. She was already sitting at the transmit panel. "How should I start?"

"First," said Clysta, "enter our coordinates." She looked in Kindra's direction, smiling at the effervescence of G'zin. "Then push the two yellow pads. That inscribes our present plotted location on the request."

"I remember now," said G'zin. "We then enter our names, ident' numbers and home planet. Then the info' we require. Right?"

"Right," interrupted Kindra. "We should ask for any personals which they have kept for us, since we left the Academy. And then, maybe we should ask for all of the news issues since the day we left. They will very likely have all of our personal material grouped and ready. It should not take very long."

The three friends spent a few more minutes deciding what else would be worthwhile. G'zin completed their request, then aimed the Bubble transmit. The target coincided with the location in deep space of the closest relay sender that was shown on the charts. The charts showing these locations were issued to memory on the guidance controls of all interstellar ships.

These senders had long ago been dispersed throughout the known and inhabited sectors of this Galactic arm. There were many, and all were automated, being self energized by their inboard ether transformers. The sender stations also had been set in locations that could send and receive the Bubbles avoiding external interference and diversion from the gravity of the surrounding stars.

Depending on the computed destination and the clear route it required, some of these transmissions could take many hours of leaping from sender to sender across the void until the final target would be reached.

Luckily, the location of Sirius was quite close to Sol in contrast to the galactic distances of the explored regions. The interval in this transmission was unlikely to be a long one.

Clysta watched as G'zin punched in the final command, sending off the small Bubble. She afterwards turned her attention to the robot. It had been standing in silence at the side of the control room doorway.

"Well Euclid. What have you got in mind for our next meal?"

The robot's visor appeared to come to life, glowing a little brighter, as it answered.

'This unit is about to prepare a delightful concoction of all your favourite dishes. If it pleases you!'

"I am sure it will," Clysta replied affectionately. "And after we have dined and if the Hyper-Visi has not cycled, you can go to work on installing the Neuro-Phasing Injector. Then tomorrow the installation of the Thought Cube can be completed."

# Chapter 40

Euclid took a little over three hours to complete the task of fitting the Injector and making it able to work in partnership with the newer systems of the Skimmer. The changes inside the updated Neuro patterns created most of the difficulties.

With the obvious exclusion of this outdated component, the newer system's revised wave fluxing devices did not allow for its reintroduction into the processes. The robot had to make a place for it.

In addition to all of this lengthy work, the robot needed extra care so not to alter the minute personality coefficients and sensory currents of the ships original guidance intellect. The loss of any of these functions would cause irreparable damage to the plotting purposes and capacity, rendering the craft a useless hulk with no means of navigation.

The three humans could only watch in amazement as Euclid carried on with the long labours of revising the equipment. Its speed and unfaltering accuracy became bewildering. As was usual with all robots, Euclid carried on with its work untiring and at all times without errors, relocating crystals, re-associating neurals, welding sensors, all in microscopic miniature.

Occasionally, each would have doubtful thoughts of the robots capacity to complete this delicate and increasingly tenuous task. But in each of them as these thoughts germinated they were internally overcome by a peculiar but pleasant feeling of complete trust in Euclid's ability. All of their doubts were cast aside.

Toward the end of the work, as they watched, it became more obvious to the small audience, that this robot was a lot more than the ordinary, standard robotics product.

Finally, the task was complete. The three humans gave a long sigh of relief when Euclid announced that the revision to the guidance console had been completed successfully.

Clysta spoke first.

"Euclid? I trust you implicitly as by now you know. But I must ask of you. Will it work?"

'Miss Clysta,' Euclid began almost with a tone of pride. 'This unit thanks you for the confidence in its abilities. This unit does confirm that all of the equipment in this craft will work in the same manner as that which it has always worked previous to the revisions. The equipment is also in a suitable condition to receive the temporal transmissions of the secrets concealed within the Thought Cube sent to you by your father, Commander Z'ee.'

"All of that toiling must have caused him to forget," said Kindra smiling. "That was, what I would say, one very long and drawn out, 'Yes ma'am'."

Just then as he finished, the signal sounded to announce the incoming Hyper-Visi 'parcel'. The others also smiled at Kindra's comment and in gratitude for the work Euclid had put into the project. G'zin quickly spun around in the anti-grav seat. She needed to check one more time, the setting of the catcher. So as not to lose the anticipated disengagement of the transporting Bubble as its content passed from the depths of Hyper Space into real space.

All three had something to read or view out of the 'parcel'. It was full of items redirected by the Mail Office at the Academy. Some items had the label-Private-being of a personal nature. Most were replies to enquiries and applications, which they had each sent off to the various Industrialist Conglomerates and some of the Laboratory Worlds that had become the trend of the last two centuries.

Clysta herself had followed up on a recommendation to take a position at one Lab' World that was being established in System BH675. It had been for a position having future prospects in the Section Directorship. She had received the reply she had been anticipating, indicating a strong interest in seeing her in person next month.

G'zin had received about twelve messages of graduation congratulations and colourful anecdotes from relatives. Many of which lived on a few of the outer star systems of the explored regions. One very precious one was from her parents that brought tears to her normally happy eyes.

Kindra had been sent a transcript from the Office of the Administrator of the Governor of Alpha Centauri. It was enclosed inside a scrambler wave which repeatedly issued the announcement 'Private-for Kindra Nymralph only. Authorize'.

"We won't ask what that is all about," said G'zin with a grimace. "Those administrators on Alpha' are a weird lot. Everything is a big secret there, you would think by now the old fears of Outer World conspiracy would have been washed away and finally forgotten."

G'zin was referring to a time, around three hundred years ago.

It was a period in Terran history, when a great amount of ambition was causing trouble between Alpha Centauri's ruling classes and the regiments of explorers who were then heading outwards to the stars beyond. These same explorers had used a small planet and two very large Alpha built satellites, as a staging point on their voyages outward. They were each within the Alpha Centauri system boundaries.

The governing body ruling Alpha's three other planets came up with a brilliant decree. The claim was that, as their long ago ancestors had been the first ever pioneers of deep space and had also been the very first Non-Solar System to be explored, they had the undisputable rights to the monopoly on all future deep space exploration.

To reinforce these contrived rights, the Alpha Republic Space Navy positioned gigantic Battle Cruisers around the system and on the major routes from Sol. A state of battle readiness was then declared.

It turned out that the most promising routes were through that quadrant and Alpha Centauri was en route. They lead to very good, promising and usable worlds that were just crying out for their development and establishment of civilization. The Alphans' defiant attitude to the outer settlers and Sol had festered. It escalated into skirmishes and almost escalated into all out war in space about five centuries ago. A number of those skirmishes took place ending in many deaths on both sides.

Finally, serious and lengthy discussions convinced the Alphans' to dismantle their battle lines and after an offer of certain royalties and guarantees, peace did eventually prevail.

It was during these years of conflict, the population and particularly the administrators of Alpha Centauri had turned paranoid. These war prepared times, left them with an unnecessarily ingrained need for secrecy, which had persisted even to the present times.

Whilst Kindra took his time viewing his correspondence, Clysta had put her messages to one side and was busy going through the items in the News Dispatch. She punched in a command code to highlight any item of news on her father's expedition. The screen display skipped through the many articles of Galactic news until it came to a stop at the sections corresponding to her selection.

Clysta reflected a little sadly.

"There is nothing in here relating too much to my father or the expedition. Just three small entries about some other inconspicuous exploration detail, that makes just minor comments about their expedition. That of course means the obvious. The Benner system that they were to lay out as they went is still not connected."

Then she turned to some of the other news transcripts, as she was skimming through them briefly.

"Here is something," she announced and turned up the volume slightly. "It's a news release from two days after we left the Academy. There is a picture of the expedition ship surrounded by a few shuttlecraft. Goodness," she said. "It looks enormous. My father told me it was a new design, but just look at the size. He didn't say it was as large as that."

At that G'zin and Kindra moved to her side to look over her shoulder as the Hyper-Visi carried on with its news report. The announcer went on to describe the release of a bulletin about the craft and its capabilities, and naming the leaders of the crew. He continued his dialogue to recount some recently disclosed transcripts telling of some minor difficulties of contact with the intergalactic ship.

During the initial outward thrust, Trans-Bubbles had been received containing routine reports and data on the trip. At about ten earth months ago though, transmissions from the expedition had mysteriously ceased it said. The report told of a new automated relay station having since been established to carry the Benner Wave Bubbles.

Although testing and checking had been continued from Sol and a few other outposts, to the relay and back, a Bubble had still not been received from the expedition and its crew. The 'cast continued to report there was recently an amount of speculation, by the staff of the Director of Galactic Exploration, that they had anticipated the present condition would be caused by exterior influences in deep space areas. They had not elaborated. The next best theory was a malfunction within the Benner transmission system on board the craft itself.

A few doom seekers had speculated, since the release of the bulletin, on other reasons but mostly they carried little respect. One in particular suggested they had been annihilated inside the dense zones, and another advanced a wild theory on invasion forces from another galaxy.

The bulletin came to an end.

Kindra had finished checking his mail earlier and having switched off his own viewer, turned toward the quiet and pensive Clysta.

"What do you say we should do?" He asked of her. "This is your show you know, the Skimmer and all. I'm game to keep going. Complete your father's request."

G'zin, also had stopped doing her own reading, her attention being drawn to the news bulletin. Likewise, she looked at her friend.

"Me too!" she said, trying to sound bright, but failing slightly.

Clysta switched off the unit she had been watching and sat up as she turned to look at the other two and then at Euclid. She was confused as a solitary thought coursed through her conscious. 'Carry on. Carry on. You must carry on,' it seemed to say.

She lightly shook her head to remove the trance. She looked at these devoted friends, saying.

"I agree. We must carry on. What do you say Euclid?"

The robot answered in a more cheerful tone than ever before.

'Miss Clysta. It is most gracious that you ask of my opinion in this matter. It has always been a priority of this unit to complete the wishes of your father, Commander Z'ee. That is to keep you from harm and have you locate and visit the world which he describes in the Thought Cube."

"I say that we should keep to the same course we started on," G'zin said with more enthusiasm. Then followed with.

"The Department of Galactic Exploration will have all of the brightest people working on whatever is creating the problem of contact. You know what 'newsies' are like. If it's not gloom, it's not good news. There is every likelihood there is a much more simple explanation to it all anyway."

Kindra nodded thoughtfully, concentrating on something that had come into his own consciousness.

Then he said. "I agree. This thing that I received from Alpha C' isn't due for their consideration for at least another four months anyway. And there is really little that we alone or anyone else for that matter can do to help in knowing what the expedition is up to. Except wait and perhaps speculate, and then speculate some more. As G'zin just said, greater minds than ours, with more chance of a solution are no doubt at work right now.

"Let's try our best to find this place and then we alone can see a place and something which only one human has seen before. It may even be exciting. Yes?"

Clysta smiled at the thought, saying with a hint of sarcasm.

"Yes. It would be a change. Well, wouldn't it? After all, life has been a little dull since we left the Academy. Hasn't it?"

They all slept long and deep but only under the influence of the sleep inducers. The excitement of the pending conclusion of the Thought Cube's translation was on each of their minds when they had retired to the anti- grav cots.

Euclid finally awakened them one by one to the aroma of breakfast once again. It consisted of the processor's rendition of real eggs and bacon, together with all of the usual embellishments.

G'zin groaned as she entered the confines of the body cleaner.

"I had forgotten all about this. We should have brought one of those 'cleaners we used on Morn. This one is likely to give me claustrophobia. Of course we would have needed a larger Skimmer."

They all eventually dressed and sat at the table to eat breakfast and enjoy. Meanwhile, Euclid had returned to the navigational console to prepare for the rest of the work of installing the Thought Cube.

A short time after they had finished breakfast, the robot entered from the control room to say.

'This unit has just now rechecked the work of yesterday and is satisfied the system is ready for the remaining function.'

Clysta stood to leave the table to bring the Cube, and turned to face the robot.

"Euclid—," she began, "That Cube might turn out to be the last and only contact with my father that I am left with. There is nothing likely to happen to erase that record, is there?"

'This element which has been installed is to extract only the guidance information and will not affect other parts of the cube,' was the reply from Euclid.

Clysta disappeared into her sleeping quarters and returned just as she had about one week earlier. She was again carefully carrying the Cube on top of the upraised palm of her hand.

With equally careful precision, the robot took the Cube from Clysta and then reaching inside the console, placed it onto the centre of the previously installed gossamer fan. It, the fan, was in the same position still spread as it was and just where it had been left earlier. With the same exacting precision as before, Euclid touched here and then touched there with an ultra fine laser welding instrument to make a number of final microscopic connections.

The result, after a minute of uncertain anticipation, was a curious pulsing sound, which came from the inside of the cube and then after about twenty beats the pulsing stopped. Very minute shining sparks amid streams of colours began to gyrate on all of its visible sides. The streams and sparks then flowed slowly and continuously downward, into the Cube's base. The effect of the streams began spreading onto the fan and cascaded down into the fine and delicate web below.

"Well," said G'zin, dreamily, "I'll not be very disappointed if it doesn't ever work at all. It is so, so beautiful to watch."

Finally, after a matter of only seconds which to the watchers seemed to last for minutes, the flow stopped and the cube became the colour of dull metal.

'The work of the Thought Cube is now complete, Miss Clysta,' Euclid said, unfazed by G'zin's remark. 'Do you wish that it be put to a test at this time?'

"I'm all for it Euclid," Clysta began. "First though, let us clean up and do a Ship Check. We will be better equipped after that, to concentrate on the results and plan our course."

# Chapter 41

The initial star track from the Cube that was to lead to the starting point in the puzzle, was not too difficult to follow. The Cube had described to their craft's guidance computer some of the coordinates and these were instantly shown in the ionized viewing display.

The vista being shown to the cabins occupants gave a three dimensional view of space filled with a profusion of stars, each of them a solitary beacon in their many varied and different magnitudes.

The panorama was being generated through a mental transcript recovered from those personal memories of Commander Z'ee and then recreated from the transmittance of what had been stored inside the alien Thought Cube.

The vision was viewed in semi-darkness. The lighting in the control room had become dimmed to a degree where it was easy to observe this vista of stars. All of the largest and the brightest stars could be noted now for the upcoming Hyper Paths' course and identification.

Kindra and G'zin each donned a Neural Hood, transferring the scene into their intellect, exposing to each a more transcendent view. This allowed them to 'see and feel' more of the subject space and its finer detail which might be lost through the eyes. By turning their own thoughts to a particular star in the image, a chart would be 'shown' to their mental picture describing in detail that particular point of light.

"According to this readout I am seeing, I can only identify about eight of these stars," confirmed Kindra, "Even with the range of the hood. This area of space must be many hundreds or even thousands of light years down the Galactic Arm."

G'zin agreed, "True, true," she said, "I didn't think this part of space was even in the record crystals. This trip is going to take a little while, you know. These distances are tremendous. The area I am studying is still in this Orion Arm but much, much closer to the core of the galactic spiral."

Kindra added, "It is no wonder the system we are to find is unknown to Terrans. It is so, so far from Mother Earth."

Clysta could not follow the view that Kindra and G'zin saw but she was following their dialogue. The computer before her, had also been following and displaying distances as they went along through their imaginary pathways.

She interrupted their comments.

"It's lucky for us my father broke this up into manageable sections. We could take days to calculate all of these Jump sequences with their distances and curves." Then, "You take the readings from directional for this first batch," Clysta instructed G'zin, "Punch it all into the comp'. Even with Hyper speed, it looks like we will take more than three days to arrive at the point where my father made the first axial change of direction. After that is reached, we can move to the next stage from his memory store and so on down. That will bring us close enough to the region where he said his Hyper Drive malfunctioned. This way, we can keep to just the more direct routes then we can stop, take the next group of readings from the Cube and start again. I suspect it will be much easier that way than trying to see the whole transcript at one time."

G'zin took all of two hours to file a directional into the guidance computer and a further two to work in a suitable course of Hyper Jumps.

Meanwhile Kindra, with help from Clysta, was busy with transferring the commands from G'zin's work into the piloting program.

"It looks like I am finished here and about ready to go," said G'zin. She explained, "I have set the Bubble to follow the coordinates heading first for Capella, about forty plus light years away from where we are now. That will be the first Jump. We can use that monster in a wide curve to gain some extra warp then on to Aquilae another one hundred parsecs down the arm. When we exit there, we can set again. After that we Jump again on to Cassiopeia, a bit tricky but it will give us another fifty parsecs at least. Then, I have located a decent tunnel, which we can jump along using three stars as directional anchors. That in itself continues,-it should be in a straight line -," she added, "For another two hundred parsecs through a few minor star fields."

"After all of that," she concluded, slightly short of breath from her lengthy dialogue, "We should arrive at an exit which shows in my own calculations is at the point in the arm about a half of the way to where your father did the first directional rotation. And Clys', if you are ready and willing, you can please do a check on these calcs'. Because, I, G'zin DeVenouire, am very 'bushed'."

She staggered mockingly toward the more comfortable lounge seat, as she added, "It won't get us any too close to the spot where your father had the Drive malfunction. But after the next series we will be only one and a half Standard Days travel from a location quite close. At least by my reckoning, anyhow."

"You really know your stuff, G'zin," Kindra said, appreciative and smiling, "And beside that, you can make it all sound so interesting too."

Clysta quickly poured over the readout and could find no fault with the route G'zin had described. She then spent a little more time carefully following the tracked star route, checking briefly with her own unit all the salient computations, but still there was no detectable miscalculation. She did not expect to find any either as her trust in G'zin's abilities was growing fast.

Turning away from the computer, she said.

"Your calcs' are all fine by me G'zin. Do you check as ok Kindra?"

Kindra nodded slowly deep in thought. Euclid, who had stood in silence through all of this time and discussion, spoke.

'I have followed the calculations that you have been working on, Miss G'zin. This unit did notice that a cloud of stellar dust does exist at three degrees tangent to the Jump number three. It would be wise, if you will not mind the suggestion, to pass that point a further three degrees to the zenith. Distortion of the Hyper Bubble will be better avoided.'

All three looked at each other then at Euclid. G'zin looked back at the console, punching in commands, to see the relative sequence of the cloud Euclid had spoken of.

"There goes old perfect again!" Kindra said, smiling and awaiting the result of G'zin's inspection.

"D'you know he could be right. In fact, I'll bet a whole 'Skoon Dilly' he is," exclaimed G'zin. Her reference was to a very costly aquatic delicacy, native to her home world. "I thought I had compensated by allowing sufficient clearance. Better that we be safe though. Let me have a few minutes to make a correction then we will be right on."

When the change was complete, Kindra was again at his own console to quickly feed the revision into the pilot program.

G'zin turned to look at Euclid, smiled and said, "I don't know yet how you do it, Euclid, but thanks again."

"And Kindra and I, we will second that," added Clysta.

The last exit from Hyper Space was just the same as the two previous ones-smooth as silk. No jolt or nausea, just the usual routine and imperceptible feeling of a shift.

"I think I am becoming addicted to this," said G'zin. "It is almost sensual," then, looking at the screens view, "Wow! Just look at all of those stars."

All eyes were turned to the one hundred and eighty-degree image of space ahead. Countless millions of points of light could be seen. The density of the seemingly closely packed stars gave the illusion of an almost solid sheet of brightness, with hardly any of the black background of space able to show through.

The reality was of course the copious quantity of stars existing close to the hub of the galaxy. Though each star was separated from its neighbour by no less than five to ten light years of vacuum, the intensity from the volume was one of almost solid bright light.

The craft had exited Hyper Space many hundreds of light years from that particular region but the same enormous distance from it did not take away the overpowering sensation of its nearness.

The Skimmer, following their exit from Hyper, was still travelling at ninety-five percent of the speed of light. Even at their present speed, in deep space the distance that could be covered in many days would be hardly negligible in astronomical terms.

Clysta pulled their attention from the view on the screen. She set the control for the view to a lower intensity.

"So far, so good. Now," she said, turning to her friends, "The messages in the Cube indicated that my father and his party turned at this point toward the edge of this plane in the direction of where the Sagittarius Arm joins with our own Galactic arm. Then, following a short period of Hyper Drive the malfunction in his systems occurred."

"I would like to get started on those readings before we eat. If you don't mind Clys'," Clysta signaled her to do so, with a movement of her hand, "Give me a little time to secure those coordinates," G'zin asked. She already had the contacts closed, opening up the sequence from the Cube, "Can you adjust our direction to match my figures, Kindra? With a full screen, we will soon see the same view your father had from this position, Clysta."

In only a short time the ship began to rotate on its axis and the view on screen moved slowly from the full and compact star field to a view of a thinning of stars. Even as the quantity of stellar bodies could be seen to decrease, there were still more than a person could count easily in a day.

"Now we are coming to the really hard part," said Clysta. "Do you recall that practical test we had to take at the Academy? The one where we were left out in space and had to find our own route back? You remember it don't you?"

"Yes," said Kindra, "I remember that one very well."

G'zin nodded in recollection.

"Well, I suggest that it is a good method to try out here," said Clysta.

G'zin added to her suggestion, "Yes of course. We can input the direction from the Cube, and then assume a temporary blindness. Use a time sequence, that we can get also from the Cube, and like an arrow, we follow it through."

Now it was Kindra's turn to add, "We are very likely to encounter stars though, which are bound to create a deflection curve. That will surely lead us to an unknown percentage of trial and error. Will it not?"

"That is true Kindra," agreed Clysta, "But if we take it slowly, and keep back checking on our calculations like we did before, we have a firm chance of success. Also the systems on board are twice as good as those we had on the Academy's older ships."

Kindra and G'zin nodded in answer slowly, then G'zin said cheerily, "Well, I am ready. It worked before and there is no reason it will not work here. Right?"

"Right!" Kindra answered firmly, "But first, lets relax for a while. Time up to now is on our side. We have all been beating ourselves to get this far. We need a rest before the next hop."

It was many hours later that the three friends once more started out on that very complicated task. One that could end in the location of a lone star then its planet. A planet that was home, to a race of beings that had been seen by only one Terran. That Terran was Commander Z'ee.

# Chapter 42

The computers on board the Skimmer had incorporated more sophisticated and updated crystals giving a few advantages over those they had used on their tests at the Academy. One major improvement being its speed. Another function amongst the many was an ability to demonstrate with clarity a sequence testing of stellar calculations showing its outcome without moving along the suggested path.

They were able also to follow by using the hoods and viewing systems as the star course was evolved.

Two hours of rigorous sampling went by, but showing a zero in their results. Of the small number of stars the computer had isolated, some were comparatively young and without planets. Two others had minor satellite like bodies revolving around them, and there were three, which were red giants. Those type of stars in particular, would not support a planet with the Terran type of life.

The three friends sat back in their seats, each of them exhausted from their collective efforts. They had by now been at their combined calculations and investigations for more than a half of a Standard Day.

"What we are really trying to find is almost a place in space where there is no star," said G'zin, thoughtfully. "If you remember, your father said that the star we are seeking from the Cube has no charted record."

"You are quite correct G'zin," replied Clysta in a voiced disappointment, "I had forgotten that fact. But however are we to find our goal, if these charts we are using do not have a record of what we are trying to locate?"

"We didn't really expect that it was to be easy," offered Kindra, trying to dispel the gloom. "G'zin's idea is the right one, but we will need to take many examples of the formula before we find the correct location. At least we have the point of commencement supplied by The Commander. We also have a good idea of the direction."

Euclid entered the control room carrying some much needed refreshments.

'If you will excuse the intrusion on your discussion and calculations,' the robot began. 'There is a general routine to the formation of all stars from spatial content. That routine is known to follow a pattern which can be determined by mathematical order.'

The three carried on with the refreshment, each puzzling over the statement from the robot and looking to each other for the answer to its reasoning.

Clysta's face took on a meditative expression, slightly blank, studying some sporadic inner thoughts. Then, hesitating slightly, she said.

"That is it. Of course! That is what Euclid was saying," Then turning to the other two. "Where there should be a star in accordance with the calculable parameters, and we find the star charts have not indicated one, that is the likely place for the star and that planet. Does all of that make sense?"

"It should make sense," agreed Kindra, thoughtfully, "The possibility is of course very much regulated by the star density in that local position in the arm and the types of stars around that same position. There are some other factors that do come into play also. You get what I mean though, don't you? It is following your own trend. Isn't it, Clysta?"

Clysta answered, still a little unsure.

"I think that is what I attempted to put in words. What do you think, G'zin?"

"I think I get your drift, that is both of you," G'zin said, carrying along in her mind, the line of discussion that Kindra had started. Then she suggested, "The closer to the centre of the Galaxy, the more stars, the farther out and so on. Right?"

"But it is all calculable," stressed Clysta. "Now though, we have to handle double or more of the calcs' but it is worth a try," then she turned to look straight at the robot, saying, "Euclid, what is it that you do? On each time we have reached a point where we are stuck, you have always given us a push. A little hint or suggestion. I say again. How are you doing it?"

'I am at your service and here to assist you, Miss Clysta, at all times. Commander Z'ee directed me that I was to do so.'

With that, the robot turned on its metal heels and left the control room, with the three friends watching it depart, each more unsure of the true abilities of this one particular and becoming more and more peculiar robot.

It took many hours of test after test after test, to narrow down all of the possibilities, which they had accumulated. In the many instances, they would run through the sequences by using the computer to extend their calculations along the direction that had been installed into the Cubes memory. In all cases the outcome was a star that was already entered in the charts.

The hours of concentration began taking its toll. They were each beginning to show signs of fatigue and inwardly ready to give up and to find another formula. Kindra had just about completed a run that appeared to be headed for the same result as all of the others, when G'zin spotted something. She said almost in a whisper.

"Hold that location Kindra," she was afraid to speak louder, "I think that one may be it."

Clysta, who had been sitting at another computer station trying to organize a few more patterns, stood up from the seat and walked across to look over the shoulders of her friends. She was saying quietly to herself, "One more time. G'zin never quits'"

"What do you see?" Clysta asked, then aloud.

G'zin pointed to an area of space in the holo' image.

"There," she said softly, still afraid to speak too loudly, "By that cluster."

"I see it," confirmed Clysta, enthusiastically, "You mean there to the North West and Azimuth? I see it. It is a larger than normal volume of just empty space. I can't be absolutely sure but it does appear it ought to fit the requirements we are trying to assemble. What are your opinions Kindra?"

He stood up and stretched with his arms high above his head. Then dropping his arms to his side indicating his fatigue, he said.

"Just set your impressions and I'll double check your calcs' later if you don't mind, please G'zin. If you'll excuse me, I'm all in," Kindra said wearily, as he staggered across the control room toward the anti-grav lounge.

Clysta smiled wanly, in total agreement. She placed her hand gently on G'zin's shoulder and said.

"Me too. It has been a very long and hard day and we have accomplished a great deal, even if we have only eliminated some firm possibilities. It will be better if we stop and rest, maybe have a real break and perhaps watch a few of our vidis for a change. That definitely means you too, G'zin. Just punch save, and we will check it again tomorrow."

"Good, G'zin said with a bright smile, "And I think that it's about time too."

She wiped her hand across her forehead in a mock display of weariness, saying "Phew". Then she pressed the appropriate pads and continued, "I honestly thought you two were never ever going to give in and call for a stop."

# Chapter 43

After a long rest the trio set to again in an attempt at proving the area from the last test could be one that could prove fruitful. It was uncertain and the uncertainty was infuriating to say the least. They had decided, finally and after some debate, that they should try by moving onward. They put away the hoods and set out to go to find G'zin's last computed location and check the area in question.

This time they were to go in person.

The passage they were taking was one with no intermediate jumps into or out of Hyper Space. It had to been their intention to try to follow the same pattern which the lonely expedition of Commander Z'ee had traveled a few years before. More or less it was a blind shoot, even though they themselves had complete control of their ship's Drive systems.

The time period, of passage through the other dimension, bore a large part of the actual analysis. And the minutest amount of its deviation would cause them to exit in an area in space entirely different from that which they were trying to find.

The Cube had given the duration, taken from the Commander's thoughts, of the period between entering and exiting Hyper Space. The major dilemma was, when coursing at Hyper speeds, seconds would account for billions of kilometres of normal space.

G'zin had, during the earlier hours, been rerunning all of their computations of the day before. Next, she set the position of the area of clear space they had viewed in the holo'. Kindra soon had the craft under way and they all retired to there anti -gravs and the cocoons. He had then sent the Skimmer into Hyper Space for the short trip and the vessel had just exited.

They all quickly and expectantly looked at the view on the screen as they each climbed from their couches.

Nothing. Just empty space. Stars of all magnitudes and assorted types shone around them at a distance of many light years. But the area they were now in. No prominent star. Nothing.

"Secure this location and put it into memory, please G'zin," said Clysta, "We will check the closest stars via some short Hyper Jumps."

Taking a radius of up to fifty light years, there were a number of the stars that were red giants and a few brown dwarfs. Some were relatively too young and two that were in the range of Blue stars. They finally selected and settled for three stars.

"These three appear to be most likely," said Clysta, viewing the readout of the spectral evaluation, "They show some of the signs of almost having the correct value and magnitude to be able to support Terran type life."

"If there are planets," She thoughtfully corrected herself. She said no more but inwardly she had little confidence that any one of these would be the right star.

All three stars, they found on closer investigation, had no planets at all.

They returned a little dejected to the earlier hyper exit point and G'zin offered a solution.

"The location we are trying to find you know, depends on exiting into normal space at the absolute instant in time equal to your father's trip. Even microseconds will make such a vast difference in distance terms. Why not back up a little in hyper terminology. If that does not reveal anything positive, then we should return here and advance ahead of this location."

"It might work," added Kindra. "Our course is after all, following precisely the correct direction described by your father. Keeping to that line, we must find the star, if it exists at all."

Kindra was showing signs of strain from the lengthy trial and error that this trio was going through. G'zin noticed his last comment. She said quickly with enthusiasm.

"It does exist, Clysta's father said so."

Clysta let the moment hang. Then.

"Ok," Clysta agreed, "Let's try."

Reversing down their original course was attempted first. This time following the second exit they came upon a star, which after carrying out a quick spectral analysis, done by Kindra, showed to be of equal magnitude to a G.2 star.

Clysta carefully checked the charts. She had input the coordinates into the library files to find out what details if any were listed about the star directly ahead of them. This star's location came up on the screen, confirming to their chagrin that it had been previously recorded. It was recorded though, on the star charts, as a K.5 star and even carried the Terran registry identification number of L6529. The column listing planets was left blank. No zero, just blank.

"How odd," Clysta said, as she rechecked the chart and registry. She found no mistakes in her location input, "That kind of error is almost unthinkable."

"That's true," Kindra agreed, more enthusiastically, "And most peculiar, don't you think. I recommend we should move up closer and really check it out." At least, he thought to himself, it would be something to break the drudgery.

Clysta nodded in silent agreement, then she said.

"G'zin, please calc' an orbit at around one hundred and seventy million kilometres and we will see if this star has a planet of some sort, Then added. "Any sort will do."

There were three. Two that were smaller and too close to their sun to be capable of supporting life of the carbon type, or any other kind to be specific. The keen eyes of Kindra spotted these two right away, as he scanned the space surrounding the stellar furnace.

Clysta was first to see the third body.

"There! There is a planet. See!" she announced as she adjusted the magnification to the viewing screen, "Just left of the star, and it looks to be a big one too."

"I see it," the others chimed in unison, seeing what Clysta was now enlarging on the screen.

"We should move up closer," said G'zin, "At our present speed we should be alongside in three hours. Then we can have a good look at it. It could just be what we are looking for."

The Skimmer coasted along as the three friends occasionally watched and took spectral readings from the planet. At one hour away the final reading left them in a sullen mood. There was little to no chlorophyll in the spectrum from the planet. There was a large content of what could be similar to carbon but the atomic structure of the molecules was wrong. And readings showed a large amount of gamma radiation from most of the surface. The final readings though as they closed in on the planet also showed it to have an atmosphere but with a low oxygen content.

"How ever could this be?" Clysta asked of no one in particular. She was thinking mainly about the record they had read earlier about this star.

"There is an atmosphere. There is also an amount of liquid. The readings show it as being an equivalent or close to our class for water."

"The diameter is close to being good enough for Terran uses," added Kindra, "Almost twelve and a half thousand kilometres. Gravity just over one 'G'."

At two hundred thousand kilometres their fears were justified. The entire planet surface was a mixture of greys and blacks. What water like liquid they saw was a shade of brown from this distance. They faced the planet on its daylight side with the star behind the ship.

"I will move in and set up to formal orbit at two thousand kilometres and lay in anti-grav to start approaching the surface," informed Kindra, "G'zin, would you mind scanning for anything of interest?"

"Already doing just that," G'zin announced as she placed the scanning hood in front of her and began her survey.

After spending fifteen or more minutes of checking, she said, "There is a large body of water or something similar. It appears to cover the surface of the planet to the left of the meridian, from pole to pole. It appears to almost encircle at least three sides of a very large landmass,

I think. I can't make too much of it at this distance though. It could be a large ocean of sorts."

After ten more minutes, G'zin once again spoke up.

"It is an ocean as I said before. Pretty bad though. We have reached directly above the other shore and all of the liquid looks quite black. What are you reading Clys'?"

"Not a great deal at all," she replied, "The surface cover, if there is or was, all looks to be completely dead from my analysis board."

Clysta had been taking more spectral samples this time of the actual surface, to give an indication of the character of the skin of the planet.

"I am receiving sporadic readings of volumes of gamma radiation too, some of it is at dangerous levels," she added.

"We are now entering the upper atmosphere," warned Kindra, "There is not very much cloud cover and the density of the air is low. I think I will drop straight down from here if you two agree."

"Ok by us," agreed Clysta, still taking readings, "But slowly Kindra please. We don't need to awaken a sleeping giant or two on our first pass. Keep to the daylight side too though. We may as well use the natural light of the star."

G'zin spoke out of the scanner hood, "Hold that position, Kindra. I see a large area of reflecting surface. I don't think it is water or whatever this planet possesses," Then, after a pause, "There, I see another but larger this time."

"I see it on the view screen now G'zin," said Kindra, "Should I close the distance Clysta, and get a better view?"

"Yes, do that," she answered, "But let's hover at fourteen hundred metres. The gamma radiation comes and goes in waves, almost like a wind. It is extensive around here and I think its effects may grow to critical."

G'zin put away the hood and joined the other two as they watched the screen and looked down on the growing planet below. She occasionally manipulated the scanner, watching the results on the smaller screen.

The screen view rotated to show a wide vista of the planet below them. All around from the centre under their craft to more than a hundred kilometres radius was sheer and unexpected surface clutter. Directly below was the area, which G'zin had seen as being the origin of the reflection.

Amongst the black and weathered or eroded surface confusion were wide and crooked stripes of some kind of a glittering metal. These lay as if unnaturally embedded into the course undulating surface around this extensive area. The stripes, of almost a flat surface, ran in all directions but still in what appeared to be some preordained pattern.

"Can you make out anything which might be called life, G'zin?" Clysta asked. G'zin still operated the scanning device.

"I don't see anything other than a moss or lichen on some areas of the surface, let me focus in on some of it. There, I have one."

G'zin took a few seconds to study the materials and its analytic constituent readout. Then she said in surprise.

"Wow, it's mobile, watch. It's only moving slowly but it definitely is moving. Hold everything and I will transfer to the screen."

Half of the view screen was taken up by the highly magnified image of what G'zin had seen. Observed from above, the material was flat and almost a fur-like texture and brown in colour. It was difficult to assess its thickness from this point above it. The area of surface it was covering could have been ten or twelve metres square, more or less.

The substance moved slightly in a jerky motion, possibly fifteen centimetres then stopped. After a short wait, the jerky movement occurred again, stopped and then began again.

"Its progress is only slow, but it does move," confirmed Kindra as he watched, "Does that indicate it is alive?"

"I suppose it does," Clysta answered, "Alive, sure. But intelligence may be another matter."

"You said you saw some other areas of the same stuff. Didn't you G'zin?" Commented Clysta.

"Yes, over here," said G'zin rotating the view to the left. Finding the spot, she focused and then she continued, "There it is, this one appears to be a much larger piece than the other."

"It looks to be cleaning the ground it is covering," Kindra said,

"See-right behind the stuff. That metallic material there is much brighter than it is on the leading side of it."

"Maybe it is feeding on the corrosion of whatever the substance is. Almost as if it was cleaning the surface as it progresses," G'zin suggested, in agreement.

Clysta changed the subject slightly, saying.

"I have just come to a conclusion. I think this whole area of surface we are looking at is the remains of a large city. Levitate upwards a thousand metres, slowly please, Kindra. We will see if my guess is right."

From the higher elevation they could now observe some of the detail they had missed on the earlier descent. The screen now showed what could only be interpreted as being the layout of an expansive metropolis but with nothing that was greater in height than one metre. Or even less.

"If it was a city, where has it gone?" G'zin asked, "It surely hasn't corroded into this state."

"Who can tell?" Clysta answered, "If the distribution of that metallic substance is anything to go by, my first guess is some kind of vehement destruction. A war perhaps?"

"Perhaps," Kindra agreed, "But one of such tremendous ferocity, I would say."

"And that would account for the gamma radiation around the planet," added G'zin.

Kindra had another thought.

He said, "But something here just doesn't make sense! That this world or planet has been out here, with all of this destruction. And all of the explorers in the past centuries have never stumbled onto it before us?"

"It does seem a little strange and unbelievable I agree. However, I suggest we make a quick survey over the whole planet," Clysta suggested, "Just to check for any life or if anything moves faster than that carpet. Something was here at sometime in this planet's past. We just may find something or even someone here with near to Terran intelligence."

"Or better?" She added, concentrating on the screen.

Kindra flew the Skimmer on manual and did a general wide survey pattern. After two hours, all they found was more of the same type of destruction to large areas they assumed to have been cities, and many smaller areas similarly laid waste. Possibly they had been towns of smaller content. All of the regions they passed across were almost flattened. G'zin remarked that there was little if any high ground. It was as though even these had been reduced to a moderate flatness by some awesome power.

Over everything they looked at where structures might have existed, there were the sporadic areas of creeping furry blanket substances, going through the same unending cleaning ritual.

"Whatever did all of this, must have happened a few thousand years ago," said G'zin, "And if weapons were used to do it, they must have had tremendous power. To waste a whole world the way this has been wasted. Wow!"

"I wonder what is in the oceans," Kindra said.

"I would rather not know for now," hinted G'zin, "It is possible there are the same clean up creatures that are on the land areas. Carrying out the same service of keeping the world tidy."

Euclid, the robot had been wandering in and out of the control room, serving refreshments and generally keeping everything in order. It stopped its work and stood now behind the group watching the screen. It then looked toward the graphic displays showing conditions in and around the craft.

Turning to Clysta, the robot, not having spoken in some time, said.

'Miss Clysta, may this unit interrupt the inspection of this planet. If you will kindly view the radiation graph, you will observe there has been a much increased amount of life threatening gamma emissions. The interior of the ship and its occupants are soon to be in danger if the condition persists. In keeping with my directions from your father, it is imperative that we leave immediately. Please.'

"Jumping Stars!" Clysta exclaimed, "I had missed that. Kindra. Let's get out of here. Fast, please. It appears there is nothing much left of anything and I am sure and it is obvious that this is not the planet we are trying to locate. We may as well get back to the quest that we came out here for."

Almost as Clysta had finished speaking, the Skimmer, having levitated in haste, was already entering outer space. Then it continued to speed on its way, directly away from the planet.

# Chapter 44

It was mid-day ships time, another day later.

Once more, the Skimmer had been back along the original path sequence, in and out of Jumps. Each exit from Hyper had given similar results to those before. Stars that were too small or too large, or stars close to correct type but without a planet.

One star had all the correct details but on close inspection its three small planets were cinder-like, as if burned up in some giant experimental furnace. On the surface, nothing was growing. A small amount of liquid, which could have once been water, settled in shallow oceans. The profiles of the landmasses were showing traces of higher water levels but overall, each of the planets appeared to have been put through a brief state of a star nova.

"It couldn't have been a stellar explosion," said G'zin, looking at the disastrous leftovers of the middle planet on the screen. "Those fissures there," she indicated, "would have been leveled off with molten rock. This place still has mountains, valleys and all the contours of a natural livable planet. But evidence of probable scorching everywhere."

Kindra agreed adding, "Such devastation though. What ever could have caused it?" They stood in silence for seconds. Then, Kindra continued, "Whatever happened, nothing could live through that. And for what it is worth, it seems to have happened a long time ago. Too long for any of these three planets to have been visited by your father, Clysta."

"I couldn't agree more," Clysta confirmed, "Total devastation. What now?"

The three friends went silent again. Then Clysta spoke.

"There is nothing in the backward direction," said Clysta, "I vote we leave this system in the records and head for G'zin's original cluster, after we have eaten. Then we can move forward along her plotted route. Agreed?"

The move ahead and past the cluster had all of the same results they had met before, only this area had still less of the star type they were seeking. There were just not any signs or indication of a sun possessing a blue planet as shown to Clysta in the Thought Cube's transmission.

On what was recorded by the trio as the fifty third exit, to inspect a suitably specific star, they once more chanced on the discovery of another planet carrying the same marks of a mostly devastating conflict, with close to total destruction of all except the areas of and close to its polar regions.

G'zin had left the others to the piloting of the Skimmer and the jumping in and out of Hyper Space. She had been quietly and dexterously entering and then pouring over the myriad computer calculations, checking and rechecking and then checking again.

Finally she stopped and as she stretched to remove the fatigue, spun around on the anti-grav seat to face Clysta and Kindra and said,"I have spent the past two hours going over all the calcs' of yesterday and back checking all of the readouts even in longhand. I still keep coming up with the identical results. The worst deviation that I am able to come up with is about one hundredth of a second in degree terms. That is down to the diameter of the Solar System in five hundred light years of distance. And that amount of deviation, from my course calculations, could only be caused if we entered the grav' field of a giant."

She looked again at the computer, saying, "We must be missing something. It just isn't possible that with all of our combined technology and the equipment at hand, we are coming up short in all of our efforts." Then, saying more to herself. "What ever must it be?"

"Ok," Clysta said, interrupting G'zin's thoughts, "We must return to our starting point, where we turned onto this trajectory from the down arm drive. We will go through it all again. Recalc' and recomp', then we will give it one more try. We are here and so far must be on the right track. The system is supposed to be uncharted and you can bet it is going to be very well and cleverly concealed or it would have been discovered long ago—."

Her words drifted off as she finished the statement. A sensation like a cold haze seemed to enter her head and then disperse. A thought was left behind, 'unless it is screened'. Then she forgot that it had happened.

"Right on Clysta!" Kindra agreed, not noticing Clysta's puzzled look. Then jokingly, "Ok G'zin, if you please. Liven up those coordinates and I'll have us back there in a jiffy."

They did just that. They spent the remaining hours checking and then double checking and then they checked again. They spent so many hours at this, the trio finally gave up and collapsed in their anti-grav sleepers and all slept soundly until a wake up call from Euclid and breakfast.

"Here we go!" Said Kindra, setting the drive in motion.

The exit from Hyper Space was at exactly the same point in space as their first attempt had been. Frustration was beginning to build inside the control room, as Euclid returned to stand in the middle of the floor. The robot looked directly at the view screen. It was showing all of the stars that were now becoming more familiar to these travelers.

The robot then turned slightly on its heel and faced its vision panel directly in Kindra's direction. Kindra then, unknowingly, returned the look as a puzzled frown crossed his face.

Kindra opened his mouth to say something, then hesitated for a second, thought, then started to speak.

"Something is really amiss here," he said.

"You bet!" Said G'zin in exasperation, as she and Clysta both turned to face him, "But just what?"

"Look around this sector of space," he answered. "There are stars there," he pointed, "There are two there, and over there are others," and again he pointed.

Clysta and G'zin followed the direction of his pointing finger.

G'zin asked the question, "So?"

"So shouldn't there be a star over there or somewhere close to that area?" Kindra answered, indicating an area of clear space.

"We can try to prove your theory," said G'zin, "It will take only a few minutes. Let me project the possibilities on the comp'," she crossed the floor to the console. "The program is still in the crystal."

In just two minutes G'zin had the computations finished. She transferred the results into the holo' imagery.

"Your idea seems to have some merit Kindra," she said as she pointed at three flashing spots of light in the array of stars, "Those are possible locations taking a balance of interstellar matrix and star density which is available."

"I suddenly got a flash of thought, that a star is possibly missing from there," Kindra tried to explain, pointing. "There should be something there, in that volume of empty space. What do you think Clysta?"

"My father, in his message, remarked that these beings on the planet were far in advance of Humans," Clysta answered slowly as if in thought. The haze she had experienced earlier returned then suddenly cleared leaving a thought.

"What if..." She stopped in mid sentence, then, "What if their intelligence is so much advanced that they have a method of hiding their whole home system? The star, the planets, everything. My father could have stumbled past their defense, or whatever it is, when he finally escaped from his blind flight through Hyper Space."

The others waited for her to continue with the theory, but she was once more deep in thought.

"I know this will sound really silly," she said breaking her temporary silence, "But I had some kind of weird thought yesterday, it comes back now. Something like, well, that the planet and its star are screened from view from outside."

"If that is true or even possible," interrupted G'zin, "They could be out there in that area of empty space. This could also be the logic of why the system has been undiscovered. As it has up to the present time."

"If that is the case," Kindra added, "Then we need to duplicate the details exactly, of the exit point that your father and his crew of robots found. And to me, the only way to do that is, our accuracy must contain the same luck he had in exiting in his dive from Hyper Drive. But that is what we have been doing all of this time, is it not? We are definitely missing a very important factor."

Kindra was saying, almost speaking his thoughts out loud, with the robot, Euclid, still looking unobserved by all, in his direction.

"We have direction…we have starting point…we have Hyper Shift…and time…and," then a thought from nowhere came into his head. "…Drift?

"That's it," Kindra was almost shouting now. "We forgot. Drift. It has been a number of years since your father's expedition and space and the stars together with their orbiting planets, they have all moved and the space between has, you know, expanded and distorted somewhat during that time."

"Of course," agreed Clysta with enthusiasm, "We didn't make any allowances for the drift in space. But wait a second. Any movement in space is relative is it not? I mean. The stars, the dust, the gases and all of the planetary systems, they all move at the same rate. Yes?"

"True, but only here in this space," admitted Kindra as he pointed in a gesture toward the deck-plating below their feet. "But we are looking for a something, a star system which your father stumbled out of Hyper Space into. All of that has a very different relationship to the here and now reality. Everything changes in Hyper. Only inside the protective Bubble is anything as we see it."

Clysta was nodding slowly, recalling some forgotten studies.

Kindra continued.

"Remember back to the words of Professor Philmax and what he told us two years ago. 'When a body enters that dimension, time and motion are irrelevant as we perceive them, because they just do not exist.'"

G'zin interrupted, saying, "Oh! I remember that one very well. I just could not get it right until you, Kindra, gave me some assistance. Einstein's Theory of Relativity does not hold water as it did for a thousand years under the ancient laws of Physics. Under normal conditions everything works along those lines, but the relationships are completely changed and a new set of circumstances takes charge. And do I ever remember that one! I for one spent weeks and weeks and—." She trailed on.

"On the top of all that," Kindra explained, "The comp' does not know of the system's existence. And even though it does, as it should, by and under our requests, the experimental runs we have accomplished showed us only what was in its crystals. It just did not know anything else."

"You are right Kindra. Thanks for reminding us," added Clysta, "I know we must now be on the right track, but the calcs' will likely be astronomical, if you will pardon the pun. I really hate to have to say this, but we will have to return once again to our original location at the turn point in the down arm Jumps—."

Clysta, after pausing, added to her statement.

"—And start all over again," Whilst the other two mockingly, mimicked the words, moving their lips in silence.

# Chapter 45

Their first attempt of this new series found nothing but clear space.

On the second run, they were honoured with success. It was definitely, an uncharted star. It was a yellow star. And it appeared friendly and that term could only be used loosely.

The ship made its exit from Hyper and was still quite some distance from the star and therefore they had no definition of where the elusive speculated screening began. All of the stars outside of this area of space were still completely visible regardless of the invisibility of the system from the outside.

To confirm their suspected success they had immediately carried out a check using the assorted triangulations exploiting the charted stars around the sector to check and be doubly sure it was not a star in the ship's records. They each sighed in relief when one after another of their calculations came up blank and it was then fully confirmed. This star was not.

How it was hidden from view outside of the system, they were unable to comprehend. But at this time of jubilation and wildly uncontrolled celebration of their accomplishment, they really did not care. It was many minutes after the jumping around and hugging in the control room had come to an end. They settled down to a toast to their suspected conclusion with a glass of the Royal Dew that G'zin had saved for just some such occasion.

Euclid did not join in. The robot stood at his usual position in the control room, soundless and as inconspicuous as a humanoid robot could be, whilst the trio fully enjoyed their well earned celebration, with ample enthusiasm.

Some time later when Clysta had almost filed away the last and final configuration she said to Kindra, getting back to business.

"Kindra. Please bring up the magnification. We need to know just what is likely to be ahead of us before we proceed any further. I know my father explained these people were friendly, but those visions I have had in my dreams keep recurring and they are nagging at me constantly. I would rather be aware if there is anything ahead which is likely to be a big surprise."

The screen's view changed, by degrees, as Kindra operated the control. First the star ahead grew in size until it filled the screen. The glare became automatically filtered to an acceptable level so not to cause the three watchers any distress.

G'zin was finishing off checking the spectral analysis and reported.

"Well, it is showing as a G.1 star with a ninety-five percent similarity to Sol. The other five percent gives a few elements, which I recognize from my own star hosting our planet Fryl. There are a number of isotopes showing up that I cannot decipher at this check but I will leave the comp' at work on those. Otherwise the star is pretty well regular in our own terms."

Kindra had begun panning the screen view from side to side to locate anything, which may be a planet.

Clysta said," I will have the gravitometer establish the orbital plane to give you a better positioning to explore for planets. Just give me a few more minutes and I will transfer the readings to your board."

"There it is," said Kindra after ten more minutes of searching the void. "One planet. Will you take the readings G'zin and do a spectral on it, while I explore around a little more."

He then split the screen and carried on with his search.

"I'll work on the orbit and diameter whilst you do all of that, G'zin," said Clysta and they all got down to their tasks with some of the left over enthusiasm. It was as if all three of the friends had been granted new energy after having their recent success of finding what might be their target.

Meanwhile Euclid, now that each of them was busy working, wandered in and out of the control room once more carrying out its menial duties. Sometimes it would pause to look to each station, as if the robot itself was checking that all was being carried out with suitable correctness.

Kindra was first to report.

"The only other items I can find are a rather large and elongated gaseous body, extremely dense and a few smallish planetoid types at a series of extreme orbits. Nothing else of real merit."

Clysta was next.

"The orbit of this planet shows at one hundred and fifty-two million kilometres and the diameter of the planet itself is fourteen thousand two hundred kilometres. Its revolution rate appears to be" she paused, "four hundred standard days," she paused once again, then, "The rotation is about thirty-six Galactic Standard hours. Hmm," she added pensively, "That is a long day. What did you come up with G'zin?"

"Wait just a little," she answered, "Ah, here we go."

The screen spilled out its final readings and G'zin had the computers voice, report on the findings. In a clear and concise voice, it recited, 'The planet is equal in quality to ninety-seven point nine, nine, six Standard One.'

Standard One is the human existence quality of the planet Earth. That benchmark is used as the basis for all planets throughout the known galaxy.

'The atmosphere is Terran breathable with a point zero two percent increase per volume of oxygen and a corresponding decrease in the element carbon dioxide.'

The computer continued with its analysis.

'Gravity is assessed at one point zero three two G, Gamma and deteriorative radiations are very good. At Earth acceptable levels.

'A background radiation of an excessively high wavelength is evident, but is unknown to this equipment. All samples and their analyses have shown that all radiation except the latter, which are unknown at present, are to be safe to Terrans.

'Specifics can be added if required.'

Clysta replied to the last quote, "That will not be necessary, computer."

The machine voice went silent.

Then Clysta added, "That radiation. It could be a concern, but if my father visited here for sure," she paused and looked at the robot as if for input. None was forthcoming, so she ended, "It did him no harm that I was able to witness."

"I have found a satellite," interrupted Kindra, "It is just outside the planet's shadow, I am magnifying. Now!"

"I see it," confirmed Clysta, "G'zin would you please check it out too and find out what we can expect from there?"

Shortly after, G'zin gave the others a reply herself.

"Not quite so rich in elements as the planet, but it is interesting. This satellite has a slight amount of atmosphere. Not so hearty as the planet, but funnily enough with all the same ingredients as the planet," She paused a second then, "That is odd, I am getting readings of internal heat, only a little, but heat all the same."

Clysta added, "My calcs' show a diameter of about thirty-one hundred kilometres and some. The revolution rate around the planet is slow, too slow to give an accurate reading at this point, and I cannot see any proof of rotation yet."

"Are we ready to move closer?" asked Kindra. He was endeavoring to hide his eagerness.

"I think so," was Clysta's reply. "Can you plot a course to take the ship in and keep the satellite between us and the planet? Like you did at Morn. Bring us to about half the distance away from where we are now and stop. I would like a better view of the planet without being too close. I am still getting that same queer feeling. I just need to be sure of what is ahead before we move into too close quarters."

As Kindra began his plot, Clysta then turned toward Euclid who had once more been watching all of the events as they passed, seemingly full of interest. She said.

"Euclid. You have in the past, served almost as a sixth sense to us. I would really appreciate it if you would stand close and keep on doing the same for the next little while, please."

'This unit is at your service, Miss Clysta, as always. Thank you for the invitation,' the robot answered politely.

"Now that was better and far, far shorter," said Kindra with a wide grin.

All eyes were now on the view screen. The Skimmer traveled inward at a slightly sideways and decreasing trajectory toward the star. Their speed was at close to light speed and closing in on the orbit of the presently distant planet. Under Kindra's skillful control, the transition was smooth and clean.

Clysta had had second thoughts about moving in closer to the satellite too soon. Many of her dream sequences had left a feeling of foreboding and now she imagined inwardly that caution should prevail. She had suggested they stay in this outer orbit for a while longer just to study the system and make sure they knew more about their surroundings before moving directly inward.

The ships night period came and they all slept well. Even Clysta slept soundly, without the repeat of her now almost always expected and recurring dreams of warning and the subsequent apprehension. Kindra and G'zin both had intermittent and pleasant dreams of fond recollection of each of their home planets.

The next day the decision was made to have the Skimmer moved into a steep and descending orbit toward the lone planet.

Clysta called for more magnification when they had reached a point at three million kilometres outside of the planets own orbit.

"My original readings still hold," said G'zin to the others, "Oxygen and nitrogen balance are good on the planet. The satellite is confusing though, with a diameter of only three thousand kilometres plus, how does it hold on to an atmosphere? Physics says it just isn't possible. It must be losing some to space. Whatever the reason its chemistry would make it suitable for us if it were a lot more dense."

"Hold that position will you please Kindra?" Clysta said quickly, "Boost up the magnification and let us keep all eyes on the planet's own outer edges."

"What are we looking for?" G'zin asked.

"I am not sure I know what I expect to see," Clysta replied, "It's just a feeling, you know, a premonition of something just not quite right.

Blame it on my dreams I guess, it's a little like I have been forewarned. I would rather take a good cautious look before making any kind of contact."

The Skimmer was parked now, in visually stationary orbit, on a line with the satellite and keeping the planet behind that. Their movement was quite imperceptible except by watching the shifting of the stars behind the two bodies ahead.

Sitting in that position they each took turns watching the screen. This position would give them a good view of the area of space at the edges of a half of the planet now being eclipsed by its satellite. The robot had served refreshments, whilst they waited. It had helped by breaking the anxiety that they all could feel building inside the craft.

G'zin was about to ask her previous question again. They had been here now for two hours or more. She was cut off as her mouth opened to speak.

'There,' Euclid motioned toward the screen. The robot had also been given a shift of watching the planet. 'This unit wishes to report a flash of reflected light.'

"Where?" Clysta and G'zin said together.

The robot indicated the area in the screen with a metal finger.

"Kindra, boost up the magnification as high as possible," said Clysta, then to the robot, "I see it Euclid. Now we must see in detail what it was that caused the flash."

# Chapter 46

"Whatever is that?" Clysta said in amazement, "That is no craft I have ever seen on the Galactic Federation listings. Look at the size. Can we do a check on the comp' and see if I am correct? It could of course belong to this world, couldn't it?"

"I'll do it now!" answered G'zin, not commenting further.

The ship they had seen on the screen was large, although they had no parameters with which to judge, except the experience of using the instrument. The craft shown on screen consisted of a very large sphere covered with many long and very slender conical spike-like projections radiating outward.

The spikes almost covered the entire surface of the central sphere, and behind this and connected to the sphere by a group of long and slender tubes was a geometrical arrangement of more tubes and radiating vanes.

G'zin was still going through the ship's catalogue. Without looking up she was the first to speak saying.

"D'you know, I have seen a shape like that sphere with the spikes before. There is a fish type creature from my home planet, Fryl. It has a very close resemblance to that ship. If I recall, it was brought from Earth. It was used once long ago to help in cleaning up some of our fresh water lakes. It removed some kind of dangerous chemical from the water. The name of the creature escapes me now, but it sure resembles that craft. Much, much smaller though."

The strange vessel had no markings that were visible. This fact alone made it almost non-Terran. Under the Federation rules of space fairing of course, a ship without markings was deemed a violator or even a pirate, whom this craft could very well be. That though was a very slim chance especially due to the efforts needed to locate this most secretive position in space.

Kindra spoke up next.

"What is that behind it?" They were all looking at the view screen. "Hey, doesn't it look similar to the one which your father's expedition was using? Like the craft they showed in those news items we received, you remember. The latest ones on the expedition," he added, "That is strange. If it is that same ship, then whatever is the expedition doing here? Surely your father is not here now and has disregarded the very wishes of these people of the planet."

Kindra went silent. Thinking that he had already said too much.

"That other ship has got to be from the planet," prompted G'zin.

She was finished searching through the ship's records of old and new craft. "Nothing in here. You remember the catalogue that we chose this Skimmer from. There was nothing in there like it at all and they were all of them, the latest in designs. I checked for centuries back too. It could be another un-issued design and was to be a part of the expedition? You know? Kept a secret or something."

Clysta had remained silent, as the others had been all this time conjecturing on the scene before them. She then said, after G'zin and Kindra had become quiet.

"This is all coming back to those visions in my dreams again. I know it will be hard to believe but that ship now I see it, has been a part of some of my nightmares. For the last few sleep periods some nights before we got here."

She turned to the robot and asked, seeking a solution.

"What do you conclude from all of this, Euclid?"

Euclid had been watching the screen closely, and answered Clysta.

'Miss Clysta, it has not been my intention to keep my past history a secret, but the correct questions have not been asked of me.'

The robot continued. 'This unit was the first in experience in a compliment of two robots which accompanied Commander Z'ee on the trip that was concluded in the area of space where we are now situated. It was remarked by the inhabitants, and I noticed it was at the time quite true, they had long since abandoned space travel and have no use of it.'

Euclid seemed to pause, seeming to give the statement credibility, then the robot said. 'That vessel is not of this system. I estimate from my memory banks it is also not of a Galactic Federation design. It is therefore logical to say, it is from a region outside of the Galactic Federation's own jurisdiction and government of planets.'

"Then why is the expedition's ship here and close to that strange craft?" It was a question Clysta asked no one in particular. Euclid gave an answer.

'That question requires an answer which will command an amount of speculation,' said the robot. 'It is a mode of which this unit is not yet capable if executing.'

Kindra had seen something and was now focusing the view onto the expedition craft.

"Look at the marks on the side of the federation ship," Kindra said as he pointed. "There, doesn't that look like damage from an explosion. Maybe even a blaster scar?"

On the side they could see, a number of panels toward the power plant systems were twisted and torn. There were also marks of heat and possibly pressure damage.

"It looks like it could well be," agreed Clysta, "But it could also have been caused by a number of other things; a collision with a large piece of space debris, or something. Anything!" She added with a tone of inner doubt.

"I for one don't like the looks of all of this," G'zin began, when in the same instant there came a high pitched whine from the output of the interspace radio monitor.

The sound continued for a number of seconds then stopped. A mellow but authoritative voice followed. It had a sound of a small bell tinkling and slightly accented, but still spoke in an eloquent Terran. The sounds filled the whole of the ship and was now not emanating from the ships internal contact system.

"We are addressing this message to the craft in outer orbit."

The sentence was repeated once again. Then following a short pause it began.

"We suggest that you do not reply to this message." The voice gave the impression it could be robotic as was usual to signal any incoming vessels in Federation areas. Apart from the accent it could have passed for an Earth tongue. "We recommend you leave this system immediately. We have a condition which is life threatening. We repeat, do not reply to this message, your reply will be monitored by others and you will be in danger."

"Quickly," said Clysta, "Find where that transmission is originating from."

"Euclid and I are already on to it," answered G'zin watching the readout before her. Euclid had already set the equipment into motion as they were listening.

One more time the message came seemingly from the fabric of the ship and then all was quiet as the transmission came to an end.

"It is coming from the satellite," said Kindra and he then double checked as an automatic indicator on the inlay on the screen showed the location. "There!"

The focus was adjusted as they watched, and the picture zoomed to show a long narrow trench on the moon's surface. A readout chart alongside automatically gave depth and particulars of its other dimensions, along with other details of atmosphere and chemical constitution.

Clysta announced.

"Well I don't intend to leave just because of a warning over space radio or whatever that was. I am not going anywhere until I know what a federation craft is doing here. And particularly that craft. The craft my father is supposed to be somewhere else in."

She turned to G'zin and Kindra. Embarrassed by her outburst and the way her statement must have sounded. She quickly added.

"I am sorry if I sounded selfish, but I really need to find out if that Federation ship out there is the one which my father is on. And if it is, why is it here? Please forgive me."

"You need no forgiveness Clys'," Kindra answered quickly, "We are with you all of the way. But by the look and size of that other vessel, this time we could have bitten off more than we can chew. Wouldn't you agree?"

They all watched the screen in silence, each studying the possibilities individually. Then G'zin smiled one of her usually pleasant smiles, saying.

"Come on Kindra. We have been through all sorts of scrapes before now, and always come up ahead. I would like to suggest something. Let us first go to the satellite. We can then find whomever or whatever is relaying that message. To my way of thinking it has almost been an invitation anyway. I myself would go just to find out who has the cheek to tell us to go away.

Then we will probably get some answers to Clysta's questions. Afterwards, we can assess the danger. If it seems to be too big for us to handle on our own, then we can high-tail it out of here and try to find someone to help us deal with it."

She looked across the deck at Euclid and then added.

"And beside all that, we have Euclid. We all are aware how he can make up for many of the things that we find impossible."

Kindra, feeling a little uncomfortable, said.

"Please, don't misinterpret what I just said. I am only trying to be cautious. I am saying, that craft out there could be very dangerous and a retreat may be the better action in this case. Even get some reinforcements, then come back and find out what has happened. What do you think of that idea?"

Clysta was silent. She was thinking of what both Kindra and G'zin had said.

"Who would believe us?" Clysta contended, "Whom do we contact? It could take months of waiting around at various offices and The Galactic Center. Then, to find someone, anyone who would first listen to our story about an uncharted planet. And then believe it is one that we found through an unheard of Thought Cube. And then there is a strange ship. Then how do we explain away our suspicions? No. We would be labeled just 'silly students' with nothing better to do. Don't forget, also this system is not on any Federation charts."

"She is right Kindra," added G'zin, "Who outside of this ship would take any notice of us and our impressions?"

Kindra looked at the other two, then at the robot who, though it seemed impossible, had once again the improbable, but faint resemblance of a smile across its face. With a change of spirits he suddenly overcame his trepidation, saying.

"You are correct in what you say, the both of you. I have to agree with you. We really have no alternative. I will set in a course and make ready to pilot the ship to that spot right there."

He pointed at the screen to where it showed the satellite in close up, indicating the location shown by the target left by the original locator setting.

# Chapter 47

Kindra closed down the Ether Motors when the mass of the Skimmer had caught the attraction of the 'moon's' light gravity.

Using the anti-grav' layer he proceeded to let the craft coast downward in the direction of the rift seen earlier. The scar, in the satellites surface which was the rift, increased in size on the screen again as they approached. As the three friends watched, they could now see it was formed by two very high and sheer cliffs. The almost vertical sides dropped downwards from a flat plain for more than three kilometres to a level area half of a kilometre wide. It was at a point within this deep gorge to where the earlier transmitted signal had been traced.

After falling for a further fifteen minutes, Kindra sent the Skimmer at a reduced rate of speed and began slowly descending into the trench between the now jagged cliff faces. Kindra then came to a stop and hovered at point two hundred metres below the high plains as they took check readings of the sheer surfaces on each side.

Satisfied there were no obstructions visible below them, Clysta motioned to Kindra to recommence their descent.

The whole area above had no signs of prominent vegetation, but as they got lower into the canyon there was a moss growing in patches in the crevices of the vertical shear face on each side. On closer examination, in the ghostly twilight the moss was changing and becoming softly luminous and with a yellowish green colouring.

They were now close to the base of the rift where the mossy growth now appeared to cover the whole floor and then extend past the areas they had observed in their descent, fully to about half way up to the top. Higher than that, there was only a rocky and virtually smooth surface covered here and there with small areas of the same moss. Still, no other vegetation was evident.

Kindra had piloted to, the approximate region where he had tracked the signal, but could make out no signs of a beacon or of an antenna.

"This place is really spooky," commented G'zin in a observation about the almost twilight effect, "Where would you say that signal came from?"

"Hard to tell from where we are now," Kindra answered, "I think I will have the ship spiral slowly downwards, that way you two can monitor the scanner and locate anything giving a recent energy output. You too, Euclid."

Without the vision of the passing view of the cliff scene outside the ship, it was impossible to believe the Skimmer was even moving. Kindra had finally reached a point at one hundred metres from the surface forming the bottom of the rift. He looked at the others.

"See anything yet?" Kindra asked.

"Nothing at all," Clysta replied softly so not to loose the concentration of the group.

"I am going to hover at fifty metres from the floor of the rift and then rotate slowly," Kindra suggested. "Watch for the same and see if there is any light from the cliff face. Euclid, you operate the infra-red scanner for heat traces."

'This unit will gladly carry out your request, Master Kindra,' the robot answered politely. The other two just smiled, and continued watching the screen.

With the screen on full size scan, the Skimmer proceeded lower and came to a stop, then it started to turn on its vertical axis. They all watched as the cliff face before them moved away and disappeared into the dim distance, then the other face moved toward them in reverse.

Part of the way through the second revolution, Euclid pointed in silence and Kindra brought the craft to a halt, saying.

"What is it Euclid? What did you see?"

Clysta had seen it too.

"The infra-red is showing a large disc of heat at the base of the cliff, we must have missed it on the first pass," she said.

"Look," G'zin interrupted, "Isn't that a light?"

They all watched as the tiny but bright beam of light shone at the Skimmer. It was coming from a position close to the bottom of the shear face before them. First it became brighter then died then grew in intensity to half of its previous power. It then cycled two more times and finally diminished to nothing and disappeared.

"It was a light," G'zin confirmed doubtfully, "But it was not there for very long. Do you think it could have been meant as a signal?"

"Move up closer toward that point there, Kindra," Clysta requested as she pointed, "Go slowly though and everyone be alert."

Kindra moved the Skimmer down and almost touching the surface forming the floor of the chasm.

"I had better put the legs down, just in case we are forced to land. I wouldn't want to scratch the underside of the anti-grav' veneer," He said, as he pushed the pad to complete his suggestion.

Deftly and under complete balanced control, he moved the ship very slowly and in a horizontal direction, toward the location of the earlier pulses of bright light.

The craft had approached a spot at one hundred and fifty metres away from the base of the cliff when a large opening formed magically in the mossy face ahead. It opened to reveal a circular tunnel beyond, dimly lit but sufficiently large to take their ship with some room to spare.

Just as suddenly, the ship began to move forward and toward the opening.

"Hold it Kindra," cautioned G'zin, "We don't know where the tunnel will lead us."

"I am not controlling the motion," he said, startled. He was pressing the appropriate pads in his attempt at holding back the craft's movement. "We are moving ahead without my commands. There is nothing I can do to hold us back, the anti-gravs' do not respond at all. Nothing does."

There was little the three friends could do except watch in apprehension as the ship approached and then entered the tunnel in the face of the high cliff. With the wide view on the screen they could then see the opening, which was now behind them, close in on itself and disappear.

Kindra, finding he could no longer control the motions of the ship, just stood, his hand resting at the edge of the control panel and watched the screen.

The craft carried on in its forward motion until, after about one hundred metres, it came to a halt and finally was lowered, coming to rest on the floor of a much larger cavern. This new area became more brightly illuminated as the Skimmer settled down onto the areas glass smooth floor.

"Whatever all of this means, I may just as well power down. Lucky I put down the landing legs," said Kindra as he manipulated the controls and switched off the anti-grav' as a precaution.

Once again the same tinkling voice they had heard earlier out in space, came from the walls of the ship saying.

"Please disembark from your craft. We of this system are non-violent and will do you no harm. The atmosphere inside this chamber is quite satisfactory and safe for Humans to breath."

"Well, they seem to know we are humans at least," G'zin remarked.

"I suppose we have no real alternative, have we?" Clysta conceded. "Let us go and see who they are. But first, should we break out the weapons?"

Euclid had been his usual silent self and was stationed between them and the passage to the air-lock. The robot spoke.

'Miss Clysta! I have recognized the voice of the person who is speaking from outside the ship. It is that of a high official of the planet we have sought. You may take my word, what he has said is the truth, and he may be called a friend. Weapons will not be required.'

"Euclid! Euclid, my kindly and friendly Robot."

The greeting of welcome came, in the same delicate and tinkling voice they had heard previously and in clear Terran. It was from a being standing some distance before them.

The being had a stature equal to human, of what they could see at least.

It was tall and slim but the bodily features were hidden under a one piece garment. The garment was of a material made of a sheer gold like filament. The covering hung from the shoulders of the being, all the way to the floor of this chamber where they were now all standing.

Clysta noticed immediately a resemblance to those people shown in the Thought Cube's transmission. The body, taller than an average human by 150 mm and slender, was totally hidden beneath the gown. The only part visible was its head that was held high and proud. The head was slender and slightly to a point at the top and was devoid of any hair, even eyelashes or eyebrows. The being's eyes were more round or circular than those of human and completely of a bright blue colour. The small and lipless mouth and not too prominent nose features were in the same place as human. Their shape had a trace resemblance to feline contours, lending to its face an aura of distinction.

The most prominent feature to G'zin and Kindra was the skin colour. It was a light shade of blue and appeared translucent and to glow or even a suggestion of radiating so slightly.

The being glided soundlessly toward them. It turned from Euclid to face and survey the three humans.

"If you came along with Euclid, then you too must also be friends," the beings tinkling voice said. There was an emphasis on the word 'must', "I suspect the warning of danger which I have given to you whilst in outer space was of little use or consequence."

Clysta and the others looked at each other and smiled. They had difficulty arriving at a decision on what was the gender of this being standing before them. The cover or gown it wore, concealed any and all details that would give any clues to their combined query. Even the being's feet, if there were feet, were not visible. On guarded but closer scrutiny the material of the gown would change into a flowing and gaseous state whenever the being moved and then transform again, reverting into the fabric like state while it was standing still.

Only the head of the being remained exposed at any time, even during the times when it was in motion.

Euclid spoke. 'This unit wishes to introduce you to three humans who have come to visit your world.' The robot half turned to indicate each as it announced their names. The name of the being was notably not mentioned.

With each of the names, the being would give a form similar to a smile and then a shallow bow of the head as if in greeting. The complexion of their host was such that it was impossible to guess its age, except Clysta herself guessed it must at least be an adult of the race, who stood before them.

After Euclid had completed all of the introductions and, although still leaving the other's name unsaid, the being began to speak again with the musically bell like voice.

"Welcome to you all on behalf of our planet. It is most unfortunate that you are here at this present time, but you have arrived at the most difficult one in our recent history.

"You were given a purposeful warning that you should leave this system because we have a group of visitors. These visitors are aliens whose craft is now in orbit around the planet. They have proven themselves to be extremely unsavory in their demands of our planet and our peoples."

Clysta finally found her voice and interrupted.

"That must be one of the two craft which we could see from the outer orbit."

"Yes," the being answered, and before she could carry on, it added.

"But please, now you have arrived you must come this way. We have much more comfortable places where we can talk," the being motioned, "Through here."

The being guided them toward the far side of the floor to the smooth wall marking the limits of the cavernous area. As the being ahead of them advanced, its gliding body movements if any were still well concealed under the cover of the gown.

As the group approached the wall, a change came over their surroundings. The area they had been in and the Skimmer which was behind them all disappeared and they found themselves inside a smaller room with the same smooth glass like floor and four walls of a similar material but coloured in a pleasant shade of yellow. The ceiling, if there was one, was not visible, the view upward was of just a comfortable lightness without a surface or any parameters.

At various places around the floor were oddly shaped blocks, which G'zin took to be some kind of seating but their shapes did not seem of a design to be able to give much comfort.

"This is our study and relaxation room," said their host, "Will you please be seated?"

They each looked around intending to find the best item to sit on. It soon became apparent that comfort would have to wait until later; whatever these items were they were not about to give them much satisfaction.

As if responding to these thoughts passing through their minds, three of the shapes closest to each of them went through a metamorphosis as they watched. The oddness in shape was converted into the configuration of a seat identical to the one present in each individual's own thoughts.

"Wow," exclaimed Kindra. The seat was moving up to him and shaped itself around his lower body, "Now isn't that something?" As he relaxed and moved into sitting position, the object formed around him and supported his body.

Clysta and G'zin took positions each onto a seat apparently of their own individual styling. Their host crossed the room to another shape, which was of a colour different from all of the other pieces around the room.

Two smooth hand like appendages with long slender fingers appeared to cut through the material of the being's shroud where no opening was previously visible. It was the first indication that the being had any appendages, but then the hands described a flourishing motion and the shape answered by increasing in height to meet the now outstretched fingers. A further transformation took place as it changed now into a style of console with many circles and stripes of various colours on its upper surface.

Their host pressed two fingers of each hand into the consoles top surface. Almost immediately, three of the other pieces on the floor were transformed. These became low tables covered with stone like, bowl containers each holding a number of smallish shapes of a crystal substance in a variety of vivid colours.

In another surprising development, the tables magically slid across the floor and stopped, with one at the side of each human. The host then spoke again.

"We have found that the offering of refreshment is a necessary precursor to pleasant relationships. You will no doubt find the crystals are most delightful. Please do help yourselves and I will begin to introduce myself."

Pausing for a second or two, the strange being began.

"My given name, you will find, is not within the range of your Terran vocabulary. You may therefore find it much easier to use its equivalent in your own language. You must call me by the name of Wyyrrum."

G'zin was the first to take up one of the offered coloured crystals and experimentally placed it onto her tongue. Wyyrrum continued his dialogue.

"My race," he began, "Is a one which is bound unto peace and absolute non-aggression. We have isolated ourselves here for many, many of your centuries-I believe the term is correct-of Standard years.

"Some time ago before your arrival here, we were bewildered to find others had found it necessary to penetrate our defense of invisibility and locate and visit our system.

"There are now two other intergalactic craft beside your own here and they are in orbit around our home planet. One of these vessels is from a planet whose star name, by which we know it, would most likely be equally hard for you to pronounce as my own name is. That vessel does contain though representatives of a world that is in a group of stars far, far away from here, at the near edge of the next spiral arm of this galaxy.

"The other," Wyyrrum continued, "Of which I am sure by now you have become aware, is a craft from your very own region of this galactic section. We need to give you caution, the former stranger to this system is undeniably a fierce aggressor of the most severe magnitude. They have made it quite clear to my friends, that they are here in this region to make conquest of this zone of space and are to use this very area as a starting base."

Wyyrrum paused to give the statement time to settle.

Before Wyyrrum could continue, Clysta interrupted.

"That second craft in orbit," she said, "The one from our own region of space. We did see it and I am sure that it is one which my father, Commander Z'ee, departed in with an expedition toward our neighbour galactic arm. Please, what can you tell us about the state or condition of the craft?"

Wyyrrum looked at Clysta, then his strange facial features transformed, taking on a look of sudden recognition.

He said, "But of course. Z'ee is your name function. You must be the offspring of Professor Z'ee," Wyyrrum had a little difficulty with the 'ee, "I did not perceive the relationship when Euclid gave it in the introduction of you. How unknowing I must have appeared. You must accept my apology. You see, actual words or vocal names, or offsprings, have little reverence or uses on our planet and I unknowingly missed the connection."

"I understand your confusion and have taken no offence," Clysta said politely and becoming a little uncomfortable, "But I certainly think my father, he is now a Commander Z'ee," she added equally politely, "Is on that craft."

Clysta then said eagerly.

"Please, then can you tell us? What is their situation? Is my father safe? Please. I need to know."

"Finish your refreshments while I tell you all of which I am able," was Wyyrrum's answer as the being settled into a seating mold of its own.

The gown, which continued to move around under its own volition, had then changed once more to its previous solid looking state. It though, still persevered with its concealment of any of the beings limbs.

# Chapter 48

Euclid stood, inconspicuous in itself as usual, at the edge of the floor close to the extremity of the chamber. There were no openings or doors visible anywhere. Only the plain but pleasantly coloured surfaces. They did not appear to be walls, as the three friends had known them but only visual boundaries to the area. Almost, they were just as a vision marking the perimeter of sight.

Oddly, the three friends did not have any feeling of apprehension at all at being confronted by this alien. Clysta thought, to herself, that alien was quite the wrong term as the trio were the aliens here. They each found it a little strange that there were no sensations of fear amongst any of them. Or any feelings of danger that this being just might be not a friend and could have other plans for anyone who had found a way in to this system as they had done. The fact that this race could conceal their star and its planet was proof of powers in excess of anything these three friends could imagine. In contrast they sat, strangely calm, attentive and unperturbed, as they listened to what Wyyrrum had to say.

"I remarked previously that the citizens of my planet are a peaceful people," Wyyrrum began in the same tinkling bell like voice.

"That condition though, in our prehistory, has not always been the case. Many, many revolutions ago, or to be more precise as calculated by you Terrans, more than eight thousand years in your own Mother Planet's time. Our own ancestors and forbears were of an extremely violent and warring race. It was not until they were finally responsible for a great catastrophe that they were brought to their senses.

"Since those distant times, even travelling through space has been avoided, with the exception of short visits to this half world. We have become solely interested in the fulfillment of the mind. Our wish is only to be left alone and to enable us to carry out that objective. We developed that effect long ago of making this system invisible, only to ensure the privacy that we so strongly desire."

"Your father," the being looked toward Clysta, "Was the first off-world person ever to stumble onto our secret in all of that length of time our protection has been active. It created quite a problem to our planners. When he left, we could not take a chance of having our location known to anyone else; therefore we had his subconscious prepared with a blankness thus preventing him from revealing the location of our star to anyone. It was done in the interest only of maintaining the secrecy we so strongly desired.

"With this we thought our secret was once more safe and we would not be discovered again. Then the unfortunate incident of his meeting with these aliens has come about, and the eventual capture of him and the crew of their expeditionary ship."

Confusion entered Clysta's thoughts. Thoughts about what he had just said.

'If they did not want my father to reveal the secrets of this system, then why—-?' She opened her mouth to interrupt at this last revelation, but she was unable to make the words form, then her thoughts became confused even more, then a portion of those thoughts were erased.

Wyyrrum himself said, as if in answer to a part of her unspoken statement.

"Yes. Your father is with them. He and his crew are, I suppose, kept as hostages, or even prisoners."

He then continued, "The members of the alien ship have taken delight in informing the populace on our planet, of their savage capture and interrogation of the captive crew. It was revealed they used some form of a mind and memory scanning device to discover many things. Things that were of secrecy. Such as, the power and capacity of the Terran Stellar Navy forces. Details of their weaponry and the central administration functions were also disclosed. And finally somehow, we can only guess, as it was not meant to be, from the subconscious of Professor Z'ee I suppose, the concealed location of this our system and its planet.

"It was likely the concealment of our star and planet, which has given it the attraction to their cause. It will obviously help them to hide their own intended base during their planned expansion.

"I must say here that from our knowledge of the Professor and the intended erasure of our system and its location from his consciousness, we truly believe any information given would have been involuntary."

Clysta became pale as the story unfolded, and she finally interrupted Wyyrrum, her previous thought forgotten.

"For some time now, I have been having a number of visions in unaccountable dream sequences. They have mainly been of my father, and on some of the past occasions, I have had those that left me with a feeling that he is in danger. Can you tell me of his location and also," she added, concern in her voice, "Is he well?"

Wyyrrum took his time to answer.

"I do know he is with the aliens as I said. And he has been shown to us on occasion along with some of the people of the crew. They appear to move them on and off the planet in an erratic fashion, possibly to stave off any attempt at a rescue.

"At the present time I am unable say where he or any of the other Terrans of their vessel's crew are. It was my good fortune to be here on this satellite when they first arrived in their close orbit around our planet."

Wyyrrum's head bowed slightly and his facial features took on a slight look of sadness, as if recalling the event. Then their host returned to the original posture and continued with his dialogue.

"It has been my delegation for some revolutions past, to visit here and supervise the many items of equipment we have installed. I check periodically the progress of a series of regeneration formula with which we are experimenting. I have therefore been able to stay here to carry out the work, which I was here to do, uninterrupted. I have now also set as my other and additional function, to be as a sentinel. Be here to warn off anyone who might, just as you have done, find a way of accessing or even stumbling into our system."

G'zin had listened in silence. She then asked,

"How long did you say that these, these, aliens have been here? With the Terran crew as captors?"

Wyyrrum appeared in thought, then to answer he continued.

"Approximately one of your years ago. These beings arrived here at our system and we first monitored them located in an outer orbit around our star. They stayed in that orbit for almost a half of that period of time.

"During this interval of time, I had made the trip to this base. At the time we were uncertain of their intentions and I am not delegated to be concerned about visitors. I myself had therefore left our planet and it was in the time following, I was informed that the two craft reduced their orbit to one setting them where they are at the present. They have been in that same orbital position for a number of what your kind consider as months I believe.

"They spent two of our days in orbit around our planet then almost immediately made a surprise and unannounced planet fall in a shuttle type of vehicle which seems to have the capability of carrying up to twelve of their kind. They have done some damage and caused an amount of pain to my fellows and have made some serious threats to us. They have also made it quite clear that this, as I made reference to before, is to be their base and they intend to stay here until their conquest is completed."

"Your race must outnumber them," G'zin stated, "Surely your own people are capable of overpowering and stopping them?"

"My people have been peaceable for so many centuries," explained Wyyrrum looking at G'zin, "It is inconceivable for them to use force. All weapons of every kind were destroyed long ago and it was then decreed, never again would they be manufactured. It is not our will or our need to fight with them."

"Even in defence of your planet?" Kindra followed, surprised.

"Even that is not possible to us," Wyyrrum answered.

"But you cannot just stand around, whilst these beings work on a plan to invade," argued Kindra, "It involves not only your own world but, if their threat comes true, the whole of the inhabited planets of this section of the Galaxy."

"I can understand the meaning of your statement," Wyyrrum answered. There was no passion in the still tinkling voice. "But there has been a conditioning amongst my race which has evolved over the centuries. It was brought on by our long, long past history. That conditioning makes force of any kind against another being, strictly unacceptable. If they were to threaten to kill everyone on the planet, we could not retaliate."

"And your leaders?" Kindra asked in bewilderment, "You do have a governing body down there," Kindra pointed at the still strange surface that was beneath his feet, "A planetary committee, or something like that. What is their opinion?"

"The population of my world does not carry the structure of administration that you humans have become accustomed to. We have no leaders as you know of them," Wyyrrum said in answer.

"We eliminated those ideals and their need many of your own centuries ago. Inhabitants of our planet need no rulers or even elected administrators. We each are aware of the others needs immediately. We then are able to fulfill one another as a whole."

Clysta began to wonder how that could be, then left the question for a later opportunity.

Clysta asked, "And in a situation such as the one happening now. You have been told by these beings of what they intend to do and have even taken forceful action against your people. What is to be done against them?"

"Nothing will be done." Wyyrrum's answer had a finality that was immovable, even though, there was no tone of sadness recognized by the listeners.

Clysta was doing her best at trying to hide her frustration at the almost defeated attitude that Wyyrrum described, of these people on the planet below. She then asked.

"What can I do then? It seems my father has been taken prisoner and is with these beings from another part of the galaxy. And possibly both he and the crew of the federation ship are in danger of eventually losing their own lives. I must find some way to see him. And if it is necessary then, I must try to rescue him and make him safe."

She glanced toward G'zin and Kindra and then at the robot Euclid. Wyyrrum then said, answering the question.

"I cannot recommend what action you can take with the exception of leaving this system and getting far away."

After a short pause, Wyyrrum continued. "These beings are no doubt savage and powerful. They have demonstrated that to us most fully. I have avoided telling you, that these invaders have caused the extermination of a large number of my people. They have also shown to my people a few of the humans- -," Wyyrrum paused, then added, "Being tortured? All as a small expression of their own savageness."

With firmness and a feeling of resolve, Clysta stated.

"Leave here, I will not do. Now I have found what I have been somehow dreading, I intend to stay until my father is safe."

She turned to look at her friends.

"G'zin and Kindra. You two may leave if you like," she said, "I will not need to inquire of Euclid's assistance, I know that answer before I ask. He will follow me wherever I go. But I must confront these beings somehow and, if the visions in my dreams are any proof, then I must try to rescue my father from them. It must be done at all costs before it all becomes too late. Believe me," she looked in the direction of her friends. "I will not feel anything bad toward either of you two if you decide to leave here."

Kindra sat a while as if in deep thought, then scratched the side of his head, saying.

"I really don't know why I am saying this, but you may as well count me in. We have already gone over this before we got to this moon. What are you going to do G'zin?"

"I would probably only leave and then get myself lost out there without you two and Euclid," she condescended dryly but with a smile, "Besides, who knows? It just might even turn out to be a lot of fun."

Clysta was not too surprised at the answer from both or her friends. But she asked.

"You are sure? Do you really want to stay? To do whatever we can."

Without any hesitation, they both answered together with enthusiasm.

"Yes."

"Well Wyyrrum," Clysta said, after a short pause, "I should say that is our answer. We are staying until this is over. If you can, would you please tell us all you know about these beings? Give us a chance, any chance available, to enable us to defeat them. Anything you can do might be helpful. If it is in your power to, give us some assistance, as what little help your own policies seem to allow. We are all together in this and I for one intend to do everything I can to thwart their own plans."

Wyyrrum had become seemingly confused by the strength of conviction shown in Clysta's statement. The being turned to face Euclid and asked.

"Euclid. Are these young people capable of carrying out such a hazardous project?"

Euclid answered immediately.

'The time which I have spent in the company of these three humans, bequeaths me to give the only answer possible to your question.'

The robot turned to look directly at Kindra with the visor aglow and strangely with its metal features showing a trace of what could only be interpreted as humour. It then turned back to face this strange being, Wyyrrum.

'Yes!'

# Chapter 49

Wyyrrum's large round eyes closed and he sat in silence, on one of those moulded shapes. It was as if he was in deep thought for almost five seconds of time. Then the eyes opened and Wyyrrum began to speak.

"Then I will give you whatever assistance of which it is in my own power to give. First, you will need to know how to find these-shall we call them-aggressors.

"They have been using, as their base on the planet surface, an area close to a place we refer to as The Old Centre. There is some sentimentality amongst my people attached to that location. It is the last remaining of the three locations where our ancient planetary government used to gather. It is located in the centre of a major city and I, am led to believe from what I know about our history, that particular city is one of our oldest. It, the Old Centre, is also where all of the many records of the history of our world are stored."

Wyyrrum continued.

"The city is located on the shore of the planet's largest land mass and at all times it is a place where many of my people congregate.

"I am not certain what the nature is of the weapons these aggressors have brought along, but they have some, which can be devastating I am informed. They have proven their power by vaporizing two of our most precious structures. Those structures were also most unfortunately occupied at the time. The attack caused the instant annihilation of four hundred and twenty three of my people.

"I said before that I was here at this base when they made planetfall.

I know most of the occurrences because I have been in constant contact with some of my fellows. They have informed me of events as they unfolded.

"I have been told there are twelve of these beings in their landing force, three of which are addressed by the others as if they are leaders. One of these three would seem to have supreme power over all of the others. That alien is the only one of them who makes whatever contacts it deems necessary with our people.

"These beings seem unable to comprehend that we in this system have no need for their kind of existence. We have informed them we wish only to be left to carry out our lives in the peace we have developed in ourselves."

Kindra frowned and said, interrupting Wyyrrum's dialogue.

"Can you not eject them, surely you have some weapons and an equal or a more advanced technology?"

"I am able only to repeat. We have no desires to use force of any kind," answered Wyyrrum, "All weapons of our history were destroyed a long time ago. Even those having the smallest of power of them all, does not exist any more."

Clysta mentally studied the facts of the predicament, and then she asked,

"Wyyrrum. If we were to go to this place the aggressors are occupying, would we get any help from your people? If we were to fight, do you know if any of your fellows would join in?"

"My people cannot understand the use of force. They would not know how to help you," was the reply.

"Tell me Wyyrrum," G'zin said in mounting frustration, "It is surely not possible for a whole race to stand in defeat without some form of retaliation. Is yours the only race on the planet?"

"We try to ignore the latent fact which is the answer to your particular question, G'zin," said Wyyrrum consciously. The being once again, eyes closed, sat as if in meditation. Following the same span of time as before, the eyes opened.

"It is a subject rarely remembered amongst us and one which brought some shame upon our distant ancestors. I will tell you what I must though it pains all of us.

"A very long time ago, at a time in our history I have mentioned before, our ancestors caused the death of two planetary systems and their whole civilizations. That is, all except a small few of the inhabitants.

"It was all the result of continual warring over feudal territory and wealth. Weapons of destruction evolved to such an extent that the outcome was three planets became useless hulks. Another, the largest body in another system was left flat and radiating harmful elements, from the incessant warring.

"Before the final devastation, a small group of its inhabitants, only about three hundred, were evacuated and saved. They were moved to our planet here to restart, in an attempt to save a civilization, which had been mostly destroyed and in a small way, make amends for these mindless mistakes.

"These refugees of our error, who now number around two thousand or more, live on an island off the major land mass that I told you of earlier. I myself have no immediate contact with the people as it is outside of my own delegation of endeavor and not a part of my responsibilities."

"What are they like?" Clysta asked, "I mean to say, do they have the same non-aggressive policy as your people? Or are they of a different disposition?"

"They have no reason to be any different," Wyyrrum answered her. Though the statement appeared to lack conviction. "Their culture is of a different variety. They have some use for rewards, whereas our existence is reward enough to us. They have no reason for force as they are self governing and have good relations in trade with their neighbours on the mainland. I do know, two of their traders were in one of the structures that these aggressors vaporized. So it is likely they will have a plausible cause to dislike those creatures who did it."

Clysta looked down at the crystalline floor of the chamber where they all sat in a circle. She was trying to come to a decision on the next path they must take.

G'zin and Kindra were sitting quietly and now and again each sampling the crystal refreshments. They also awaited Clysta's response, knowing inwardly what it was likely to involve.

Many seconds of silence passed with no-one saying a word. Finally Clysta looked up and said.

"I think you may have just brought about the possibility of a plan. It could be a useful way for us to gain access into the city. I think I may have a strategy, which could be the means of getting up close to the aliens. Would it be possible for us to land our craft on the island you talked about?"

"It could prove to be dangerous if these aggressors discover your craft—," answered Wyyrrum, cautiously.

"It is a risk we need to take if we are to carry out a confrontation with these beings," interrupted Kindra without hesitation.

Kindra's face took on the closest approximation of a concealed smile, and in the direction of Clysta as he said the words, realizing he had fully committed himself again.

Then he followed with, "Could you also tell us some more of the people who inhabit the place? I remember you used the word refugees. Possibly to inform or give us some insight into what they are like."

Wyyrrum looked from one to the other. In the clear bell like voice the host said.

"It is obvious you are each committed to your plan to stay here. I appear to have little alternative but to give you all the assistance that I can.

"This structure," a hand like appendage appeared through the fabric of the gown and waived to display the surroundings, "Has access to a library which contains some of the history of these people, and ours too. That should be helpful. Perhaps it will provide sufficient background to satisfy some of your needs," Wyyrrum offered, and then continued.

"I will also make contact with one of my fellows who has a close relationship with those island dwellers. He is more able to make some arrangements to have them receive you if and when you arrive there."

# Chapter 50

They had waited until a period when the alien ship had just slipped behind the large sphere of the planet. In that way their descent toward the planet would have a better chance of going unseen by any observers who might be inspecting or observing the surrounding space.

Kindra had set a course for the Skimmer to approach the planet in a direct line, further using its mass as a screen from the craft of the invaders. Both of the interstellar craft were luckily in a stationary orbit following the rotation of the planet below. That trajectory held them directly above that city where the Old Centre could be found and subsequently their shuttle when the aliens were using it to descend and travel to the planet surface.

Kindra had also decided to use the anti-grav as a means of propulsion. Using this, there should not be any drive trace elements to leave a trail, which the aliens also might be capable of picking up and then, track them later.

The trip was made at high speed and Kindra slowed their pace as the ship approached the planets' outer atmosphere. Timing had been perfect as their arrival was at the planets night side and all below them was in darkness.

"Where to now," Kindra asked, checking the rate of descent, "We will be at the surface in eight minutes at this present speed."

G'zin was watching the view screen. It was the using infra-red scan to show the details of the surface below the Skimmer.

"There is a large area of land mass on this segment of the planet. The ocean we are seeking is to the right Kindra. If we get to the altitude of five thousand metres we will be low enough to take level flight un-noticed from space."

Kindra followed G'zin's suggestion.

"Go lower and hover at two hundred metres when we are above the ocean and clear of the coast, Kindra," Clysta said, watching the screen. Then, "G'zin, comp' up the route to the island. Euclid, your reactions are a little quicker than ours. Stand close to Kindra's side again, please. Watch the screen for anything you might see as dangerous."

Then she added, "I'm sorry Kindra, do you mind?"

"Not one bit Clys'," he answered quickly, "Place yourself right there Euclid."

'Thank you, Master Kindra', the robot said as it approached.

"Plot's in Kindra," said G'zin, "I have set an irregular course, just in case we are seen or tracked. We really do not know what equipment these aliens have on their craft up there," She pointed toward space. "We can't be too careful."

"How long before we are into daylight?" Clysta asked, "The infra-red is good but I will be feeling a lot easier when we have normal vision."

"From my reckoning, at the island it is just coming up to dawn," was the reply from G'zin. "The rotation here is about twenty-five percent longer than our Standard Day. That puts us about…" G'zin tapped in some figures to her computer, then, "I should expect we will take another one hour and twenty minutes to reach daylight at our present speed."

"And the island? How much after?" Kindra queried.

"That should be five minutes later, if we continue," G'zin concluded.

"Ok," interrupted Clysta, "We should stop and hold the position when we are into full daylight. Keep the horizon between the island and us. We can check the area with long range scan.

"Then we will go in slowly."

The Skimmer was still in motion as the star, which was the sun of the planet, came over the horizon to meet them. The sky was changing from the deep black of night and all of its multitude of stars, to a deep bronze colour at first. The daylight progressed into a light gold as the intensity of brightness increased when the full light of the sun finally took over from night.

The exterior sensors registered no movement around or above and beyond the limits of the horizon.

Kindra slowed to a stop at the calculated spot above the ocean and hovered using the anti-gravs to hold the Skimmer in place. They all were studying the ocean around through the screens view as the daylight became stronger.

Kindra noticed some turbulence in the otherwise calm and brassy coloured sea.

"Is that something swimming?" said Kindra, pointing, "I think I saw a tail or a fin."

Clysta and G'zin both looked at the screen, trying to see what it could have been.

"I don't see anything, only that area of turbulence, there in the ocean. Let's get a little lower," Clysta said, "We may see it better through the water if we hover directly over it."

"I should think, with all of this ocean there are likely to be lots of sea creatures," G'zin commented as the craft descended to a height of fifty metres. "Don't you agree?"

The turbulence had stopped and the ocean once again became as still as before. Only a slight swell was evident. No wave action at all.

"It looks as if whatever it was has been scared off or gone to find a meal," Kindra remarked jokingly.

"Look, over there," said Clysta drawing their attention to another part of the view screen. "That sail like thing. There, that's another, and another one over there."

In the distance, around a half of a kilometre away, they could make out the three triangular shapes almost ten metres high, their colour was a deep purple. They rose from the surface of the sea straight upwards and were moving through the water at speed as though following each other, like ancient ships in line.

Clysta, her eyes still on the movement in the distance, asked,

"Did you ever see anything like those when you and my father were here before, Euclid?"

Euclid did not give an answer.

The robot had been attracted to another part of the screen. That view showed an image of the water directly below them, where the turbulence had ceased earlier.

In an instant, Euclid had placed a metal hand gently over that of Kindra's hand, which was stationed on the Skimmer's levitation pad. Kindra was still watching the triangles that appeared to be coming closer. The three friends had missed the movement unfolding below.

Rising out of the water immediately under the craft, was a giant mouth. So large were its proportions that it could be no less than forty metres across. It was difficult to decide what kind of beast or being was attached behind the mouth, as it was all that was visible from inside the ship.

Kindra, taken completely off guard, just had the time to see the hundreds of sharp and pointed teeth filling the screen's inlay view as Euclid forced the levitate pad toward the 'ascend' position.

The craft reacted and began to rise away from the impending menace to avoid whatever was likely to happen next. It was then that four long and tentacled appendages appeared from behind the still wide open and now accelerating mouth. Those appendages all stretched, to reach upward in an attempt to make contact with the ascending Skimmer. Each had rows of many suction cup-like attachments, which ranged from small, to very large, all along their wet and shining surfaces.

G'zin, only fractions of a second after the beast rose out of the ocean saw it. She let out a scream then said in an urgent voice.

"Go right, quickly."

The creature was now somehow gaining on the craft and it continued to stretch and reach out with all of the arms. Whatever this beast was, did not intend to let the ship escape. The ship's movement to the right came just in time and it caught the frenzied beast by surprise. The change of direction was too quick for it to follow. The impetus it had somehow gained was carrying the marine giant upwards, the tentacle arms now flailing outward to the side, as if frenetically, in the direction of its target.

The view of the sea creature took the breath from the three visitors.

Now they had a full side on view of its tremendous and monstrous bulk as it continued to rise to a height of more than two hundred metres.

It was all of five hundred metres long and covered in a mixture of scales and bristly hair and of a dark green colour. Four large ball-like eyes could be seen on their side of the beast, behind the gigantic and still wide-open mouth. Its trajectory peaked in a narrow curve when its full length was clear of the ocean and then began its descent back to the sea.

In a final attempt to connect with its intended prey, the creature gave a flick of its long trailing thorn covered tail in the direction of their ship. Then gravity took over as it plummeted downwards, into the ocean and disappeared from view.

"Phew!" Exclaimed a pale and shocked Kindra, breathlessly, "That was close. Thanks Euclid, there is another we owe you. That time you really saved our bacon."

'Bacon? Bacon?' Echoed the robot in confusion.

"Just an old saying, one you likely cannot comprehend," Explained Kindra, "But thanks all the same."

All signs of the monster had now gone and the sea below was quiet again. G'zin said in an anxious voice.

"Perhaps we should travel the remainder if the way at a slightly higher altitude from here. I just hope this is as high as they can jump in this area."

Kindra had the ship moving very slowly forward as, their attention was once again taken by the triangular shapes. By now, they were travelling closer and in the general direction of the area of water, above which the Skimmer was now hovering.

They watched in silence as the creatures continued closer and towards their location.

Suddenly, as they had seen earlier, part of the ocean surface between these shapes and the onlookers, turned into a frothing area of turbulence. Then, as if following in the same ritual they had just experienced, what must have been the same or even another similar creature emerged and rose clear out of and above the water. It appeared to accelerate as it flew at a high rate of speed through the air in a shallow curve, to descend on the middle of the three triangular shapes. With its huge mouth open wide, the creature easily swallowed whole the triangle together with whatever was attached and hidden below the water line whilst crashing one more time into the sea.

Clysta broke the stunned silence that followed the display. The two remaining triangular shapes were fast leaving the area in opposite directions and eventually disappeared, becoming completely submerged below the ocean surface.

"You were right the first time Kindra. There really was something looking for a meal and I don't expect that beast is afraid of anything. Now, I think we should make landfall as soon as we can. I for one, have seen enough of what is in this ocean for today."

# Chapter 51

The remainder of their journey across the wide ocean was uneventful.

The sky by this time had become a rich golden colour and was still cloudless. A number of flying creatures passed them by, travelling in the opposite direction, just as they made visual contact with the shore of the target island ahead.

Wyyrrum had advised that they would be better to approach from this particular side, as the mainland was closer to the opposite coast.

The beach at the ocean's edge was of a vivid red colour and at their elevation it was difficult to make out if the surface was of sand or just of rock.

The Skimmer crossed the beach at a low speed. For a distance inland the surface, which was unmistakably farmed and tended, was covered with vegetation consisting mainly of a tall 'V' shaped growth. From their present altitude the plants looked to be about sixty metres high, with the two main smooth trunks soaring with no foliage at all, just topped of with a sizable bunch of gourd like fruit, most very large and in many different colours.

"It seems as if these are all being cultivated," said G'zin making an observation and pointing toward the view on the screen. "See, they are set out in neat rows in all directions. What do you suppose they are?"

Euclid waited until the others did not answer, then in the usual metallic voice said.

'On our previous visit to this planet, we did not know of the presence of this island. I did observe something of a similar smaller shape to these items being used as a food source. They were also used in a manufacturing process on the mainland.'

"Probably, they are grown as the main produce on this island," Kindra added, "There are certainly lots of the plants, whatsoever use they may be."

"See," interrupted G'zin, and adjusting the focus of the screen, "Up ahead. Those over there, they look like they are buildings of some sort. It must be the town that we are meant to visit."

Clysta said.

"I think we can make for a lower altitude now, Kindra. I don't expect there are any big surprises coming from this plantation."

Kindra did as Clysta had suggested, and also slowed the pace of motion. The Skimmer descended to just a few metres above the tops of the tall tree-like growths, still continuing with its erratic course. When they were at twenty- five hundred metres from the town they had seen ahead, an open area came into view that would be the one Wyyrrum had also described to them.

"I'll make for that clearing and land," said Kindra. "It must be the right one, it's the only clear area around."

Still watching the screen as the Skimmer came to rest, they could see three beings that were waiting at the extremities of the open expanse. They then started to walk in the direction of their now landed craft.

"Those must be the welcome committee. I hope," remarked G'zin. "They look a little different in appearance to Wyyrrum though. Don't they?"

Beside their different attire, the three were of different heights to Wyyrrum, the tallest being less than two metres and the smallest about one metre and a half.

"I suppose they are most likely to be of a different people too," Clysta commented, "After all. Their ancestors did come from another planet."

# Chapter 52

The larger of the two spacecraft in the close planetary orbit, had been left with a small service crew of four. They had been given the duties of maintaining their ship and its systems with each of them having specific duties to perform.

Two of them were under their leader's orders to see to the general requirements of maintenance and the regular monitoring of the large storage freezers. The other two of this skeleton crew had another additional duty.

Of these two, one crew member was the ship's navigator whose major responsibility had been to guide this enormous vessel across an unthinkable measure of space, unscathed. And now, today he was bored. He had been bored most of the time since they had finally arrived here at this point in space.

The other was a languid crewman who had the divided duties of a part time cook-part time monitor crewman. Each of these two had the split duty of visually checking, through the ship's scanners, for any sign of suspicious movement, which might occur on the planet's surface. In particular, that portion immediately below their ship.

Their leader, the Captain, of whom everyone on board had taken an instant dislike to, from the very beginning of their long voyage, had left very strict orders to these two observers on the ship. They were not only to carry out visual checks by scanner, but also view the scanner records when they were off duty. That was an order. The Captain did not trust anyone who was out of his sight. This last order was just in case they might have missed anything important or perhaps had fallen asleep during their watch periods.

The navigator had finished his turn at watch some time ago and had left his partner at his post, to salvage some of the frugal refreshments from the galley.

Unknown to the cook-crewman and unseen by him, it was during this his watch, that the Skimmer had passed across the planet surface fractionally within range of their scanners. He though was once again dozing, half asleep, as was his usual habit. He was still in a shallow slumber when the navigator, his station superior, returned and stepped to the control room.

Quazraam, as the navigator was named, knew from past experience that the other was most likely to be sleeping at the console. He crept around the musty and damp room unheard by the semi-conscious crewman, with much effort he kept his rock hard and pointed feet from making the slightest of scratching sounds on the deck's stone surface. Keeping as close to the side of the doorway as his large sectional body would allow, silently he approached the shaped stool which was supporting his sleeping watch partner. He carefully placed his refreshments onto the side desk top, then Quazraam stabbed out in a vicious arc with one of the leading of his four legs. He deftly caught the supporting stool and flipped it out from beneath his slumbering comrade.

The heavy crustacean body of Kraklac toppled and fell like a stone onto the rock-like deck of the compartment, landing with a loud and resounding crunch onto its back. With a lightening agility and a quick push on the strong front mandibles, Kraklac rolled and effortlessly bounded onto his support legs. He quickly took up the instinctive defensive crouch, ready to attack the object that had interrupted his slumber.

Quazraam ducked to avoid the heavy claw that was now swinging in his direction. The claw passed by and hit the desk top with a reverberating clack then went on to upset the fresh container of the sticky green fluid refreshment, which the navigator had just placed there.

Quazraam, his fury building, caught the still flailing appendage in his fighting claw and, twisting it with all his strength, forced Kraklac off balance. Trying desperately to regain that balance, Kraklac found himself bent over face down and almost onto the floor. He had by now lost most of his previous drowsiness and was cursing loudly.

"I am away from the board just a few Clats and, as usual, you immediately fall asleep," said Quazraam angrily, looking into the beady eyes of his captive. He was still twisting the appendage and applying pressure. "Well, now you will have to go to the galley and get me another cup of Mallio Juice, and then you can clean up that mess you just made. And be quick, or I just may report your continual sleeping on the watch to the Captain."

With the last word of his threat, Quazraam gave the other a hard and swift two legged kick into the other's mid-rift as he released, sending Kraklac skidding and tumbling across the floor in the direction of the corridor outside.

Still cursing and grumbling loudly, Kraklac picked himself up and ambled down the passage in the direction of the galley, defeated.

"I'll report you to our illustrious Captain, I will," He said, mimicking the other as he went.

Quazraam turned about and picked up the overturned stool and then sat at the screen to continue with this interrupted shift of monitor duty.

The heavier of the two claws opened and seven slender and dexterous finger like appendicles extended from within. Quazraam rested them to fit inside the tapered holes in the surface of a small sphere and began to focus the view screen to suit his own vision. The viewer then began panning widely over the region surrounding the city below them.

"Now I will need to go through all the strips again, all because of that 'Donzoe'," Quazraam grumbled to himself, "But that can wait, I am sure we missed nothing. I can easily do it later. Maybe tomorrow. Or leave it even to the day after that. Who really cares? Nothing happens down there anyway. Not with those Claks."

The view on screen focused to show the large expanse of the city and the surrounding hills from above. Panning the screen, the instrument cycled the territory for a hundred Siilens around, even to the inhabited island offshore. Quazraam had been ordered by the Captain to watch the island particularly. He had said its inhabitants were-'not as docile as the fools who occupied the city'.

Little did Quazraam know then, as he watched the quiet island, just what he had missed. By but only a few minutes of time, he missed the view of the Skimmer as it came in to land after passing across the wide ocean.

He had, and more importantly because of his same misfortune to have been struggling with his watch partner Kraklac, also lost a chance at taking one of those large rewards usually due if he had been able to report the sighting.

The four visitors made their way down the short ramp from the Skimmer as the three local beings walked closer.

One more time the humans were taken by the immense size and the unusual openness of being on a planets surface. One of the three ahead of them raised a hand in welcome.

They were of a human physical shape, shorter in height than the average Terran, though similarly proportioned. The skin of these beings this time had a bright pink cast and also these people had hair. It was of the same golden colour in all three and confined to just the back parts of their heads. Each wore it tightly formed, held by a clip device from behind. Their features bore a similarity to human except the ears were small and hardly noticeable and the nose was most distinguishable. Where Wyyrrum's features had a slight feline appearance, these were definitely canine.

"Welcome to our land of Murayssa," said the one in the middle, in clear Terran but spoken with a slightly musical lilt. All three wore the same style of attire. It consisted of a tight trouser to the lower body and then a loose brightly coloured coverall hanging down to the knees.

"My name is Qqo, this is Helf, and," indicating the shorter, "This is an offspring, Feru."

They then all dropped their arms to their sides and displayed their open palms to the visitors.

The visitors, not knowing exactly how to return this strange greeting, just bowed slightly as Wyyrrum had before.

Qqo continued, seeming to be distant in his manner.

"Wyyrrum has been in contact through another and has asked that we expect you and make you welcome. Please walk this way."

The three humans and with the robot following behind, walked away from the ship.

"At least they don't seem to need that silly quarantine which we were forced to go through on Morn," Stated Kindra.

G'zin concurred, "That's good. We must be immune to everything anyhow, following that treatment," Then looking at the ground beneath her feet, she continued in a low voice, "This surface seems to be almost alive, it moves but it is also hard."

Feru, the smallest of the trio, had overheard her comment and explained.

"We on the island are able to grow all materials which we need. The surface we are walking on is a type of vegetation that has been developed through hybrids for surfacing."

G'zin said quietly, so the three locals did not hear.

"I wonder. Do you remember that material on the last planet we surveyed? The one with all the radiation?"

Before Kindra could respond, Feru was continuing with a definite amount of pride in his dialogue.

"Even the clothing we wear and the dwellings are produced by strains of plant life. We grow each item naturally. Very little of which we use on this island is manufactured."

Clysta looked back to watch G'zin who had crouched to touch the material beneath her feet, and exclaimed in a shocked voice.

"Hey! Where is the Skimmer?"

Both G'zin and Kindra turned to look back to see also that the craft had disappeared.

"Do not fear," Qqo said in a calming voice, "Your craft is quite safe. A light diffusing pattern is protecting it from view, particularly from above. You are able to locate its position by that orange triangle, there on the surface growth. But we must now move on to cover quickly. Your strange garments will make you conspicuous."

Looking ahead at the buildings, Clysta observed to the side of the path they were following, two more orange triangles with patterns and a green one further away. She asked.

"Are those markers for showing concealed items also?"

"Yes they are," Qqo replied.

"And would they be air or space ships or something similar?" She asked again.

"We have many devices which to us do not blend too well with the beauty of this island."

Feru had answered this time but did not explain what they where, "We find a screen helps to keep the appearance of the area clear, clean and attractive."

By this time they had left the clearing and, after being guided past a number of various sizes of strange shapes, they finally came to a stop. They were at an opening or entrance into a large smooth building having a round and bulbous appearance. Their hosts motioned them to continue inside. On the interior, when they entered, they found it partitioned into rooms and levels and emanating everywhere with a bright concealed almost sunny illumination throughout the very spacious interior. All around there was a pleasant sweet smelling and fresh aroma.

Anticipating their curiosity, Helf spoke to them for the first time. It was in a voice of a higher pitch than the other two, still musical and almost having a feminine inflection.

"Yes, as you can see, this is one of our dwelling hybrids. It took two revolutions of our sun to grow. It is still growing but it has almost reached its maximum for this species. We do have a grower that will produce a much larger volume in less time. That growth we keep for use as meeting places."

"Now you must make yourselves comfortable," interrupted Qqo. "We will serve refreshments, after which you will have the time to tell us of your purpose for visiting the island of Murayssa."

# Chapter 53

During the ensuing conversation and discussions, these hosts showed an outwardly grateful attitude to their adopted planet's people for all that they had.

Inwardly and mostly concealed, the three visitors noticed it was a little different.

The Murayssians could not completely camouflage that hidden enmity which was for the race that had destroyed their own original world so many centuries ago. The memory, even after that lengthy passage of time, was still running deep. Occasionally a comment made by one or the other, would sometimes expose the buried feeling to these three visitors from another planet.

Time and its passing had of course managed to erase most of the worst memories. The welcome and kindness they had been shown by the changed generations of people of this world for these same centuries, had been valuable in defeating most of those memories.

Occasionally during the conversation, the minor cracks were still visible through a heavy facade of gratitude. Feru, who being perhaps of a younger age did not show these same signs.

The same hatred for anyone who may have an aggressive intention was also now directed at these creatures that had arrived from outside the boundaries of this arm of the galaxy. These descendants of the original refugees did not wish another reign of terror. One, which was likely to evolve, from these alien visitors. They, who had shown a visible delight in their attempts at terrorizing the people around the mainland and particularly in the Old Centre.

From the outset of their stay, the only contact the three friends had on the island was with the hosts Qqo, Helf and of course Feru. This short visit had been planned that way.

The three friends listened to the mostly one sided dialogue from their hosts. Finally Clysta thought it time to talk about the purpose for their being here on this world.

"We three and the robot have come here because my father recommended I visit this world of yours. He planned for us to receive a reward in his name. That was before he disappeared on his way to the next spiral arm of the galaxy. Then when we arrived in this system, we saw the two ships from our view point in space."

She then explained briefly about her father and the expedition, but did not speak of any other details. She described succinctly their meeting with Wyyrrum leaving his whereabouts unmentioned.

"I have good reason to believe, my father is a prisoner of these creatures along with some of his colleagues," explained Clysta.

Qqo was silent for a while and sat as if trying to make a decision, and then finally he looked at the three friends, saying.

"We were asked to give you whatever assistance we could. We of course have no weapons of any kind. Even the mainlanders do not possess anything able to match those these creatures have brought with them. I imagine Wyyrrum has explained to you, this planet has known peace for so long. Even the word peace itself has no meaning except as a reflection of times past. It is said there are a few ancient devices in the Old Centre. They might be useful against them perhaps in some kind of retaliation. But I have been led to believe, they are sealed in a vault somewhere in an underground chamber to remove them from temptation and keep them out of harms way."

Kindra looked at the other two. Then he asked.

"Do you think, perhaps these aliens would know of these weapons. They could easily have learned of them and have intentions of breaking into that vault."

"That is a possibility of course, but they will first need to know of the whereabouts of the vault and not many of the ordinary population even know of its existence," Quo answered, then looking furtively at Helf.

Helf saw the mistake, which Quo had made in referring to a most guarded secret. Even many on the mainland were not privy to that kind of information. Helf quickly changed the direction of the conversation.

"Please tell us. What is it that you yourselves intend to do?" Helf asked, "You must have some kind of plan? I suppose that first you need to see these aliens. So what can we do that will be of help to you?"

"Can you at least help us to get close to them," G'zin began. "We have…"

Clysta held up a hand to stop her in mid-sentence.

Then Clysta interrupting, said, "That way we can at least get a good look at them and assess their power. Then we will decide on which course of action," Clysta added with caution, "If any, that we must take."

The three islanders looked at each other then Qqo spoke.

"I think it can be done. It may not be easy but we can try. I am sure you understand it is also going to be dangerous. It will be impossible to go in your flying machine. You will need to leave it here on the island."

Quo leaned forward in his seat, and continued.

"The day after tomorrow is our day to visit the mainland. We go there each third day, along with a number of other islanders to trade our wares. You will need to dress as one of us of course. These creatures it seems from some reports I have had, have an intellect that allows them to see everything which is not usual. We will need to make changes to your faces—at least to appear to resemble ours."

G'zin was about to protest. But Helf cut her off.

"We can do it to last only temporarily, do not fear. Your hair will need to be changed, that can be done easily too. You two are slightly taller," indicating Clysta and Kindra. Then, looking to G'zin.

"Yours will be a matching height to ours."

Quo looked at the Euclid, puzzled.

"But the robot," he held back. Then, "It will need to remain here on the island. It will be too difficult to disguise."

Clysta said firmly.

"We will not go without Euclid. He is a very important part of our group and he must accompany us at all costs."

Quo rubbed his shallow chin. He once more looked at the robot then, as if rethinking the new problem.

"It will be just too difficult as I said previously," Quo went silent. Then Feru spoke for the first time.

"I have an idea that may work. The robot can be dressed as a roving seller. We will need to work harder in its case. They dress much differently than the normal merchants. And they carry their samples with them. That will assist in concealing much of the physical oddity. But perhaps with luck, the alien visitors will be too preoccupied with some other matters to notice."

Quo and Feru spoke to each other at length and debated the full possibility of a disguise. Finally Quo conceded and Feru volunteered to assist in an adequate costume for the robot.

This being settled, the visitors would have a chance to relax and make plans for the day after tomorrow when the trip to the mainland was to take place.

Kindra had been baffled since his first meeting with these dwellers of this planet. He thought a change of topic now might come as a tonic to the group.

"Tell me one thing," started Kindra, "It has been puzzling me since we met with Wyyrrum and now I am having the same trouble with you people. I know it may lead to a sensitive answer, but I cannot make up my mind just, which is masculine, and which is feminine and what relation the difference in an individual's sex makes on this planet. As you can see with Terrans the difference is most obvious."

It was also obvious their hosts were a little puzzled by the question and it was Qqo who answered.

"On this world, we do not have use for a reference of the sexes as it seems from your statement, your people are accustomed to. I, Quo, am decision maker number one in this set. Helf is the number two. Feru is the offspring of our communion."

Helf took up the next part of the explanation.

"This makes for a balanced output of product and duties. After two revolutions of our star, Qqo and myself exchange relationships and duties and carry on then with the change of our respective positions completed."

"Later," Qqo once again took up on the dialogue and continued, "Our offspring Helf will, after three more revolutions of our star, form a half of a set of two to carry on their own particular functions in the community and become producers."

Kindra thought for a moment taking it all in, then, "I think I got the answer to my question. Simple and efficient. Do you not think so, G'zin?" He asked with a sardonic smile.

"Sounds a little boring to me," she replied quietly.

Clysta heard and succinctly changed the topic.

"So. When and how do we change and get made up for the trip to the mainland?"

"Tomorrow is early enough to begin the changes in your appearance," Qqo answered, "Meanwhile we must show you to your quarters. Then after, we will show you some of our products and tomorrow a little of our home island. We can also make a selection of the correct apparel later tomorrow. Later in the day, we will prepare some merchandise and be ready to leave at sunrise the following day. We will also teach you some of our customs and marketing methods to make you ready for the event of questions by other inhabitants and of course the invaders."

On the morning of the third day, they gathered at the loading area for the trip to the mainland. Their group was not the only one crossing today. At least thirty other island dwellers were assembled, each giving the apparent customary showing of their palms to each group as it arrived.

The others traders did not outwardly show if they had noticed the difference in the build of the visitors and therefore the disguises appeared to be effective. Euclid had itself been disguised well enough in the clothing of the recommended travelling tinker, who it was earlier explained, always completely covered their heads by the hoods on their garments.

No-one amongst those gathered seemed interested in talking to these newcomers. It gave Clysta a feeling that perhaps somehow they were hiding their awareness, and she thought, also were possibly aware of their intentions.

Although these inhabitants of the island had simple needs, their technology was evidently far in advance of what they actually exposed.

Walking was the means of transport in physical terms. But heavy loads, such as produce were moved by levitation. How it actually worked, the three humans were unable to find out. They could only guess and watch as Qqo looked carefully at his pile of gourds. They had been placed on an unusual stiff mesh type of material with an almost transparent quality.

He then proceeded to walk around the outside of the pile with a long pencil like object, drawing an imaginary circle as he went. Qqo then stood back. To the surprise of the three humans, the mesh and the pile lifted from the ground about two or three centimetres and hovered.

"We are now ready to leave for the mainland," Qqo announced.

When they set off in the direction of the dock, the hovering goods followed along, untethered, behind them.

G'zin along with the robot, had earlier fulfilled a scheme to return to the Skimmer on the pretence of picking up some of their personal equipment. They had returned in good time to witness the group moving off.

"These people are so full of surprises," she said jokingly. And then she explained for the benefit of their hosts.

"I have brought along some medical supplies and some inter-talks. I also have those long range viewers. They may come in handy."

She had returned with a backpack with the items she had described. Euclid also had a parcel containing some items she had not mentioned and was making an excellent attempt at concealing its bulk.

The crossing of the strait to the mainland was by a type of transport that once again had the visitors confused.

They were to ride across the water on a flat surface that was of a similar looking material to the one, which their hosts and others who were gathering at the crossing point, had each used to carry their goods.

It was just less than transparent, flat and felt hard to their feet. The goods were each placed in designated areas on the material. This fabric too was mysteriously levitated at a slightly higher elevation than before. But in this case, it was hovering above the water of the small bay harbour.

The 'craft' was square and must have been thirty metres or more to each of its sides, though its extremities were this time hard to define. It just faded at the edges. The passengers spread out to sit or stand in groups as they prepared to leave the island.

Propulsion was another new mystery to the newcomers. It was moved through two large and oddly shaped sails. They were a conical shape in design again floating and secured to nothing they could see. But after the craft got under way, its speed was considerable.

"I notice you do not use any type of fuel in your daily life," said Kindra with interest. He was trying to locate where the wind was, which was apparently propelling this craft. The sea and the air around them were both quite at rest.

"We found ways of controlling the natural elements of our world many revolutions ago," Helf replied, not explaining further. "We have learned how to put these elements to work without wasting anything at all."

On the distant horizon they soon could see the shore of the mainland. In a short time they had arrived and the levitated craft simply floated of the surface of the ocean and onto a wide flat docking zone. A number of similar flat transports were each docked around the same area, indicating that other traders were here before them.

The port town on the shore of the mainland was large and filled with people who were coming and going about their business.

It was a clean and well organized centre for the merchants. Its buildings consisted mainly of coloured pyramid shapes that were again levitated above the surface. It was explained that these were there mostly as a protection from the elements and to give shelter from the brightness of the sun.

Feru told the three strangers that behind the port and inland, was the city whose name was Ffulamen. It was the centre of business of this, the planets major land mass, with these islanders. Although Wyyrrum had explained previously that the planet had abolished the need for economics long ago, it was obvious the local people here and particularly the islanders, enjoyed its adventures.

"What a beautiful city," G'zin said in awe at the view, as they left the area of the port, making their way through the crowds.

Quo left the group to deposit his merchandise with one of the established sellers. He returned shortly and suggested they head in the direction, which would lead them to the Old Centre.

They arrived at an area where a crowd was gathering.

"This is our motion station," Helf informed them.

Transport here on the mainland was once again on foot. Helf went on to explain that distances could be covered by stepping onto lanes formed in wide strips of short and strand like vegetation.

They appeared to have a similarity to that hybrid as was on the island on the area where they had landed the Skimmer. The difference in this area though, was these lanes of vegetation, waved in a forward motion, as if in a perpetual flow. And each lane was of differently coloured stripes.

It soon became obvious, whilst they watched other travelers, that the colours were an indication to show the varieties of speed. A passenger would move onto a strip and off the passenger would go. Then to alter the speed of travel the rider stepped from one colour to another to increase or decrease the pace.

"I suggest we stop acting as sightseers," Clysta warned, "We are supposed to be here as local merchants."

She turned to check the robot Euclid that had been wearing the disguise of a tinker with some effort. It had mastered the crouch and walk but some of the movements of the arms still looked mechanical.

Clysta carried on, asking in the direction of Quo.

"Will this track get us close to the Old Centre?"

After Quo had nodded in confirmation, Clysta continued.

"Wyyrrum told us briefly it was something of a central administration area or building. The Centre also is where he said the creatures had landed their shuttle and made it their present headquarters. If so, then that is where we should go to start."

# Chapter 54

Quazraam cursed.

One of the other two crewmen had just left his small resting room after informing him that the Captain had just called for him. He knew what he wanted. He was expecting to get from him personally, a full report of the watch of the two days before.

He had been putting off checking the scanning of that period for most of that same day. The Captain did pretty nasty things to any one in charge of the watch, if they had not the report ready when he called for it.

He went down the dim corridor to find Kraklac.

He found him slouched in a side room close to the main control room, doing nothing in particular as usual.

"The Captain just called," he informed his comrade, "He wants a full report. And quick."

He moved up close to Kraklac, and forced his body to its fullest height.

"I warned you that your sleeping on the watch would one day get us into trouble," he said as he vented his impatience. He took a wild swing with the larger claw at Kraklac's head section.

Kraklac, dopey as he usually was, was always ready for an attack. He had anticipated the action and ducked just in time, his skull section shrinking into the socket in the upper body shell.

"Awe, shut up your cawing," he said venomously, regaining his full posture, "We can do a speed scan, set to show up on anything that isn't usual. That way we can be through before the next call."

"Ok. But be careful not to miss anything," Quazraam said in agreement, "You go now and start up the monitor, I will follow soon."

In single file they both left the small room, Kraklac heading for the control room, Quazraam stalling, needing to give him time to let him start up the equipment. The control room was occupied by the crewmember that had delivered the message.

"Anyone for chow!" Came a voice from the doorway.

The creature entering the control room was the fourth member of the maintenance shift. He was carrying a large stone bowl of live and squirming Xlynx Slugs.

"These are fresh out of the Farm Bins," he said, as he made crude gurgling sounds.

He rummaged through the thriving heap and pulled out three wriggling fat ones and threw them into the air over toward Kraklac's head.

A long and slender whip flashed out from its socket at the back of the head of the other. Quazraam, who had now entered, had caught the slugs short of mid flight before the slower moving Kraklac had had time to focus on them. Then, even before Kraklac had moved his head to look upward, they were already in the open feeding slot that was the mouth, half way down Quazraam's upper torso.

Quazraam then growled and pointed.

"This 'garbage' here only eats after we have finished work and not before. Now. Out, Zimskik and leave us alone, we have work to do. You too, Slurge. Out!"

He lashed out with a leg but missed as Zimskik scurried for the safety of the corridor, the bowl still held tight to his body. Slurge followed, skittering along with his upper shell stooped low so not to make an easy target for the likes of Quazraam.

The two creatures, now alone, returned to their task.

They watched the screen as the records and time flashed by.

"What was that? See. There."

After watching the screen for what seemed ages, Quazraam's keen vision had finally seen something, a movement on the ocean.

"Back up a bit," he instructed the other.

"Ah, its only a fish, nothing else," suggested Kraklac as usual, obstinately.

"Reset the magnification will you, and reverse the strip to the frame before the fish," Quazraam ordered, exasperated at the other's attempt at laziness.

This done, the viewer went over a rerun but this time it was at a slower speed.

"There, that flat shape. The one above the fish. It's a flyer," said Quazraam, "Increase the magnification some more."

Kraklac adjusted the control.

"Now that is a new design. I haven't seen one with that shape on this planet before. Have you?"

Kraklac was not very interested. He had already missed two meals and his insides hurt. All he wanted to look at was a large bowl of fresh Xlynx slugs.

"How should I know, I'm just a replacement cook. You are the brainy one here. What do you think it is? It may be some kind of bird."

"That's no bird. See. Those markings. They look familiar to me," Quazraam said.

Then, thinking more to himself, 'Where have I seen those markings and that design before?'

Quazraam was just too weary to pursue it any farther. It had been ages since he had slept well. With his troubles he was having with Kraklac and his doziness. He needed a good rest. He had also been studying this sequence long enough, besides making his reports sound correct. He too was ready for a meal. He added as he increased the viewer speed.

"Whatever it was, that big fish missed a meal. Let's see further."

He set his mind back to the recorded scanning and started again.

"Look. It is making toward the island," The navigator followed the progress of the strange shape. Then later. As he watched its progress, "Did you see? It has landed."

Once more he thought. 'Where was it I saw those markings before?'

"So it landed. What does it matter? So it's a flyer. So what?" Kraklac was slowly edging off his seat as he moaned his dissent. Quazraam's attention was now fully on his screen. Kraklac continued. "I am getting hungry and I need to eat. I'm going."

With the fastest motion he had made in days, Kraklac dived for the opening to the corridor and then disappeared, leaving only the sound of his four spindly legs clacking toward the galley. Quazraam spun around intent on stopping Kraklac, but he was too late.

He decided he too needed to eat, so he switched off the scanner screen and left the recorder to run on automatic. He dropped from the stool and ambled off down the passage, he himself heading toward the galley. He had a report that would satisfy the Captain for now. He also had something else he would follow up on later. Whilst the other three were asleep.

# Chapter 55

The Terrans and their local hosts stepped from the mover at Qqo's signal. The group was now approaching the centre of the city, which was marked by a structure of a kind the three visitors had never seen before.

It was almost fantasy-like with an unmistakable appearance of its age, though not through decay but by its aura.

The structure held a look of majesty and reverence, both at the same time. Its formation was mainly of a series of spirals, slopes and towers mostly of a dull gold, interspersed with glass spiral designs adorned with crystal inlaid ornaments and projections in random but appealing locations. All adding to the enhancement of its beauty.

On all sides of the edifice, as far as they could see, was an enormous and spacious courtyard, also of a glass or crystal material. The surface, which was hard, was transformed into a comforting softness when touch by their feet. Its thickness was incalculable, as it was as clear as air and the bottom appeared to be far into the planets depths.

G'zin spoke what was in her mind, whilst taking in the view of the structure.

"It looks much like the father of the museum we visited on Morn."

Her two friends nodded their silent agreement and carried on. They all progressed on foot around and to the other side of the great structure and Qqo halted them and pointed ahead.

"There. That is the creatures shuttle," he said, a trace of sadness in his voice.

Spoiling the beauty and reverence of the area was the shuttlecraft of the aggressors. It was large and unsightly. It was an ugly brown colour and consisted of twisted and irregular pipes around an oddly shaped central pod. It stood, almost with a crouching and threatening appearance, on six spindly legs to cover an area of the glassy courtyard, now badly scorched.

There, beneath it, was a shallow charred pit carved obviously by the reaction motors of the ship, or whatever these creature used for propulsion and descent control.

The group stood in silence. Then G'zin spoke.

"I saw a vidi' once when I was at my early school. That looks very similar to an animal of the sea they were showing us in one of our lectures. I remember, on my planet, it being called a-a-'Crabbolicci'. I think."

"See that slight shimmering of the air, there, about ten metres around the legs," Clysta motioned with her head to avoid pointing. "It has to be a deflection field of some type."

Euclid had been silent up until now and said in a low voice.

'My sensors are confirming that fact Miss Clysta.'

"Well, that settles that. We can't just go up and knock," said G'zin, then she asked. "Have any of your-err, set,-seen any of the creatures?"

"No, we have not had that opportunity," Qqo answered quietly. "We have been informed of their outward appearance though. From their description, they are quite unpleasant to see, nothing at all like us, or you in form. We have in the oceans of this planet, a crawling creature that is very small and not of a likeable appearance. These beings have a comparison to those. These visitors, I have been informed, are also of a much greater size of course. It would appear these also have a greater intelligence."

"Where are they likely to be now?" Kindra asked, noticing that none of the creatures were to be seen.

Qqo answered.

"They are said to be unable to stand the stronger light of the sun, especially during its high point. They will appear when the sun has passed well beyond its midway point, toward the horizon."

Clysta whispered to G'zin.

"Make a mental note of that. It may be useful to know later."

She then turned to their guides, saying.

"We have seen enough for now, let us move away before we become conspicuous. There is a chance they are scanning the crowds at this very moment."

The group moved on and away from the central square. When they had reached a point out of sight of the craft, Qqo asked Clysta.

"What do you intend to do from now?"

"We need to find a place to sleep and eat," Clysta answered. "We also cannot risk endangering yourselves. You have been good enough to us up to this point. I suggest you carry on with your business, after pointing us toward some suitable quarters."

Feru spoke up before Qqo could give his reply.

"I have a good friend who lives here in the Centre who can perhaps see to your needs. This one was with me in our education works. This one is also from this area and knows of many things. I am sure that person will be pleased to be your guide. May I ask?"

Feru looked sideways at Quo.

Qqo's otherwise pleasant face now took on a stern and angry appearance.

"If you mean to recommend that no-good lay about, Shram," he said, trying to hide his temper. "Shram is a rebel and will never do any good,"

"But Qqo, Shram is so good at heart," Helf insisted, trying to defend Feru's friend, "Shram helped Feru through a most difficult stage. Who else is there to recommend and who lives near the Old Centre? We ourselves are not too familiar with any others who might live around this part of the city. And you must agree, Feru knows Shram much better than we do."

"I will not deny that one was the one who assisted Feru, but Shram is still a rebel and is very likely to cause upset to this planet one of these days." Qqo was beginning to loose some of his anger.

"Sounds like someone we need on our side," joked G'zin, half in seriousness.

Qqo finally conceded, returning to his original calm and pleasantness.

"But then, as you have said Helf. Whom else is there who we know well enough and can fully recommend?"

After a few second of silence, Quo continued with his capitulation.

"I suppose Shram is the only one. I will admit that one is of a most different kind to the normal. You could be correct."

"I do not like to interrupt," Kindra added, "But let us be the judge of this-'Shram's-intentions and ability to be of help. We need to find somewhere to stay in the city and we may as well start with this individual Shram. Where do we find this person?" Kindra still felt unable to establish gender.

"If Qqo will allow, I will take you immediately to Shram's own quarters," Feru said, looking and almost pleading toward Qqo.

Another period of silence went by, as Qqo appeared to think over the few if any alternatives. Then, nodding in agreement, he said.

"You may go along with them as guide and to introduce them to Shram. We will wait at the transport. It leaves at dusk," and then with finality, "Please be there."

# Chapter 56

The route taking them to the quarters used by Shram, Feru's friend led them through the centre of the city and away from the place where the alien craft had landed. On a scale of one to ten, this city came easily up to ten. Buildings were immaculate and clean. The designs were mostly functional, with exteriors of such an unusual individuality that was not wasted. Each one of them was matched to its neighbour so as to blend all into one in every direction.

They travelled quite some distance, mostly on foot. A part of their trip was by a stretch of the moving pavement material. On one of the wide avenues, they passed what was left of one of the buildings, which must be one of those they had been told the aliens had destroyed. A large space torn from the always spectacular flow of the avenues was all that remained. To accompany its absence was a large, shallow crater with heat burnt scars around it on all sides.

The avenues the group passed along were generally inhabited by scatterings of people. All of the passers by that they did see were attired in the same style of clothing as that of their first contact, Wyyrrum. Some of their textures were varied and the colours differed but basically the effect was still the same. Hands and feet were concealed and each carried nothing at all, neither parcels, or purses, or goods.

After a lengthy period of walking through and past people, mostly solitary and groups of no more than three, G'zin made her observation known.

"Feru, there appears to be a distinct range of texture and colour of the fabrics worn by many of the people here, although the styles are similar. Does this hold some significance, or is it some kind of style change?"

"You are most perceptive, G'zin," Feru replied, "Although the people of this city have no need for rank or status, there is a certain flow of responsibility and service in the duties accredited to each of them. This is shown as a relationship in a community position which each holds. That is then indicated in the form of their dress, by material and by colouring."

"We would have a tendency to call it a uniform, or something like that," Clysta suggested, trying to help in the definition. "Is this the same?"

"Well almost, though uniform is a term of the past," Feru continued trying to answer the questions as the carried on walking. "I am not too well versed on the more violent parts of our history, but I will attempt to answer some of your questions. This planet's people have endeavoured to put behind them what a uniform represented in the past and try to disassociate the meaning. This system was a way in which position or function would be obvious without advertising the fact. Variations in the colour and material are a way they can display a persons duties in the community, small though some might be, without reviving those old status patterns."

"This sounds interesting," interrupted Kindra, "Please, tell us more of how it works."

"It is a little confusing, even for me sometimes. On the island, we have not the same needs for its formulas," Feru confessed, "But I will try to explain."

"Everyone on this world, when they reach a certain age, becomes a Plan Controller. This is a state when the person is given responsibility in the city's well being. Leading up to that stage each is on a sliding scale which ends in finally achieving that position."

"And clothing acts as an indicator to others of what level the person is at," Kindra said.

"Precisely," Feru answered, then added, "But without badges or reward."

"Sounds like an easy system," concluded Clysta, "And what about your people on the island? You say you are not a part of all this."

"We are not included in any control of the mainland. Whether it be city or out-city," said Feru, "Our race, as you know, is not of this planet. And even though it was many centuries ago, we still maintain some of our previous beliefs. One of them is that real rewards should be given for effort."

They were now approaching an enormous pyramid set back from the avenue. The visible triangular sides were of a translucent texture. As Clysta studied the surfaces they took on never ending visual changes generating an appearance of waves. These waves were of the many spectral colours moving ever upwards, toward the pinnacle that was the top of the structure.

"That flowing motion reminds me very much of the 'Thought Cube'," G'zin said to Kindra in a low whisper.

Feru informed the three friends.

"This is the place where my friend Shram dwells."

Feru said the words with a little added pride. He then beckoned them to follow as he led them to an opening in the base of one of the sides at ground level and guided them into the interior.

Once through and inside the opening, Feru stopped at a screen to one side of the narrow and confining hallway. There he touched a strip, which must have been some form of control. Feru stood facing the screen in silence. The others stood, with Euclid, waiting for some sound or response from the device.

Without saying or apparently hearing any sound, Feru turned back to the others, saying.

"We are fortunate. Shram is presently within his quarters and says we are welcome to go inside, there we will be able to meet with him."

Feru motioned them to follow. He led the way once more, this time farther into the structure. The interior of the pyramid beyond the entrance was quite unexpected.

An area that previously was before them and empty, opened wider the farther they walked into it. The effect was outside the comprehension of the three Terrans but, as if by optical illusion, the walls and ceiling around them appeared to move away as they progressed, giving the impression of never ending space.

It advanced to a state of not being inside a structure but outdoors. The illusion, if it was illusory, was so very convincing. All around were pleasant sights of scenic views and a number of small animals and flying things. A soothing tinkling musical sound was in evidence all around them. All was serene and exceedingly appealing to the eye and the ear.

"We will make our way to Shram's space by way of the 'transport'," Feru said, "Come this way, please."

Straight ahead of them was a vertical glass like shimmering form rising out of the material of the floor to a height of three metres. As they approached it, the substance changed to an upward flowing mist. The visitors immediately recognized the similarity to that same kind of medium from the gardens on Morn. They each left unsaid what was going through their minds, saving their comments until a later time when they could be alone.

"Follow me. Just walk into the mist," Feru said, as he motioned to G'zin.

G'zin hesitated and looked toward Clysta. The three friends then looked at each other and then at Euclid, who stood behind the group, impassive as usual. Each of them was unsure of what the relationship in this medium might mean.

Kindra was first to ask, hiding his true question.

"What is it? Where will we be going?"

"Oh" Feru said slightly embarrassed, "I must apologize. I did not remember. You are not accustomed to the major dwellings on this planet," he then turned to face the visitors, saying, "This is a transport, and it is quite safe. See, I will demonstrate."

With that, he turned on his heel and walked straight into the substance and disappeared. This gave the three friends a short time to voice their puzzling speculation between themselves, but before they arrived at a conclusion, Feru had returned.

He was now dressed differently in a dress tunic and a purple sash around his waist.

"Is this demonstration adequate?" Feru asked.

They all completed their part of the charade by sounding puzzled but convinced. So Feru once more gestured toward the medium, saying, "G'zin and Kindra may go first, then you and your robot, Clysta. You need not be concerned about the effects on Euclid. This will cause it no harm. Then I will follow you."

Clysta moved in her turn along with Euclid toward the illusion. The robot accelerated and positioned itself to pass through the medium first, and a half of a step ahead of her. The result was slightly different than on Morn, somehow smoother, but still similar to passing through an open doorway.

Clysta emerged to stand inside a room looking around and then into the deep dark eyes of a tall and handsome person, who to Clysta was most undoubtedly male. This being had many more attributes, with more definite facial features. Almost more Terran even, in appearance but not quite. He was holding out his hand in a mostly unusual form of greeting for this world. He was dressed in a loosely fitting top and three-quarter length loose fitting slacks. This attire was most totally unexpected in relation to others of this city who they had seen on the outside.

'A very unusual medium, is it not Miss Clysta.' Even Euclid's own reference to the transport was trying to maintain their charade.

Clysta caught sight of G'zin, who had been first through the transport. The eyes of the diminutive female from Fryl, were aglow and the smile was showing its intensity as she moved closer to this person who must certainly be the one named Shram.

Feru entered the area and began immediately to introduce the Terran visitors and Euclid. He then introduced Shram.

G'zin, still glowing, looked long at Shram. Clysta watched, slightly amused that Shram was becoming uncomfortable, having noted her attention too. She decided to ask a question after the last of the introductions had been completed. Her curiosity was peaked and had got the better of her.

"I am pleased that you are able to receive us Shram. I must ask a question and you may find it very impertinent, but in my case it will need to be answered eventually, even if it were only to avoid some future embarrassment. I am puzzled at what sex you might be? You look to be dressed as a male of our race. But up until now you are the only one of the mainland dwellers who I have seen dressed in anything other than a total body cover. I must say that your people are confusing us and particularly me, no end."

"That is easy to answer," said Shram, "We are not divided into sex as you, from the question, are possibly conditioned to. Our people do not need the divisions given by the different sexes. We each share duties and carry on life not knowing any of the confusions or complications brought about by such a system."

"Then what about propagation?" Kindra asked, joining in on the discussion.

"That is done simply through design, as and when it is assessed as being necessary by the High Committee," Shram answered.

He continued, "Almost all of the planet's population is of a nil-sex ideal. It has been this way for many hundreds, even thousands of revolutions of our star."

"So that means you are essentially all of the same. Males are as females and females are as males," G'zin suggested a little embarrassed at her interpretation of the answer. She was now eager to hear Shram's reply for the most obvious of reasons.

"Well, almost. Our bodies have the differences yours probably have, but ours are of no consequence to the individual. We have a system of total equality," Shram finished.

"Of course," Feru added, "The people of my home island have a slightly different approach to the system, but since our race made this world our home we too have come to adopt its virtues."

Feru continued, "But my good friend Shram is not saying it completely the way Shram himself wishes it. Shram has earned that label of Rebel, which my father warned you about before we left him and Helf. Shram came by that title because he feels, along with a few others, that a return to the difference in the sexes has been long overdue. That is why I myself like to refer to Shram as he, as in male. It may mean little in the difference in the sexes which you are yourselves acquainted with, but that is Shram."

"Then," interrupted Clysta, "If it is not too awkward for Shram, we too should put to use the same gender class we are used to, and we will consider him as a male."

Shram caught a brief glimpse of the intoxicating flashes from G'zin's eyes and found 'he' had difficulty speaking his next words. Catching 'his' breath 'he' said.

"That is fine by me. Though what it means to me may be something we will have to leave perhaps until a later time. The actual differences I mean," then, quickly changing the topic, he asked.

"I was told you require some kind of help. I will endeavour to do whatever I can that is useful to your needs. My friend Feru here informed me you would need shelter too. We can easily make those arrangements later. But first you must all make yourselves comfortable and we will discuss your plight over some refreshments."

# Chapter 57

"Tell me more about your world?" asked Clysta, "We have been told a little by a person called Wyyrrum and then some more from Quo and Helf, the islanders. I would like to hear the point of view of someone closer to our stage of life. In all cases your people are described to us as a gentle race of beings."

"We are that many times over," Shram began, "We have been this way since probably many thousands of your years in our own past. You say you have already met with Wyyrrum. You were lucky. Wyyrrum does not usually make contact, except under severe or certain consequences. I have seen him myself, only once. He must have told you of the 'Wars'. They are part of a past history even farther back in our time, when our ancestors took over this sector of the Galaxy, by force in most instances. In those times our people were of a very fierce and dominant nature."

"One item we have missed in all of our discussions with the people of your world is its name," G'zin interrupted, "What is the name you use for it?"

"We have become so insular in our thinking," Shram said, "We hardly ever use a name, but it was once known as Vedanne. I suppose that is as good as anything to call it, even now."

"The Vedannians of the past had explored this region of space many Quads ago," added Feru. "Our planet where our race originally lived was one of their earlier discoveries. It had at the time, a well developed civilization but had not the capability of advancing too far into space. At least that is how it is told on Murayssa."

"A Quad by the way is equal to one hundred and fifty of our own Star Revolutions," explained Shram, interrupting Feru. Then he once more took charge of the dialogue.

"The original explorers, and I suppose you may call them colonizers, did many good things to and for the planets they had discovered. They worked in many ways of making desert worlds livable and improved those already bearing any kind of life. Many became populated and prosperous and interplanetary trade flourished. That trading eventually generated into fierce competition, which in less than ten Quads had turned into warring between the various traders."

"A vast and uncontrollable change had come about," Shram added, and then continued, "It was a disastrous change. Jealousy progressively took a hand, territories were being disputed, first over the lesser populated of the worlds, until these became the first battleground. Self made War Lords were in command within a short time and more devastating weapons were invented to force their will. After a time whole planets, that were being fought over, were reduced to the same barren lifelessness they had originally been developed from."

"Wyyrrum was able to show us records of the planet where Feru's ancestors came from," Clysta said, "That one seemed to be the last big battleground. What was it which caused the change to what your people are today?"

"My people avoid any discussion on that period, but I call it simple conscience. It is said that one was the battle which changed it all and brought them to their senses," Shram answered.

He continued once more, "There was nothing left to fight about. Unless you count our untouched world of Vedanne where it had all begun. Some of the War Lords had been killed in the battles on other planets, but their instigators were still secretly running the wars from this planet. A movement had been started years before the final end of that part of history. It, the movement, was trying to halt these horrible and useless wars. It had almost become too late. This planet was sure to be next."

While Shram stopped to take a sip from his cup, Feru took up the story.

"There was only Mure left you see, of all the original inhabited planets. That is where my ancestors are from, we ourselves named our adopted island Murayssa from that name. Although it is still known by the Vedannians, using the name of Darz. The fiercest of these War Lords had entrenched himself on Mure and was developing devices of horrendous destructive power. The last remaining independent armies surrounded the planet and blasted the surface with unimaginable force, killing and destroying everything in sight. They are said to have had a weapon, which caused a reaction in the metabolism of the planet surface. It activated amongst other things, a deadly radiation killing almost all of the remaining people who had managed to survive the onslaught. A surviving handful were evacuated and brought here. We are the descendants of what remained of those refugees."

"That was a sad era in our history," said Shram, "So sad it is rarely recalled. It is though, the first lesson we are aware of after birth, and though inwardly everyone of this world knows of it, they just do not need to talk about it."

Kindra asked,"And what became of those armies, were they allowed to live following such devastation? And their weapons and their leaders-where did they end up?"

"History tells us they were," Shram said in answer. "Though only in isolation. The movement of reconciliation had developed into a larger proportion of this planets government. When those armies had been convinced of the futility of carrying on, the fighting stopped and they too were isolated. The weapons? We are not to know. It is thought that they were all destroyed.

"This whole planet was purged of war and its evils. Individual leadership was abolished. None of our people were ever to become outright leader of any group or level ever again. It took many revolutions of our star to remove the scars left by those Quads of battle and useless destruction.

"A new beginning was made and the remaining people of Mure were given their island, Darz, or Murayssa as a place of their own. In the main it was to make amends and beseech forgiveness. It was also in an effort to try to rekindle the culture they had been deprived of."

"That was not all though," said Feru, interrupting Shram.

Shram nodded his head in recognition and continued, "The Committee of the peace movement, convinced it should never be allowed to happen again, decided it was best to isolate our planet and its peoples from the rest of the Galaxy. Almost taken as being given a sentence for their wrongdoings. It was decreed they had to ensure that any other race of people, perhaps from a world far away, would never learn of the secrets and have knowledge of those devastating weapons. They were afraid of a recurrence of the power and devastation we had wrought.

"For the longest of time, those following after this did not venture into space again. They developed into an introverted race, changing and learning new meanings to life and its pursuits.

"Then as a final safeguard, they set up the Screen, that same one which now conceals our star system from outside view. We have hidden here ever since that time."

Shram had finished his dialogue and sat in silence, obviously thinking of the planet's past and its effect on his world of today.

"You are well informed in the history of the things your people seem ready to hide," Kindra said.

"That is how I became known as a rebel," he replied, "I have not been as others are, who try to hide and hope they will forget. I could be easier termed an enigma. I do not know exactly why or where I gained these unusual traits but I have them. My mind is not as most that are found on this planet. I am inquisitive and have been blessed with a sense of intuition."

Euclid had been stationed to one side of the group, in silence. The robot interrupted Shram, saying.

'This unit has endeavoured to develop those same qualities in the patterns within my own Nega-Fluid mentality. It is a sequence my makers did not find necessary to my purpose. I have not yet had the ability to complete that function. It is a well developed mental quality held highly throughout the Terran civilization. It keeps Earthlings always looking ahead, always seeking answers. It is one that someday I will develop. '

"That sure was some speech, Euclid," expressed Kindra. He thought it was time to dissipate the seriousness of the past few minutes of Shram's dialogue. "I suppose that could be the reason behind a few of Euclid's peculiar actions I have had some trouble understanding. I just never thought it out, him being a robot."

Clysta turned to face Shram, who had been sitting, legs crossed, on the floor. She asked.

"You must be obviously aware of these beings presently in orbit."

"Oh! Yes," he answered, passionately.

"You must also know they are travelers from beyond our arm of the galaxy? And what do you see in the visit?"

"I think they have come with only one purpose in their mind and that is to set a base for hostilities," Shram began, "On the second day after their shuttle had settled down on the planet. It was just outside the city at the time. A group containing seven of the city's senior people was detailed with instructions to see these aliens and to greet them to our world.

"The aliens had not been outside of their craft up to that time. They had remained concealed inside the ship and our people had no idea what to expect. The group's purpose was to make welcome whoever the aliens might be. They were to be invited to participate in a meeting with more of our peoples and show them through the city.

"The appointed elders arrived at the landing place and waited for some time, close to the alien craft. By the use of some device within the strange craft they were drawn inside and disappeared.

"One day later, their dead and mutilated bodies were expelled. Just cast out onto the surface in the area in front of the spacecraft. They had all been drained of their body fluids, and just left as if they were a used dried fruit.

"These creatures have since been seen outside the craft on occasion but have not announced any other intentions of contact with my people. On each third day they would lift off and return into space presumably to their ship in orbit. On their return, they would circle the city and each time, pick out and blast and destroy a building. They then land in a new area. The last landing though was a little different. This time they landed in the Square of the Old Centre and have been in the same place for four days and have not moved back into orbit or to anywhere else since.

"I wonder why the Old Centre? Isn't that where your people, Quo or Feru, said the records of your history are kept?" Clysta asked, turning to Feru.

"Yes, it was Quo who said it was," Feru answered a little embarrassed, as he avoided the look from Shram.

Shram then said, "That is information which is not supposed to be known by the majority of the people. I believe it is also close to the sealed vault where the records of the ancient weaponry are kept. That may have some significance."

"What have your people decided to do, the people who are of a responsible level?" G'zin asked once again looking at Shram.

"Nothing. Nothing at all," Shram's reply was almost a retort, "All that has happened is complete lack of concern for the matter. The population just goes about their business and their studies as if nothing has been going on. So far as I see it, except for that unfortunate welcoming group, they are ignoring the visitors. It is as if they expect the aliens will go away one day and leave us in the same peace we knew before."

"Have you seen any of these creatures?" Clysta asked.

"Yes, twice, but only from a distance," Shram answered, a frown crossing his face.

"I was at the rear of a crowd at the edge of the city when they landed. Oh, it must have been their third or forth landing here-I believe. A second time was in another place they landed at, closer to the Centre. Three of the creatures left their craft on that occasion. One thing I have noticed is it is always a long period of time after they had made a landing.

"I am sure they must have had been scanning us from the inside, before these three finally exited the ship. They are not like us at all, or anything I have seen near here. The body is a like a hard and polished shell. They were of different sizes but the average appeared to be more than half again as tall as I am. I was too far away to see many other details but I am told they have claw things up at the front and walk partly upright on four spindly legs."

'If you will pardon this interruption to your description,' said Euclid again. 'My records along with a recent description given by Quo, show a depiction similar to that which makes these beings comparable to a Lobster. A crustacean, which is an inhabitant of the oceans of Old, Earth. I also show a record of a creature also which is a land animal and inhabits the mountains on one planet in the Proxima Centauri system. Both are small in size and of lower and almost negligible intelligence.'

Feru interrupted saying, "My elder, Qqo new of someone who was quite close and said she saw beings brought out of the craft who appeared to be similar in bodily proportions to ourselves but dressed differently. There were three or four of them who the creatures paraded around and they were all on a tether. Almost as if they were displaying them to the onlookers, they said."

"Wyyrrum said he knew my father was with the aliens landing party," said Clysta. "That must be why he knew, but how?"

"Whatever happens anywhere on Vedanne, Wyyrrum knows about it," Shram suggested, this time with conviction, "Wyyrrum is one of this planet's oldest. And wisdom comes with age."

Clysta sat back in the chair. She glanced at her friends Kindra and G'zin, saying. "I am sure now the dreams I have had in the past had a meaning, almost a premonition. The whole scene is becoming clearer now. In some I have even had a distorted vision of a creature to one side. I remember the creature that Euclid has described, and it was a creature quite similar in appearance to that. In all of those strange dreams of my father, there has been the feeling of dread. I knew there had to be some sense to them right from the start. Now I am sure of it."

Feru was the one to ask, "What do you intend to do?"

"There is only the one thing to do," Clysta said without even studying the implications, "I must find a way to rescue my father. And if at all possible, his crew and companions."

"If they are still alive." Clysta added with a tone of sadness.

# Chapter 58

The next day Clysta awakened the others early. Euclid was busy making breakfast arrangements with the strange food dispenser. It took a while to get through to the auto system, as the memory circuits just did not recognize the voice pattern of the robot.

Shram was eventually awakened. Euclid was having a lengthy and anxious dialogue with the meal dispensers command circuits. Finally, Shram took over and ordered them all a selection of crystals similar to those, which had been served at the island home of Feru.

These really are tasty," said G'zin as she popped a third crystal into her mouth, "Are they grown or are they just processed?"

"They are both. Those you are eating grow naturally and some of those over there are manufactured," was the answer given by Shram, especially for G'zin, "In simple terms, the system in the unit transports the molecules via wave generation. The crystals are then grown through magnetic attraction on the disc in the unit. The flavour is through molecular selection, by the equipment to match the individual's order."

"Now that has been settled," said Kindra to stop the conversation from leading into another lengthy narrative. He then turned to Clysta and asked, "What are your plans?"

"First I would like to get close to their shuttle craft," she replied. She in turn then turned to face Shram.

"Yesterday, we were taken to the Old Centre to see the alien ship. Whilst we were there, we could see what appeared to be an opaqueness of sorts, close to the base of their craft. Something akin to what we know as a force deflection field. It was enveloping the area around it. Do you know if it is or could be so?"

"I myself noted that when I saw their landing craft on the second time," Shram slowly answered. Then, "It could well be. I made comment about it to my companions, but to be honest they were completely uninterested in the whole matter. The people here just don't care who these beings are, or what it all means. I have felt so frustrated about it. I suppose you people are up until now, the only ones who have shown any real interest in them or their real purpose. Excepting for the occasional sightseers from other districts, who are few if any."

"Well," Clysta broke in, "If what you say is so, then I expect not much help from the City's inhabitants."

She stood up from her seat and continued, "If you don't mind I would like to leave now to revisit the area where they have landed. We need to take a good look around. I may come up with an idea.

"But whatever happens," she added, with final conviction, "From now on, I am going to undertake to make things right and I do not intend to let anything get in the way."

"Now I remember!"

Quazraam, who had been up to now partly laying and partly hanging from his delegated suspensor lounge, tilted his large body and swung his four pointed feet downward and onto the course deck. He clacked rapidly with his right claw as he headed in the direction of the other lounger where the motionless and dozing Kraklac lay.

"What is the matter now?" Kraklac cawed as Quazraam rolled him over. Sleep was still fogging his brain. "Do you never stop? You have been keeping me from sleep for all of this rest period, with your scudding and clacking up and down and in and out of the corridor."

The eyestalks retracted into the beings headpiece as Kraklac made an attempt to regain his previous unconscious state.

"Those markings!" Screamed Quazraam, now close enough to begin tapping at Kraklac's head with a claw, "I have remembered where it was that I saw them last. Now you get up and man your station. You lazy 'Gonzo'."

He grabbed at one leg of the grumbling Kraklac and, holding it tightly in one mandible, tugged at it until he fell from the cot onto the floor. Then, clacking through the doorway, he set off in a hurry down the passage with the other in tow skidding along on its back, his other legs flailing around in the air.

Quazraam was headed for the large ship's control room and the viewing equipment.

Pushing the half awakened Kraklac onto the stool with one claw, he extended the appendicles of the other to switch on and adjust the controls of the scanner.

"Now. Wake up. Find the shot of that flyer from three daylights back," he ordered. "And magnify. I want to see it up close this time. Real close."

Kraklac had still not regained his full consciousness, so it took a while to locate the position on the recording unit. Meanwhile, Quazraam had to occasionally clip the other on the side of the head just to keep him awake. After a second run through, Quazraam finally saw what he thought was the part he needed.

"Stop!" He shouted in a growl. Kraklac did as he was bid, "Back up fifteen frames. There it is, freeze that," bellowed Quazraam as Kraklac almost overran the frame again. "Now, switch over to this ships exterior scanners. I want to see the little 'Swaddy Boat' we caught at the edge."

The screen view changed to a blurred picture whilst the internal signals could sort themselves out. Slowly the picture took shape and displayed the view of local space as could be seen through the eyes of these alien creatures.

"Move the view around toward the prisoners ship, you sloth, shapeless Gross," screamed Quazraam, "This find could get me down to the surface. Instead of watching you sleep all of the time."

Kraklac sleepily zigzagged the view until the captured Terran ship came into sight.

"Improve the focus," Quazraam instructed the other. The view changed and the outline and silhouette of the Terran craft slowly took shape. "There. On the side facing toward us," whispered Quazraam jubilantly, pointing at an inlay portion of the screen. "Those markings. Looks like a star and nine rings," they were visible now in the light of the local sun, "Now see the same type of marks in that craft on the island. They are the same. Aren't they?"

"Are you asking me or are you telling me?" Kraklac said half way through a yawn. "Anyway, what do I care? It could be or it may not be the same. The colours are different anyhow."

"Look closely, see the pattern," instructed Quazraam, getting exited now about his find, "Also the lines of that ship on the planet, and the profile are similar. Have we seen anything or any craft like it on this planet up to now? No. Then I'll bet you one hundred Clinger Slugs, that vessel and the one we caught are from the same system. And it's not from here. Am I correct?" Quazraam demanded of his sleepy partner. "Now…why?"

# Chapter 59

Clysta and the others stood inside of the building, which was now known to them as The Old Centre. They were close to what could be best classed a window in one of the exterior walls of this cathedral like structure. The portal itself was invisible to anyone on the outside of its decorative exterior, but from inside the view outward was clear as open air.

Shram had brought them here and stood with them looking outward at the scene below. Feru had, most reluctantly, returned earlier to meet with his family elders. As planned, he had returned to his off shore island home. It had been a little later than his instructions from Quo, but he had promised before leaving, he would make it back to the island and the irreverent delay, would probably bring only a mild scolding.

Shram had taken them to this structure and then when once they were inside, to an upper level placing the group some fifteen metres above the level of the square outside. This location now gave them the unobstructed view they needed of the aliens ship standing outside.

The sun had already climbed into the morning sky and as they were told to expect, the side of the craft opened slightly and a ramp descended. It extended downward to rest on the surface of the square below, now blasted by the heat of midday.

Clysta, using a long range viewer saw a movement inside the craft.

"There, one of the creatures is leaving the shuttle. It definitely looks crustacean like in form, see!"

Kindra, who also was using a viewer, replied, "Yes. I see it. There is

SPACER

another behind that and it has stopped on the ramp. Now it is coming down."

As they watched from their unseen place, six more of the strange creatures exited down the ramp to the crystal surface and spaced themselves to form a wide, part circle around the opening in the side of their ship.

The last to leave, the smallest of this group of the aliens, came down the ramp pushing ahead of it a black sphere of about a half of a metre in diameter on some kind of levitating mat.

The largest of the aliens ambled up to the black sphere and took a position behind it. This alien was taller by almost a half of a metre than its companions. At the best guess from their vantage point, they each looked to range in height from two and a half to three metres.

This particular being had a bright blue and sparkling sash tied in a cross fashion around its upper torso. It had also a number of heavy jewelled rings and some ornamental bracelets around the two forward appendages, each of which ended in large pointed pincers.

The large alien gave out a loud snarling sound and then roughly pushed the smaller one away then took up a position behind the device. It stood, in a half crouching fashion, facing the small crowd of onlookers that had now begun to gather, possibly inquisitive at what was about to happen.

It then pressed the pointed ends one of its claws, into the top of the black sphere.

The small round head swivelled from side to side. Through their viewers, the onlookers could see the two stalk like extensions that carried what must have been eyes. The eyestalks waived around in a non-stop observation of the crew and the crowd in the neighbourhood. Then a tube telescoped from its main upper body. At this distance they were not sure just where it came from, but it began to release sounds, which were indistinguishable to all who were watching.

After a minute or more had passed, of the alien's jabbering sounds and realizing he was not being understood, the eyestalks turned to look down at the sphere before it. It adjusted the position of the claw, and then once more began to make its noises. Now speech could be heard.

"The instrument before me is our Translator," it said. The sound of its speech was harsh and demanding, losing nothing of its aggression through the processes of the machine. The resulting emission was accompanied by a series of whistling noises. "If anyone in this scrawny crowd of weakling can understand what I just said, then make it known by signal. Now!"

There were no more than twenty-five Vedannians gathered around the ship who were actually listening to what this creature had said. Many others were either passing through the extensive courtyard area or facing away in groups showing no interest at all in any of the new happenings at the craft.

A number of the spectators turned their head as if to signify that they had heard then turned away to carry on with other their other matters. Others looked on, as if only partly interested. The crustacean turned around to look at one of its companions, appearing to say something in its own guttural tongue. The claw twisted again into the black sphere, then it once more faced the onlookers.

"It seems some of these soft skinned slime cannot yet understand what I am saying," it said, more to the friends behind it, than to the crowd. But this time the creature had altered the device again, making its speech much clearer and louder.

That was of course if anyone in the square was really listening to what it had to say.

Though some of those originally there were now moving away, a number of the passers by finally began to show some slight interest in the voice from the sphere and the crowd closest grew to around thirty.

Once again the alien spoke, using the device. This time it used an even more commanding tone.

"We demand the maximum attention from you all to our requests, and we will not take lightly to any delay or refusal. By now you are aware we have come here to determine if your miserable, sterile planet is suitable for our superior race. We have decided it will be sufficient for the time being and we are to stay here. We have brought along embryos of our own stock and they are ready now to bring down to begin our colonization. When we are satisfied that the environment is fully suitable, we will begin soon to move in more of our population into this sector. Be warned you cannot stop our expansion. We have with us now, weapons and devices of destruction the like of which you have not yet seen. Even never dreamed of. And we cannot be defeated. We are masters of our own sector of the star field. Any resistance you may have in mind will not be tolerated."

Clysta, along with the others, had heard the commands and the threats.

Kindra spoke first, "It sounds like the aliens do mean business."

Clysta nodded her head, deep in thought, and then she said, "The speech translator. It was not a transmission by the airwaves was it? It was more like mental stimulus but I am sure it was not telepathic. Strange. It appears to have also a good range and is not blocked by structures."

Then she turned to the robot. "Did you get it all Euclid?"

'Yes Miss Clysta, but I also experienced sounds being transmitted by the air and at a very low frequency. It is possibly at a range which is not receivable by humans.'

"Whatever the device is or how it works," said G'zin, "That creature does not intend to have any friends here."

The alien at the craft turned once more to face its companions. Almost with a sneer and a gibbering noise it said something else in its own tongue, likely unsavoury by its sounds. Then again it turned to face the small crowd.

"You there. Yes you standing by that ugly growing thing," It was using the Translator again as it pointed with its free claw to one of the Vedannians who was standing alone.

"Yes you. Come over to me. Now. Now I say."

The lone spectator, realizing it was the subject of the alien's attention, calmly started to move. It glided over, in the same fashion as all Vedannians, to face the large crustacean and stopped two metres from the shimmering protective medium. Beyond that point and on the inside and just ahead was the alien.

"Now you soft skinned 'Bydkin'. I don't think I like you. You do know what a Bydkin is, do you?" The creature towered above the

Vedannian. The local showed no visible sign of fear. Almost ignoring the menace of the creature's voice as it continued, "Well we don't like them either, so we eat them. Whole. And that is only if we have nothing at all left to eat."

A gurgling sound that could have only been taken as laughter at its own humour, came from the device. The other crustaceans, appearing to have also enjoyed the comment, dipped up and down on their four supporting legs loudly making the same sounds.

The speaker continued.

"I want to see the leaders of this, this…" It waived a large claw around indicating the city. "This monstrosity where you all seem to want to live."

"We call it Centre City," the local said calmly, quite unconcerned by the other's comments. The alien must have heard this through the translating sphere.

"It speaks!" The crustacean said in mock surprise, "Well, whatever it is that you name it, it is still an ugly heap of Clinch dung," it retorted and again a gurgling sound. Then it continued. "Now, wherever these leaders are to be found, I want to see them here, in front of my ship. You get them here to meet me when that star," he pointed at the sun, once more with a claw, "Is down to its last quarter cycle of this day. That is all."

The creatures behind this larger alien then, one at a time, pulled back toward the ship to re-enter it. The larger alien who obviously was now being recognized by all onlookers as the leader was last to climb the ramp.

Half of the way up, it turned and again began speaking through the Translator, which it was towing backwards up the ramp. It said in the direction of the now dispersing groups of locals, "All of you. Just in case you misread my intentions. Watch and I will give you slime-slugs a demonstration of one of the least powerful of our weapons."

It took a stick like item from the side of the black sphere and pointed it at the same bush where the Vedannian had stood previously. The creature then emitted a sound likened to a command and the shimmering around the ship ceased. A low whistling sound seemed to come from the end of the device gripped in its claw, then the bush and the ornate planter it stood in, evaporated into nothingness.

Almost immediately afterward the shimmer reformed.

With the same bellowing sounds of its laughter, the giant crustacean followed its companions into the ship and disappeared from sight.

# Chapter 60

"Humph," said Shram. He said nothing more.

The others of the group with the exception of Euclid, who could never show any real signs or expression of emotion, just looked down on the scene. The small and mostly unconcerned group of locals at the front of the aliens ship were since dispersing. Others, who had been or now were passing through the area, still gave no token of their attention to what had been said or what had just transpired.

Kindra was the first to make a remark, "No-one down there appears to be too interested in what has just happened. See, the one the creature just spoke to. He, or is it a she? Who can tell the difference except a Vedannian? It isn't even concerned about what just took place. Even that demonstration of its weaponry. What does it take to excite your people, Shram?"

Shram tried to ignore that last sentence from Kindra. He answered.

"I recognize that person, it is Mekwa. A junior, and is what you would refer to as a female, though only in your views. She is not at all high in the system and does not have any contact with any 'leaders' as the creature named them."

"Do you know her well, Shram?" G'zin asked.

"Not very well," he answered, "I participated in a series of lectures with her and a number of other scholars. That was more than a half of a revolution backwards."

"This is just totally amazing," Kindra said in astonishment, still closely watching the square below them. "These aliens produce a minor weapon which has those destructive powers and all around the bystanders carry on as though nothing has happened. Look at that crowd. No-one is even excited. Not even a police person."

"Police person?" Shram was confused at the reference.

"You know," said G'zin, "The police. People who are needed to uphold the law and keep the peace."

"We need no-one on Vedanne to tend to matters such as those. We have no-one who holds that kind of position."

"I suppose not when I think about it long enough. Nothing so bad has happened in centuries. Then what about those leaders she was asked to produce?" G'zin queried, "Are there any, and do you think they are going to be here by the time the alien has requested? He said something meaning late in this day, did he not?"

"It will only be, I know, that nothing is to happen," Shram tried to explain, "We have no police people as you just called them. They do not exist on this world. And the leaders you mention. We have only those I have described as part of the system of High Committee.

"She, Mekwa, has no means at all of contact with them. In fact I myself know of no one who does have contact. And if they were aware, they must be too busy to arrive here to see these aliens."

"What is next then?" Kindra asked, showing exasperation as he turned from the transparent wall to face his friends, "It would look like we have some time to wait before the aliens put in another appearance. I expect that at least is going to be very, very interesting."

"What are the chances of finding or contacting the Vedannians who met with Clysta's father?" G'zin queried, "They are the likely ones to have at least an opinion about all of this. After all, Professor Z'ee meant her to meet with someone when she arrived."

"The only thing is," said Clysta, who had not said anything up to now, "I don't have a clue as to whom it was to be. The"...she stopped at that, feeling she was suddenly unable to describe the Cube "...letter really did not give any details."

She turned to face Shram. She was still a little confused at the sudden omission, so she said, "Can you at least recommend a person, someone, who will have something to say about all of this. A seer or an elder or someone."

Shram slowly shook his head as if in deep thought. Finally he said, "I can only bring to mind people who will not become involved. We have no one here in the city, at least that I am in contact with. Nor even anywhere close by for that matter who is any part of the present- 'Committee'. I have read in some very old texts of history of what was termed long ago, 'The Gathering'. It was a peculiar title but they operated many, many numbers of revolutions ago. But then I have not found any trace of a similar arrangement in these present times. I suppose it would be that type of representation, which should be the one to meet the aliens. But I surmise they are no longer required and do not exist. We have no need any more."

Euclid interrupted the discussion. 'Please excuse my adding to the conversation. I have in my memory section from Commander Z'ee's previous visit, a name of and a person who was called 'Zemmn' in Terran tongue. That person was of great age and appeared to be of great wisdom.'

The three friends first looked to Euclid then all turned to look at Shram, inquiringly.

"Zemmn?" Shram repeated the name. A puzzled expression passed across his face.

Clysta asked.

"Do you know of this person, and where he can be found?"

"I am aware of Zemmn. It is he who is the Keeper," Shram began, "He is most inaccessible. But he does appear, only very occasionally, in the Old Centre. I do not see any possibility of him seeing anyone without a very good reason. There are persons who have had appointments to see him and they have taken upwards of one whole of our stars revolution to take place."

"I may be speaking out of turn," said Clysta, "But I should estimate that this thing outside is as good a reason as any for him to do something out of the ordinary."

Clysta was slowly losing patience. The fact that not any of the general populace cared. And here were a group of aliens who had brought death and destruction to the almost tranquil peace of this planet. And most of all, maybe her father was their prisoner.

She added. "What better reason does this Zemmn need? His knowing my father and of the arrangement for me to visit. Who knows? He just might find that is good enough of a reason to agree to see us," she ended adding a little sarcasm for emphasis.

"I would like to suggest," Shram rather cautiously replied, "That you wait until after the aliens deadline. At that time, you may be better able to judge your next actions."

"Yours may be a good idea," retorted Kindra, "But time may be running out Shram. Do you have any idea what these aliens might do the next time if they don't get their way? There is no guessing what other tools of destruction they may be carrying. This world of yours could be reduced to a cinder not much unlike those you told us of from your planet's past."

"Of course, you may be right," Shram conceded, though still only abstemiously. "Come this way. I will take you to the Centre's administration. There I will at least make the appropriate application to try to find a way which will gain you an audience with Zemmn."

# Chapter 61

Inside the alien shuttlecraft, all of those in the crustacean crew were taking their slumber. This period was the one they all enjoyed. It compensated for that sleep they had lost while they were in transit across this region, scanning all of the possibilities for planetfall.

The crafts interior was hot and it was steamy.

There were two large tanks of fluid where the members of the crew could wallow and enjoy these periods. It was a throwback to their long evolutionary stage when they had finally left life below water and become surface dwellers.

The ancestors of this species had once inhabited those deep and saline based oceans on their home planet. Its land surface had since been their habitat for a little more than two thousand years. Only a very short period of their history during which they had speedily evolved into a fully land bound and savagely intelligent race of creatures.

They had developed into the most dominant creatures of all those which were the inhabitants of their own world. Eventually, Space Travel came to them, partly through a freak action and then, through their savagery and force they had conquered the neighbouring star systems in their segment of the Milky Way galaxy.

A signal broke into the peacefulness of the odd gurgling and splashes that were a part of the tranquillity of this respite. The crewman, who was appointed the responsibility of monitoring the link to the main craft above, closed the contact.

"This is Klatzu. What do you want?" Demanded this one, who was the smallest of this crew. He was the same alien that had towed the spherical Translator down the ship's ramp.

"I must talk with the Captain," was the reply, equally demanding. The crewman recognized the voice. It was Quazraam, the navigator up there above them in their deep space vessel.

"Oh, its you is it," Klatzu snarled, "He is busy in his tank, and he is not to be disturbed. And you know what that means, don't you Quazraam? The last time that happened. I was the one who interrupted his rest. It took me three Qu'anzers to re-grow a lost leg. That creep snipped it right off. Just one snip was all."

The thought was still strong in the crewman's memory.

"Listen you runt," said Quazraam, knowing any lack in its size was the most vulnerable attribute to any one of this race of creatures, "I have some important information that the Captain will need. He will need it right now. It is very important he hears what I have to say. If it waits any longer and he finds out you are the one that held it up, the Captain will have all of your legs off. For dinner."

Quazraam added, "Especially when he hears that you were too afraid to wake him. Heh, heh, heh!" He gurgled into the mouthpiece.

Klatzu thought it over slowly. He still felt the pain of the lost leg.

"I'll tell you what I will do," The crewman had no real intentions of cooperating with Quazraam, "You just tell me, what it is you need to tell the Captain so urgently, and then I will be the judge of its importance. Ok?"

"Not on your miserable life Klatzu, you slug," Quazraam had dealt with the likes of him before, "Then you can take all of the credit. No, no, no!"

"Please yourself," Klatzu said, still not about to take a chance of waking the Captain, "Up to now it's only you and me knows you have your information."

A pause. Then Quazraam decided.

"I'll wait. Open transmission immediately the Captain is out of the tank. Don't forget though. I have a record of this conversation."

The crewman was just about to throw back at the other, an especially ugly comment, when the transmission closed from the craft out in space.

Klatzu, now deprived of some satisfaction, returned to his original task of scanning the Vedannians down here, outside of the shuttlecraft. He mumbled curses to himself, in disgust, whilst watching them as they went about their stupid everyday 'doing nothing' business.

# Chapter 62

Shram lightly touched the strip with one finger. The mist appeared instantly, fifteen centimetres from the wall surface from the floor to the ceiling. Then, turning to the others, he said, "This is instantaneous, just as you experienced yesterday when Feru brought you here. All you do is walk into the mist. It is quite safe. I have set the coordinates of where we are going. That includes you too, Euclid."

The three friends still did not say anything regarding the similarity to the procedure on the planet Morn. They had discussed it the night before when they were alone and had somehow agreed it may be better to keep it to themselves.

Clysta turned to look to Euclid, who once again was ready to accept Shram's confirmation of its safety.

Clysta watched as G'zin and Shram entered first, followed by Kindra, then she nodded at Euclid saying.

"Right Euclid, now it is our turn. Let's go."

Clysta was this time going to try to feel the transports effects. The other times she had used it, she just didn't have the opportunity. She thought on this occasion she could study the action more closely.

She cautiously put her left foot into the mist, but could feel nothing but a slight chilling of the skin. Letting her foot fall onto the yet invisible solidness beyond, she then moved forward permitting a half of her body to pass into the medium until her face was within it and it had almost surrounded her head. There came a strange blankness and the same chilling of the skin persisted, but no more than that. She decided she was gaining nothing by the experiment so she let the remaining parts of her body carry on, millimetre by millimetre, through or into the mist.

There was though this time, a surge. It was slightly different than the previous occasions. As if the particles or even the atoms of her existence had accelerated. But even though she had previously been prepared to study the sequence, it came and went so fast, it was over before she could get her mind tuned into any proper analysis. She thought instantly of the occasion on Morn when she had first entered the mist medium.

To her shock and surprise the exit this time was into an area without visible walls, though something within told her it was or must be an enclosure of some kind. She turned to look back and saw Euclid exiting the mist that was now behind her. The others, her friends, who had gone ahead were nowhere in sight.

She stepped back toward the mist and Euclid moved to the side to let her pass. She put her hand out to touch it. The medium was now changed into a material of sorts. Solid as stone to the touch and cold. But still visually moving in misty swirls behind the surface hardness.

Clysta tried to choke back her feelings of panic and fear, saying to the robot, "Something is very wrong, Euclid. Can you see the others anywhere out there?"

Though she had said it, she really was not sure where 'out there' was.

'I cannot see them, Miss Clysta and my detectors find no trace of anyone ahead,' Euclid answered in its usual calm and metallic voice. 'I was following closely behind you. I did not see anything until we arrived in this place to find you ahead of this unit.'

"What is this place and where are we? And where has Shram gone?" Clysta was now beginning to turn the panic into latent aggression.

'My sensors indicate a solid mass ahead, around and over us although it is not visible in the recognized light reflection perception,' the robot answered. 'But I can sense that it is moving in many directions; therefore I cannot calculate what its distance is. Although I calculate the medium must be close as its maximum and minimum distances are registering an average of approximately twenty three metres from where we now stand.'

'In an endeavour to give you the answer to where?' Euclid continued his dialogue. 'This unit is unfamiliar with these surroundings. As to the whereabouts of our good friend Shram is'…The robot's explanation went unfinished. Clysta cut the robot off in mid sentence.

"Ok," She said a little exasperated, "That will be sufficient, Euclid, please. I now see that we are alone," then following a brief pause, "I have just noticed also we are not standing on anything. Solid that is."

Clysta was looking down to where her feet were. They were level, but whatever was supporting them was not visible. She looked at the robot's feet and the effect was the same. Nothing.

Another thing was obvious. Although the area was generally bright, there seemed to be no source of light. Up, down, or anywhere around them.

"Let us try walking," she said to Euclid, taking a tentative step in a forward direction, "So far so good, follow behind me, Euclid. And keep your sensors active for any kind of obstruction which might be ahead."

Their forward movement did not mean much without solid and visible terms of reference, but progress was obvious, even if only in the action of their feet.

'Whatever this strange medium is that surrounds you and this unit, Miss Clysta," the robot began. 'There is something of an opening in the materials existence. The opening is immediately ahead of you Miss Clysta and it is amply large so that we both will pass through.'

"What is beyond the opening? Can you make anything out?" she asked.

'There is another area similar to this volume that we now occupy, ' was the reply.

Clysta could somehow feel or imagine the opening although it still was not visible to her. But she knew they had passed through. The substance that was underfoot was still not visible along with whatever surrounded them.

Two more steps into the other area Euclid had forecast, and Clysta stopped her forward progress. Euclid also came to a halt and they stood in silence. The lighting appeared brighter here and as Clysta became accustomed to it, slowly the parameters of the area became solid.

Clysta had a strange feeling that she was somehow familiar with this place. She had been here before. She could not be too sure when it was, it could have been a dream maybe she thought to herself. But she discarded that thought almost immediately. She had been here in person but could not say for sure when or why.

It was a large room twice as long as the width, and the walls were high along with the ceiling that was higher in its centre. Almost church like in appearance, or as close as she could remember from some vidis of Old Earth. The shape was not a square, more octagonal with an elongated axis. The only other room she could bring to mind having any similarity would be the Academy Commissary. But this was perhaps smaller and was mystically developing a beauty that transcended even that place.

The room's features slowly came into view from the haze. Its lines and the columns, the colours and shades, each fresh shape, all were of a nature unknown to any Terran structure.

Clysta walked slowly forward into this new area and stopped again after three paces. The gallery had now fully materialized out of the nothingness they had just passed into. She stood in amazement as more and more detail began to develop into shapes, almost out of the air within, adding to the grandness.

Inside an area of seemingly focused bright light in the middle of the room a large table now took form and was followed by an arrangement of seating. The intensity of the light increased though not so bright as to hurt the eye, and people shapes now formed, once again from out of the nothingness.

Finally, the shapes ended their slow transition to become the same as Vedannian in size and feature. And as mysteriously as all that had happened, they became living beings with features that she could understand.

A voice spoke. It was not unlike the voice of Wyyrrum, and of the same slight tinkling of a bell sound. But Clysta could not be sure if it was the same person. She was inwardly sure though it was coming from a being who was of great age and most likely of great intelligence. Such was the impression the sound made on her soul.

"Ah! Miss Clysta Z'ee of Planet Earth. Finally, you have found your way into our place. A little soon, but we do wish to welcome you, to this our Committee. The same as has been named to you as of times past as 'The Gathering'."

# Chapter 63

These figures she observed ahead though visible were slightly diffused, as were all of the other parts about what appeared to be a most ornate of rooms. The view she got was similar to looking through a piece of misty glass, or even perhaps a slightly unfocused lens. But still, the details were clear and distinct if her eyes were to look and be concentrated directly upon them.

Clysta's eyes continued to focus and she panned to and fro to quickly take in what she could of the scene and commit it to memory. She thought that she had mistakenly been transported to this area by some glitch or mistake and did not believe she would be here long enough to see all there was to see. The members, who had been announced as the Committee, had an ambience about each of them. They all had distinct bodylines but the outer edge of their profile radiated outwardly and halo-like.

She finally let her eyes settle on the grouping at the far end of the table, to locate the person who had been speaking. It appeared to be the one who sat the farthest from her. That one was no different than those on each side, though there appeared to be some unexplainable feature that made Clysta confident in his superiority above the others. The table was long and its surface resembled a polished wood of a most excellent quality. It took up most of the visible area, though she constantly had difficulty reasoning the exact proportions of it. There were six others, all of them seated three each side of the one she had taken as being the speaker. All were in high backed chairs, which by their shape, proportions and placing, gave the group an appearance of some extremely regal council. The figures that were here in the group, were each turned slightly to face in the direction of Clysta's and the robot, as always, at her side.

The seven figures all had the same appearance and dress though the upper part of their bodies was the most she could see. It consisted of the similar style of flowing body covering gown as was worn by those in the city. The quality though, brought back her memories of the visit they had had with Wyyrrum. Theirs though on this occasion was of a substance she assumed as being far superior to any she had seen on or of the planet. She had no idea what the material was but the patterns and designs in it were of such intricacy and from what she remembered of the day before, if this covering registered status, then the group before Clysta must be of a very high order.

"Where am I and what has happened to my friends Kindra and G'zin?" Clysta asked, firmly but not demanding.

"They are in a safe place," answered the original speaker.

'That did not answer my question,' she thought to herself.

"Are they prisoners?" She asked.

"We have no necessity for the confinement of anyone or as you call it, prisoners. All beings are free. Your friends will come to no harm," The answer came once again from the same speaker at the end of the table.

The visual effect was to Clysta extraordinarily confusing at first. But as the person spoke, the speaker's body and its features gained more solidity, and then it would fade and return into its previous state.

"Then please explain to me, why is it that I and my robot Euclid are here and they are not?" Clysta said. She needed to know. For the first time that she could remember, Clysta was a little afraid.

"We thought it necessary to allow you an interview," The speaker two spaces to the right of the one who spoke first had given the answer. The same odd visual transformation occurred with this speaker, as had the one before.

Then, the being continued, "We have been aware of your presence and have also watched your search in this area of space around our star. We have also taken note of your ability to find us without any real or true co-ordinates. It showed a great deal of intuition, ability and skill."

"That effort was not all my own," responded Clysta, "My two friends were an equal part in the work."

"Quite a commendable statement," said another voice not really directed at her. Although it was one of those at the table, Clysta was not able to identify that speaker's position.

She could not be really sure if these beings before her were really speaking, maybe it was some kind of telepathic speech. Anything might be possible from this race, even that this Committee could really not be here at all but be only a projection of some kind.

"However," Once more the original speaker began, "We have observed your progress. And, though limited assistance has been given by the planet's inhabitants, we know you have come to a decision. It is an obvious wish to pursue a course which will endeavor to find your father, Professor and now the Commander Z'ee."

"So you know of my father then?" she said.

"Yes, we do," The reply came from the central figure.

"And you will also know then, I intend to rescue him if it is necessary?" Clysta was quick to add with conviction. "I have been sure for some time now, that he is a captive of those aliens who have occupied the plaza outside the Old Centre. Though I must admit, I am not sure just where they may be keeping him," she added sadly.

The Group around the table did not reply.

The assembly sat in silence as if studying between them in their silent and motionless state, what their next decision might be. Now, Clysta observed, the room had become completely visible. The lighting had increased and brightness was everywhere. She looked from side to side spellbound at the beauty of her surroundings. All around her had become solid and not infracted and unfocused. The ornamentations and the effects, which she could now see clearly, were truly breathtaking. Though alien to her eyes, the designs, the furnishings and the embellishments gave a pleasure, which to her appeared most normal and instinctive.

Clysta waited in anticipation of some kind of condemnation, to any intention of force on her part, but none came. Finally she spoke, "So please tell me," keeping a controlled respect in her voice, "Why am I here, in this place?"

The person at the middle broke the group's silence.

"A number of your years ago, your father stumbled into this system quite by mistake. Fortunately for the population, he found his way to the planet's surface. Whilst he was here, he did the planet's occupants a great service. He rectified a malfunction in their main Food Regeneration process. The system had run for so many of your centuries unattended, the people had quite forgotten how it had been built and they found its repair to be, most unfortunately, something which was beyond their own abilities."

"During his stay here," the speaker continued, "your father exhibited certain qualities which had been all but forgotten in our many eons of isolation. He told us something of you his daughter and we recommended to him we would welcome seeing you. We permitted him to secrete from us the device you know as a 'Thought Cube' and with its help you should be allowed to commence on your journey in an attempt to locate the system.

"Your father of course as you are aware, by use of another device we have not needed in a considerably long time, had the location of our planet erased from his consciousness. At least that was the design."

The speaker turned slightly and looked to one of the others, reprovingly.

"We really did not feel you would be able to find your own way here unaided," he added. "It was arranged to give you an amount of assistance and if necessary, guidance. So we adapted the robot, which has been your companion. It was subjected to a number of improvements before your father left here, unknown to him of course. The work appears to have met with some success as, here you are."

"What you are telling me," Clysta remarked, a little surprised at what the speaker had said, "Is that I and my friends have been guided here."

"That is almost true," This time it was another of the group who answered.

410

"You have proven that you had within you those same qualities which your father had shown to us. Guidance was not required, just the enquiring intelligence. The other would follow and come naturally. The use of Euclid in all of this was as a means to ensure the path you were sure to follow was clear and safe."

Clysta turned to Euclid, saying. "You knew all along, and you did not tell me?"

'I apologize for any encroachment on the area of disrespect. It was truly without intention. I was carrying out a particular program.' The robot answered.

"But how?" Clysta was confused, "We were at the controls, G'zin did the comp' work and Kindra piloted the Skimmer. They were more a part of the plans and decision making. I think I can understand now, Euclid's work with the cube and its installation in the guidance systems was programmed here on this world. But the work of planning our route, that was ours."

The central speaker explained, "Euclid's Neuro Fluid brain was modified in such a way as to send out some specific signals, similar to telepathic impulses. These adaptations were made to enable the robot to transmit certain prompts to the thought patterns of yours and your two friends."

"So we were guided to this system," Clysta stressed.

"Not quite," was the response, "We had our reasons to ensure you arrived here safely. But we had to be sure you would succeed using only your own methods and your intuition. Except initially, the first start required to be introduced by the Cube."

Clysta was silent as she tried to bring to memory the few parts of their trip where either Clysta or the other two could possibly have been prompted unknowingly. Awareness slowly began to surface.

"That explains—," Clysta's thoughts drifted over the sequences they had been through. "The flashes I received when our efforts were not working. And then Kindra too. He made an astounding assumption when we had exhausted our options. Euclid was the prompter!" Clysta concluded.

Finally, seeing the light, "Now I understand how we got to be here,"

Clysta stopped, thought, then added in the direction of the first speaker, "I have yet to understand. Why?"

The speaker who was at the head of the table began again. He looked from side to side at his comrades almost with a pride in Clysta's answer.

"Our race of people, as you have been told, has not used conflict in any form for many of your centuries. Our only major reason for existence is now the progression of intelligence, along with the peaceful future of our galaxy. Many eons ago, even before our period of savagery, we set out on a course of probing Mathematical Probability. We have used it as a tool to forecast the effects of our galaxy's varied inhabitants on each other. And to make an effort to control their consequence on the peace we wish to maintain."

Another of the group took up the topic as though it was his speciality.

"Eons before it happened, we were able to correctly forecast the rise of your Terran civilization from its inconspicuous star. We foresaw its inevitable spread into the stars around that region of the galaxy. But before your ancestors could be allowed to take up the inescapable expansion through space, they had to learn to coexist in peace on their own world."

"We had the means to use a number of procedures at our disposal to restrict their advancement of interstellar travel. Until those our prerequisites were met and had finally endured.

"During our work of forecasting in the other parts of the galaxy, it became obvious there would be an equal probability of an intelligence duplicating or being even superior to your own Terran civilization. The location of this race was estimated, though still unknown at the time, to be somewhere outside of this Galactic spiral.

"Our predictions of this other intelligence were proven correct when a certain planet developed a race of beings with greater intelligence than all of its other species found inhabiting that planet. The planet was in the region you call by name 'the Sagittarius Arm'. But then, a thousand revolutions ago, one of our probes surveyed a cluster in a region other than the one we had forecast. There were beings, which had altogether escaped our attention and had unpredictably heightened their intellect. They had become thinkers and in that they had begun to understand. Then, after an unprecedented short time of only four of your centuries had passed, we noticed a drastic change in their evolution far exceeding our previous projections.

"We had recognized the pattern in our determinations for forecasting the growth of one or possibly two dominant and warring species. Our observations and probability calculations now said they, the second strain, would overrun the region and some intervention should be necessary.

"One of those inhabitants had somehow become developed at a faster degree than we calculated. It was all too suddenly at a stage where we were unable to correct their advancement without the use of drastic measures. Measures which; we were incapable of carrying out. We had had our own troubles and were in no position to administer that doctrine.

"They have since developed enormously and have overrun their own and also some neighbouring planetary sectors. They have also demonstrated they have no concern for the many inhabitants of the planets in their region. And they will not allow the development of another race that is likely to become a threat to their own future. These beings are of such brutality they either make their neighbours into their own slaves or simply annihilate them from existence.

"The craft that is now in orbit around Vedanne is one of that race's scout and seed expeditions. It is similar to the expedition that your father was sent on in the direction of their arm of the Galaxy. But their motivation is not the same. How they found this star system is not clear but we can be sure it could only be by a mind scan, and one which through its sophistication has the ability of extracting many things."

Clysta broke in, saying, "My father. He is a prisoner of those creatures. I know that now. Can you then at least tell me, is he still alive?" She craved some kind of positive assurance from someone. These beings here, whoever they were, must know.

"We can only hope," the central speaker answered this time, somewhat sadly, "And then hope that he is in good health. For those beings have no reverence for other races or even other living creatures."

# Chapter 64

"This is Captain Laslas here! What do you have for me," the giant creature said with a snarl, "That it is so important, you almost had the ignorance to interrupt my soak?" The Captain was in his usual hostile disposition.

"Captain Laslas,-Sir." The navigator Quazraam squirmed on the stool as he began, "If it pleases you to give me an audience…"

The Captain cut him short with a wave of his jewel encrusted large claw.

"Just cut out the fawning gobbledygook, you slimed Lassbin, and get to what you have to say to me. And you had better make it extra quick and extra good!"

Quazraam heard the chuckling off screen that must have been from the com' watch Klatzu. 'At least the creep had remembered to get the Captain to contact me,' he thought to himself.

Once more Quazraam started.

"Sir. I have been checking the planet's surface around the city as you ordered and I have noticed something, which I wish to bring to your attention. Sir."

Inwardly, Quazraam had hated this particular Captain for the most part of this voyage. In his many Quads as space navigator, he had known others on other ships, but this one was the worst. Though Quazraam could mix it and win with the best of any of the crew, being so far away from the home planet, he had no alternative other than to sound, and act subservient.

"And what is this something that you have found?" asked the Captain.

"Captain. I wish to remind you of the reward you have so graciously promised for anyone giving useful information," Quazraam said in his lowest voice possible.

"Yes, I remember," the Captain said in an equally low voice. Then he spoke louder so that all in the shuttle would hear, "But only if I, and only I, find that it is warranted. Now out with it and then I will decide about what reward you deserve."

"Captain," Quazraam began, "I have a visual record of a craft which I believe is a stranger to this planet. It is almost similar to the one that you yourself crippled out in deep space. The one we have in tow. With those soft shelled creatures inside."

"Let us begin at the beginning, Navigator," the Captain growled, not really too interested. "How can you tell it is not of this planet?"

"Captain. I am good at shapes and this one does not appear like anything I have seen here before," was his reply.

The Captain knew the navigator was good at his work, though he had no intention of ever showing it or allowing any favour. He placed himself closer to the spheres view of Navigator Quazraam, saying, "So what else is there? If there is more, then give!"

"Captain, Sir," He knew he now had the Captain's attention, "This is an enlargement on the top side of that craft," He turned a control and the Captain saw at his end the transmitted close up of the uppermost side of the Skimmer. The transmission zoomed, showing the identification markings.

"Now, Captain, see this," Quazraam continued. Using a split screen, the transmission was showing another view alongside the first. This new scene was of the side of the captured vessel in space above.

"Do you see the same round pattern in those markings, and the colours, they too are the same. I don't know what those other markings are for but those two look very like each other."

Quazraam was correct. The Captain's interest was aroused. He was though, always successful at hiding it. Laslas slid the claw, which was out of sight of the scanner. It pushed a contact starting the device to store all that was to follow.

"So what do you make of it, Quazraam?" This was not the Captains usual way of addressing crewmembers. He very rarely used their names. Only the work titles, or worse.

The navigator noticed the subtle change, storing it away for future use. He answered quietly.

"Sir. These things that populate that planet do not have any flying machines. They don't seem to need them, although it has puzzled me. Why? Then suddenly after we have been here for almost a revolution of the star, there appears this," Quazraam pointed at the image of the Skimmer.

The Captain leaned up still closer to the sphere.

"Ok, keep going," he said.

Quazraam continued, "I have been thinking. These two craft must be from the same place. Or grown or manufactured at the same place. So. Is it a rescue craft? Is it just a coincidence? There has got to be a reason."

"Then," he continued, "It occurred to me. There was something else. I started to think. How do these beings on that planet move around their surface without any visible transportation of any size? Maybe they have secrets. Maybe even weapons or something useful to our own planet, which we can take back home when our tour is over. Then I got to thinking of all those rewards for a few of those secrets."

Quazraam stopped his dialogue. He had said enough, he thought. A silence descended. And now all the navigator could hear from the transmission were the gurglings and splashings of the other shuttle crewmen in their tanks of ooze.

After more than ten seconds that passed like minutes, the Captain broke into the dense quiet.

"I will think over these things and get back to you," the Captain cut the transmission.

The Captain did not take very long to make a decision. The giant crustacean used his personal channel to make contact with the main craft in space.

"Navigator Quazraam!"

The Captains attitude had mellowed. He spoke into the transmitter in a quiet tone, "I your Captain will honour the code. You are now

416

promoted two levels on the strength of the information you have put before me. But be forewarned. If it leads me nowhere, you are to be demoted instantly by three levels. Do you understand what I have just told you?"

Quazraam, his round hard head nodding his agreement, said nothing.

The Captain would not take a nod. He said, now with some of his old aggression, "Say it Quazraam."

"I agree to your own terms Captain," the navigator said. He realized he had lost the ploy he was trying. If things did not work out, he was now trapped into the Captain's own conditions.

"Now," the Captain demanded, "You will take the smallest shuttle to the captives craft. You will then immediately relieve those dopey guards of four of those scrawny captives. I want you to make sure you bring the one who said he is the Master. You remember. The one that always has so much to say."

The Captain continued, "Then, you will bring them down here, dock on the top of this shuttle as is customary and transfer those four to this, my shuttle.

"We will send the small shuttle back with the obnoxious slug infested garbage handler we call Klatzu. I think it is now his turn to go on planet watch. Did you get all of that Navigator?"

"Yes Master."

After the transmission closed, Quazraam waived the front antennae around and around in circles showing his elation. Then he ambled with a proud and swaggering gait, down toward the ship's galley. He was planning to grab a hamper full of his favorite Clinger Slugs as a personal prize to himself. He could use the time it took to descend, whilst gobbling them all down on his way to the surface of the planet below.

# Chapter 65

Clysta began, "I am almost too afraid to ask the same question again, but now I feel I must.

"I came here because of a suggested message from my father. My friends and I arrived by a route, which at least was occasionally prompted by a robot that you programmed. And now since I arrived, I find my father is a captive of a bunch of thugs. These thugs appear to be on a course to eventually destroy or enslave all other civilizations. Maybe even throughout this whole galaxy. Now my question again is this."

Her eyes were on the head speaker as she took a deep breath.

"Why, am I here?"

The speaker who sat at the centre of the group spoke again.

"It has been explained to you on other occasions, we and those on Vedanne have a distinct aversion to force of any kind. It has been that way for the preceding five thousand of your own years and is inherent in the very fibre of all of our peoples of this planet. It has been a part of our history and is so deep even the loss of our individual lives would not change it. We cannot do harm to another intelligent being. Whomever or whatever that being may be."

Clysta remained silent as she listened to the explanation.

The same speaker continued.

"In our theories of Probability, we have concluded that with the type of civilization which these beings represent, if allowed to carry out this visit unchecked, they will be the forerunners of a period that is to create total subjugation.

"An altered set of equations so complex will take charge and the result is the eradication of your own race in less than two hundred revolutions. Such is the true nature of these creatures."

One of the others at the table then took up the dialogue.

"We have developed a number of variables to our theses. It is not possible for us ourselves to generate a course of action from these. Our Probabilities conclude only paths, which take your centuries of time to unfold. We are also unable to detect short-term answers.

"But there is something which does become obvious," the same speaker continued, "In all of our variations the same range in time develops into an obvious point where changes are created in the pattern.

"That point is in this present time we now occupy. If a change does not take place, then the sequence will not be altered. The events of which our learned Director has spoken will undoubtedly happen."

It was the first time Clysta had heard a title used to indicate anyone on Vedanne. The 'Director' took over once more.

"We have become convinced of our variations. The fine points are invisible to us. One item is in every variation. That is. A being from another sector of this spiral arm changes the sequence. Your arrival on Vedanne, your ability and strength to carry you through adversity, all of these indicate our Predictions and the variations can be correct."

Clysta was momentarily stuck for words.

Then, "What?" Clysta said a little breathlessly, "You are trying to tell me, that I am this one who is meant to remove the threat you have spoken of?"

A hard silence took over the chamber. Clysta was not quite convinced of the truth of what she had been told. Inwardly she was afraid it might all be true.

She asked, "Why do you yourselves not remove these aliens? Why not dispose of or even oppose their influence on this Probability which you talk of?"

The second speaker responded, "We cannot fight. We, nor the populace on Vedanne will not and know not how to use any type of force. Our violent prehistory has made it impossible. It is not in our ability to do anything that will lead to consequences to bring harm to another being. No matter what that being is capable of."

From another at the large table came a similar answer.

"It is becoming more important a change be started quickly. The one who has the ability to start that change would appear to be you, Clysta Z'ee."

Clysta silently recounted all she had heard. She took a deep breath and then began almost to herself. Repeating her earlier thoughts.

"I came here because my father told me there was something here he wished me to receive on his behalf. I found he is now a captive of a race of beings, which you have forecast will predicate disaster upon our section of the galaxy. You yourselves will not or can not defend against that impending doom for one reason or another."

Still running over these thoughts, Clysta was again silent. The gathering of these, who she took to be representatives of the Vedannians also were silent as they each looked in her direction.

She turned to the side to face the robot.

"I am unsure, Euclid, if you are still likely to attempt to prompt my thoughts—," she said. Then she began slowly turning to face the assembly and added still speaking to Euclid.

"—But I have all of the reasons not to take up this idiotic proposal just suggested by these members of this group.

"One thing though I must do. I have yet to have the solid proof that my father is here, with these aliens. If he is, then I must find a way, which will enable me to rescue my father. If, in the course of my efforts, I am able to stop the threat these creatures are predicted of being," she stopped for a second, "Then that is good and so be it."

The speaker at the head of the long table said as though in answer to her fears.

"You need have no concern. The robot had no influence in your decision. Now this audience must end."

Clysta, surprised at the Directors words and their finality, said quickly.

"Not so fast, if you don't mind. I have only accepted the course that I alone must take to help my father escape. I will need help and I am not yet sure what. My friends Kindra and G'zin will be involved also. They will be a part of the end result and the plan. I will need to ask them if they are willing to help."

While she was saying the last few words, the group had begun to fade into its earlier misty and unfocused state. Even the table and the room itself was becoming nebulous and out of focus. Just as it had when she first saw this strange place.

A voice made itself felt and seemed to be far inside her head.

It was saying, "You will be given some assistance. In a limited way."

Within seconds, all was gone, the gathering, the elegant room with its furnishings. Gone. Clysta and Euclid were standing alone once more surrounded by the same opaque medium they had arrived in before the meeting.

Clysta looked hard into the misty gloom.

In the distance ahead, she could now see the Transport mist moving slowly toward them. Clysta was not sure if they had been turned around or were in motion or, even if the medium was. Without moving a step they became engulfed in it and just as suddenly they were both stepping out into a large and well illuminated hall.

Shram with G'zin and Kindra were slowly walking onward toward a throng of Vedannians and away from where she had entered the new area.

Then Kindra turned, to see that she and Euclid had exited the mist safely and were following behind. He made no remark when he looked at her and the robot. Kindra seemed as if unaware of their presumed delay in the exit Clysta made from the Transport Mist.

She was then suddenly struck with the realization that oddly, though a length of time must have elapsed, they all three must be equally unaware of that period of time she had been absent from the grooup.

# Chapter 66

The landing the small shuttle made was not one of its textbooks best ever. And it certainly did not go unnoticed.

The navigator Quazraam never had been known for his landing skills. Navigation yes, landing no. Especially with his having to work with and judge the lower gravity possessed by this abominable planet.

Quazraam's alignment was correct and the securing lugs were in their catch position. But he had cut the thruster just a few micro-seconds too early. The effect on the craft was to cause it to almost fall the last few metres instead of landing smoothly on the top of the larger, stationary main shuttle.

A reverberating clang sounded throughout the larger ship. Instantly a scream of curses and insults rang out from the previously relaxing crew inside.

Quazraam's passengers, the Terran prisoners, had been secured in the net like suspensors. These had been designed for the bulkier shapes of the aliens and were therefore larger than was comfortable for the Terrans. The four of them were bounced around as they each tried to grab at anything in reach, if only in an attempt to reduce the pain. Pain that was being inflicted by the electro-charged manacles securing them in their positions.

Before the vibrations had time to stop, Quazraam clacked rapidly across the floor to the captives and towered over them menacingly, his eyestalks twitching this way and that way.

"Now. Everybody on their useless soft shelled feet," he warbled the command in his own tongue. The four prisoners could not interpret the words verbally without the sphere, but Quazraam's intent was quite obvious by his tone. He picked up the stick like weapon from its hanger and gestured with it to reinforce his words.

Each prisoner was released one at a time from the manacles. Before they could relax, Quazraam had grabbed at them then secured each one by the wrists to the short tether attached to one of his legs.

He prodded the leader, Commandeer Z'ee, and then pushed him toward the airlock. The Commander watched the alien weapon as he said in a low voice to the others.

"This one cannot understand us without the talking sphere. Take it carefully and watch for my mark. I think we have been brought to the surface of the planet again. It sounded a lot like the other time when we landed on top of their largest shuttle."

Quazraam gave the tether a sharp pull and pointed to the now open connection into the tube leading into the other craft below. Approaching the large opening, they could see beyond its edge and into the gloomy interior as a rush of the hot and humid atmosphere escaped into their space mingling as it did, to become equalized.

Luckily, the oxygen and nitrogen mix of the aliens' home world was close enough to being compatible to that of their human captives. The humidity and the ever present aroma of rotten eggs though had taken some time to overcome. But these Terrans had now been in captivity for many months and had little alternative but to accept the conditions and become acclimatized.

One more time, Quazraam motioned toward the opening, then disconnected the tether from his leg and watched the four prisoners climb down the tube.

The aliens, in the crew of the shuttle below, were each of varying sizes. All had much more bulk than their captives. Three of them who were not now in the soaking pits showed an amount of secret and guarded interest in this visit from above, the others continued with their soak and slumber.

The Captain of the expedition was the largest of all. This alien was more than three and a half metres in height, if he was to stand upright. But due to the structure of the exterior skeleton, a crouching stance was normally all that any of these aliens could maintain for any stretch of time.

The others of the crew in this craft, there were seven in number, ranged downward in their comparative sizes to one who was the smallest. That one alone stood slightly taller than a tall human.

In the eyes of the captives, the aliens had an appearance similar to a mix of the Earth type Crabs and Lobsters. Using all four legs to stand and move around, they were capable of great speed. Their stiff joints in the upper legs though, reduced their directional qualities.

They had more body strength than the Slint Ox of the planet Quantre. The two pincer like claws, on front facing mandibles, had strength enough for lifting and obviously also to be used as weapons.

These claws had developed in unequal sizes during their evolution. Inside of each was a set of retractable flexible probes, five inside one and eight in the other. These probes, similar to Terran fingers, had given them the dexterity required to develop as a tool on their home planet. This item alone, together with their strength, had resulted in giving these beings the major advantage for their evolutionary superiority over the other species on that world.

On the uppermost segment of the forward facing part of the body was the creature's head or brain case. It was retractable and set into a pocket in the hard shell in the front and was small in comparison to the other parts of the creature's crustacean body.

The head had two eyes. These were also retractable. Each eye was placed at the ends of two flexible stalks with the ability to swivel in each and every direction.

Their ugliness was enhanced by a gash like deformed orifice that was the mouth. It was full of writhing worm-like feelers and was used only as a feeding slot and was closer to the base of the upper body section. The sight of it always brought to the Terrans a feeling of nausea and revulsion at the times when the aliens began their feeding. Twice each day they would repeat the ritual of forcing the still live and writhing food into this slot with one claw, whilst instinctively guarding their large stone dish with the other.

The Terrans began their decent, one after the other, into the hot and steamy interior of the large shuttle. Captain Laslas did an ambling, rocking about face from the screen he had been watching. Commander Z'ee caught a view of the visually distorted picture. It was of the square outside. He recognized it from his last visit, three or maybe four days before.

The Captain put out a long and crusty leg to reach for the Translator sphere and dragged it across the floor of the shuttle, to a position between the Terrans and himself. He then extended his speech tube, a loose slim trunk like appendage located on the underside of the lower body section.

After adjusting the device he started to speak.

"I suppose you are wondering why we have been so good as to offer you another look at the surface of this ugly and disgusting planet." The interpretation by the device was clear and correct. Even the Captain's vehement tone came through and none of the intent was lost.

Commander Z'ee was himself over two metres tall, but he was still compelled to look upward at the towering alien. He said in a faked subservient tone which he found always pleased his captors.

"You are correct, as always. We were deep in wonder," he looked at the picture on the viewing sphere. "Captain!" He added quickly, remembering the last time he had forgotten to attach the title when he answered.

"That is good," said the Captain with a sneer, having had the response he liked from the captors. He then straightened and stood taller as he went on.

"My Navigator," he pointed to Quazraam who still held the tether, "Reported to me personally a sighting of a strange craft. It is one that my Navigator has not seen before and is not aware of on this world of useless beings."

The other six aliens who made up the crew had now become interested in the presence of the four Terran captives and were now fully attentive to what their Captain had to say. Each of those out of their soak pits were moving about and feigning an attention to their duties, but closely following the Captain's words. The rest in the pits had turned their eyes onto the prisoners.

"What do you know of any flying craft which these worms might use on this planet?" Captain Laslas asked. He now included the other three prisoners as he fixed them all with his gaze.

"My fellow members are not familiar with this planet," the Commander began, maintaining the charade, "I have informed you previously-Captain-I am the only Terran to have visited this world and that was purely by accident. My stay here was not for a very long period of time."

The Captain's eyestalks extended from each side of his head, "Then what kind of craft is this one?"

Growling, he pushed a control and the viewer changed. The picture now showed the frame of the close up of the Skimmer.

Commander Z'ee knew immediately. It was a ship by one of the designers of the Galactic Union Shipyards. The crest was so visible. He only hoped the aliens had not noticed his sudden change of facial expression, slight though it was. He turned to face his three captive companions, keeping a calm posture.

The Commander winked an eye at the others, who had also seen the resemblance.

"What do you think, Manchoo?" The Commander said aloud. It was directed toward the man who was Science Director with the interrupted expedition.

"I do not recognize that craft," lied Manchoo in a calm voice. The other two just remained tight-lipped and shook their heads in negative confirmation.

Captain Laslas screamed into the Translator.

"You are lying. All of you are lying. I can tell you are lying, you soft shelled Magworts." He grabbed a weapon hanging on his belt at his side. They each knew what it was. The Electro Whip.

"Now we will begin again." The whip touched the Commander only once. A sharp painful shock left its mark, and he winced at the agony.

"My navigator is no fool. He has recognized those ugly markings," the Captain pointed the whip toward the spheres view, "He says they are the same as the markings on your scrap heap of a ship," he then prodded the Commander one more time with the whip for good measure.

The Commander went to his knees in pain and as he caught his breath, he said from between his teeth.

"I cannot understand why you and your navigator should say that," he managed to say again in a lie. Then as the whip approached his chest area, he added " – Captain," then he slumped to the rough floor, faking unconsciousness.

He had understood immediately how a craft from their same sector of space had arrived at Vedanne. They too could be lost just as he himself had been long ago. A sudden thought began to form in his head. But the Captain, now standing over him, had diverted the effort from its completion.

Another prod came from the whip, and violent pain was again the reward for his slowness in adding that one word-'Captain'.

# Chapter 67

"Sorry for the delay," said Clysta testing apologetically, "But Euclid and I…"

"What do you mean? Delay," G'zin asked.

"Well I thought…" Clysta started, then it occurred that somehow, they might not have taken so long as it appeared to her. She quickly thought it would be better to say nothing until later. She changed the topic, "Where to now, Shram?"

Shram, who had not taken particular notice of Clysta's entrance into the area, continued in his efforts. He was trying to locate the appropriate request display through the crowd of Vedannians

He turned to face Clysta saying, "This is the Hall of Requests. It is where we are directed when a particular answer is needed. I know we can arrange an audience to get us to Zemmn from here. I just have to locate the correct alignment."

He looked toward a wall to their left and then continued, "There is the listing I need. It is the green wall over there."

Shram guided them through the crowd of what were possibly three or four hundred or more people of a range of local classes, each apparently intent on their own enquiries. They arrived at the base of the wall he had indicated.

A design of lines and patterns totally meaningless to the Terran friends covered the wall from end to end and up to a height of almost two metres from the floor. Discs, some polished and some coloured, were set at intervals appearing to coincide with some of the lines, but even these meant nothing also, as their randomness formed no pattern either.

Shram walked through a group of the other visitors to this gigantic Hall and stood close to the wall. He placed an open hand onto one of the discs, which was coloured and pushed with a twisting motion, once to the left then over to the right.

"We will wait a short time for our reply," he said.

"Is that all it takes?" Asked G'zin, surprise in her voice.

"It takes our intentions from our touch, and possibly a little more that will take a lot of explaining," he replied, smiling back affectionately at G'zin.

In less than one minute, a figure of a local appeared before them. It was positioned with almost the rear half of its body inside the wall. It was smaller than the average Vedannian, about half size.

Then the visitors realized it was a very perfect holograph. The holo' spoke. 'You wish an audience?'

Shram responded, "I am Shram Ioo't. I require an audience with Zemmn."

'What is the necessity of this audience you request?' The holo' asked.

"My friends have requested I help them to form a conclusion in a particular problem," Shram said.

A silence took over the discussion as if the request was being processed. Then the figure spoke again.

'Zemmn is presently in a series of discussions which are to be concluded one and a half rotations from the last light of this one. You may take an allocation after that.'

Shram turned to face the others, his face showing his disappointment.

"Take it," said Clysta quickly, "It may turn out to be the only help we can get."

"I am pleased to have that allocation. Will you register it for us, you have my title," said Shram as he turned back to face the image.

'It is registered,' the holo' said in reply. 'You will be contacted at your quarters at the time allocated.'

Then the holo' disappeared, and the wall returned to its previous pattern.

The friends wandered away from the wall and made their way to the outside of the building, finally arriving in a small parkette where there were trees and flowers. All of the growing things in and about the city were very strange in appearance to the three Terrans. They eventually sat on some equally strange looking seating, although to their surprise it was unusually comfortable.

Euclid stood as usual in the background.

Clysta turned to speak to her friends.

"I have been thinking about all of this," she began, "Perhaps we should try to sort our problem out in our own way. There is little doubt that the Vedannians in general have not the ability to repel these intruders. Their acceptance of the craft in the square, the damage it has done and the deaths it has wrought. Without any kind of retaliation whatsoever makes it most obvious, that retaliation by them is just not going to happen."

She then looked at Shram, saying, "I would not wish you to become a part of any plan we may come up with, Shram. It could be one, which would be against your will, or one that might put you yourself in danger. But we are in need of help and if there is anything you can do, I for one would welcome it."

Shram, looking puzzled, answered quickly, "I would be glad to help, if it is in my power. It would certainly improve on anything I have planned for the immediate future. I already have the history, short though it might be, of being a different nature than most other people of Vedanne. For one thing I become bored at the lack of pace in my fellow Vedannians. Perhaps this is to be a turning point in my life and even our own history. Who knows?"

"Thank you," said Clysta. Then, "If you can give whatever help you can, starting say as suggestions as to what is available. Or even anything to increase our knowledge of the city."

"Of course," he began with some enthusiasm, "I do have a fair knowledge of the Old Centre. I was not born here, but I have lived here most of my recent-we shall call it for your sakes,-'years'. I have also done lots of exploring in and about, and a little self-education on many things. It has been those actions, which gave me the title of nonconformist or 'rebel' I suppose. These though may be put to some use."

Clysta then turned to G'zin and Kindra.

"I know I keep asking you two this same question," she smiled, "I intend to somehow rescue my father, and without a doubt it is going to be dangerous."

Before she could say more, Kindra interrupted, taking her hand in both of his and saying.

"Clys', I guess you will have to include me. I sure am not returning to our sector, without showing those things out there some of what we can do. What do you say, G'zin?"

"One more time," she answered, "Just don't try to leave me out. I wouldn't miss this for two worlds."

Clysta continued smiling at her friends' ready agreement to stand at her side. She then became serious, saying.

"Now we need to have a plan, and I think I know what we must do. First Shram. I think we need added mobility. These mist things, the transporter systems. Are they able to relocate themselves in other places? You know what I mean. Able to be projected, say into an area other than a station? In those where we have seen or used them, they have been inside structures."

"I think I understand what you are looking for," said Shram interrupting her, "You are thinking of perhaps a terminal that will reposition to any pre-calculated location and be able to transport into and out of at will."

"That is the general idea I am trying to develop, and it may fit into a plan I have been formulating," said Clysta.

"That concept has not been used for hundreds of our planets revolutions-years," he corrected himself, then he said as he thought. "I know some of the basics, but I also know it requires a variety of complex manipulations and considerable work in computations. I am good but I may not be good enough to give you the results you are looking for."

"Do you have access to any records of the methods?" Clysta said.

"I have access to some details at my study area," Shram answered, "But I am still unsure if I can do the necessary computer work."

"G'zin is one of our Academy's top students," Clysta said with inward pride, as she winked at her female friend, "Show her your notes and the basics and I'll bet she will be able to do the rest."

For the first time in her young life, G'zin was speechless.

"Now," Clysta started once more, still facing Shram. "How long do you need to find our answers?"

Shram scratched his ear-lobe as he thought. G'zin watched him closely, her eyes beginning to shine.

"It should take us the remainder of today to find and then check the studies," he said thoughtfully, "Then G'zin and I can start to put together a phase to generate the medium, after which you will need to tell us where you intend to use these remote transporters. I say we can be ready the morning after tomorrow."

"The way I see it," said Clysta, "we may need it earlier than that. If you work late tonight and start early tomorrow, can it be ready in the afternoon?"

"I will know better later today," he said, "Is that ok by you G'zin?"

"Of course," G'zin answered, now radiant, "Now. What do you have in mind?"

"I will explain later," Clysta, answered, "G'zin! You and Shram get going. Help him in any way possible, and take care. Kindra," she turned to face him, "you and I will return to the Old Centre square with Euclid. He may be able to do something useful for my plan as well. I want to see that shuttle again. I also need to be there when they find out no-one has still taken them seriously. We will meet back at your quarters, Shram, if you don't mind. Is dusk o.k?"

Shram looked at G'zin and then nodded his acceptance of the timing.

"Oh, and G'zin," Kindra got close and added in a whisper. "Your eyes are on fire."

"Kindra?" Clysta had not noticed. "Remind me please to check our parcel. I am convinced we will get a chance to use it now for sure."

# Chapter 68

Commander Z'ee could only watch.

One of the Terrans who had been brought along, down to the planets surface, writhed in agony on the hard and course rock-like deck inside the shuttle. He and the two others were each secured to an anchoring device set in the floor to stop them going to his aid.

The injured man had just been subjected to a demonstration of the aliens' idea of amusement. It was also an effort to try to soften up the Commander's resolve. Commander Z'ee was still continuing to conceal what the truth might be of the strange craft and that it was familiar to him.

The torture had been executed by two of the larger aliens. Each gripped the man, holding him by using the tentacles inside its pincers. One of them was holding on to his feet and the other his arms. They had then begun pulling in opposite directions, whilst the navigator Quazraam prodded and tormented the poor screaming man with the Electro Whip.

His shrieking from the pain was loud enough to cover even the raucous gurglings of obvious enjoyment the other crewmen were making as they continued to goad the antagonists. It was a mercy that the man blacked out and finally passed into unconsciousness.

"Now that one didn't last very long," leered Captain Laslas into the translator. The now limp and silent body of the tortured man was considered useless and so it was thrown into a corner of the large control room.

"Why don't we try another?" The Captain looked toward the other two and pointed to the Science Officer, Manchoo.

"Ok ok," Commander Z'ee finally had seen enough pain inflicted. It was time to try to bluff it out with this Captain. He must possess some kind of weak link somewhere.

The Captain ambled across the floor, his leg joints clicking and stopped to face these three secured captives. He towered over the Commander and set one of his extended eyes directly on him.

He said into the translator device, "You have finally found it is better to speak about that craft. Yes? Now tell me all that you know."

The Commander hung on the Captain's first words. Then timidly,

"I agree those markings on that other craft you showed us, are of a similar type," he said. He waited as the device translated his words to the aliens' language, "But I swear I do not recognize what they are," he lied, hoping the machine did not pick up any inflections which his lying might cause. "It could be a ship from anywhere outside of this system. It could also be lost, just like I was when I first came here years ago."

"That is a better answer and one I am beginning to like," the Captain said, "But it is not enough and I need more. You are still hiding something from me. You will tell me all you know."

The Captain made a quick jab at the man Manchoo with his whip.

Commander Z'ee knew now he had to manoeuvre and out-think this wise creature that was Captain of their mission and he also knew it would not be easy. At least the torture had been stopped for the time being. This one had not made it to his present rank and position from nothing. He was obviously very intelligent, alien or not.

Commander Z'ee faked a flinch and raise an arm, as if in protection from an anticipated blow.

"Captain Laslas," he began, still in the same timid voice, "Just suppose then, that ship was to be from somewhere in our own same sector. If it is from one of our group of planets, then they have seen our ship in space and are surely aware that we are here and they will now be trying to locate us. Even if you keep us hidden inside the shuttle, they will still find out we are here.

If that is so and they do not see us, they are sure to go or even send for reinforcements or they may even go back to their star and bring help to try to locate us. But if they see us they will realize we are your captives and are likely to hold off any firm plans of action."

"What opposition can you weak soft shelled slugs put to be a match against us," said the Captain boastfully. The alien pushed his torso into an almost upright stance. "We are strong. We have completely eradicated all forms of opposition in our own Royal Empire. We know of your own futile defenses. There is no-one in the whole Galaxy who is powerful enough to defend against our might."

The Commander had to chose his next words with care.

"Your ship is large and strong, but the crew you have is only small in number. It is also only one lone warship and if a squadron arrives from my people then a battle will surely break out and the consequences are predictable."

"Would this please you?" Captain Laslas said and a tone of obvious sarcasm leaked through the translator.

"Not in the least," the Commander replied. He lied again, "That means when any battle breaks out involving your ship, all of our lives would obviously be at risk and mine in particular. I am not at all intending to endanger that.

"And I have no wish to bring death to anyone of my crew and I will do my utmost to prevent its happening. That would stop of course at the sacrifice of my own life."

The alien Captain's body turned slightly as he made sounds in the direction of his crew. The translator sphere had some apparent difficulty with the conversion, but to the Terrans the sounds were easily recognized as noises and sneers of disgust.

It was impossible to guess if the Captain had come to a decision about what the Commander had been intimating. But as a token to this alleged weakness, he turned slowly, faked a look in another direction, then fiercely swung his smaller claw up and around. It caught the Commander with an almost anticipated and glancing blow, as he was ducking out of its path.

The blow had sufficient force to send him skidding and rolling across the rough floor of the ship. His semi conscious body came to an abrupt stop as it fell into an open drainage trough, with the tether pulling tight and straining at his ankle.

Clysta, Kindra and Euclid, passed through an arch forming one of the many entrances into the Old Centre Square from the city outside. Their arrival was just minutes before the smaller shuttlecraft commenced its lift off from the top of the larger main shuttle. They stood in the shelter of an overhang and watched as it disappeared into the distance on its way to space.

Kindra remarked, "I wonder just what that was doing down here and why is it leaving now?"

'Possibly Master Kindra,' said Euclid in answer. 'It was delivering supplies.'

Clysta was looking about the square and taking in all of the details of the surroundings. The area was still busy but by no means crowded. A number of Vedannians were passing through the area and none appeared to have been interested in the shuttles noisy lift off. There was also no sign of that 'committee' requested by the alien leader.

"Well," said Clysta, having come to a conclusion, "It is just as I expected. There has been no attempt to fill the aliens demand for an audience."

Then she indicated with a movement of her head, "Look, over at the other side of the square. Isn't that the one who was instructed to summon the elders or some kind of delegation?"

'That is quite correct,' Euclid confirmed. 'Mekwa was the name used for her by Shram. He referred to the person as being of the female gender.'

"Let's make our way slowly over there, to her side of the square," Kindra suggested, "We need to be closer. We can see just how the aliens take it all when they find she has returned unaccompanied."

The three were still disguised and dressed in the fashion of locals. They did not find anyone who was taking particular notice, as they took a circuitous route to the area where Mekwa stood. They came to a stop a short distance behind the female with the alien vessel some thirty paces ahead of them.

It was now close to the time the alien Captain had promised they would return to the outside. After a short wait, a hissing sound announced the opening of what was likely the air-lock in the underside of their crab like alien vehicle. Within a minute a long sloping ramp descended to the ground below. After another five minutes of waiting, the first of the aliens emerged.

The two friends and Euclid moved closer to the Vedannian female and stood in a circle so not to appear to be fully interested in the craft or its occupants.

Kindra spoke in a whisper, whilst trying not to look directly at the shuttle.

"You were quite correct, Euclid. I remember now. That one looks just the same as a Lobster. That was its name. Possibly these beings are a little more streamlined, not as many plates and sections as I remember of those from Old Earth. But these are equally as grotesque. And also they are gigantic."

"I wonder what quirk of evolution made a creature as awkward as that is, able to conquer space flight?" Clysta said in an equally low voice.

'It is a possibility the original work on that was completed by another weaker species and they were unable to defy these creatures the use of the inventions and developments,' Euclid said trying to form a satisfactory answer.

"You could be on to something there, Euclid," Kindra said in agreement. It then occurred to him, Euclid is still just a robot. How ever is he able to make such conclusions? He thought it better to let it go at that. He continued, "I suppose with those monsters, anything can be possible."

"I would like it if we were a little closer," said Clysta quietly, "We should close this gap between us and the girl."

As they moved slowly, two more aliens exited their craft, clicking and clacking down the ramp. One of these was the largest alien in the group, the same one that had done all the talking earlier. The other was much smaller and again that one had the task of pulling the sphere on the sled.

The larger alien went through the same ritual as the time before and turned from side to side as if making sure the crowd was aware of his exit from the shuttle.

The large claw touched the sphere and for the first time they could see the flexible finger like probes as they were used to manipulate the device.

"If there are those of you who did not get it before," said the Captain, "I am the Captain of this shuttle and of the great and mighty warship we have left circling in orbit. I said I would be out in the star's last quarter, and here I am.

"Now. I am ready to meet with that shell-less someone who is in power in this place. Where are the ones I said before, that I wanted to see?"

The creature's small head swivelled around. With the eyestalks moving in different directions he closely covered the crowd. The number of Vedannians in the square by this time was slightly more than when he had descended the ramp earlier in the day.

The female Mekwa, who the Captain had spoken to before, walked slowly and deliberately toward the front of the small congregation.

"It was I whom you asked to pass on your request," she said in a level voice. She looked directly at the alien.

The momentary silence was deafening.

"Well!" The alien Captain roared, "Where are they?"

Without a sign of intimidation, Mekwa said in a strong but still bell-like voice.

"No one is coming to meet with you."

The translating sphere did its work in reverse, slowly but effectively. The Captain got the reply and stiffened his support legs to stand a little taller. He started to make louder noises into the device.

"What do you mean?" the Captain said, in a bellowing translation.

He repeated the translation with a mimicking tone, "No one is coming?" He went on, "Are your slimed cored leaders too afraid to stand and face a being of superior strength and might?"

"That I cannot answer," she responded, in the same calm and clear voice as before. "I can only report that there is not anyone who will be here to meet or talk with you."

As had happened here before, the small crowd were once again starting to separate and disperse, some seeming to have lost interest in the events. The girl Mekwa was standing, still facing the towering alien Captain who was inside the protection of the ships encircling force field.

"We will see," the alien said in a menacing tone. Captain Laslas swiveled his head, leaving one of his eyes facing the Vedannians. He then snapped out in his own gibbering voice what sounded to be a command.

A tubular probe about one metre in length extended from an aperture in the front facing plating at the top of the vessel. It had the appearance of a gun barrel but as everything about the alien's designs, it was of a course texture and did not possess any really smooth lines.

The Captain made another sound, similar but especially different from the first command. As Clysta and the others watched, the shimmering around the ship faded away.

Clysta and Kindra stood and watched in silence.

Kindra spoke first in a whisper, "There. The force field is going down. Now that could be very useful!"

With a dull crackle the probe began a discharge of sorts. A slight discolouration of the air occurred immediately in front of the tube. It then spread outward in a narrow stream heading in the direction of a small group containing four of the Vedannians a little to the left of Mekwa. The discolouration then expanded to cause the same effect around and then enclosing them all.

The device ceased its action and withdrew into the craft and disappeared, leaving the group encased and sealed in a transparent jelly like substance. The four remained standing just where they were with the substance holding them captive. It appeared they were still able to breath but were unable to escape from the confines of the material.

Within less than a second, the air immediately around the craft had returned to its same shimmering. The protective field had been regenerated.

Once more the Captain spoke into the sphere, "Now! You see these miserable excuses for intelligence," he pointed at the encased Vedannians using his smaller claw, "They are to stay there exactly as they stand, until someone with authority arrives. We will give you until the next star rise.

"I have become weary of your ignorance. If I receive this same stupidity and there is nobody here by the time I have said, we will use those," the Captain pointed, "As a supplement to our food. I should think they would even be very tasty from what I remember of those we had before."

He turned his attention back to the messenger. The alien still towered over the female, Mekwa.

"Now, do you understand what I mean?" he said.

With both eyestalks standing outward, he looked down at her, menacingly.

Mekwa answered.

Once again she said just as calmly as she had done previously, "I will do what I can."

The large crustacean stood as if stunned at the coolness of this diminutive being. In his frustration, the Captain's eyes swivelled to the rear to ensure none of his crew who had joined him outside could be seen to have recognized the futile attempt of frightening this thing standing before him.

"Next!" Dismissing the matter, the Captain stretched to its fullest height in an endeavor now to attract the attention of others in the square.

"We have inside our ship, a few prisoners. They are similar in appearance to you and possess your same kind of soft-shelled bodies. We easily tracked and captured these and their own useless ship while it was a great distance outside of this area of space."

He turned toward the shuttle. This time all around could hear the translation when he screamed toward the opening at the ramp.

"Bring out those slug-like weaklings. I want them out here in full view for all to see."

Some of the Vedannians, who were now leaving the area, stopped to see what it was that the alien had to show. Others who were not, or appeared to be not interested, carried on with their business talking softly in groups as others wandered in and out of the large square.

Clysta got a sudden premonition. What she was about to see would make those dreams she had been experiencing, all come true. The two of them and the robot stood their ground, trying their utmost to fit into the small crowd.

First the feet and legs of the prisoners appeared at the top of the ramp, Kindra whispered just loud enough for the small group to hear.

"Those are feet and legs of an offworlder. They are most definitely not Vedannian. See, their garments are the same fashion that ours were back at Sol."

Inch by inch the torso came into view reinforcing Kindra's statement. It was eventually obvious there were three who came to the base of the ramp and stopped and they all were most definitely Terrans. They each wore the standard one-piece suit. Loose, but following the body's shape. And being a light blue, in colour. They all were a little grimy, stained and pale looking, but each of them was leaning against the other and trying their best at managing to stand upright.

On the left side of their tunic just above the breast each wore the glistening star inside a gold wreath. It was the insignia of the Galactic Federation.

The alien Captain spoke in a mocking tone.

"These here are a sample of another race of weaklings that are inhabitants of this section of our galaxy," the Captain tried to emphasize the word 'our'.

He looked at the captives, saying, "This part of our galaxy it would seem, just breeds weakling. If this is the best this sector can produce as a defender, then our mission to take over in this place is going to be very, very easy."

Clysta's eyes were glued to the top of the ramp about thirty or so metres away. They took on a look of apprehension as a fourth prisoner came into view. Whomsoever it could have been, that person was staggering from side to side. Then, just as the shoulders came low

441

enough to be in line of sight, one of the aliens that was following close behind gave the newcomer a forceful push. It caused the Terran to stumble and stagger on the course sloping surface and trip then fall. He rolled head over heals for the rest of the way to the base of the ramp finishing sprawled on the smooth surface that was the square below.

She could not be absolutely sure but it appeared as the person fell, to be a male. Clysta was craning her neck also in an attempt to be not obviously interested, to see as he got to his feet. He looked to be drunk and ended facing away from the small crowd of onlookers, then he staggered and turned to take in a quick unnoticed glance at the audience. It was a male as she had guessed and now even the grime and pale appearance could not conceal his features.

Clysta gasped, then, in a whisper.

"It's – it is, my father."

Euclid quickly held her arm, as if to warn her not to reveal her presence. Kindra took a half a pace into the front of her also, to block the possible move she might make toward the alien craft.

"I must go- -," she said, still in a whisper. Euclid's metal hand tightened the grip on her arm but still gently.

Then realizing the error she was about to make, she said, "Ok, I understand. It will do no good to make any unplanned moves at this time. But later!"

Kindra said, "We have been here long enough. If they do have a scanner that is monitoring the crowd, we should make like the rest of the Vedannians. We must appear not interested. Let's move away, slowly."

They leisurely sauntered through the spectators moving outward in an irregular course and from the scene, stopping occasionally and trying their best to remain inconspicuous.

Commander Z'ee was feigning to be stunned, though looking carefully at the small crowd through half closed eyes. He was sure he might see someone he would recognize from his earlier visit to this planet. Although his two previous landings with the aliens had been unsuccessful, he was also in hope he himself would be recognized.

And then there was the new craft. It had to be from the Terran sector. Maybe—.

In the fleeting seconds he speedily scanned the small groups outside of the protective barrier. He could see no one he could recall. But then, the Vedannians all looked the same.

His attention was taken by a group of three Vedannians who seemed to be leaving the square in a way more direct than most other spectators had in the past. Then one of the three looked back, the other two in the group did not.

The Commanders eyes focused on a face he did acknowledge.

It was hidden beneath a loose hood but that could not hide the angular lines of the face in the shadows. The being's walk was more deliberate and not so fluid. And the robe it wore did not completely camouflage the angular frame from the practiced sight of the Commander.

The face he saw in the shadows of the hood was undoubtedly the face of a robot. This fact made his heart beat a little faster.

# Chapter 69

Clysta and Kindra with Euclid had made their way on foot back to Shram's quarters. The other two, G'zin and Shram, had still not returned from their investigations of the transporter systems. After a few hours of waiting mixed with thoughts of the captives, Clysta briefly outlined to Kindra a plan that had been developing in her head. After a while and just as a golden dusk had begun to descend, G'zin and Shram exited from the room's transporter. Clysta and Kindra were heartened from their morose of the last few hours. G'zin's eyes had in them a glow they has not witnessed lately and one which was most unmistakable.

Shram stood close to G'zin almost touching her. His face a look that was most unusual in all of the inhabitants they had seen on the planet, up until now.

The reason for both of these states was equally obvious to Clysta and Kindra.

After saying their hellos Clysta excitedly related their experience in the square and the sighting of what she said must have been her father the Commander.

She then asked. "Now tell us. What did you two find out about the systems of the Transporter?"

G'zin answered quickly. She was surreptitiously watching every move that Shram made.

"We first visited Shram's learning place. It was enormous. And it was stocked with all kinds of devices of learning and tools of experimentation. Anyhow, we poured over the system designs and found what was a little used function of the processes. The main system uses routines that are way above my head but Shram convinced me that he understands it all. It could be made, with not too many major adjustments, to vary the location of what is termed a Transponce Focus. I think. Is that right Shram?" she looked to Shram for confirmation. He smiled and nodded his verification.

She then continued, "Normally the mist is set in its individual location permanently. The Vedannians have had little or no reason in making them mobile. That is since the time when they were sited were they are now.

"The stations are positioned in the most convenient places for their normal uses any way. This seems to have been worked out centuries ago from what we were able to assess from those records. And beside that, there is one close at hand, almost in every locale."

"So how do we move one then?" Clysta asked.

G'zin became serious now. She tried to explain, "We examined some rather old records and found the address of a place where the devices were originally manufactured. We went there and it was also very large, and very empty except for some devices that have been there to for a long, long time. We rummaged around again and found another address which was of a location for a kind of storage area for extra – 'Focus devices'-and went over there to investigate.

"The place was closed up and hadn't been opened for what appeared to have been ages. Anyway we got inside. I won't bother you with the details of how. But it was dark and a little dusty. And—."

She looked sideways at Shram. He was smiling.

"Anyhow. We found some of what we need to set up a random locator,-that is what it is known as in our terms -, and I am sure it is able to do what we need. Shram says so anyway. It can be activated through a holo' vidi' and, would you believe, kind of put into use the thought waves of the user as a guidance medium."

G'zin continued her dialogue, going over some of the workings of the procedure, with a few intermittent prompts and corrections from Shram.

Clysta and Kindra both listened in silence as they described what they had learned and found.

Then, Clysta asked them both, "Now for the big question. Are we able to move an exit to the Old Centre Square?"

Shram who had remained mostly quiet through G'zin's dialogue, except for his prompts and guidance, spoke first in an answer.

"I will need to make some internal program changes first. The Square is a unique condition. There is a certain anomaly making it almost hallowed. There has long been a sort of barrier or defense set up there to the Transporters' systems."

"How long will it take to set out this new program?" Clysta asked almost afraid the answer would create a long delay in the plan.

"Perhaps with G'zin's help…" Shram went quiet for some seconds, eyes closed, as if meditating, "If we begin early, we should have a system operational by mid-morning. Will that be good enough?"

"That will do fine," Clysta said, brightening and with a smile. She then explained the final plan.

The four friends had relocated in a large and almost empty room which was inside one of the least used or maybe unused buildings in an area of the inner city. They were sat in a circle around an odd shaped console riding on a suspensor field. Euclid had taken his usual position in the background but at full alert awaiting orders.

Shram had told them he had found he could use this place as a handy workshop and that he had frequented it from more than two revolutions past to develop a few theories relating to his education. It was most unlikely Shram said, that they would be disturbed, as he had never seen anyone in this building for all of that time he had used it. He also explained it was now reserved for his use alone, now making it more remote they would be disturbed.

Shram touched his finger to a spot on the side of the console and immediately a projection assembled itself seemingly from out of nowhere.

A scaled down holo' showing the targeted main square was now being transmitted to the area which was in the middle of the clear floor and showed some of the surrounding structures and most of all, the alien craft at one side of the projection view. The finer details, filtered out presently along with any of the local populace in the area, Shram had added, would be completed by the transmission when their plan was in action.

Clysta turned eagerly toward Kindra, "Are we ready to go?"

Kindra nodded.

She looked at G'zin and Shram. They nodded their readiness also.

Then Clysta looked at Euclid, saying.

"You understand, Euclid, I need you to stay here to listen, so you will not be with me."

The robot gave his reply.

'This unit understands, Miss Clysta, but it is against my program to have me become separated from you. I will do so only as it is your bidding.'

Clysta then added, looking at the transmitted view of the large alien shuttle.

"At least the small shuttle has not returned, that means the captives are still here."

Shram had managed to obtain some garments, which were of a higher grade. They would help to make the two Terrans appear to be more of importance and in keeping with the traditions. Just in case the aliens had themselves worked out the relevance of clothing and materials.

The first part of the strategy was that Clysta and Kindra were to go into the square and act as representatives of the planet. This was just the start though, to Clysta's elaborate strategy.

When all was as prepared as they could make it, Clysta said finally, "Ok. Here goes! G'zin! Start up your calcs'."

G'zin smiled and immediately went to work, deftly moving her speedy hands about this new artifice which was to control the location of any entry and exit from the transport devices.

Clysta and Kindra walked across the room and then into the newly generated panel of mist. It had been created at the farthest end wall of this room from which they were to operate their action.

The exit they had chosen was a regular one inside the Old Centre foyer. As usual, their exit was unnoticed and all about them were Vedannians moving in regard to their regular daily duties, or non-duties. Some, who were having discussions with others and some moving about in their own isolated studies.

From here they walked the short distance to the ornate arch that led them to the outside and into the open square. Across the crystal pavement stood the large and foreboding shape of the alien craft just as it had been the last time they had seen it, and the prisoners.

The time was now mid-afternoon.

Already, the ramp was down and an alien, who looked to be one of a smaller stature, was slowly patrolling the area on the inside edge of their protective force field. The extended eyestalks rotating to take in all that there was to see around the landed craft.

"That thing must be some kind of weapon it has strapped onto its back," guessed Kindra. He spoke just low enough for only Clysta to hear.

The weapon was a configuration of jointed tubes ending in a course barrel, possibly of a larger thickness than that of the hand held one used on the planter a few days before. The device was secured, even perhaps bolted, to the rear skeletal plating of the alien.

Kindra added, still speaking in a low voice, "This must be their idea of mobile heavy armaments. Its operation is most likely by the alien bending downwards to sight in on any level and firing."

There were a few Vedannians inspecting those locals who had been encased in the strange jelly substance. Occasionally one of them would touch test its consistency, then walk away as if satisfied with its findings, still with the same disinterest as always. In what appeared to be slightly more in number than before, a crowd had gathered and were standing around the front part of the craft. These still arranged themselves in the same fashion as the other times, not really looking at the shuttle and showing only slight interest in matters as a whole. In other areas of the square there were also larger numbers, moving around although still with the same previous unconcerned attitude they had always presented.

As Kindra spoke, two more aliens came into view and ambled down the ramp, pushing before them two of their Terran prisoners. Then three aliens followed and on reaching the bottom of the ramp started a gibbering conversation in their own language. Without the translating device it was not possible to understand what they were discussing. But the menacing prods, with stick things, which sparked on contact, at the two captives left the impression they had some game of antagonism planned.

Clysta put her hand to her mouth and spoke into a small, concealed disk, "Can you see all of this, G'zin?"

"The picture is coming in very clearly," was the reply heard through tiny earpieces that all of them carried, "And the zoom works well too. When are you about to start?"

Clysta was attaching the speech disk to the collar of the gown she wore, so that it resembled a part of a shoulder crest. The other parts of the crest on her shoulder were a micro vidi' transmitter.

She answered, "We will wait a little longer, they look to be coming out of their ship. I want all of them outside before we start the masquerade."

Then, she spoke to Euclid. The robot had moved up to the holo' of the scene of the Square.

"Ok, Euclid. Take your position, but do not move yet, await the command from G'zin."

Euclid watched, inside the room, the scaled down image of Clysta as she spoke. The robot then moved to the end of the large room to be ready to step into the mist medium.

Finally, back in the Square, the other four aliens came into view at the top of the ramp. They were pushing before them the other two prisoners. Clysta's heart began to race. Now she was certain. She could see that one of these really was her father. He was more alert now. This time he walked upright, with his eyes guardedly darting to and fro, scanning the crowd. He was looking for another sighting of that robot he was sure he had recognized the day before.

Mekwa, the latent messenger once again was present in the square at the fore of the milling Vedannians. She was standing roughly in the same place as she had been on previous days.

The alien Captain looked out at the crowd and saw her. He clacked his way up to the force field and positioned the sphere between both of them and began gurgled into it in his own tongue.

"You there!" came the same demanding tone, "Yes you that I gave orders to before. Do I get an audience with anyone of importance today?"

To give his demand some weight one of his eyes swivelled to focus on the block of alien jelly substance encasing the Vedannians. They were still showing small signs of life but were noticeably fatigued. The Captain raised a claw indicating the captives and said in a louder and mocking voice.

"Well!" He demanded, "Do we get to taste these prepared delicacies or do we not? That Cloriclat covering has a property our cooks use to preserve and tenderize some of our food. He also uses it to keep everything we eat living for a long time. We always only eat our food while it is still alive. Dead food is not good for us."

Mekwa answered, this time in a slightly trembling voice. As before, she told the Captain that she had not been informed that anyone would be making an appearance.

Expressions did not show on the exterior skeleton of the immense crustacean, but it was obvious he was displeased with the reply. He quickly turned to the alien with the device on its back and screeched a command in his own language.

The small alien dropped immediately into a crouching stance, causing the weapon to be aimed at the crowd, which by now had increased. A second alien moved into place at the side of the now positioned weapon. This one was holding a form of control loosely secured by cross webbing to its front upper plating.

The second alien looked through swivelling eyes on fully extended stalks at his Captain. This one was awaiting the next command.

"Are you getting all of this, Euclid?" Clysta spoke softly into the disk in the crest. "It looks as if something is about to happen."

'Yes Miss Clysta, I am hearing everything,' was the reply, equally low.

The Captain gibbered a command in his own language once more.

450

As if in reply, the shimmering field around the shuttle dissipated. Almost at the same instant the Captain's next command was translated.

"Fire!!!"

The weapon was activated by the upright alien. Nothing was visible at the weapon itself but at a distance of twenty metres, a narrow blue white stream of energy extended away in a straight line. The beam did not last longer than a millisecond as it hit the encasing jelly with a resounding 'plop'. The jelly substance was instantly vaporized and disappeared. The captives who had been encase within its confines were momentarily released, but their freedom was short lived as in the next millisecond they all were vaporized too.

The Captain gave his interpretation of a gleeful sound over the translator as he said.

"We wouldn't have wanted to eat them anyway. If those last captives were any example, I don't expect they were very tasty."

The other aliens behind him made sounds, which could only be translated as raucous laughter at the events.

Another barked command was made and the weapon was once again aimed, this time toward one of the many ancient monument structures that graced the square.

"Fire!"

Once more the command came through the translator.

The same silent stream of energy this time took a corner off the metal plinth forming the base of a decorative sculpture across the square.

The obelisk, all of twenty-five metres high, toppled to the side. As it did, it hit another piece of beautiful and ancient sculpture and pushed that over. As both heavy objects teetered and then tumbled to the surface of the square, ten or more of the onlookers who were unable to move quickly enough out of the way were struck by the tumbling weighty debris and killed instantly. As the conflagration disintegrated others who were standing close by were hit creating injuries of varying magnitude.

"This is too much. I suggest it is time to move," said Clysta, slightly shocked at what she had witnessed, "Be ready for my signal G'zin. You too Euclid."

As Clysta and Kindra came into the open, they heard the reply of readiness from G'zin.

Together and with deliberate and authoritative movements, their steps hidden beneath the coverings, both disguised Terrans approached the front of the crowd. Clysta took note that only a handful of the Vedannians had moved toward the tumbled edifices, showing some signs of curiosity at least, with most of the others still maintaining their usual less than caring strolling about and their previous coming and going. Altogether, the latest show of power by the aliens had still had little effect on the locals gathered here. Not a murmur of remorse had been uttered, by the locals for those dead and injured.

As they walked toward the shuttle in the distance they heard a loud command from the alien Captain. It was the one they had associated previously with the force field screening.

Kindra whispered into the talk piece, "The defense is up again, I trust you got it all Euclid."

'Yes Master Kindra. This unit executed your instructions precisely,' the answer came back.

# Chapter 70

Commander Z'ee had watched the aliens' reaction to the reply given by the Vedannian. He was unsure if it was male or female. The Commander had also seen the destruction of those edifices in the far corner of the square, though he could not see what the cost in lives could likely have been. He had also been watching the groups of locals hoping these aliens had not seen his eyes move furtively about inspecting the faces he could see. Then, his attention was drawn to a movement at the large decorative archway, which he remembered, from years before. He also recollected it had led into one of the buildings he knew as the 'Old Centre'.

He could not be too sure at this distance, but it seemed there were two Vedannians who were making their way slowly and deliberately in the direction of the aliens craft.

There were others who had moved about in the usual pattern indicative of their non-involvement, which had gone on for so many days before. But these were definitely coming this way. That in itself was a strikingly different conduct for these people.

"It looks like we are to have a meeting at last," said the Commander quietly, toward his fellow prisoners, "Be ready for anything that looks like it is a way out. There are two Vedannians on their way across the square. This could be the diversion I have waited for; at least it is something new. If that damned screen stays down longer than one minute, we may as well make a run for it."

Commander Z'ee knew all too well he had talked too long even in a low voice. He was to be reminded by a lash strike from an Electro

Whip across his back from one of those guards standing close behind them. It was accompanied by the usual gurgling command for silence.

The two locals advanced and stopped at the outer limits of the defense screen. The alien Captain looked down on them, his eyestalks rotating to and fro as he viewed these two, checking for any sign of weapons. He studied them long and hard, realizing these two must represent something higher than all these other cattle that populated this square. If only from the outer skin they had about them.

He waived over one of the other aliens to stand by his flanks as he positioned the translator ahead of his towering body. He began to speak.

"Only two?" he said with disgust. He raised his body higher to look across the square, checking for any more who might be coming after these. Then satisfied these were the only emissaries. He concentrated on these before him and continued.

"So. Finally. You have come to your witless senses. Do you require a further demonstration of our weaponry to get you to bring out a larger number of your kind? We have much more that we can show you. Our gunner needs a little more practice and the last one is but a small tool of destruction that we have brought with us."

The Commander was on his knees and in some pain from the last lash but was all the time trying to recognize the face of one of the Vedannians. Something was strangely familiar; the eyes appeared different, a little more oval. Not much unlike a Terran. The face too, it was also Terran in shape, the bone structure more pronounced, but somehow different.

One of the representatives spoke.

"We are of the High Order. Under these most unpleasant circumstances, we feel we must still bid you a welcome…"

The speech of the disguised Kindra was cut short. The aliens started to give out loud gibbering and cackles of their sounds of mirth. They then started the bobbing up and down action on their spindle legs, as they began heckling at the statement.

One of the Terran prisoners whispered just loud enough not to be heard above the raucous noise of the aliens screeching.

"It spoke in Terran. Did you hear?"

"I heard," said the Commander, "A good thing the translator sphere does not know the difference. I am sure their faces have had some kind of alteration. That one must be a male and the other one I think is a female. If I could only see past the heavy make up, I am sure she is Terran too. What is more important, I am almost certain I recognize her."

The alien Captain regained his composure, what small amount he was able to draw upon. Turning he looked down on what he had taken to be the diminutive inhabitants who were to be the representatives for this miserable planet.

Once more through the translating sphere, he said, "Well. I will ask you one more time before I show you how much more damage we can do. Where are the rest of your miserable leaders? Is this all that we are to see? Why are there not more of you-and with some of your riches? That is the least of the treatment we are accustomed to on our other conquests."

Kindra replied with a lie and a touch of reverence.

"There are others, and they are preparing for your visit. We have been selected to show you into the Great Hall within the Old Centre. It is there in which we have the records and all that we value of our great civilization."

"That is good. It is a start," the Captain said in reply after listening to the translation. "I intend to send along two of my best soldiers to see this hall and inspect it. I myself don't trust you or anyone that you represent."

He turned to face his crew, signaling to one and then another who were to accompany these hosts. He then said in a loud gibber with the intent that the sphere would translate all of what he was saying and transmit it. Especially toward these two 'Vedannians' standing there before him.

"Do not let us have any errors. If there are any signs of treachery, vaporize them all, starting with these two."

In the room where G'zin and Shram along with Euclid waited for their action to start, they sat at the console alert to the happenings up to now and watching the performance on the holo'. Before them the strips of coloured lights and patterns, which partly were the controls of the system, gleamed brightly.

They could see in the holo' where the crustaceans had positioned their Terran prisoners, slightly to the blind side of the group of aliens. Their leg tether had been secured by a hooking device to a ring on a supporting leg of the craft. The aliens were not too concerned about anyone on the inside of the protection of the field and paid no great attention to these weaklings. So long as they were secured, that is.

G'zin and Shram, constantly alert, quickly covered the operation sequence as they awaited the signal from Clysta. Otherwise, all inside the room was silent.

Over the talk disk contact came the voice of Clysta.

"We will gladly take your representatives to inspect the Great Hall. You need not have any fear of us, the people of Vedanne only wish you peace and will do you no harm."

The Captain made the sounds to command the lowering of the screen field.

G'zin spoke to Euclid, "Was that the same screen down command, Euclid?"

'Yes, Miss G'zin, it was the same inflection of the guttural tones, giving the identical sounds and connotations...' Euclid went on.

"Thank you Euclid," G'zin said to stop the robot, as she jovially shook her head. "Now be ready."

They then heard Clysta say.

"We are ready if you are. Come this way, please."

This was the signal for which G'zin had been waiting.

"Now," she said to Shram.

Shram's palms danced across the many strips on the console with a fluid motion as if playing some musical instrument. In the room's holo' image before the pair, they could both see a transporter mist now beginning to form.

Their plan was now taking shape. G'zin, who was watching the holo' closely, said to Shram.

"Move it a metre closer to the Terrans. That will put it a metre inside the line of their protection field," then an instant later, with a wave of her arm, "Go, now Euclid. Go."

At the order, the robot stepped into the mist at the wall of the room and was gone. The holo' image of the square showed the robot stepping out of the now adjusted mist close to the side of the alien's shuttle craft.

In the square, the Captain of the alien ship was just finished with dispatching one of his best crewmen and the navigator Quazraam, to accompany these new shell-less creatures. He had been busy giving them the additional orders, in their own tongue to be sure to return with something of value. They were also to bring along some new hostages on their return.

The creature, with its scaly back facing the direction of the Terran prisoners, had missed the instant in which the square shape of the transporter mist magically formed out of nowhere. It was part of the plan that the ships protection screen be inactive before the medium was formed, mainly as a precaution against its failure to transmit inside of that area. The friends could not take a chance, as they were unsure if the medium could be passed through the protective field previously surrounding the craft.

One of the crewmen gibbered something, which was likely a warning of surprise in the Captain's direction, whilst another just looked on in shocked amazement. That one was just watching, stunned by the peculiar form that was the robot as it emerged.

Euclid had removed the robe and disguise. It now was showing humanoid limbs and torso with their solid and metallic exterior. It was a most unusual sight to the aliens. They had not seen anything like it on this planet before, or maybe even on any other for that matter.

The robot spoke confidently in the direction of the prisoners.

'This way please, Commander Z'ee. It is most important that you all enter this medium with much haste. Do not be concerned, you will come to no harm.'

The Commander too was surprised. He spun around to face the robot and immediately recognized the face that was Euclid. He turned to the others, saying.

"This is a friend. Hurry, we are leaving."

As they all took a step toward the mist, they were reminded that all four were secured together and the tether had been fastened around a supporting leg of the shuttle. Euclid in one fluid movement reacted by reaching out and snapping the tether at the anchor. The robot wasted no further time as it instantly scooped up the two Terrans furthest from the mist and carried them bodily, one in each metal arm, toward the medium and its imminent safety.

At the same moment in time, the Captain, alarmed by the crewman's noises, began to turn to see what he had missed behind him. One of the other aliens dropped a claw to its side to reach for a weapon in a cradle attached to the plating at the side of one of its forelegs.

"What trickery is this?" Captain Laslas screamed in his bewilderment and confusion. He was now fully turned, enough to see the first two Terrans disappear into the square of swirling mist. He screamed out a command to the one who now had the weapon partly drawn, to fire and destroy their escaping prisoners.

In the next split second, all five had passed into the transport and were out of sight, just as the alien opened fire in their direction.

As the charge of fierce energy left the muzzle, Shram, who had watched the events in the holo', closed down the instrument and ducked, shouting out.

"Everyone down on the floor!"

His movement was well timed as the leading portion of the energy bolt followed the transportation and exited into the room where he sat with G'zin. It ended its travel by cutting a smouldering but otherwise harmless scar in the wall opposite the now cancelled mist.

G'zin was first to speak as they all rose to their feet again.

"Commander, please let Euclid tend to your needs, whilst we now get your daughter out of there."

It was a bewildered Commander who finally said.

"My daughter? You mean, Clysta?"

# Chapter 71

Clysta and Kindra stood their ground, whilst looking past the large alien, and watched as the Commander and the other three Terrans were assisted into the transporter by the robot.

They could almost feel the rage mounting inside the hard exterior skeleton of the alien Captain. A scream was emitted from the sound tube of the Captain. It was a command to reset the protective field, but the order had been too late as the mist began to fade into nothingness. He began to draw his own blaster hanging at the side of his front left leg, at almost the same instant that the crewman's shot had followed the escapees, then stopped at the futile gesture.

He next turned to face the disguised Clysta and Kindra. The creature was so enraged he moved to charge through the instantly reforming protection intending to vent his vicious wrath on these two puny Vedannians. Only a quick instinctive warning from his navigator Quazraam, still inside of the screen, as to what such a passage through the field could do. It stopped the Captain in mid stride.

Captain Laslas stood glaring at the two local figures outside of the perimeter, with savage revenge in his ball like eyes. Two separate commands rung out from the noise tube, and the screen began once again to dissipate.

One of the smaller aliens reacted to the other order and prepared to leave the zone accompanied by Quazraam. Their instructions were now to capture these two alive.

"We had best get away from here," said Clysta to her companion. "Move toward that space in the crowd, there over by those shrub things."

Whilst the action of rescue had taken place, the Vedannians in the square had begun to watch with interest all of the incidents, but not for any other reasons. Now the flurry of action had all passed, they returned to their usual pace and non-involvement. This day had become once more the same as any other common day.

Kindra turned his head to look over his shoulder as they left the area immediately in front of the Captain. He saw the two aliens following after them at a speed greater than he had anticipated.

He said to Clysta who was walking at his side, "I suggest we begin running. These things are really moving and they're gaining on us!"

"That is roughly in keeping with our plan, I would say," Clysta responded, a little whimsically, and then taking the advice she picked up the pace slightly. A second later she was speaking into the inter talk on her shoulder.

"Transporter please G'zin, and make it snappy."

One second later, the now familiar sheet of mist started to form ahead of them, but it had made an appearance slightly to the right of their target and two strides farther away. They just had time to change direction and enter it before the two aliens following, reached out with their large claws to grasp at them.

With their claws outstretched and the loud screams of derision thrown by their leader, the Navigator and its confederate alien, faltered in their stride as they were racing onward toward the strange apparition. They were confused as both aliens saw the friends disappear from view after entering into the strange mist.

"Follow them, you scum. Go after them and don't dare to return without their entrails!" The Captain screamed, both in his effort to vent his rage, and in the panic mounting inside his shell. He was now afraid of having lost his prime advantage. Now he was also loath of his failure and what this crew around him might think of his future as leader.

Four valuable prisoners had been stolen away from him and mysteriously taken he knew not where. And these two representatives of this useless breed of beings had managed somehow to disappear from his sight.

It was there inside the workroom, where G'zin and Shram operated and controlled the mist transport, that Commander Z'ee was now quickly regaining some of his strength. He had been handed a large tumbler containing a drink of a strange but palatable pink fluid. It was a preparation of fast working healing agents and antibiotics with a few vitamins. These medicines had been prepared by the Vedannian, Shram and especially for this operation.

The other three ex-prisoners had since been placed in relaxers and were to be allowed to recover from their past ordeals at a slower pace. The Commander crossed the room to watch the holo' showing the action in the square. Whatever the concoction had been, the drink was taking a speedy effect. His strength was coming back and all the pains of his long capture were fading as if by magic. His senses too were fast increasing. He was still a little shaken by the suddenness and speed of their rescue but inwardly very pleased with its apparent success.

He had been baffled though by the statement made by the young female who appeared to be a Vedannian. She was sitting with another at this elaborate and confusing instrument and he was now wondering whom these two young strangers could be. And what was that about his—daughter?

The Commander then remembered that perhaps the robot Euclid might give him some answers. Just as he was about to open his mouth to ask, he heard a vaguely familiar voice from the region of the holo'.

The call, from his daughter Clysta, came over the inter talk and his heart missed a beat. Seeing in the holo', the aliens who were in pursuit and closing the gap behind these two Vedannians. It was going to be very close.

In the next instant, Clysta and Kindra leapt out of the mist and into the room.

The Commander now more than confused turned to see the two Vedannians he had just seen on the holo', stepping into the area at the far wall. They then turned, scrambling one to each side as if in anticipation of the next horror.

"Phew! That was close," said Clysta, and in the same breathe, "Hello father, I am so glad to see you are safe."

"Watch out," shouted G'zin and Shram in unison, "Here they come!"

Quazraam the alien navigator was first.

He exited from the transporter on to the highly polished floor surface, lost traction and immediately started to spin around on his four articulated legs. He was doing the best that he could, keeping his balance and at the same time trying to gain a little traction from the very slippery floor beneath him. The ever alert alien, as he spun, was quickly taking in the view and the number of fresh antagonists before him in this new and very strange place.

The second alien, slightly more cautious at entering the unknown, was following close behind. He was not quite so brave as Quazraam and faltered as he entered the strange chamber from the mist of the transporter. The shock of what he could see stopped him at his first step into the room.

Ahead though, Quazraam was quickly drawing his sidearm.

He had it in his mind to destroy instantly whomever it could be that was responsible for having caused the rage of his Captain to fall down upon him.

G'zin, anticipating the move, was ready. She deftly produced a concealed stun gun, one of those, which she had brought from the Skimmer these many days earlier. Levelling it at the sliding and gyrating alien, she pushed the button to release a stream of nerve stunning pulsations.

The weapon G'zin was using did not fully have the same effect as it did on a Terran nervous system. The beam caught the alien at the claw holding the sidearm, impacting at one of the many joints, just as it was about to fire. In place of the predicted slackening of the muscles, the alien's appendage became stiff and its grip on the mechanism with it. The sidearm was engaged.

"Watch out," yelled Commander Z'ee, "It's about to fire."

The second alien had now come fully into the room at that same instant. Quazraam was now completing his uncontrolled slithering turn and had gone through one hundred and eighty degrees. The now out of control discharge from the sidearm, caught his partner on the upper abdomen, cutting the beast clean into two pieces. The accompanying concussion sent the writhing remains rearward and into the mist, just at the moment Shram had closed it down.

With a plop, the mist and both halves of the dying alien with it, disappeared.

Quazraam, still conscious but unable to regain control of the disabled claw, showed no other effects from the still fully operating stun gun. The alien extended itself to its fullest height, let out a chilling scream and made a frantic charge toward the diminutive G'zin, his object adversary.

The closest to G'zin was the Commander. He moved immediately into the alien's path and crouched. He was ready to defend this female whomever she might be, barehanded.

Euclid had other thoughts, as its brain had calculated the odds of the projected actions outcome.

Leaping across the room the robot jumped high and landed on the back of the towering alien. The robot's metal hands then took a firm hold of the small head. The alien faltered slightly in its forward and skidding rush. It shook its whole body from side to side, in a vain attempt to dislodge the thing that was pulling backwards so hard until finally, all in the room heard a grinding snap.

The alien navigator staggered for just two more steps then its four legs buckled and spread out widely. The towering crustacean crumbled in its track and crashed to the floor, its appendages twitching to and fro in the final throes of its death.

Many seconds had passed before Kindra broke the silence.

"You are not supposed to have the ability to do that, Euclid."

'Master Kindra.' The robot said as it climbed from the fallen beasts back. It seemed to have already calculated the rules related to its action. 'Two or more humans were in peril of instant annihilation. In addition, this now terminated alien is not human and never will be human. Those are unarguably sound and acceptably programmed qualifications for the actions that were taken by this unit.'

# Chapter 72

"Now for the others," said Clysta, after the shock of first combat had dissipated. Clysta, while wiping away a part of her disguise, quickly brought her father up to date on her plan.

"We can have time for other things if we can defeat these alien creatures, but we must keep up the pace," she said, then indicating her friends, "By the way, father, say hello to G'zin and Kindra from the Academy at Europa. And this is Shram our friend and a very special Vedannian."

"Now we go into Plan B," said Kindra, smiling. He had not bothered to remove his make-up or the Vedannian apparel.

Clysta turned to Euclid, saying.

"Are you still able to duplicate the sounds that will make the defensive screen disengage?"

'Yes Miss Clysta, this unit is capable of copying any sounds received into the receptors, and making an exact duplicate of the deep guttural notes whilst repeating the reso…'

"Please Euclid," Kindra said with wide grin, stopping the robot in mid sentence, "Later you can explain."

"Ok then, let's get going. Shram?" She indicated to him with a wave of her hand that the mist should be re-energized. Then, "You first Euclid and you understand just what you must do."

'Yes, Miss Clysta,' were the only words this time in the robots reply.

The alien Captain was angry and confused. What had happened to his two crewmen? It began to pace to and fro inside the protection that had been replaced. What was this unusual and mysterious vapour that could make things disappear? And why was it taking those two so long to return?

It was not possible that members of his master race could be defeated. Especially by such slug like spongy looking creatures as those they had found in this area of the Galaxy. Why, he thought to himself his anger mounting, these weaklings were merely fodder to the lowest of beings.

The Captain paced up and down, keeping at a close distance from the shuttlecraft. In his rage, he missed completely the reforming of the transporting medium nearby and just fractionally outside the limits of the defensive energy screen. The next thing he did not see was Euclid's second exit, then standing and quickly studying the positions of the other aliens.

He did though hear the sounds Euclid made. They were an identical imitation of his own command to lower the defensive shielding. They were loud and clear enough for the crewman inside the shuttle, who was always so fearful at his Captain's rage and anger, to operate the shield controls without delay.

Immediately the screen was discontinued, the panel of mist appeared without a sound at a location closer to the craft and well inside the area that was usually protected.

Kindra exited and moved quickly to stand confidently, legs astride, in front of the surprised Captain, with Clysta following close behind.

"Hold your ground!" Kindra said in the direction of the towering Captain.

The alien could have little comprehension of the words Kindra had used, but it was certain he new what was meant. Pushing at the frontal sections of the Captain's upper skeleton was a weapon. Captain Laslas immediately recognized it as the one belonging to the missing navigator, Quazraam.

The alien stood absolutely still.

Clysta, who had followed closely behind Kindra, paused for an instant to be sure that Kindra's stand was working and turned to face two others of the crew. They too had heard the command to lower the screen and becoming inquisitive, had clacked around the shuttle to see the reason.

One of them was the first to see the two Terrans holding their Captain at bay. It immediately brought up the weapon at its side as Clysta, in anticipation, raised the small hand blaster and took aim. It was another of the contents of G'zin's surprise package. The alien was a little too slow.

A blue white beam cut a slash into the upper part of the alien's body and it crashed to the ground, still alive but with its motor nerves severed. Her face paled as she watched a green fluid escape from the gaping opening in the shell. Then within seconds the downed alien began to twitch in its final throws of death.

Kindra took a quick glance over his shoulder then returned his attention to the larger bodied Captain.

"You will be the next," Kindra said, once again prodding the Captain with this strange weapon. He was not too sure if the firing mechanism was in the places that his fingers were ready to manipulate. But the cowl around his smaller hand hid all of this from the alien.

A jibber from the Captain brought the other alien to a halt about six metres away.

Commander Z'ee stepped out of the square of mist. He caught the look of surprise that was evident in the alien eyes of the Captain, saying.

"Yes. It's me and I am back!" He said as the mist behind him silently cancelled.

Moving cautiously to the side of the stationary aliens, held at bay by his daughter and Kindra, he removed their side arms from the cradles at their forelegs.

He looked back at the towering Captain, saying to Kindra, "You keep him there, Kindra," then to the robot, "Come with me Euclid! We must disable the shuttle. We cannot give them any chance to contact the main ship."

He moved toward the ramp.

Slightly distracted and upset at the death she had created, Clysta missed the smaller aliens next movement. It had produced from a pocket, concealed under a plate of its skeleton, a sharp cutting instrument, not unlike a curved knife. Euclid though had better hearing and heard the slight scraping sounds from the joints just as the robot was about to step onto the ramp.

Turning, the robot saw the alien, now preparing to throw the knife, and raised the level of its voice in warning.

'Miss Clysta! You are in danger!'

The alien's throwing claw hit the crystal floor of the square, still with a hold on its knife, severed by the blast from Clysta gun. The alien came on, its rage unchecked as Clysta calmly leveled the blaster for a slicing beam and pressed the button.

She once more looked down as the second beast died at her feet. In a low, trembling voice she muttered sadly as if the corpses were able to hear.

"That was not at all necessary, you know. You two are the only things I have ever put to death."

Commander Z'ee reached the top of the ramp ahead of Euclid. Somewhere in the craft there were three other aliens unaccounted for.

'They have got to be in the control room,' he thought, so he made a turn in that direction.

The interior still had the typical rank and rancid aroma the Commander had grown to hate. It was very humid even though the ramp and airlock had been open for more than an hour now. The lighting was not bright but still effective, giving sufficient illumination to see well.

Up an internal ramp they both went, turning to the right into the feeding area. There ahead was one of the missing aliens. It was the smallest of the whole crew.

It was also busy feeding. The preoccupied alien did though hear the sounds made by the two newcomers.

The eyestalks turned slowly around without having its head move, to focus on these intruders.

'Maybe it's one of the crew, here to take away my bowl of Slugs again,' thought the creature. It then saw who was behind it.

With one eye on these intruders, the other eye rotated on its stalk and located its weapon hanging on a rack behind it. Making a fast scrambling move toward its weapon holster the startled alien fell over a stool, stumbled and lost its balance missing the weapon completely. Rolling over, it quickly regained an upright stance on its four legs, turned and charged. Both of its claws were, dangerously gyrating and snapping at these trespassers.

Euclid moved in front of the Commander, to position itself between the two. With a strong upward thrust, Euclid caught the alien underneath its main section. The robot, taking advantage of the creatures impetus, then lifted upwards to send it flying up and over their heads to come crashing down head first in the corner of the compartment.

The Commander crept around the centre table to check its condition. He felt around the upper body of the unconscious alien looking for signs of life, and then said in a low voice.

"Well Euclid. It is either dead or very unconscious! At least, it shouldn't be any trouble for a while."

He then stood and motioned the robot to an opening in the course wall at the other side of the table.

"Just two more to go," the Commander said, "They are likely to be in the room where the guidance controls are. This one we have time to come back and secure later."

They crept, silently as possible, along the wide passage, which the Commander knew would lead them to the targeted room. Stopping at the opening, he peered carefully around the edge of the plating to look inside.

There ahead some ten metres away, were the last aliens to be accounted for. They both stood on all fours at the control console, observing the happenings outside on the monitor sphere. They were making sounds in low tones, possibly trying to decide what was best to do. But the Captain had conditioned these two beasts so well they could not make a decision on their own. So they stayed here where they were, gibbering and gurgling in quiet panic.

Either through premonition or its acute senses of smell, one of the aliens let its eyes swivelled to see what it was that stood somewhere behind them. The shock was too much.

The alien operator pressed a contact that energized the outside speakers. It started to jibber and scream in its own tongue into the square outside, to warn their Captain that there were captives loose on their ship.

Unable to get a response both of them turned. They each took the same attack stance that their other comrade had just minutes before. Then one of them charged.

"Stand to the side," came the cool voice. It was from Clysta.

She had decided to follow them and was now right behind. Both the Commander and Euclid moved back into the passage as Clysta took careful aim and pressed the button on the hand blaster.

Acrid smoke cleared inside the control room to reveal one of the aliens, sprawled headless on the course floor close to the opening. The second had been cut into two sections where it stood and now lay in a pool of green ooze-lifeless and sprawling across the console.

Kindra was alone outside the shuttle. He was still holding the alien weapon at the upper body of the towering Captain, and occasionally glanced toward the ramp. He was trying to see where Clysta was and if she was over the ordeal of the last little episode.

She had walked up the ramp and out of sight and now was nowhere to be seen.

He called out her name.

"Clysta?" He waited for a reply, then, "Are you o.k?"

The sudden screaming from the alien inside of the shuttle was now being broadcast over the exterior speaker and it startled him.

The Captain took this new distraction as a chance to gamble. This Captain had earned many honours, almost too great to number, for his victories in battle. He would not allow himself to be outsmarted by such weaklings. Not even this one that was now holding one of their own weapons to his body.

Kindra's head was turned away though in the corner of his eye he saw the movement. But it was too late. The alien brought up a claw with the appendicles extended and rapping them around the muzzle of the weapon, wrenched it clear away from its frontal plates.

Kindra, whose fingers now became disarranged from the firing controls, had no chance to operate them. As the instrument left his grasp the alien in the same movement brought up and around the other claw to strike.

Kindra knew what would be next. He swivelled his body around to the direction away from the anticipated blow as the claw connected with his rib cage. The effort was not a waste. It avoided the penetration by the keenly sharpened points but still the impact sent him sliding and spinning across the crystal surface in a state of semi-consciousness. He came to a stop, landing at the underside of the ships ramp luckily out of target range from the Captain.

Switching the regained weapon to the other claw, the rearmed Captain made ready to do combat. He backed slowly away from the shuttle, eyestalks waving and looking in every direction. Looking briefly at the two carcasses and cursing, he then stopped to face the ramp, anticipating that the Terrans would surely leave his ship by that route.

The Captain's wrath was now directing all his senses in anger at the ramp. He had forgot completely about the dazed adversary now out of his line of sight. He thought only of the prizes he would receive from his distant superiors after this small victory that was coming. Both ball like eyes were fixed on what he could see of the ramp and his sound receptors were tuned to hear these two legged slugs as they approached from the inside.

'Here they come' he thought to himself, as Clysta led the victors out of the alien craft and started down the ramp. He had taken time to place the translating sphere to his front with the free claw working the controls. He wanted them to hear his own words of victory.

He waited until they were in his line of sight.

With the saliva of his anticipation dripping from the wide feeding slot, he spoke into the sphere, "Halt, you slimy shell-less creatures. You think you are able to hold conquest with the Honourable Captain Laslas of the Imperial Navy and win? Well, you have lost and your miserable attempt at that conquest has failed."

So concentrated were his senses in holding his quarry that the Captain missed for the last time the silently reforming transporter just a few degrees at his rear and beyond his peripheral vision.

G'zin silently exited with the two handed blaster raised and ready. This time there had to be no mistakes.

At his last word, the alien received a full charge of the blue white plasma that first severed the appendage holding the weapon, then it seared a large hole into the side of its upper body. The immensely strong Captain, surprised but apparently unaffected by its wounds, turned to charge this new enemy and for each step forward received another blast. The third finally finished him as it cut into his upper body, concluding with a wide gash that finally severed the small head.

The crustacean's last movement was as it fell to the smooth glassy surface in a distorted heap of smouldering exoskeleton.

"Have no remorse, especially for him," said Commander Z'ee, "They were each of them a cruel and soulless fighting machine. That one was the worst of all. Death or mindless slavery was all they intended for any other race."

They stood outside the shuttle surveying the corpses of the aliens.

"What do we do next?" Kindra asked.

"Clysta," the Commander said, turning to his daughter, "Whatever your plans are from here on, we now have their starship to worry about. My crew, or what is left of them, is still on our expedition ship and the aliens disabled it some time ago.

"Their main craft is carrying in it a Queen of their species and she is bearing with her hundreds of egg things. Their plan was to find a suitable planet and leave her to propagate."

G'zin asked, "How many more aliens are there up there with this Queen?"

"Not more than three, awake that is," was the Commander's answer. He continued, "She and a number that form her entourage are in a state of sleep. These," he waived an arm to indicate the dead crew, "Are others of the party who have awakened to scout for a landing.

"They have been piloting their ship and preparing for the big event. Then there are also three armed aliens on guard on our own ship."

"Is there any chance they will be aware of what has happened here?" Clysta asked indicating the bodies.

"I doubt that very much," answered the Commander, "This Captain, and all of his crew for that matter, led a very singular and solitary life. Savage fights used to break out concerning secrecy and the Captain had total control of everything. No, I don't think the crew would call the ship above in fear of the Captain's rage. And of course, he himself would not be party to admitting to any fear of danger. Just to save face and maintain his honour."

G'zin spoke, "Then there is only one thing to do. We must go to their ship and do something. Anything, which will put a stop to this invasion."

Then she looked at Kindra, then Euclid, saying, "Take Euclid with you Kindra. See if you can operate this vessel. Our ship is too far off, and time is important."

"That is a good idea," agreed Clysta. "Father, are you strong enough to help? I expect you saw some of the operation of the drive system and you must have a slight idea of how this ship was flown."

"I spent months with these beasts on and off, always under guard though," the Commander explained, "I can probably be of some help. There are a few of the things I did see. Though I didn't get much of a chance to watch them operate their ships for any length of time. Let me try."

"Anything will be useful father."

Suddenly, it came to Clysta that in all of this time and through the dangerous action, she had not yet touched her father. She moved toward him eyes filled to overflowing with tears, threw her arms around his neck and held him tight.

Trying her best to stop the sobbing she managed to say.

"I am so glad you're alive and safe, I have so much to tell you and ask you. But first…"

"But first we have to stop the Glantrx. I agree," he interrupted, wrapping his own arms around her to give a hug in return. He disengaged, and stood at arms length looking hard at the daughter he hardly knew any more. Then, with a finger, he carefully stroked a tear from her face.

# Chapter 73

The alien shuttle slowly lifted from the charred surface and carefully climbed upward from the square.

Euclid had studied the unfamiliar systems briefly, and with some help from the Commander the robot had finally managed to power up the equally strange energy units.

'Now I am about to redirect the power to energize the ascent coils,' Euclid informed this 'new crew'. 'Master Kindra would you please be so good as to place three of your fingers into those three holes above this unit's left hand implement. The Glantrx were blessed with at least eight appendicles to the left claw and it appears that all are necessary for vertical flight.'

They all felt the energy and strong vibrations from the vertical thrusters.

"Well," the Commander whispered, almost too afraid to say it loud, "We appear to be off the ground at least."

Euclid spoke again, 'Master Kindra? Now would you push on that slide whilst this unit will operate this disk, please?,

With a surge the alien craft accelerated at an angle to the vertical, taking all of the occupants by surprise.

'If you will please excuse the inaccuracy of my operation of this strange craft...,' Euclid started to explain, but Kindra cut the robot short, saying.

"Euclid, Euclid. It's quite all right. We understand the craft is strange. Just get on with straightening it out."

Euclid eased the pressure slightly and the ascent slowed and became more vertical. Upward and upward it rose gaining speed each second.

Leaving the planet's atmosphere without any further errors, they watched the craft's strange view screen. There was a vague similarity with that of the Skimmer, in its control and transmission except for the control it required more fingers to operate. The picture quality was pour but they accounted for that as being due to the differences of the aliens' visual capacity.

Panning with the screen and following a straight line course, they finally located the giant alien mother ship with the Explorer ship following along in its synchronous orbit. Euclid had finally become more able to control the alien shuttle and with Kindra's help the robot moved it closer. When they had approached to a distance of almost five kilometres the three friends were able to appreciate the enormity of this gigantic intergalactic vessel.

"Wow!" Kindra said in an understatement as the gap closed, "That is one big ship, just look at it."

"It was built for invasion," confirmed the Commander, "Have no doubts about that. It is filled with many devices of mass destruction. Now we must act swiftly if we are to put a stop to their plans. And stop them we must."

Then, he spoke to the robot, "Move up a little closer Euclid, but take it slowly from here. And try to keep the flight smooth, we do not want to make them suspicious."

G'zin interrupted, "Now I remember. It was an Erachin or something; I have been trying all of this time to recall that creature on Fryl that the alien's ship resembles. Now we are up close it comes back to me. That was it, an Erachin."

Euclid added.

'You are quite correct, Miss G'zin. That creature to which you refer, was known as The Sea Urchin on the planet Earth, and only reasonably small. It is almost extinct there as the oceans are now extremely polluted and are too much for that species. Many have been harvested during the past and have found new homes on other planets to assist as purifiers of water.'

The Commander looked at the others with a smile.

"Is he always so eloquent and descriptive? I cannot recall."

"Not half!" Kindra answered quickly. Then, "Thank you for the nature lesson Euclid."

Commander Z'ee tried to bring their attention to the matter at hand, saying.

"Euclid, you see that clear circular space between the group of radians dead ahead? Guide the shuttle toward it and look for a light beam."

As he finished, a growl then a jibber came from a grill in the top of the console.

"That is likely their docking call sign," said the Commander, "We will try to ignore it. If they let us that is."

'Perhaps if this unit-sorry Master Kindra-I-use the same sounds back at them,' Euclid said. 'I may help to confuse the creatures.'

"Maybe if you can change it a little, one way or the other, it may even double the confusion. Do you not agree," added Clysta.

'I will add the sound which transcribes as Captain Laslas,' added Euclid further. 'I can still bring that to memory and it will give it some authority.'

"We can only give it a try. What have we got to loose?" Kindra responded.

"Ok. But let us wait a little longer before we do," said the Commander in agreement, "Laslas never did respond to these subordinates right away. They will not be sure what it means if they get an answer too fast."

Euclid waited as planned. The seconds advanced into minutes as the distance to the mother ship became shorter. Finally the Commander nodded to the robot and it immediately made sounds, which so far as they could tell, matched those they had heard earlier. Then a long silence as they all watched the screen.

Near the area where the targeted point of light was being emitted, a panel slid upward then another moved to the side to reveal the interior of what they all knew to be a docking bay. Although the entrance to the bay was only a minuscule percentage of the surface of the enormous ship, its size was immense. Large enough to take a craft four times that of this shuttle.

"When we land," said the Commander, "We will open up the ramp but we will stay inside. One of the crew will come with a type of decontaminating equipment, for the security of the interior. They did it every time when I was on board before, something to do with maintaining the safety of their Queen. Everything gets the treatment, even those of the crew. We must be ready to overpower that one first, then there should only be two more left that we need to be concerned about up here."

The craft entered the opening and hovered momentarily above the immense floor of the cavernous shuttle dock. Kindra and Euclid quickly closed down the power systems after the craft had settled onto its support legs. As the Commander next stood by the control to lower the ramp Kindra breathed a sigh of relief at their successful flight. They all then went to stand before the viewer screen to await the arrival of the promised decontamination operation.

Their wait was not a long one. Watching the spherical screen they saw the giant doors of the airlock close. Then the expected alien crewman emerged from a passage close to the craft. He was equally as tall as the largest of the other aliens they had seen before. The only major difference appeared to be that this one had a body which was slender and likely lighter than all of the others had been. The Commander opened the airlock and lowered the ramp

The creature towed behind it a sled that seemed to float along about twenty centimetres above the course floor. On it were a number of pear shaped objects, of a material resembling rock and red in colour. A tube or cable came out of each, which ended at an instrument not much unlike a horn.

"This is the one and that is the equipment I told you about," the Commander said, "He will walk right up the ramp," he then turned to G'zin saying, "Pass me your hand blaster. I know this one all too well. Now, all stay inside here and wait. I want to go to meet it alone."

Blaster in hand, the Commander walked soundlessly out of the control room, his obvious intention being to confront the alien.

Seconds of silence passed as the three and Euclid waited. The next thing they heard was the growling jibber that was the usual and now familiar speech of the aliens. Almost, they could perceive the surprise in the tone of the alien's sounds, as they imagined its shock on being challenged by the unescorted Human.

The next sounds were the unsavory and blasphemous remark from Commander Z'ee, followed by the staccato whine that was the discharging blaster. Then silence reigned once again.

Clysta left the room at a run leaving the others behind and was first to arrive at the enclosure at the top of the exit ramp.

Her father was standing over the holed and smoking corpse of the alien. Clysta moved to his side as the others followed her out. She placed her arms around his waist as he put an arm about her shoulders, saying angrily.

"This one I wanted for myself. He and another of these beasts murdered two of my science team right in front of the rest of our group. Tore them apart they did, piece by piece. This was too easy a death for that particular one."

He regained his previous manner and continued.

"We must find the other two now, before they miss the usual noises and come looking for the shuttle crew," he turned to Clysta and G'zin, "You two stay here and try to raise our ship, use the call sign-The Galaxy Explorer-the transmitter in that control room is adequate. It works in a similar way as ours but you have to remember about those fingers of theirs. It may take you a while but the channel is open and our people will be listening and should hear you."

He continued, "They are under guard, but the Glantrx don't understand Terran. Tell them what we have done when you get through, and have them start up their part of the surprise I have long had planned for this day."

"And what are you going to do?" Clysta asked, almost knowing the answer.

"I am going to find those other two before they do come looking. They are likely to be inquisitive and want to see why the big shuttle is back. I will take Kindra and Euclid with me," he answered.

Turning to them he asked, "Are you game?"

Kindra nodded his answer. The robot did not need.

"But Father…" Clysta began to object.

"No butts Clysta," he answered, "I owe this to the men and women in our team who have died in the sport of these creatures. They are about to have some revenge finally, and I want to be the one to get it for them."

"Now Kindra. Do you still have a weapon of any sort?" He asked.

Kindra's reply was to turn and reach around the opening inside the enclosure, and say. "I still have this."

He turned again holding the cone shaped weapon that had belonged to the navigator, Quazraam.

"Will this be good enough?" He said with a smile.

At the far side of the huge dock where they had landed stood the smaller shuttle that Quazraam had used when he transported the Commander and the other three prisoners to the surface.

Though the lighting in this area was not bright, it was just adequate for the Terrans to see by. All the surfaces, the floor, the walls and even the ceiling above as far as they could make out were all of a course texture, almost rock like. The atmosphere throughout had a sticky and humid heavy quality that though uncomfortable to them was normal for the Glantrx.

Kindra had stopped for a second and was kneeling and inspecting the floor. Even though it was a course texture it shone with a strange cleanness, the same was apparent in all of the other surfaces.

The Commander, who was leading the way, halted in his stride and tried to answer Kindra's unasked question about the phenomenon.

"It has something to do with the material it is made of. It seems that all of this ship and all of their other craft are constructed from a kind of rock, not much unlike the types found in our own regions of space. The closest explanation I could define was that is grown or somehow spun. The outer hull itself grows. Then the aliens have the mechanical and technical equipment installed."

Then, changing the subject, Commander Z'ee said, "Now keep with me. I remember it was this way, to the left. The corridor leads to their communications area."

Cautiously they turned a corner in the corridor they were following, and the Commander went on in a low tone.

"I was told most of this by one of the alien guards over the months that we were held in captivity. We were brought on board for some of their games. This particular alien explained, very boastfully I might add, that all of their technology is the benefit of one of their enslaved species. They were described to me as 'physically inferior but mechanically superior'. They are the ones responsible for the design and building of the equipment and machinery to propel these ships and the shuttles."

Euclid interrupted the Commander's explanation.

'I have been quite confused by endeavoring to find an appropriate reason for how these clumsily constructed creatures could be responsible for the development of such sophisticated equipment as these machines are. The matter is now clearer.'

Kindra just nodded his head.

By now they were at the end of the long corridor, which they had taken after leaving the shuttle area. The scale and distances were greater than usual for Terrans, the Glantrx were at least double their size. Peering around an opening leading into what was the main control area, the Commander put out an arm to hold the other two back.

He spoke in a whisper, "I see only one of them in there. I will go first, Kindra, you follow when I am inside the room and keep close. Euclid, wait here and keep watch for the other one. It is possible he is on tour and may return through here."

Sitting at the console was Kraklac. His task was still to scan the surface of the planet below. Once again he was in a deep slumber.

He was dreaming of his home planet, and about all those Glantrx of the opposite sex that he had known in his long life. The alien was awakened by a prod in the side. A snarling jibber left his speech tube as he turned to retaliate, intending once and for all to end these continual interruptions to his sleep. Being in an unconscious slumber, he did not even know the Captain's shuttle had returned.

As Kraklac swivelled around, the Commander ducked to avoid the heavy claw. The alien then saw that the intruder into his dreams was

479

none other than one of those low life organisms that seemed to be native to this damnable area of space.

"What are you doing here?" The alien blurted out in his own tongue. It raised the same claw again, intending to take another swipe at this slug, and then it saw the weapon pointing into its upper body shell. With one of its eyes on the weapon and one on the Commander, the claw was slowly lowered to its side.

"You don't understand what it is I am saying, but you sure know what I mean," The Commander gave the alien a prod and said. "Now back up."

He kept on prodding and pointing to another doorway, in the other wall of the room. He was explaining to Kindra who had now joined him as he cautiously steered the crustacean.

"That opening leads to the freezers. We are going to need Euclid for this. Please bring the robot while I manoeuver this beast through the door," Once again he prodded the large alien, backing it toward the opening.

Then he added, "Once this one is in the cocoon, we can find the other and try to do the same. After these are tucked in we will then deal with the one we have trussed up in the shuttle. If it is still alive that is."

Clysta was standing at the top of the ramp that led from the shuttle to the vast bay floor. She was idly inspecting the weapons belonging to the aliens, all neatly laid out on a shelf in the rock like wall. G'zin had left the craft to explore around the landing bay area outside the craft.

Five minutes before, they had concluded and closed down the transmission to the nearby Terran ship.

"Galaxy Explorer, come in please," It had taken a number of repeated calls to finally get a response. Then she had managed to explain to the confused operations controller.

"My name is Clysta Z'ee. I am transmitting out of the alien mother ship via the Glantrx shuttle. We have taken over the alien ships and are in command of the invasion complement. We are going to come to your aid after cleaning up here. Are you receiving all of this?"

The two females waited in silence for seconds seeming like minutes.

Then, almost as Clysta was about to repeat the call the voice of a Terran came across the void loud and clear.

"Clysta Z'ee. We hear you. Are you Terran?"

"I am. We have terminated a number of the aliens and will shortly be coming to your aid. What are the numbers of aliens on that ship?"

"There are three. But are you sure you have control?"

Clysta had answered confirming that they had.

"This is the opportunity we have awaited for so long. Now I can't believe we are to get our chance at last. We are easily able to overpower these three now we know there will be no fear of retaliation from the Glantrx over there."

Clysta and G'zin were elated at the reply. Clysta's smile confirmed her confidence and described some of the events of their conflict and the death of the Captain. Finally, she suggested they close the transmission and get on with the work at hand.

The other operator asked a question, as he was just about to discontinue the contact.

"You said you are Clysta Z'ee. Is that just coincidence or is there some relation with our Commander?"

"I am his daughter."

G'zin was leisurely inspecting a few of the strange items that were set around the walls of the shuttle hangar. She had not seen one of the aliens who had been standing quietly in the shadows for more than a minute.

He had walked down one of the passage leading from the ship's galley and turned the corner and into the loading bay. The crewman though had seen G'zin immediately.

He had managed to stifle his disbelief at seeing this 'Slugvrant' all alone. Unshackled and most of all, unescorted.

Silently, so not to have its victim know it was being stalked, the ships cook slid along close to the wall in an attempt to get closer.

G'zin, still unaware of the alien and its nearness, innocently carried on with her investigation of these strange items and had no idea what many of them could be for. She moved nearer to where the alien hid in the shadow cast by the other smaller shuttle. Then she was close enough for the alien to pounce.

It reached out from the dimness and grabbed G'zin with its pincer like claws holding her in a vice like grip. Although unable to see her assailant, she knew instinctively it was a Glantrx that had taken her by surprise.

She released a short scream as the sub-crewman raised the diminutive body of G'zin high above its small head, holding her with her upper arm and lower leg. It shook her a few times then started to pull in opposite directions, but only slowly. It was intending to enjoy its sport.

G'zin, after overcoming the shock, began holding her breath against the increasing pain. Finally she found her voice and managed to call out as loudly as her pain would allow.

"Clysta, Clysta. It has me! Over here, it has me. Kill the beast. Kill it! It's trying to pull me apart."

A startled Clysta heard the cries of her friend.

Precious fractions of the following seconds began to erode as Clysta searched frantically through her thoughts. She was still at the head of the ramp, trying to remember the last place she had seen one of those weapons they had gathered from the dead aliens. She knew immediately the stun gun in her belt would be useless. Then it came to her in a flash.

Clysta quickly turned on her heel and there on the rocky shelf like projection to her left, three of the conical shaped weapons had been left, placed side by side by Kindra after the fight on the planet below.

G'zin groaned in agony as she felt the popping of a joint in her shoulder. Then there came a gathering of pain beginning in her upper chest, as the rib cage took the strain. The alien meanwhile, was making noises that could have been between joy and satisfaction at its victim. She could not hold back the scream as the alien gave her a shake up and down.

"Quick Clys' please," she called out in anguish.

Two and a half seconds of time had now passed, as Clysta reached for one of the strange weapons. Another half of a second slipping her hand inside the cone shaped cowling that was around the firing controls, as she held the massive device with the other hand. Frantically, her fingers were finding the firing rings. She started her turn in one fluid movement and headed at a run back toward the ramp and shouting out loud.

"I am coming G'zin. Hold on."

She ran at full speed down the ramp and onto the course floor of the hangar, trying as she went, to remember what Kindra had said when he demonstrated how to make these strange weapons work.

Four seconds. The ramp was course and caused her to stumble and loose her balance momentarily then tripped and fell to the floor. She rolled over in a quick twisting movement and regained her feet and continued her run toward the sound of G'zin's voice.

Thoughts raced through her mind as she turned in the direction of G'zin's whimpering sounds of agony. In her mind, Clysta went through the advice that Kindra had given.

'The two first fingers into the sockets, there.' She raised the device, now to waist height, 'Next. Two fingers through the rings, where are the rings? Ah, there they are.'

She could now see her friend and the Glantrx. She shouted out loud, "I am here, G'zin."

"Push and pull," Clysta breathed, saying out loud to no-one in particular, trying to take careful aim. But the weapon was too heavy.

The alien carrying G'zin high in the air had moved from the shelter of the smaller shuttle and was now in full view of the space around the larger one.

G'zin, still high in the air, was beginning to loose consciousness as the pain through her body grew in intensity. Her hip joint was now straining as she, half unconscious, saw through closing eyes the flash of energy from the direction of the fading shuttlecraft.

The beam of savage white energy was enough to bring daylight to the area, as it sliced the air toward the alien, passing by it only centimetres to the side and burning into the wall behind.

The alien saw with one swivelling eye, this other, new intruder. It anticipated the next discharge and began to lower the helpless G'zin as a cover for its head and upper body section.

Clysta muttered as she steeled herself for the next shot, this time holding the weapon steady.

"I am way ahead of you, you ugly sadistic creep!"

She tucked her elbow into her waist and dropped her aim to hit the alien's legs, just below the last joints. With a sweeping motion, the weapon's beam of super heated plasma sliced across and through each one like cutting through butter.

The alien now partly legless, dropped straight down and onto the hard floor of the hangar with a crunch, still with G'zin's limp body held before it.

A screeching sound of agony was emitted from its speech tube as it tried vainly to retain its upright balance. Then in a sudden last ditch effort at regaining a victory; the beast threw the unconscious G'zin in an upward arc, in the direction of the energy beam.

Although the time was immeasurable, this alien's protection had now been lost. Clysta had a clear shot at the main body section. Just one.

She never saw that last shot hit its target.

G'zin's limp body struck her friend full in the chest, shortening Clysta's jubilation as she was knocked over backwards and onto the floor. The blow of the impact had enough force that she lost consciousness, and lay with G'zin's disjointed body resting and entangled on the top of her.

# Chapter 74

Clysta awoke with a start. She had been dreaming of gigantic Lobster like creatures, maybe a hundred of them. And G'zin and Kindra and herself were trying to fight them off by hand and were fast losing the battle.

Her eyes had opened to a place that was familiar yet not really. She lay quite still awaiting another rush of the giant creatures, and then slowly came the realization that she was at rest on a Medi-bed inside a well lighted room that felt safe.

Looking to her left, she could see three more of these beds, all of them empty. She turned to the right and a sharp pain made her wince in agony.

Her eyes focused on the face of another person on the bed next to the one she was occupying. It was G'zin, her friend. Clysta tried to rise but found she was restrained, not by belts or webbing but by something that fit like a skin. Possibly, she concluded, it was a field which allowed small movements but would stop her getting up.

"G'zin," she managed to say in a whisper. There came no answer. A sudden weakness overtook her.

Then she lapsed into a calm and peaceful sleep.

Her father the Commander, sitting by her bed, continued.

"Kindra contacted your friend Shram on the surface. He made arrangements to have G'zin taken to one of their medical centres down there. We tried to mend her injuries but we were losing ground and it was almost too late. The damage to her internally was so extensive and our equipment could not handle the trauma and the repairs speedily enough."

"Is she going to be o.k?" Clysta asked weakly.

"They have said she will, but it will take at least two months," he replied.

"That is good," she said, relieved. Then asked, "So what about you and the expedition? What is to become of that?"

The Commander looked at his daughter long, before he made to answer.

"We have decided we must carry on with the mission. My technicians have rigged the alien ship to return in the direction from where we believe it came. All of its inhabitants and what is left of the crew are sleeping now, and if their trip takes two hundred years, it will be too short."

"And what will happen if you meet more Glantrx? What then?"

"We have a good idea of which area of their galactic arm they dominate and we are intending to give that a wide berth," he replied, "The way we see it, their dominance indicates the possibility of more friendly species that might wish to find a way to be released from that same dominance."

"If that is the case, if you are going on," she said quickly, "I want to go along."

The Commander's face became serious and he began shaking his head.

"I wish I could take you along Clysta, but you must stay in this arm at least for now. It would be unfair to my crew and the mission. We all accept that we owe our lives to the three of you. Only you have to understand. The people who form the expedition have been selected from many and all had loved ones to leave behind. I cannot expect them to agree to my breaking the rules and the conditions that we all took up from the start."

"But Father, I want to come with you," she argued a little sadly.

"I know you do," was his reply, "And that would please me very much. But there is so much for you to see and do and learn yet. You have a future ahead still to explore, and then there are your friends, G'zin and Kindra with many more yet to meet. Believe me, this is the kind of trip you can look forward to in your own future, but not now."

The Commander was still trying to put together the words that would convince her. He added.

486

"The most important job that you have to undertake is delivering the evidence of this attempted invasion of our space. I have prepared a record and a visi' which I want you to deliver to the Controller for this expedition. He is a good man and he will listen. But it will not be as easy to make others in higher places do the same. You will be useful in relating the events live and in person."

Clysta sat quietly, while she thought over her father's words and what he had tried to say. Then she agreed, "Your arguments are not very convincing, but I suppose you must be right as always. When are you planning to leave?"

"We have a few things still to repair," he started to answer, "The Glantrx did a lot of surface damage to our drive, but nothing very critical. We will be ready for a test in forty-eight hours or so.

"We have had a little help with replacement materials-from the Vedannians-and those have helped to reduce the time for repairs considerably."

Clysta winced as she sat up quickly, saying, "The Vedannians. I had forgotten them! What will happen to their secrecy now? It has been something they have maintained and almost cherished, for so long. Won't they now become exposed through all of these events?"

She stopped and a thought came back to her, something from the past.

Then she remarked, "They owe you something don't they? A reward? You remember? From the time you were here last."

Puzzled, he studied his daughter for a few seconds, then answered.

"What reward could that be? The events that have happened here in these last few days are reward enough for anyone. You, arriving with your friends. The plotting and the fighting so we would be free, and who knows, even the whole Galaxy too one day. That is the only reward I would ever need."

He then said, "I don't really think I know how it was done, but it is almost as if the Vedannians themselves knew it was to be this way."

"I'm sure I know!" Clysta said with conviction and related to her father some of the experience when she met with the Committee of the Gathering.

# Chapter 75

Clysta watched the transmission as the Galactic Explorer vanished into Hyper Space. They had retrieved their Skimmer from the island and were in the control room watching the visi' screen. The Skimmer was now parked in a large landscaped area, within the city, close to the Old Centre.

Kindra was standing with Clysta. Euclid stood silent at the opening to the sleeping quarters, once more awaiting a call to attention. G'zin was still at the medical centre, recovering from the injuries inflicted in the last encounter with the Glantrx.

The Vedannian doctors had worked long and hard to save her life, but many more weeks would be needed before she could be strong enough to leave the hospital.

All outside was in darkness as Clysta turned from the screen, which now showed only the millions of stars surrounding this once more peaceful planet.

"We should go to see G'zin," said Kindra, finally breaking the silence that seemed to hang like a cloud inside the craft.

"That is a good idea," Clysta agreed, "I'll just put away these comp' crystals, then we will be off. You come along too, Euclid!"

G'zin had finally regained consciousness the day before, and when they arrived at her bedside they found Shram in his usual spot. He was sitting in the same place he had occupied for all the many days before. G'zin and Shram had developed more than a mere bond when they had been working together on the transporter system.

G'zin was wide awake when they entered and they were occupied with looking deep into each other's eyes.

"Are we interrupting anything?" Kindra said with a wide smile as he entered.

"Sure looks like it to me," added Clysta and adding to the most obvious situation, "I think we should go out and come in again."

"Oh! Hello you three," G'zin said, cheerily. She gingerly turned her head to the side in order to see them.

'Good morning to you Miss G'zin and you Shram,' the robot said graciously. Then. 'I trust that you are well Miss G'zin.'

Shram, who had been holding on to G'zin's hand, blushed slightly and looked uncomfortable but did not release the hand. G'zin gave his a squeeze, saying, "Don't take any notice of these two, Shram. They have a weird sense of humour."

G'zin's whole body was encased in a mould of a blue coloured moss like substance, which pulsated softly. Her hands and face were the only parts of her body that were exposed.

Clysta asked of her latest examination by the doctors.

G'zin explained.

"The medics tell me I will need a month or maybe even two more before I can even think of leaving the hospital. That is when this moss stuff is to come off. So, Shram said he would keep me company until that time."

Kindra asked, "What are your plans after you are repaired and well enough to travel?"

"That depends," she responded. She looked to Shram, Shram then looked nervously up at Clysta and Kindra, then at the robot. Finally his eyes stopped at G'zin's.

Once again he was blushing, only now it was a brighter hue. He began to say, stammering at first but his voice became stronger as he continued.

"I,…I…, we…we, I hope you will not mind, but I have asked G'zin to stay here on Vedanne. I can help her to recuperate first and make sure she heals properly. After that she can decide if she wishes to stay here longer, and I hope she will. With me."

This time it was G'zin's turn to start to blush, even through the dark tones of her skin.

She replied, teasingly, "That will depend on how well you look after me, won't it?" Then, to the visitors, "And what are your plans then, will you three be going anywhere?"

Clysta, who was not surprised at this turn of events, said, "I need to return to Sol and somehow get the story of this invasion to the proper authorities. That will mean I will have to leave you here. I don't want to do that if you have not yet made up your mind."

G'zin's face gave a wide grin, as she said, "That was really all I needed to give me the push I was looking for. I am staying here. And what about you, Kindra?"

Kindra looked puzzled. Then he said, "Hey! This is all too fast. But do you know, I really wanted to return to the planet Morn. You all remember that pleasant place," Kindra gave a fake shudder.

He continued, "I want to return there and see my brother again. I would seriously like to help him out, and of course be with him. I never really spent enough time with him when we lived on our home planet. You two do not mind do you?"

"Not one little bit," the two females chimed together. Clysta then added, "But won't that be a little dangerous. The search for your brother will very likely still be going on."

"Dangerous?" He replied, grimly, "What is danger after this that we have just been through? I feel like being in dangerous situations is becoming a part of my life at least."

"If you look at it that way, I suppose you can be right," Clysta tried to agree, then stressed. "But you be careful."

Then, in a brighter and more cheerful vein, "Well, it appears we have all sorted out our futures for now," She looked at G'zin, "Now you are in good hands, Euclid and I will be leaving in two days. We can make landfall on Morn if you can be ready to come along with us, Kindra. How does the timing sound to you?"

# Chapter 76

Clysta once again found herself in that same misty place of nothingness. This time though, Euclid was not with her. Just the same as the time before, she had stepped into a transporter on her way across the city and found herself here. Although a little frightened after the surprise of arriving here, on this occasion she was more prepared and her mind did not play the tricks it had previously.

Only parts of the same room had formed. This time it was a little faster, likened to a vision and she could see plainly the same furnishings before her.

Clysta could make out through the haze the seven same seats. But there was only one occupant who was in the distance, at the head of that large table.

In this misty atmosphere in the place where they were, it was just as difficult to see clearly any facial features. But when the person spoke she recognized the voice as that of the leader from the last visit.

"Clysta Z'ee. I am pleased. Our mathematical predications were quite correct. The horrors which are likely to have befallen this our galaxy are kept at bay, for now."

She hung momentarily on the last two words. Then she said, "For now. What does that mean?"

"We have not stopped at the here and now. We are predicting the future far in excess of five thousand of your years into the advancement of our existence, with a new and infinite factor of certainty."

Clysta chose the next words carefully, "Will the Glantrx be involved again?"

"The elements of chance we cannot separate. Meaning, we are unable to isolate the particular functionaries. I can say though that your involvement is to be of advantage at a time in the future. To help keep these events from critically altering the continuum."

"Can you be a little more specific, like, when, how or where?" Clysta asked.

"It would be of little gain for you to be aware of predicted happenings in advance," was the reply, "It would only lead to complications."

Clysta stood in silence, nodding agreement to the last statement. Then changing the topic she said, "Kindra and I together with the robot Euclid are intending to leave Vedanne, in two of your days. Do you have any objections to that?"

"No objections at all," was the response. "Your stay in that system has been of immense benefit to the people of Vedanne only in a small way at the present, but the future is to have more benefit than even we expected. And your expulsion of the aliens will give the results in keeping with our predictions."

"And G'zin, what about her," she asked.

"We are unable to be specific about this female, but it appears most fortunate she was a part of your party. She can stay there on Vedanne as long as she wishes. And if she decides to stay, it is that which is destined to have a great influence on the future generations on the planet. The people of Vedanne have lived so long in their self-imposed isolation that there has become a serious danger of their own stagnation. The consequence of your visit, short thought it has been, has brought to that planet a freshness and I might say, an influence that is to have a lasting effect on the future of the planet's race. And this person G'zin will be the catalyst."

"Then before I bid you farewell," Clysta started, "I cannot get this question from my mind. How could it be that the Glantrx ended up with their invasion force here at Vedanne? The whereabouts of this system could not have been re-traced from my father's subconscious if you, as it was said, had them removed when he left this system before."

Silence.

"That then leads me to think. Were they drawn here? That this was some kind of pre-arranged scheme. Could it be, I am close to the correct reason for all of this?"

The mist suddenly dissipated around the person at the head of the long table. He began to explain as the whole area around them gradually became clearer.

"You are a very astute individual, Clysta Z'ee. You are close enough to the correct reason for me to complete your questions. Yes, it was a calculation to bring the Glantrx here, to our space where they could be dealt with, carefully.

"It was explained on your previous visit to this place that we had not realized the speed of advancement by these creatures. The whole truth is, we missed its growth completely before it had become too late.

"We felt it was we ourselves who were to blame for not seeing their development, so we had them guided here. Here they could be turned without the loss of lives of people who were not directly responsible. If they had been drawn to your own sector it would surely have led to a war which might have lasted for hundreds of your years."

He continued, "Our race is much older than we told you before, and we are charged with the maintenance of advancement of intelligence throughout the galaxy. They were such a threat to those advancements that, if they are allowed to have their way, it would have eroded millennia from the history of progress."

Finishing, he asked, "Is that an answer to your question?"

"I suppose it is," Clysta replied, slowly.

Then she continued, "I can understand now why my father was not aware of the device we named the Thought Cube. In it, my father's supposed message of so long ago spoke of some un-detailed reward. I presume that was some kind of lure to ensure I would come to this system. It of course is now very academic but in its own irony all of this and the saving of my father's life will be reward enough. I think the only thing I need to say now is-Goodbye!"

Clysta turned and made her way into the mist of the transporter.

A second member emerged from the nothingness and joined the

one sitting at the table after Clysta had left. The new one said, quietly, "You did not tell her!"

"It was not necessary. Her brain already has the correct neural frequencies needed."

"Can she control them?"

"Not at the present time. In a few of more of their years time, telepathy first then the others later."

"And her friends, Kindra and G'zin. What of them?"

"Theirs is not quite so strong, but that will improve. It was that which brought them together. And the one known as Kindra, he is returning to the old Base Planet you know so well."

The other looked at the first.

"What do we do with the 'Shram' thing"?

The first did not turn his head, but replied.

"It was a good thing we did. We will leave it as it is."

"And our secret?" The newcomer asked, still not quite sure he had finished his questions.

"That is to be dealt with when they leave the system."

# Epilogue

She still thought of space as her home. Standing on the command deck of her cruiser, looking out at the millions of stars she loved. In her one hundred and twenty-one years, she had seen most of the best in this galaxy. Many of them up close.

Thinking to herself, of those early years and the special friends she had known. Of Kindra and G'zin. She had often wondered what had become of them both.

Euclid! Her good friend, and servant, always there, at her side. Still with her and still at her side.

Still preferring speech, Euclid said, 'I know Miss Clysta, that as a robot I am not supposed to, but I think also of them. Often.'

Clysta turned her head and smiled. If only Kindra could have heard such poor grammatical usage from this most perfect of robots, she thought. Then once more she returned to looking outward at the infinity of space and its billions of stars.

The End

Printed in the United States
55855LVS00003B/4-60

9 781424 127658